The Fortunes of Texas: Return to Red Rock

A powerful family of Red Rock, Texas, faces a secret past…

Look for all the books in this bestselling classic miniseries!

Plain Jane and the Playboy & Valentine's Fortune
USA TODAY Bestselling Author Marie Ferrarella and
New York Times Bestselling Author Allison Leigh

Triple Trouble & A Real Live Cowboy
USA TODAY Bestselling Authors Lois Faye Dyer
and Judy Duarte

Fortune's Woman & A Fortune Wedding
New York Times Bestselling Author RaeAnne Thayne
and Kristin Hardy

RaeAnne Thayne finds inspiration in the beautiful northern Utah mountains, where the *New York Times* and *USA TODAY* bestselling author lives. Her books have won numerous honors, including RITA® Award nominations from Romance Writers of America and a Career Achievement Award from *RT Book Reviews*. RaeAnne loves to hear from readers and can be contacted through her website, raeannethayne.com.

Also available from RaeAnne Thayne and HQN Books

Haven Point

Redemption Bay
Snow Angel Cove

Hope's Crossing

Wild Iris Ridge
Christmas in Snowflake Canyon
Willowleaf Lane
Currant Creek Valley
Sweet Laurel Falls
Woodrose Mountain
Blackberry Summer

Visit the Author Profile page
at Harlequin.com for more titles.

New York Times Bestselling Author

RaeAnne Thayne

and Kristin Hardy

Fortune's Woman &
A Fortune Wedding

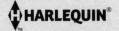

HARLEQUIN®

ISBN-13: 978-0-373-60237-7

Fortune's Woman & A Fortune Wedding

Copyright © 2016 by Harlequin Books S.A.

Fortune's Woman
Copyright © 2009 by Harlequin Books S.A.

A Fortune Wedding
Copyright © 2009 by Harlequin Books S.A.

Special thanks and acknowledgment to RaeAnne Thayne for her contribution to Fortune's Woman and to Kristin Hardy for her contribution to A Fortune Wedding.

Recycling programs for this product may not exist in your area.

Printed in U.S.A.

www.Harlequin.com

CONTENTS

RaeAnne Thayne

Fortune's Woman

Chapter 1

What was the punk doing?

Ross Fortune stood beside a canvas awning-covered booth at the art fair of the Red Rock Spring Fling, keeping a careful eye on the rough-looking kid with the eyebrow bolt and the lip ring.

The kid seemed out of place in the booth full of framed Wild West art—photographs of steely-eyed cowboys lined up on a weathered fence, tow-headed toddlers wobbling in giant Tony Lamas, a trio of horses grazing against a stormy sky.

Yeah, he might be jumping to conclusions, but it didn't seem like the sort of artwork that would interest somebody who looked more wannabe rock star than cowboy, with his inky black hair, matching black jeans and T-shirt, and pale skin. But as Ross watched, the kid—who looked on the small side of maybe fourteen or fifteen—thumbed through the selection of unframed prints like they were the most fascinating things in the world.

Ross wouldn't have paid him any attention, except that for the past ten minutes he couldn't help noticing the kid as he moseyed from booth to booth in the gathering twilight, his eyes constantly shifting around. The punk seemed abnormally aware of where the artist-vendor of each booth stood at all times, tracking their movements under dark eyelashes.

Until the Western photographs, he hadn't seemed much interested in whatever wares the artists were selling. Instead, he had all the tell-tale signs of somebody casing the place, looking for something easy to lift.

Okay, Ross was rushing to judgment. But something about the way the kid's gaze never stopped moving set all his alarm bells ringing. Even after the crowds started to abate as everybody headed toward the dance several hundred yards away, the kid continued ambling through the displays, as if he were searching for the perfect mark.

And suddenly he must have found it.

As Ross watched, the kid's gaze sharpened on a pink flowered bag somebody had carelessly left on a folding chair.

He moved to take a step forward, his own attention homing in on the boy, but just at that moment somebody jostled him.

"Sorry," muttered a dark-haired man in a Stetson who looked vaguely familiar. "I was looking for someone and wasn't watching where I was going."

"No problem," Ross answered. But when he looked back, the kid was gone—and so was the slouchy flowered bag.

Adrenaline pumped through him. Finally! Chasing a shoplifter was just what he needed right now.

He had been bored to tears all day and would have left hours ago and headed back to San Antonio if he hadn't been volunteered by his family to help out on security detail for the Spring Fling, which was Red Rock's biggest party of the year.

At least now, maybe he might be able to have a little something to relieve the tedium of the day so he couldn't consider it a complete waste.

He stepped out of the booth and scanned the crowd. He saw his cousin J.R. helping Isabella Mendoza begin to pack away the wares at her textiles booth down the row a ways and he saw the Latino man in the Stetson who had bumped into him standing at a corner of a nearby watercolor booth.

He also spied his despised brother-in-law, Lloyd Fredericks, skulking through the crowd, headed toward a section behind the tents and awnings, away from the public thoroughfare.

No doubt he was up to no good. If Ross wasn't on the hunt for a purse snatcher, he would have taken off after Lloyd, just for the small-minded pleasure of harassing the bastard a little.

He finally spotted the kid near a booth displaying colorful, froufrou dried-flower arrangements. He moved quietly into position behind him, his gaze unwavering.

This had always been his favorite moment when he had been a detective in San Antonio, before he left the job to become a private investigator. He loved that hot surge of energy before he took down a perp, that little thrill that he was about to tip the scales of justice firmly on the side of the victim.

He didn't speak until he was directly behind the boy. "Hey kid," he growled. "Nice purse."

The boy jumped like Ross had shoved a shiv between his ribs. He whirled around and shot him a defiant look out of dark eyes.

"I didn't do nothing. I was just grabbin' this for my friend."

"I'm sure. Come on. Hand it over."

The boy's grip tightened on the bag. "No way. She lost it so I told her I'd help her look for it and that's just what I'm doin'."

"I don't think so. Come on, give."

"You a cop?"

"Used to be." Until the politics and the inequities had become more than he could stomach. He didn't regret leaving the force. He enjoyed being a private investigator, picking his own cases and his own hours. The power of the badge sometimes had its privileges, though, he had to admit. Right now, he would have loved to be able to shove one into this little punk's face.

"If you ain't a cop, then I got nothin' to say to you. Back off."

The kid started to walk away but Ross grabbed his shoulder. "Afraid I'm not going anywhere. Hand over the bag."

The kid uttered a colorful curse and tried to break free. "You got it wrong, man. Let me go."

"Sure. No problem. That way you can just run through the crowd and lift a few more purses on your way through."

"I told you, I didn't steal nothin'. My friend couldn't remember where she left it. I told her I'd help her look for it so she could buy some more stuff."

"Sure kid. Whatever you say."

"I ain't lyin'!"

The boy wrestled to get free, and though he was small and slim, he was wiry and much more agile than Ross had given him credit for. To his chagrin, the teen-ager managed to break the grip on his arm and before Ross could scramble to grab him again, he had darted through the crowd.

Ross repeated the curse the kid had uttered earlier and headed after him. The punk might be fast but Ross had two major advantages—age and experience. He had chased enough desperate criminals through the grime and filth of San Antonio's worst neighborhoods to have no problem keeping up with one teenage boy carrying a bag that stood out like a flowery neon-pink beacon.

He caught up with him just before the boy would have slipped into the shadows on the edges of the art fair.

"Now you've pissed me off," Ross growled as he grabbed the kid again, this time in the unbreakable hold he should have used all along.

If he thought the boy's language was colorful before, that was nothing to the string of curses that erupted now.

"Yeah, yeah," Ross said with a tight grin. "I've heard it all before. I was a cop, remember?"

He knew he probably shouldn't be enjoying this so much. He was out of breath and working up a sweat, trying to keep the boy in place with one arm while he reached into his pocket with the other hand for the flex-cuffs he always carried. He had just fished them out and was starting to shackle the first wrist when a woman's raised voice distracted him.

"Hey! What do you think you're doing? Let go of him right this minute!"

He shifted his gaze from the boy to a woman with

light brown hair approaching them—her eyes were wide and he briefly registered a particularly delectable mouth set in sharp, indignant lines.

He thought she looked vaguely familiar but that was nothing unusual in a small town like Red Rock, where everybody looked familiar. Though he didn't spend much time here and much preferred his life in San Antonio, the Fortune side of his family was among the town founders and leaders. Their ranch, the Double Crown, was a huge cattle spread not far from town.

The Spring Fling had become a large community event, and the entire proceeds from the art festival and dance went to benefit the Fortune Foundation, the organization created in memory of his mother's cousin Ryan, that helped disadvantaged young people.

Ross was a Fortune, and even though he was from the black-sheep side, he couldn't seem to escape certain familial obligations such as weddings and funerals.

Or Spring Flings.

He might not know the woman's name, but he knew her type. He could tell just by looking at her that she was the kind of busybody, do-gooder sort who couldn't resist sticking her lovely nose into things that were none of her business.

"Sorry. I can't let him go. I just caught the kid stealing a purse."

If anything, her pretty features tightened further. "That's ridiculous. He wasn't stealing anything! He was doing me a favor."

Despite her impassioned words, he wasn't releasing the boy, not for a moment. "I'm sure the Red Rock police over at the security trailer can sort it all out. That's where we're heading. You're welcome to come along."

He would be more than happy to let her be somebody else's problem.

"I'm telling you, he didn't do anything wrong."

"Then why did he run from me?"

The slippery kid wriggled more in his hold. "Because you wouldn't listen to me, man. I tried to tell you."

"This is my purse!" the woman exclaimed. "I couldn't remember where I left it so I asked Marcus to help me find it so I could purchase some earrings from a folk artist on the next row over."

Ross studied the pair of them, the boy so wild and belligerent and the soft, blue-eyed woman who looked fragile and feminine in comparison. "Why should I believe you? Maybe you're in on the heist with him. Makes a perfect cover, nice-looking woman working together with a rough kid like him."

She narrowed her gaze, apparently unimpressed with the theory. "I'll tell you why you should believe me. Because my wallet, which is inside the bag, has my driver's license and credit cards in it. If you would stop being so cynical and suspicious for five seconds, I can show them to you."

Okay, he should have thought of that. Maybe two years away from the job had softened him more than he wanted to admit. Still, he wasn't about to let down his guard long enough for her to prove him any more of a fool.

He tossed the purse at her. "Fine. Show me."

Her look would have scorched through metal. She scooped up the purse and pawed through it, then pulled out a brocade wallet, which she unsnapped with sharp, jerky movements and thrust at him.

Sure enough, there was a Texas driver's license with

a pretty decent picture of her—a few years younger and with slightly longer hair, but it was definitely her.

Julie Osterman, the name read under her picture. He gazed at it for a full ten seconds before the name registered. He had seen it on an office door at the Foundation, next to his cousin Susan's. And he must have seen her there, as well, which explained why she looked slightly familiar.

"You work for the Fortune Foundation, don't you?"

"Yes. I'm a counselor," she tilted her head and looked more closely at him. "And you're Ross Fortune, aren't you?"

He should have recognized her. Any good cop—and private investigator—ought to be more tuned in to that sort of thing than the average citizen and be able to remember names and faces.

"I don't give a crap who you are," the wriggling teenager in his grip spat out. "Let go of me, man."

He was still holding onto the punk, he realized. Ross eased his grip a little but was reluctant to release him completely.

"Mr. Fortune, you can let go anytime now," Julie Osterman said. "It all happened exactly as he said. He was helping me find my purse, not stealing anything. Thank you so much for your help, Marcus! I'm so relieved you found it. You can go now."

Ross pulled his hand away, surrendering to the inevitable, and Marcus straightened his ratty T-shirt like it was two hundred dollars' worth of cashmere.

"Dude's a psycho," he said to no one in particular but with a fierce glare for Ross. "I tried to tell you, man. You should have listened. Stupid cop-pig."

"Marcus," Julie said. Though the word was calm enough, even Ross recognized the steel behind it.

Marcus didn't apologize, but he didn't offer more insults, either. "I got to fly. See you, Ms. O."

"Bye, Marcus."

He ambled away, exuding affronted attitude with every step.

When he was out of earshot, Julie Osterman turned back to him, her mouth set in those tight lines again. He was so busy wondering if she ever unbent enough to genuinely smile that he nearly missed her words.

"I hope you haven't just undone in five minutes here what has taken me weeks to build with Marcus."

It took him a few more seconds longer than it should have to realize she was wasn't just annoyed, she was fuming.

"What did I do?" he asked in genuine bewilderment.

"Marcus is one of my clients at the Foundation," she said. "He comes from, well, not an easy situation. The adults in his life have consistently betrayed him. He's never had anyone to count on. I've been trying to help him learn to trust me, to count on *me,* by demonstrating that I trust him in return."

"By throwing your purse out there as bait?"

"Marcus has a history of petty theft."

"Just the kind of kid I would send after my purse, then."

She fisted her hands on her hips and the movement made all her curves deliciously visible beneath her gauzy white shirt. "I wanted him to understand that when I look at him, I see beyond the mistakes he's made in the past to the bright future we're both trying to create for him."

It sounded like a bunch of hooey to him but he decided it might be wise to keep that particular opinion to himself right now, considering she looked like she wanted to skin him, inch by painful inch.

"Instead," she went on in that irritated voice, "you have probably just reinforced to a wounded child that all adults are suspicious and cynical, quick to judge and painfully slow to admit when they're wrong."

"Hey, wait a second here. I had no way of knowing you were trying for some mumbo-jumbo psychobabble experiment. All I saw was a punk lifting a purse. I couldn't just stand there and let him take it."

"Admit it," she snapped. "You jumped to conclusions because he looks a little rough around the edges."

Her hair was light brown, shot through with blond highlights that gleamed in the last few minutes of twilight. With those brilliant blue eyes, high cheekbones and eminently kissable mouth, she was just about the prettiest woman he had seen in a long, long time. The kind of woman a man never got tired of looking at.

Too bad such a nice package had to be covering up one of those save-the-world types who always set his teeth on edge.

"I was a cop for twelve years, ma'am," he retorted. "When I see a kid taking a purse that obviously doesn't belong to him, yeah, I tend to jump to conclusions. That doesn't mean they're usually wrong conclusions."

"But sometimes they are," she doggedly insisted.

"In this case, I made a mistake. See, I'm man enough to admit it. I made a mistake," he repeated. "It happens to the best of us, even ex-cops. But I'm willing to bet, if you asked anybody else in the whole damn art fair, they would have reached the same conclusion."

"You don't know that."

He rolled his eyes. "You're right. I completely overreacted. The next time I see somebody stealing your purse, I'll be sure to just watch him walk on by."

The angry set of her features eased a little and after

a moment, she sighed. "I hope I can convince Marcus you were just being an ex-cop."

Despite his own annoyance, he could see she genuinely cared about the boy. He supposed he could see things from her point of view. He had a particular soft spot for anybody who tried to help kids in need, even if they did tend to become zealots about it.

"I can try talking to the kid if that would help," he finally offered, though he wasn't quite sure what compelled him to make the suggestion. Maybe something to do with how her eyes softened when she talked about the punk.

"I appreciate that, but I don't think—"

A woman's frantic scream suddenly ripped through the evening, cutting off whatever Julie Osterman had intended to say.

Julie's heart jumped in her chest as another long scream echoed through the fair. She gasped and instinctively turned toward the source of the sound, somewhere out of their view, away from the public areas and the four long rows of vendor tents.

Before she could even draw a breath to exclaim over the noise, Ross Fortune was racing in the direction of the sound.

He was all cop now, she couldn't help thinking.

Hard and alert and dangerous.

She was too startled to do more than watch him rush toward the sound for a few seconds. It always managed to astound her when police officers and firefighters raced toward potentially hazardous situations while people like her stood frozen.

She knew a little about Ross Fortune from her friend Susan, his cousin. He had been a police officer in San

Antonio but had left the force a few years ago to open his own private investigation company.

He was a trained detective, she reminded herself, and she would probably do wise to just let him, well, *detect*.

But as another scream ripped through the night, past the happy laughter of the carnival rides and the throbbing bass coming from the dance, Julie knew she had to follow him, whether she was comfortable with it or not.

Someone obviously needed help and she couldn't just stand idly by and do nothing.

Ross had a head start on her but she managed to nearly catch up as he darted around the corner of a display of pottery she had admired earlier in the evening.

Probably only ten seconds had elapsed from the instant they heard the first scream, but time seemed to stretch and elongate like the pulled taffy being sold on the midway alongside kettle corn, snow cones and cotton candy.

She ran after Ross and stumbled onto a strange, surreal scene. It was darker back here, away from the lights and noise of the Spring Fling crowd. But Julie could still tell instantly that the woman with the high-pitched scream was someone she recognized from seeing her around town, a blowsy blonde who usually favored miniscule halter tops and five-inch high heels.

She was staring at something a dozen yards away, illuminated by a lone vapor light, high on a power pole. A figure was lying motionless on the ground, faceup, and even from here, Julie could see a dark pool of what she assumed was blood around his head.

A third person stood over the body. It took Julie only a moment to recognize Frannie Fortune Fredericks, a frequent volunteer at the center.

And Ross's sister, she remembered with stunned dismay that she saw reflected in his features.

Frannie was staring at her hands. In the pale moonlight, they shone much darker than the rest of her skin.

"It's her. She killed him!" the other woman cried out stridently. "Can't you see? The bitch killed my Lloyd!"

Her Lloyd? As in Lloyd Fredericks, Frannie's husband? Julie looked closer at the figure on the ground. For the first time, she registered his sandy-blond hair and those handsome, slightly smarmy features, and realized she was indeed staring into the fixed, unblinking stare of Lloyd Fredericks.

This couldn't be happening...

Ross quickly crossed to Lloyd's body and knelt to search for a pulse. Julie knew even before he rose to his feet a moment later that he wouldn't have been able to find one. That sightless gaze said it all.

That was definitely Frannie's husband. And he was definitely dead.

Ross gripped his sister's arm and Julie noticed that he was careful not to touch her blood-covered hands. *How did he possibly have the sense to avoid contaminating evidence under such shocking circumstances?* she wondered.

"Frannie? What's going on? What happened?"

His sister's delicate features looked pale, almost bloodless, and she lifted stark eyes to him. "I don't... It's Lloyd, Ross."

"I can see it's Lloyd, honey. What happened to him?"

The screaming woman wobbled closer on her high heels. "She killed him. Look at her! She's got blood all over her. Oh, Lloyd, baby."

She began to wail as if her heart were being ripped out of her cosmetically enhanced chest. Julie would have liked to be a little sympathetic, but she didn't fail to notice the other woman only began the heartrending sobs when a crowd started to gather.

Ross turned to her. "Julie, do you have a phone? Can you call 911?"

"Of course," she answered. While she pulled her phone out of her pocket and started hitting buttons, she heard Ross take charge of the scene, ordering everybody to step back a couple dozen feet. In mere moments, it seemed the place was crawling with people.

The 911 operator had just answered when Julie saw a pair of police officers arrive. They must have been drawn to the commotion from other areas of the Spring Fling.

"This is Julie Osterman," she said to the 911 dispatcher. "I was going to report a…an incident at the Spring Fling but you all are already here."

"What sort of incident?" the dispatcher asked.

Julie was hesitant to use the word *murder,* but how could it be anything else? "I guess a suspicious death. But as I said, your officers are already here."

"Tell me what you know anyway."

The woman took what little information Julie could provide to relay to the officers, who were pushing the crowd even farther back.

When she hung up the phone with the dispatcher, she stood for a moment, not sure what to do, where to go. She disliked this sort of crowd scene, the almost avaricious hunger for information that seemed to seize people when something dramatic and shocking occurred nearby.

She wanted to slip away but it didn't feel quite right, especially when she had been one of the first ones on the scene. She supposed technically she was a witness, though she hadn't seen anything and knew nothing about what had happened.

Julie scanned the crowd, though she didn't know what she was seeking. A familiar face, perhaps, someone who could help her make sense of this shocking development.

In the distance, she saw someone in a black Stetson just on the other side of the edge of light emanating from the art fair. He made no move to come closer to investigate the commotion, which she found curious. But when she looked again, he was gone.

"Oh, Lloyd! My poor Lloyd."

The woman who had alerted them with her screams was nearly hysterical by now, standing just a few feet away from her and gathering more stares from the crowd. Julie watched her for a moment, then sighed and moved toward her.

Though she wanted to slap the woman silly for her hysterics—whether they were feigned or not—she supposed that wasn't a very compassionate attitude. She could at least try to calm her down a little. It was the decent thing to do.

She reached out and took the other woman's hand in hers. "Can I get you something? A drink of water, maybe?"

"Nooooo," she sobbed. "I just want my Lloyd."

Lloyd wasn't going to belong to anyone again—not his pale, stunned-looking wife and not this voluptuous woman who grieved so vociferously for him.

"I'm Julie," she said after a moment. "What's your name?"

"Crystal. Crystal Rivers. Well, that's not my real name."

"Oh. It's not?" she asked, with a perfectly straight face.

"It's my stage name. I'm a dancer. My real name is Christina. Christina Crosby."

"How about if I call you Chris?"

"Christy. That's what people call me."

Julie offered a smile, grateful that their conversation seemed to soothe the woman a bit—or at least distract her from the hysterics. "Okay, Christy. What happened? Can you tell me? All I know is that we heard you scream and came running and found him dead."

"I'll tell you what happened. She killed him. Frannie Fredericks killed my Lloyd."

Chapter 2

Julie frowned as the woman's bitter words seemed to ring through the night air.

She still couldn't quite believe it. She had always liked Frannie. The woman seemed to genuinely care about her volunteer work at the Foundation and she had always been friendly to Julie.

She supposed no one could really see inside the heart of someone else or know how they would respond when provoked, but Frannie had always seemed far too quiet and unassuming for Julie to accept that she had murdered her husband.

"How can you be so certain? Did you see her do it?"

"No. He was already dead when I came looking for him." She sniffled loudly and pulled a bedraggled tissue from her ample cleavage. "We were supposed to meet here and take off to my place after his obligations at the stupid Spring Fling. He didn't even want to come, but Lloyd had business tonight he had to take care of."

Business at the Spring Fling? Who on earth tried to conduct business at a community celebration?

"What kind?" she asked.

"I don't know. Something important. Someone he had to talk to, he said. Maybe Frannie. Maybe he told her he was going to divorce her for me. I don't know. I just know she killed him. Now watch—her brother Ross and the rest of the Fortunes are going to cover it all up. They think they own this whole damn town."

Julie shifted, uncomfortable with the other woman's antagonism. She liked and respected all the Fortunes. Susan Fortune Eldridge was one of her closest friends and she adored Lily Fortune, who was the driving force behind the Fortune Foundation that had been founded in memory of her late husband.

"Ma'am? Are you the one who found the body?"

Julie turned and found Billy Addison, a Red Rock police officer with whom she had a slight acquaintance through the Foundation.

"I did," Crystal waved her scarlet red nails like she was rodeo royalty riding around the arena. "My poor Lloyd. Have you arrested Frannie Fredericks yet?"

"Um, not yet. Let's not jump the gun here, miss. We're going to be taking statements for some time now. I'm going to need to ask you a few questions."

"Anything. I'll tell you whatever you need to know. But I don't know why you need to ask anybody anything. It's plain as my nose job that Frannie did it. Look at her—she's got blood all over her."

She let out a dramatic sob, more for effect than out of any real emotion, Julie thought, with unaccustomed cynicism.

"Lloyd was going to leave her skinny butt," Crystal

said. "She knew it and that must be why she killed him. That's what I was just saying."

"Do you know that for a fact, ma'am?" the officer asked her.

"I know they fought earlier today. On the phone. I was with Lloyd and I heard the terrible things she said to him. She called him a two-faced liar and a cheat and said as how she wasn't going to put up with it anymore."

"How did you hear her side of the conversation?" the officer asked. "Was she on speaker phone?"

Crystal gaped at him. "Um, maybe. I don't remember. Or maybe she was just talking real loud."

Or maybe the conversation never took place, Julie thought. She didn't know what to believe—but she did know she shouldn't be hearing any of this. Any affair between Lloyd Fredericks and Crystal Rivers was not something she wanted to know any more about.

She stepped away to leave the police officer to the interview. Still, Crystal wasn't exactly being unobtrusive. Her words carried to Julie as she walked through the crowd.

"I just know Frannie made my poor Lloyd's life a living hell. And now her brother's going to cover it up. Watch and see if the Fortunes don't all circle the wagons around her. You just watch and see."

The Fortunes *were* a powerful family in Red Rock. But most of the ones she had met through the Foundation were also decent, compassionate people who cared about the community and making it a better place.

The family also had its enemies, though—people who resented their wealth and power—and Julie had a feeling Crystal wouldn't be the only one who would whisper similar accusations about the Fortunes.

What a terrible way for the Spring Fling to end, she

thought as she made her way through the crowd. The event should be a celebration, a chance for everyone in town to gather and help raise money for a worthy cause. Instead, one life had been snuffed out and several others would be changed forever, especially those in Lloyd's family.

Julie knew the Frederickses had a teenage son. Josh, she thought was his name. If she wasn't mistaken, he was friendly with Ricky Farraday Jamison, her boss Linda's son, even though Ricky was a few years younger than Josh.

Had anyone told him yet? she wondered. How terrible for him if he were somehow drawn to the scene by the commotion and the crowd and happened to see his father's body lying there. It was a definite possibility, even though the police were widening the perimeter of the scene, pushing the crowd still farther back.

Perhaps proactive measures were called for. Someone should find the boy first before he could witness such a terrible sight.

Ross Fortune seemed the logical person to find his nephew. She sighed. She really didn't want to talk to him. Their altercation seemed a lifetime ago, but she would still prefer not to have anything more to do with the man.

If she had her preference, she would escape this situation completely and go as far away as possible. It reminded her far too much of another tragic scene, of police lights flashing and yellow crime tape flipping in the wind and the hard, invasive stares of the rapacious crowd.

She had a sudden memory of that terrible day seven years earlier, driving home from work, completely oblivious to the scene she would find at her tidy little house, and the subsequent crime tape and the solemn-eyed police officers and the sudden terrible knowledge that her world had just changed forever.

She didn't think about that day often anymore, but this situation was entirely too familiar. Then again it would have been unusual if the similarities didn't shake loose those memories she tried to keep so carefully contained.

She didn't want Frannie's son to go through the same thing. He needed to be warned, whether she wanted to talk to his uncle again or not. She started through the crowd, keeping an eye out for the tall, gorgeous private investigator.

In the end, he found her.

"Julie! Ms. Osterman!"

She followed the sound of her name and discovered Ross in a nearby vendor booth with his sister and the Red Rock chief of police, Jimmy Caldwell.

Frannie Fortune was slumped in a chair while her brother hovered protectively over her. She looked exactly as Julie imagined *she* had looked that day seven years ago. Frannie's lovely, delicate features were stark and pale and her eyes looked dazed. Numb.

She wanted to hug her, to promise her that sometime in the future this terrible day would be just an awful memory.

"I told you, Jim," Ross said. "I was talking to Ms. Osterman just a row over when we heard a scream. We were the first ones on the scene, weren't we? Besides the other woman."

Julie nodded.

"You're the one who called 911, right?" the police chief asked her.

"Yes. But your officers were on the scene before I

could even give the dispatcher any information. Probably only a moment or two after we arrived," she said.

The police chief wrote something in a notebook. "Can you confirm the scene as you saw it? Lloyd was on the ground and Frannie was standing over him."

"Yes." She pointed. "And the other woman—Crystal—was standing over there screaming."

"You didn't see anyone else? Just Frannie and Crystal?"

Julie nodded. "That's right. Just them."

"Frannie? You want to tell me what happened before Ross and Ms. Osterman showed up?"

She lifted her shell-shocked gaze from her blood-stained pants to the police chief. "I don't know. I was looking for... I just... I found him that way. He was just lying there."

"Tell him, Frannie," Ross insisted. "Go ahead and tell Jim you had nothing to do with Lloyd's death."

"I... I didn't."

Jimmy scratched the nape of his neck. "That's not a very convincing claim of innocence, Frannie. Especially when you're the one standing here over your dead husband's body with blood on your hands."

Ross glared at him. "Frannie is not capable of murder. You have to know that. You're crazy if you think she could have done this."

The police chief raised a dark eyebrow that contrasted with his salt-and-pepper hair. "This might not be the best time for you to be calling names, Fortune."

"What else would you call it? My sister did not kill her husband, though she should have done it years ago."

"Appears to be no love lost between the two of you, was there?"

"I hated his miserable, two-timing guts."

"Maybe you need to be the one coming down to the station for questions instead of Frannie here."

"I'll go any place you want me to. But I didn't kill him any more than my sister did. I've got an alibi, remember? Ms. Osterman here."

"He's right. He was with me," she said.

"Lucky for you. Unfortunately, by the sound of it, Frannie doesn't have that kind of alibi. I'm going to have to ask you to come with me to the station to answer some questions, Frannie."

"Come on, Jimmy. You know she couldn't have done this."

"You want to know what I know? The evidence in front of me. That's it. That's what I have to go by, no matter what. You were a cop. You know that. And I'm also quite sure this is going to be a powder keg of a case. I can't afford to let people say I allowed the Fortunes to push me around. I have to follow every procedure to the letter, which means I'm going to have to take her in for questioning. I have no choice here."

Ross glowered at the man but before he could say anything, another officer approached them. He was vibrating with energy. Julie imagined in a quiet town like Red Rock, this sort of situation was the most excitement the small police force ever saw.

"We found what might be the murder weapon, sir," the fresh-faced officer said. "I knew you would want to know right away."

"Thanks, Paul," the chief tried to cut him off before he said more, but the officer didn't take the hint.

"It was shoved under a display table in one of the tents and it's got what appears to be blood on it. I'll have CSU process it the minute they show up. Take a look. What do you think, sir?"

All of them followed the man's pointing finger and Julie could see a large, solid-looking ceramic vase. When she turned back, she saw that Frannie Fredericks had turned even more pale, if that was possible.

"What's the matter?" Ross asked her.

She shook her head and looked back at her blood-stained slacks.

"Do you know anything about that vase?" Jimmy Caldwell asked her, his gray eyes intent on her features.

When Ross's sister clamped her lips together, the police chief leaned in closer. "You have to tell me, Frannie."

She suddenly looked trapped, her gaze flitting between Jimmy Caldwell and her brother.

"Fran?" Ross asked.

"It's mine. I bought it from Reynaldo Velasquez," she finally whispered. "I wanted to put it in the upstairs hallway."

Ross muttered an expletive. "Don't say anything else, Frannie. Not until I get you an attorney. Just keep your mouth shut, okay?"

She blinked at her brother. "Why do I need an attorney? I didn't do anything wrong. I just bought a vase."

"Just don't say anything."

"In that case," the police chief said, "I guess we'll have to continue this conversation at the police station."

"You don't have nearly enough to arrest her. You know you don't."

"Not yet." The police chief's voice was grim.

"Josh. You have to find Josh," Frannie said suddenly. She clutched her brother's arm. "Find him, Ross. Get him away from here."

He looked taken aback by her urgency. "I'll look for him."

"Thank you, Ross. You've always taken care of everything."

He opened his mouth to say something, then clamped it shut again.

"Let's go, Frannie," the police chief's voice wasn't unkind. "I'm sure it will be a relief to you to get away from this crowd."

"Yes," she murmured.

The police chief slipped a huge navy windbreaker over her blood-stained clothing, then wrapped his arm around her shoulders. By all appearances, it looked as if he were consoling the grieving widow but Julie saw the implacable set to his muscles, as if he expected the slight woman to make a break for it any moment.

Ross watched after them, his jaw tight. "This is a fricking nightmare," he growled. "Unbelievable."

"Do you need help finding your nephew? I was coming to find you and suggest you look for him. It would be terrible for him to stumble onto this scene without knowing the…the victim was his father."

He muttered an expletive. "You're right. I should have thought of that before. I should have gone to look for him right away."

"I'll help you," she said. "We can split up. You take the midway and I'll head to the dance."

He blinked at the offer. "Why would you want to do that? You've already been dragged far enough into this."

He wouldn't get any arguments from her on that score. She would much rather be home in her quiet, solitary house than wandering through a crowd looking for a boy whose world was about to change forever.

She shrugged. "You need help."

He eyes widened with astonishment, and she wondered why he found a simple offer of assistance so very shocking.

"Thanks, then," he mumbled.

"No problem. Do you have a picture of Josh?"

"A picture?"

"I can't find him if I don't know what he looks like," she pointed out gently.

"Oh right. Of course."

He pulled his wallet out of his back pocket, and she was more charmed than she had any right to be when he opened an accordion fold in the wallet and slid out a photograph of a smiling young man with dark-blond hair, brown eyes and handsome features.

"I'm almost certain I've seen him around at the Foundation but the picture will help immensely," she said. "I'll be careful with it."

"I have more," Ross answered.

"We should exchange cell phone numbers so we can contact each other if either of us finds him."

"Good idea," he said. He rattled off a number, which she quickly entered into her phone, then she gave him hers in return.

"Now that you mention cell phones, it occurs to me that I should have thought of that first," Ross said. "Let me try to reach Josh on his phone. Maybe I can track him down and meet him somewhere away from here."

She waited while he dialed, impatient at even a few more moments of delay. The longer they waited, the more likely Josh would accidentally stumble onto his father's body and the murder scene.

After a moment, Ross made a face and left a message on the boy's voice mail for him to call him as soon as possible.

"He's not answering. I guess we're back to the original plan. I'll cover the midway and you see if you can find him at the dance."

"Deal. I'll call you if I find him."

"Right back at you. And Ms. Osterman? Thank you."

She flashed him a quick smile, though even that seemed inappropriate under the circumstances. "Julie, please."

He nodded and they each took off in separate directions. She quickly made her way to the dance, though she was forced to virtually ignore several acquaintances on her way, greeting them with only a wave instead of her usual conversation. She would have to explain later and hope they understood.

She expected Ross's call at any moment but to her dismay, her phone still hadn't rung by the time she reached the dance.

Country swing music throbbed from the speakers and the plank-covered dance floor was full. Finding Josh in this throng would be a challenge, especially when she knew him only from a photograph.

She scanned the crowd, looking for familiar faces. Finally, she found two girls she had worked with at the Foundation standing with a larger group.

"Hey, Ms. O." They greeted her with a warmth she found gratifying.

"Hey, Katie. Hi, Jo. I could use your help. I'm trying to find a boy."

"Aren't we all?" Jo said with a roll of eyes heavily framed in mascara.

Julie smiled. "A particular boy, actually. It's kind of serious. Do either of you know Josh Fredericks?"

"Sure," Katie answered promptly. "He's in my algebra class. He's kind of cute, even if he is super smart."

"Have you seen him lately? Tonight?"

"Yeah. It's weird. Usually he doesn't go two inches away from his girlfriend but I saw him by himself earlier, over by the refreshments. I think that was a while ago. Maybe an hour. He might have ditched the place by now."

"Thanks," she answered and headed in the direction they pointed.

She found Josh right where Katie had indicated, standing near the refreshment table as if he were waiting for someone. She recognized him instantly from the picture Ross had provided. He was wearing a Western-cut shirt and a black Stetson, just like half the other men here, and she could see his dark blond hair and brown eyes like his uncle's.

She didn't know whether to feel relief or dismay at finding him. She did not want to have to explain to him why she was searching for him. She quickly texted Ross that she had located his nephew at the dance and waited close by, intending only to keep an eye on him until Ross arrived to handle things.

He looked upset, she thought after a moment of observing him. His color was high and he kept looking toward the door as if waiting for someone to arrive.

Did he already know about his father? No, she couldn't imagine it. Why would he linger here at the dance if he knew his father had just been killed?

After two or three minutes, Josh suddenly looked at his watch, then set down his cup on a nearby tray.

Rats. She was going to have to talk to him, she realized, as he started heading for the door. She waited until he walked out into the much cooler night air before she caught up to him.

"Are you Josh?"

He blinked a little, obviously startled to find a strange

older woman talking to him. "Yeah," he said slowly, not bothering to conceal his wariness.

"My name is Julie Osterman. I work at the Fortune Foundation with your mother's cousin Susan."

"Okay." He took a sidestep away from her and she sighed.

"Josh, this is going to sound crazy, I know," she began, "but I need you to stay here for a minute."

"Why?"

She couldn't tell him his father was dead. That job should fall to someone closer to him, someone with whom he had a relationship. "Your uncle is looking for you," she finally answered. "He really needs to talk to you. If you can hang around here for a minute, he should be along any time now."

She hoped.

"What's going on?" His gaze sharpened. "Is it my mom?"

"Your mom isn't hurt. Ross can explain everything when he gets here?"

"No. Tell me now. Is it Lyndsey? She was supposed to meet me here but she never showed and she's not answering her phone. Is she hurt? What's going on?"

"Josh—"

"Tell me!"

She was scrambling for words when a deep male voice spoke from behind her.

"It's your dad, Josh."

Chapter 3

She turned with vast relief to see Ross walking toward them, looking tall and solid and certainly strong enough to help his nephew through this.

The boy's features hardened. "Did he hurt Mom again? If he did, I'll kill him this time, I swear. I warned him I would."

"You might not want to say that too loudly," Ross said grimly. "Your father is dead, Josh."

For all his bravado just seconds before, the teenager's color drained at the words.

"Dead? That's crazy." Even as he spoke, Julie thought she saw something flicker in his brown eyes, something furtive, secretive.

"It's true," Ross said. "I'm sorry, Josh."

The boy gazed at him blankly, as if he wasn't quite sure how to respond.

"What happened?"

Ross cleared his throat. "We don't know for sure yet."

"Did he have a heart attack or a stroke or something? Was he hit by a bus? What?"

Ross sighed. His gaze met Julie's for a moment and she saw indecision there as he must be weighing just how blunt he ought to be with his nephew.

She would have told him to be as honest as possible. Josh would find out all the gory details soon enough. In a town like Red Rock, the rumors would fly faster than crows on carrion. Better for him to hear the news from his family than for them to all dissemble about the situation, which he would probably find condescending and demeaning.

Ross must have reached the same conclusion. "It's too early to say anything with a hundred percent certainty but it looks like he was murdered."

"Murdered?" Josh blinked at both of them. "You're kidding me, right? This is all some kind of a sick joke. People in Red Rock don't get murdered!"

"I'm afraid it's no joke," Julie said, her voice soft with compassion.

"Who did it? Do they have any suspects?"

Ross's gaze met Julie's again with a wordless plea for help and she thought how surreal it was that just an hour ago they were wrangling over her purse, and now he was turning to her to help him through this delicate family situation.

It was hard enough telling Josh his father was dead. How were they supposed to tell Josh that his own mother was the prime suspect?

"They're still investigating," Ross said after a moment.

Josh pulled off his Stetson and raked a hand through

his hair. "This is crazy. I can't believe it," he said again. "Where's my mom? How is she taking this?"

"Uh, that's the other thing I needed to talk to you about," Ross said.

Fear leapt into his dark eyes and he turned to Julie with an accusation in his eyes. "You said my mom wasn't hurt!"

"She's not," Ross assured him. "It's just… Frannie had to go to the police station to answer some questions."

Josh obviously wasn't a stupid boy. He quickly put the pieces together. "*Mom* had to go for questioning? They think *she* killed him?"

"Josh—"

The color that had leached away at the news of his father's death returned in a hot, angry flush. "That's the most ridiculous thing I've ever heard! If she had it in her to kill him, she would have done it years ago."

If Julie hadn't worked with troubled youth on a daily basis for the last five years, she might have found his bitterness shocking. Instead, she found it unutterably sad.

"They're only questioning her. She's not under arrest," Ross said. "I'm sure they'll figure out soon enough that your mom is innocent."

"What about his girlfriend? Are they questioning her? Or his last girlfriend? Or the one before that? I could give them a whole damn list of suspects!"

"I'm sure they'll question as many people as they can," Julie said. Unable to help herself, she laid a comforting hand on the boy's arm. Though by all appearances he despised his father, her heart ached at the pain she knew still waited for him down the road. Losing a parent was traumatic for anyone, no matter what their relationship.

Josh didn't flinch away from her touch, but he remained focused on his mother and her predicament.

"I should go to her," he said after a moment. "She's going to need me."

Ross couldn't seem to look away from that soft, comforting hand Julie placed on his nephew's arm. There was no good reason he could figure out that the sight should put a funny little ache in his chest.

He cleared his throat. "I promise, the police station is no place for you right now, Josh. You have to trust me on this."

He, however, needed to get his butt over there as soon as possible to find out what was happening with the investigation. He was torn between dueling obligations, one to his sister and one to his nephew during this difficult time.

"I'll be eighteen in two weeks, Uncle Ross. I'm not a child anymore."

"I know that. But I've spent most of my adult life in police stations and I can tell you the best place for you is at home. I'll go check on your mother."

"I want to see her."

"She won't be able to talk to you, son. Not if she's being questioned."

"Well, I can at least tell them that I know she couldn't have killed Lloyd," Josh answered.

His loyal defense of his mother struck a chord with Ross. It reminded him far too much of the way he used to stick up for Cindy, making excuses to the other kids when she would stay out all night drinking or would bring a new man around the house or, worse, would entirely forget about them all for a weekend binge.

The difference there was that he had foolishly been

trying to protect an illusion, while Josh's efforts were on behalf of an innocent woman.

"Everything's going to be okay. Trust me. She's only being questioned. I'm sure she'll be home in a short time. Why don't you head on home and get some rest? You're going to have a lot to deal with in the coming days."

"I should be with her," Josh said stubbornly.

Julie again reached out to Josh and Ross saw that once more her quiet touch seemed to soothe him. "The absolute best way you can help your mother right now is to give her one less worry. You were the only thing she thought about as they were taking her in for questioning. She insisted that your uncle watch out for you and that's just what he's trying to do. As he said, you have to trust him right now to know what's best, okay?"

Her words seemed to resonate with Josh. He looked between the two of them and then sighed. "I guess."

Ross was astounded and more gratified than he wanted to admit that she would come to his defense like this, especially after their altercation earlier in the evening. That encounter and his own honest mistake over the purse had been a fortuitous meeting, he thought now. He didn't know what he would have done this evening without her.

The thought sparked an idea—a nervy one, sure, but one that would certainly lift a little of the burden from his shoulders.

"Josh, could you hang on here for a second while I talk to Ms. Osterman?"

His nephew looked confused but he nodded and Ross stepped a few paces away where they could speak in relative privacy.

"Look, I do need to get to the police station to see how things are going with Frannie, but I don't want to send Josh to his empty house alone. This is a huge favor to ask when I'm virtually a stranger to you and you've already done so much, but do you think you could stay with him for a while, while I check on my sister?"

As he might have expected, Julie's soft blue eyes widened with astonishment at the request. "But wouldn't you rather have someone in your family stay with him? Your cousin Susan, maybe?"

Susan would come in a heartbeat, he knew, and like Julie, she specialized in troubled adolescents. But he hated to ask the Fortune side of the family for anything. It was an irrational reaction, he knew, but for most of his life his particular branch of the family had always been the needy ones.

He didn't know how many times the Fortunes had bailed Cindy out of one scrape or another, before they had virtually cut ties with her out of frustration that nothing ever seemed to change.

Even though he loved and admired several members of his extended family, Ross preferred to handle things on his own when he could. And when he couldn't, he much preferred asking somebody who wasn't a Fortune for help.

"They're all going to be busy with the last few hours of the Spring Fling. Plus, now they're going to have to deal with damage control after Lloyd's murder."

It was bad public relations for the festival, especially since this was the second time a dead body had been found while the town celebrated. A few years earlier, an unidentified body turned up at the Spring Fling. The town had only just started to heal from that.

Her forehead furrowed for a moment and then she nodded. "In that case, of course. I'll be glad to stay with Josh as long as you need."

For one crazy moment, he longed to feel the soft

comfort of her touch on *his* arm, though he knew that was ridiculous.

"Thanks a million. It won't be long. I'm sure I'll be taking Frannie home in just a few hours.

He had been far too optimistic, Ross thought an hour later as he stood in the Red Rock police chief's office.

"Come on, Jimmy. This is a mistake. You have to know that. There's no way on earth Frannie killed Lloyd."

"You were on the job long enough, you know how it works. We just want to talk to her but she's not saying a word. She's shutting us down in every direction. I have to tell you, that makes her look mighty guilty."

A white-coated lab tech pushed open the door. "Chief, I've got those results you put the rush order on."

"Excellent. You're going to have to excuse me, Ross. Why don't you go on home? There's nothing more you can do here tonight."

"I'll stick around. Somebody's going to need to drive Frannie home when you're done with this little farce here."

Jimmy opened his mouth to answer, then closed it again. "I can't make you leave. But if you really want to help your sister, tell her to cooperate with us. The quicker she gives us her side of the story, the quicker we can wrap this up."

Ross had been a cop for a long time, trained to catch subtle nuances in conversation. He didn't miss the way the police chief phrased his words. *Wrap this up* was a far cry from *send her home.*

Something about this whole thing gave him an ominous feeling. He suddenly guessed he was in for a long night.

Chapter 4

Four hours and counting.

From his perch in an empty detective's chair, Ross looked at the clock above the chief's glass-walled office in the Red Rock police station.

He couldn't think the long delay boded well for Frannie. It was now nearly half past midnight and she had been in an interrogation room for hours.

His poor sister. Eighteen years of marriage to Lloyd Fredericks had just about wrung every drop of spirit out of her. She must be sick over this ordeal.

What could be taking so long? Frannie should have been released hours ago. With every tick of the clock, his hopes for a quick resolution trickled a little further away.

When the police chief emerged from the hallway that housed the interview room and headed for his office, Ross rose quickly and intercepted him.

"What's going on, Jimmy? I need info here."

His friend gave him a long, solemn look and Ross's stomach suddenly clenched with nerves. He did not like the implications of that look.

"She's going to be charged, Ross. We have no choice."

He stared at the other man, not willing yet to accept the unthinkable. "Charged with what?"

The chief rolled his eyes. "With jaywalking. Lord, Ross, what the hell do you think, *with what*. With murder!"

This couldn't be happening. Ross balled his fists. "That's bull! This whole thing is bull and you know it! Frannie no more killed Lloyd than I did."

"Are you confessing?"

"I've thought about killing the bastard a thousand times," he answered the chief. "Does that count?"

"Sorry, but if we could prosecute thoughts, I doubt there would be anybody left *outside* the walls of my jail."

"What evidence can you possibly have against Frannie that's not circumstantial?" he asked.

The police chief just shook his head. "You know I can't talk about that, Ross, especially not with the suspect's own brother, even if he is an ex-cop and an old friend. Even if you weren't Frannie's brother, I couldn't tell you anything."

"Come on, throw me a little bone here. It's only been four hours since Lloyd's death. Why the big rush? You haven't even had time to look at any other possibilities! What about Crystal Rivers? She claimed she just stumbled onto the body and found Frannie there, but she doesn't exactly seem like the most upright, stalwart citizen of Red Rock. For all we know, she could have killed him, then waited around for somebody else to find him before circling back and throwing her big drama queen scene."

Jimmy was quiet for a moment, then he motioned toward his office. They walked in, and he shut the door and closed the louvered blinds to conceal their conversation from any other curious eyes that might be watching in the station house.

"Look, I don't know if this is my place, but you and I have been around the block together a few times, from our days at the academy together to our time in the same division in San Antonio. I respect you more than just about any detective on my force and you know I'd hire you here in an instant if you ever decided to come back to the job."

"I appreciate that. Just be straight with me, Jimmy."

"I'll just remind you who calls the shots around here when it comes to prosecutions. Bruce Gibson. That's not helping the situation for Frannie, especially when she's refusing to say anything about what happened."

Ross gazed at the other man as the implications sunk in. Bruce Gibson was the district attorney—and a particularly vindictive one at that. He was the one who chose when charges would be filed and what those charges would entail. Even if the police department wanted to pursue other leads, a district attorney could make the final choice about whether they had enough evidence to go forward with a prosecution.

And he had been one of Lloyd's closest friends, Ross suddenly remembered, had practically grown up at the Fredericses' mansion.

Gibson would be out for blood—and it would be a bonus to the man if he could extract a little of that blood from the Fortunes. Gibson had made no secret of the fact that he thought the Fortunes were too wealthy, too powerful. He was up for a tough re-election battle in the fall and from all appearances, he seemed to be making an issue of the fact that he considered himself a man of the people and wouldn't let somebody's social status sway prosecutorial decisions.

Added to that, there was no love lost between Ross and Bruce Gibson. Just a few weeks earlier, he and Ross had exchanged words over an incident involving a stable fire on the family ranch and the way the family was choosing to investigate it privately.

What a tangled mess. Any other district attorney would see how ludicrous this whole thing was.

"Can I see her?" he asked.

Caldwell gave him a long, appraising look, then finally nodded. "It's past normal visiting hours but we can make an exception in this case. It might take a few moments, though. She's in central booking."

Perhaps half an hour later, Ross was finally ushered by the young, fresh-faced police officer he had seen earlier on the murder scene to a stark white interview room. Frannie looked up when the door opened and Ross had to stop from clenching his fists again at the sight of her in a prison-orange jumpsuit.

Since his sister's ill-fated marriage to Fredericks years ago, he had seen her disheartened and hurt, he had seen her hopeless and bleak. But he didn't think he had ever seen her look so desperately afraid.

The chair scraped as he pulled it out to sit down and she flinched a little at the noise.

"Hey, Frannie-Banannie."

Her eyes filled up with tears at the childish nickname. "You haven't called me that in years."

He was suddenly sorry for that, sorry that while he had never completely withdrawn from his family, he had enjoyed the distance that came from living twenty miles away in San Antonio. He didn't have to be involved in the day-to-day drama of family affairs, didn't have to watch Frannie slowly become this washed-out version of herself.

"How are you doing, sis?"

She shrugged. "I guess you know they're charging me."

"Yeah. Jim told me. Sounds like Bruce Gibson is on the warpath."

Her mouth tightened but she only looked down at her hands.

"What happened, Frannie?"

"I don't want to talk about it."

"That's what I hear. But you told them you didn't do it, right?"

She didn't answer him. Instead she rubbed the fraying sleeve of the jumpsuit between her thumb and forefinger. "How's Josh?" she asked.

He sighed at her evasive tactic but decided to let it go for now. "He's fine. I sent him back to your house."

"He shouldn't be alone right now. Is someone with him?"

"Julie Osterman is with him."

"Julie? From the Foundation? Why?"

Because I didn't want to ask the family to bail us all out once again, he thought but could never say. "She was with me when…everything happened. I couldn't be in two places at once and I needed help and Julie seemed a good choice since she's a youth counselor and all, like Susan."

"Julie is nice."

Frannie sounded exhausted suddenly, emotionally

and physically, and he wanted to gather her up and take care of her.

Those days were gone, though. Try as he might, he couldn't fix everything. He couldn't fix her marriage for the last eighteen years. He couldn't get his young, happy sister back. And he wasn't at all sure he could extricate her from this mess, though he sure as hell was going to try.

"Ross, I need you to do something for me."

"Anything. Whatever you need."

"Take care of Josh for me. Stay with him at the house. I know he's almost eighteen and almost an adult and will probably tell you he doesn't need anyone else but I don't want him on his own right now. Help him through this, okay? He's going to need you."

"Come on, Frannie. Don't worry. You'll be out before we know it and this will all be a memory."

"Just help him. You've always been far more of a father to him than...than Lloyd."

"You don't even need to ask, Fran. Of course I will."

"Thank you." She attempted such a forlorn smile it just about broke his heart. "I can always count on you."

If that were true, she wouldn't be in this calamity. She wouldn't have been married to Lloyd in the first place and she wouldn't be facing murder charges right now, if he had been able to rescue her from the situation years ago, like he'd wanted to.

"We'll get the best attorney we can find for you, okay? Just hang in."

She nodded, though it looked as if it took the last of her energy just to make that small gesture. He had a feeling in another minute, his baby sister was going to fold her arms on the interrogation room table, lay her head down and fall instantly asleep.

"Get some rest, okay?" he advised her. "Everything will seem better in the morning, I promise."

She managed another nod. Ross glanced at the officer who was monitoring the visit, then thought, to hell with this. He pulled his sister into his arms, noting not for the first time that she seemed as fragile and insubstantial as a stained-glass window.

"Thanks, Ross," she mumbled before the guard pulled her away and led her from the room.

The Spring Fling seemed another lifetime ago as Ross drove the streets of Red Rock toward the house where Frannie and Lloyd moved shortly after their marriage.

The security guard at the entrance to their exclusive gated community knew him. His fleshy features turned avid the moment Ross rolled down his window.

"Mr. Fortune. I guess you're here to stay with your sister's boy, huh? You been to the jail to see her?"

The news was probably spreading through town like stink in springtime. "Yeah. Can you let me in?"

"Oh, sure, sure," he said, though he made no move to raise the security arm. "Jail is just no place for a nice lady like Mrs. F. Why, you could have knocked me six ways to Sunday when my cousin Lou called to tell me what had happened at the Spring Fling. Too bad I was here working and missed everything."

Ross gestured to the gate. "Can you let me in, George? I really need to be with my nephew right now."

The guard hit the button with a disappointed kind of look.

"You tell Mrs. F. I'm thinking about her, okay?"

"I'll be sure to do that, George. Thanks."

He quickly rolled his window up and drove through

the gate before George decided he wanted to chat a little more.

Lights blazed from every single window of the grand pink stucco McMansion he had always secretly thought of as a big, gaudy wedding cake. There was no trace of his sister's elegant good taste in the house. It was as if Lloyd had stamped out any trace of Frannie.

The interior of the house wasn't any more welcoming. It was cold and formal, white on white with gold accents.

Ross knew of two rooms in the house with a little personality. Josh's bedroom was a typical teenager's room with posters on the wall and clutter and mementos covering every surface.

The other was Frannie's small sitting room that hinted at the little sister he remembered. It was brightly decorated, with local handiworks, vivid textiles and many of Frannie's own photographs on the wall.

Lloyd had a habit of changing the security system all the time so Ross didn't even try to open the door. He rang the doorbell and a moment later, Julie Osterman opened the door, her soft, pretty features looking about as exhausted as Frannie's had been.

"I'm sorry I'm so late," he said. "I never expected things to take this long, that I would have to impose on you until the early hours of the morning."

"No problem." She held the door open for him and he moved past her into the formal foyer. "Josh tried to send me home and insisted he would be okay on his own, but I just didn't feel right about leaving him here alone, under the circumstances."

"I appreciate that."

"He's in the kitchen on the telephone to a friend."

"At this hour? Is it Lyndsey?"

Josh's young girlfriend had been a source of conflict between Josh and his parents, for reasons Ross didn't quite understand.

"I think so, but I can't be certain. I was trying not to eavesdrop."

"How is he?"

She frowned a little as she appeared to give his question serious consideration. Despite his own fatigue, Ross couldn't help noticing the way her mouth pursed a little when she was concentrating, and he had a wild urge to kiss away every line.

He definitely needed sleep if he was harboring inappropriate fantasies about a prickly busybody type like Julie Osterman.

"I can't really tell, to be honest with you," she answered. "I get the impression he's more upset about his mother being detained at the police station than he seems to be about his father's death. Or at least that appears to be where he's focusing his emotions right now. On the other hand, his reaction could just be displacement."

"Want to skip the mumbo jumbo?"

She made a face. "Sorry. I just meant maybe he's not ready—or doesn't want—to face the reality of his father's death right now, so it's easier to place his energy and emotion on his mother's situation."

"Or maybe he just happens to be more upset about Frannie than he is about Lloyd. The two of them didn't exactly get along."

"So I hear," she answered. "It sounds as if few people did get along with Lloyd Fredericks, besides Crystal and her sort."

"And there were plenty of those."

Her mouth tightened but she refrained from commenting on his bitterness. Lloyd's frequent affairs had been a great source of humiliation for Frannie. "How is your sister?" she asked instead.

"Holding up okay, under the circumstances."

"Do you expect them to keep her overnight for questioning, then?"

He sighed, angry all over again at the most recent turn of events. "Not for questioning. For arraignment. She's being charged."

Her eyes widened with astonishment, then quickly filled with compassion. "Oh, poor Josh. This is going to be so hard on him."

"Yeah, it's a hell of a mess," he answered heavily. "So it looks like I'll be staying here for a while, until we can sort things out."

She touched him, just a quick, almost furtive brush of her hand on his arm, much as she had touched Josh earlier. Through his cotton shirt, he could feel the warmth of her skin and he was astonished at the urge to wrap his arms around her and pull her close and just lean on her for a moment.

"I'm so sorry, Ross."

He cleared his throat and told himself he was nothing but relieved when she pulled her hand away.

"Thanks again for everything you did tonight," he said. "I would have been in a real fix without you."

"I'm glad I could help in some small way."

She smiled gently and he was astonished at how that simple warm expression could ease the tightness in his chest enough that he could breathe just a little easier.

"It's late," she finally said. "Or early, I guess. I'd better go."

"Oh right. I'm sorry again you had to be here so long."

"I'd like to say goodbye to Josh before I leave, if it's all right with you," she said.

"Of course," he answered and followed her into the kitchen.

In his fantasy childhood, the kitchen was always the warmest room in the house, a place scattered with children's backpacks and clumsy artwork on the refrigerator and homemade cookies cooling on a rack on the countertop.

He hadn't known anything like that, except at the occasional friend's house. To his regret, Frannie's kitchen wasn't anything like that image, either. It was as cool and formal as the rest of the house—white cabinets, white tile, stainless-steel appliances. It was like some kind of hospital lab rather than the center of a house.

Josh sat on a white bar stool, his cell phone up to his ear.

"I told you, Lyns," he was saying, "I don't have any more information than I did when we talked an hour ago. I haven't heard anything yet. I'll tell you as soon as I know anything, okay? Meantime, you have to get some rest. You know what—"

Ross wasn't sure what alerted the boy to their presence but before he could complete the sentence, he suddenly swiveled around to face them. Ross was almost certain he saw secrets flash in his nephew's eyes before his expression turned guarded again.

"Um, I've got to go, Lyns," he mumbled into the phone. "My uncle Ross just got here. Yeah. I'll call you later."

He ended the call, folded his phone and slid it into his pocket before he uncoiled his lanky frame from the chair.

"How's my mom? Is she with you?"

Ross sighed. "No. I'm sorry."

"How long can they hold her?"

"For now, as long as they want. She's being charged."

His features suffused with color. "Charged? With *murder?*"

Ross nodded, wishing he had other news to offer his nephew.

"This completely sucks."

That was one word for it, he supposed. A pretty accurate one. "Yeah, it does. But there's nothing we can do about it tonight. Meanwhile, Ms. Osterman needs to get on back to her house. She came in to tell you goodbye."

He was proud of the boy for reining in most of his outrage in order to be polite to Julie.

"Thank you for giving me a ride and staying here and everything," Josh said to her. "And even though I told you I didn't need you to stay so late, it was…nice not to be here by myself and all."

"You're very welcome." She smiled with that gentle warmth she just seemed to exude, paused for just a moment, then stepped forward and hugged the boy, who was a good six inches taller than she was.

"Call me if you need to talk, okay?" she said softly.

"Yeah, sure," he mumbled, though Ross was pretty sure Josh looked touched by her concern.

They both walked her to the door and watched her climb into her car. When she drove away, Ross shut the door to Frannie's wedding-cake house and wondered what the hell he was supposed to do next.

He would just have to figure it out, he supposed.

He didn't have any other choice.

This was just about the last place on earth he wanted to be right now.

In fact, given a choice between attending his de-

spised brother-in-law's funeral and wading chest-deep
in a manure pit out on the Double Crown, Ross figured
he would much rather be standing in cow honey swat-
ting flies away from his face than sitting here in this
discreetly decorated funeral home, surrounded by the
cloying smell of lilies and carnations and listening to
all the weeping and wailing going on over a man most
people in town had disliked.

It would be over soon. Already, the eulogies seemed
to be dwindling. He could only feel relief. This all
seemed the height of hypocrisy. He knew of at least a
dozen people here who had openly told him at separate
times over the last few days how much they had hated
Lloyd. Yet here they were with their funeral game faces,
all solemn and sad-eyed.

He glanced over at his nephew, who seemed to be
watching the entire proceedings with an odd detach-
ment, as if it was all some kind of mildly interesting
play that had no direct bearing on his life.

Josh seemed to be holding up well under the strain
of the last five days. Maybe too well. The boy's only
intense emotion over anything seemed to be rage at the
prosecuting attorney for moving ahead with charges
against his mother.

It had been a hellish five days, culminating in this
farce. First had come the medical examiner's report
read at Frannie's arraignment that Lloyd had been killed
with a blunt instrument whose general size and heft
matched the large piece of pottery his sister had purchased shortly before the murder. Then reports had
begun to trickle out that the heavy vase had several
sets of unidentified fingerprints on it—and one very
obvious identified set that belonged to his sister.

Added to Crystal's testimony that Lloyd had a heated

phone call with Frannie shortly before the murder, things weren't looking good for his sister.

A good attorney with the typical cooperative client might have been able to successfully argue that Frannie's fingerprints would naturally be on the vase since she had purchased it just a short time earlier, and that a hearsay one-sided telephone exchange—no matter how heated—was not proof of murder.

But Frannie was not the typical cooperative client. Despite the high stakes, she refused to confirm or deny her involvement in Lloyd's murder and had chosen instead to remain mum about the entire evening, even to her attorney.

Ross didn't know what the hell she was doing. He had visited twice more since the night of the murder in an effort to convince her to just tell him and the Red Rock police what had happened, but she had shut him out, too. Each time, he had ended up leaving more frustrated than ever.

As a result of her baffling, completely unexpected obstinacy, she had been charged with second-degree murder and bound over for trial. Even more aggravating, she had been denied bail. Bruce Gibson had argued in court that Frannie was a flight risk because of her wealthy family.

He apparently was laboring under two huge misconceptions: one, that Frannie would ever have it in her to run off and abandon her son and, two, that any of the Fortunes would willingly help her escape, no matter how much they might want to.

In the bail hearing, Bruce had been full of impassioned arguments about the Fortune wealth and power, the entire time with that smirk on his plastic features that Ross wanted to pound off of him.

The judge had apparently been gullible enough to buy into the myth—either that or he was another old golfing buddy of Lloyd's or his father, Cordell. Judge Wilkinson had agreed with Bruce and ordered Frannie held without bail, so now his delicate, fragile sister sat moldering in the county jail, awaiting trial on trumped-up charges that should never have been filed.

And while she was stuck there, he was forced to sit on this rickety little excuse for a chair, listening to a pack of lies about what a great guy Lloyd had been.

Ross didn't buy any of it. He had disliked the man from the day he married Frannie, when she was only eighteen. Even though she had tried to put on a bright face and play the role of a regular bride, Ross had sensed something in her eyes even then that seemed to indicate she wasn't thrilled about the marriage.

He had tried to talk her out of it but she wouldn't listen to him, probably because Cindy had pushed so hard for the marriage.

When Josh showed up several weeks shy of nine months later, Ross had put the pieces of the puzzle together and figured Lloyd had gotten her pregnant. Frannie was just the sort to try doing what she thought was the right thing for her child, even if it absolutely wasn't the right decision for *her*.

In the years since, he had watched her change from a luminous, vivacious girl to a quiet, subdued society matron. She always wore the right thing, said the right thing, but every ounce of joy seemed to have been sucked out of her.

And all because of Lloyd Fredericks, the man who apparently was heading for sainthood any day now, judging by the glowing eulogies delivered at his memorial service.

Ross wondered what all these fusty types would do if he stood up and spoke the truth, that Lloyd was just about the lousiest excuse for a human being he'd ever met—which was really quite a distinction, considering that as an ex-cop, he'd met more than his share.

In his experience, Lloyd was manipulative and dishonest. He cheated, he lied, he stole and, worse, he bullied anybody he considered weaker than himself.

Ross couldn't say any of that, though. He could only sit here and wait until this whole damn thing was over and he could take Josh home.

He glanced around at the crowd, wondering again at the most notable absence—next to Frannie's, of course. Cindy had opted not to come, and he couldn't help wondering where she might be. He would have expected his mother to be sitting right up there on the front row with Lloyd's parents. She loved nothing more than to be the center of attention, and what better place for that than at her son-in-law's memorial service, with all its drama and high emotion?

Cindy had adored her son-in-law, though Ross thought perhaps he'd seen hints that their relationship had cooled, since right around the time Cindy had been injured in a mysterious car accident.

Still, even if she and Lloyd had been openly feuding, which they weren't, he would have thought Cindy would come.

He was still wondering at her absence when the pastor finally wrapped things up a few moments later. With the autopsy completed, Lloyd's parents had elected to cremate his remains, so there would be no interment ceremony.

"Can we go now?" Josh asked him when other people started to file out of the funeral chapel.

Ross would have preferred nothing more than to hustle Josh away from all this artificiality. He knew people likely wanted to pay their respects to Lloyd's son, but he wasn't about to force the kid to stay if he didn't want to be there.

"Your call," he said.

"Let's go, then," Josh said. "I'm ready to get out of here."

As he had expected, at least a dozen people stopped them on their way to the door to wish Josh their condolences. Ross was immensely proud of his nephew for the quiet dignity with which he thanked them each for their sympathy without giving away his own feelings about his father.

They were almost to the door when Ross saw with dismay that Lloyd's mother, Jillian, was heading in their direction. Her Botox-smooth features looked ravaged just now, her eyes red and weepy. Still, fury seemed to push away the grief for now.

"How dare you show your face here!" she hissed to Ross when she was still several feet away.

Chapter 5

Several others at the funeral stopped to watch the unfolding drama and Ross did his best to edge them over to a quieter corner of the chapel, away from the greedy eyes of the crowd.

"My nephew just lost his father," he said calmly. "I'm here for him, Jillian. Surely you can understand that."

She made a scoffing sort of sound. "Your nephew lost his father because of *your sister!* If not for her, none of us would be here. He would still be alive. You have no right to come here. No right whatsoever. This service is for family members. For those of us who... who loved Lloyd. You never even liked him. You probably conspired with your sister to kill him, didn't you?"

It was such a ridiculous thing to say that Ross had no idea how to answer her grief-induced ravings.

"I'm here for Josh," he repeated. "Whatever you might think about my sister right now, and whatever the circumstances of Lloyd's death, Josh has lost his father. He asked me to come with him today and I couldn't let him down."

Though he *had* let him down, Ross thought. And he had let his sister down, over and over. He hadn't been able to get Frannie out of her lousy marriage. He had tried, dozens of times, until he finally gave up. But maybe he hadn't tried hard enough.

"I want you to leave. Right now." Jillian's features reddened and she looked on the verge of some apoplectic attack.

"We're just leaving, Grandmother," Josh assured her and Ross was proud of his nephew for his calm, sympathetic manner.

At that moment, Lloyd's father stepped up and slipped a supporting arm around his wife's shoulders. "That's not necessary. You don't have to leave, Joshua. Come along, Jillian. The Scofields were looking for you a moment ago."

Cordell gave Ross a quick, apologetic look, then steered his distraught wife away from them. Ross watched after him, his brow furrowed. He hadn't seen Lloyd's father in a few months but the man looked as if he had aged a decade or more. His features were lined and worn and he looked utterly exhausted.

Was all that from Lloyd's death? he wondered. He knew the Fredericks had always doted on their only son and of course his death was bound to hit them hard, but he hadn't expected Cordell to look so devastated.

Maybe Lloyd's death wasn't the only reason the man seemed to have aged overnight. Ross had been hearing rumors even before Lloyd's death that not all was rosy with the Frederickses' financial picture. He had heard a few whispers around town that Cordell and Lloyd had been late on some payments and had completely stopped making others.

It wouldn't have surprised him at all to learn that Lloyd had been the one keeping Fredericks Financial afloat. Maybe Cordell was terrified the whole leaky ship would sink now that his son was dead.

He made a mental note to add a little digging into their financial records to the parallel investigation he had started conducting into Lloyd's death.

"Follow the money" had always been a pretty good creed when he'd been a cop and he saw no reason for this situation to be any different.

"Sorry about that, Uncle Ross," Josh said when they finally stepped outside into the warm afternoon, along with others who seemed eager to escape the oppressive funeral chapel. "Grandmother is…distraught."

Poor Josh had a bum deal when it came to grandparents. On the one side, he had Lloyd's stiff society parents. On the other, he had Cindy. She was no better a grandmother than she'd been a mother, alternating between bouts of spoiling her grandson outrageously with flamboyant gifts she couldn't afford, followed by long periods of time when she would ignore him completely.

"Don't worry about it," Ross assured him. "Jillian's reaction is completely understandable."

"It's not. She knows my mom. She's known her for eighteen years, since she married my dad. Grandmother has to know Mom would never kill him."

"It's a rough time right now for everyone, Josh."

"I don't care how upset she is. My mom is innocent! And then to imply that you were involved, as well. That's just crazy."

Ross sighed but before he could answer, he was surprised to see Julie Osterman slip outside through the doors of the chapel and head in their direction.

She wore a conservative blue jacket and skirt with a silky white shirt and had pulled her hair back into a loose updo, and she looked soft and lovely in the sunshine.

His heart had no business jumping around in his chest just at the sight of her. Ross scowled. It didn't seem right that she should be the single bright spot in what had been a dismal day.

How did she have such a calming presence about her? he wondered. Even some of Josh's tension seemed to ease out of him when she slipped her arm through his and gave a comforting squeeze.

"Hi, Ms. O."

She smiled at him, though it appeared rather solemn. "Hi, Josh. I was hoping to get a chance to talk to you."

"Oh?"

She studied him for a long moment. "I have a dilemma here. Maybe you can help me out. I promised myself I wasn't going to ask you something clichéd like how you're holding up. But then, if I don't ask, how am I supposed to find out how you're doing?"

Josh smiled, the first one Ross had seen on his features all day. "Go ahead and ask. I don't mind."

"All right. How are you doing, under the circumstances?"

He shrugged. "Okay, I guess. Under the circumstances."

"It was a lovely memorial service, as far as these things go."

"I guess." Josh looked down at the asphalt of the parking lot.

"When do you go back to school?" she asked.

"Tomorrow. I've got finals next week and I can't really miss any more school if I want to graduate with my class. Uncle Ross thinks I should study for finals at home."

He and Ross had argued about it several times, in fact. It was just about the only point of contention between them over the last five days.

"I just think he should take as much time as he needs," Ross said. "If he doesn't feel ready, he can probably take a few more days, as long as he gets the assignments from his teachers. There's also the scandal factor. Everybody's going to be talking about a murder at the Spring Fling and I want to make sure he's mentally prepared for that before he goes back to school."

"What do you think, Ms. O.?" Josh asked.

Ross could tell she didn't want to be dragged into the middle of things but Julie only smiled at both of them. "There are arguments to be made for both sides. But I think that you're the only one who can truly know when you're ready. As long as you feel prepared to handle whatever might come along, I'm sure returning to school tomorrow will be fine."

"I think I am," Josh answered. "But I won't know until I'm there, will I?"

Julie opened her mouth to answer but one of Lloyd's elderly aunts approached them before she could say anything.

"Joshua? I've been looking all over for you," she said. "You're not leaving already, are you?"

Josh slanted a look at Ross. "In a minute."

"You can't leave yet. Your great-grandmother is here. She specifically wanted to see you."

Josh looked less than thrilled about being forced to talk with more Fredericks relatives but he nodded and allowed himself to be led away by the other woman, leaving Ross alone with Julie.

"I didn't expect to see you here," he said after a moment.

He didn't add that if he had seen her earlier, it might have made the whole thing a little easier to endure.

She made a face. "I decided I would probably regret it if I didn't come to pay my respects. I know Jillian casually from some committees we've served on together and it seemed the polite thing to do, for her sake alone. But more than that, I wanted to come for Josh. It seemed…right, especially as I feel a little as if I were involved, since you and I were on the scene so quickly after it happened and I was with Josh for those few hours afterward."

"Makes sense. It was nice of you to come."

She studied him for a long moment. "Forgive me if I'm wrong, but I get the impression you're not very thrilled to be here."

His laugh was rough and humorless. "Is it that obvious? I can't wait to leave. We were just on our way out. And just so you don't think I'm rushing him away, Josh is as eager to get out of here as I am."

She frowned. "How is he really doing?"

He gazed toward the door, where Josh was talking politely to an ancient-looking woman in a wheelchair. "Not as peachy as he wants everybody to think. He isn't the same kid he was five days ago."

"That's normal and very much to be expected."

"I get the grieving process. I mean, even though his relationship with his dad wasn't the greatest, of course he's going to be upset that he died a violent death. But something else is going on. I can't quite put my finger on it."

One of the things Ross liked best about Julie Osterman was the way she gazed intently at him when he was speaking. Some women looked like they had their minds on a hundred other things when he talked to them, everything from what they had for breakfast to what they were going to say next. It bugged the heck out of him. But somehow he was certain Julie was focused only on his words.

"I'm sure he's also upset about his mother's arrest."

"True enough. If you want the truth, he acts like Frannie's arrest upsets him more than Lloyd's death. He's furious that his mother has been charged with the murder and that she's being held without bail."

"Have you talked to him about his feelings?"

He rolled his eyes. "I'm a guy, in case it escaped your attention."

"It hasn't," she murmured, an odd note in her voice that sent heat curling through him.

He cleared his throat. "I'm no good at the whole 'let's talk about our feelings' thing. Not that I haven't tried, though. Yesterday I took him out on my boat, thinking he might open up out on the water. Instead, we spent the entire afternoon without saying a word about his mom or about Lloyd or anything. Caught our limit between us, though."

Why he shared that, he wasn't sure and he regretted even opening his mouth. What kind of idiot thought a fishing trip might help a troubled teen? But Julie only gazed at him with admiration in the deep blue of her eyes.

"Brilliant idea. That was probably exactly what he needed, Ross. For things to be as normal as possible for a while. To do something he enjoys in a safe environment where he didn't feel pressured to talk about anything."

"I used to take my brothers when we were kids. I can't say we solved all the world's problems, but we always walked away from the river a little happier, anyway. Or at least we stopped fighting for a few minutes. And sometimes we even caught enough for a few nights' dinners, too."

She smiled at that, as he found he'd hoped she would. "You know, Ross, if you think it might help him cope with his grief, I would be happy to talk to Josh in a more formal capacity down at the Fortune Foundation."

He mulled the offer for a long moment, then he shrugged. "I don't know if he really needs all that."

"I'm not talking long-term psychotherapy here. Just a session or two of grief counseling, maybe, if he wants someone to talk to."

Ross thought of Josh's behavior since Lloyd's death. He had become much more secretive and he seemed to be bottling everything up deep inside. Every day since his father's murder, Josh seemed to become more and more tense and troubled, until Ross worried he would implode.

He had seen good cops take a long, hard journey to nowhere when they tucked everything down inside them. He didn't want to see the same thing happen to Josh.

His nephew wouldn't share what he was going through with Ross, but maybe a few sessions with Julie would help him sort through the tangle of his emotions a little better. He supposed it couldn't hurt.

"If he's willing, I guess there's a chance it might help him," he answered. "You sure you don't mind?"

"Not at all, Ross. I like Josh and I want to do anything I can to help him through this hard time in his life. I would say, from a professional standpoint, it's probably better if he gets some counseling earlier rather than later. Things won't become any easier for him in the next few months, especially if the case against Frannie goes to trial."

"It won't," he vowed. He was working like crazy on his own investigation, trying to make sure that didn't happen. "I can't believe such a miscarriage of justice would be allowed to proceed."

"You were a police officer," she said. "You know that innocence doesn't always guarantee justice."

"True. But I'm not going to let my baby sister go to prison for something she didn't do. You can be damn sure of that."

Her mouth tilted into a soft smile that did crazy things to his insides. "Frannie is lucky to have you," she said softly.

He deliberately clamped down on the fierce urge to see if that mouth could possibly taste as sweet as his imagination conjured up.

"We'll see," he said, his voice a little rough. "If Josh is willing, when is a good time for me to bring him in?"

"I've got some time tomorrow afternoon, if that works. Around four, at my office?"

"I'll talk to Josh and let you know. I don't want to force him to do anything he's uncomfortable about."

"From the little I've learned about your nephew, I don't think you could force him to do anything he didn't want to do. I'm guessing it's a family trait."

He actually managed a smile, his first one in a long time. He was suddenly enormously grateful for her compassion and her insight. "True enough. Thank you for all your help. I've been baffled about what to do for him."

He didn't add that he felt as if was failing Josh, just as much as he had failed Frannie for the last eighteen years.

"You're doing fine," she answered. "Josh needs love most of all and it's obvious you have plenty of that to give him."

She touched his arm again, as he realized was her habit, and Ross felt the heat of it sing through his system.

He wanted to stay right here all afternoon, to just let her gentle touch soothe away all his ragged edges, all the tangles and turmoil he had been dealing with since Lloyd's murder and Frannie's arrest.

What was it about her that had such a powerful impact on him? She was lovely, yes. He had known lovely women before, though, and none of them exuded the same soft serenity that called to him with such seductive invitation.

"Sorry that took so long. We can leave anytime."

At Josh's approach, Julie quickly dropped her hand from his arm and Ross realized they had been standing there staring at each other for who knows how long.

Josh shifted his gaze between the two of them, as if trying to filter through the currents that must be zinging around.

"Um, no problem," Ross mumbled. "I guess we should go, then."

They said their goodbyes to Julie, and he couldn't help noticing that she looked as rattled as he felt, something that probably shouldn't suddenly make him feel so cheerful.

Julie studied the boy sprawled in the easy chair in her office.

For the past half hour, Josh had been telling her all

the reasons he wasn't grieving for his father. He talked about Lloyd Fredericks as if he despised him, but then Julie would see flashes of pain appear out of nowhere in his eyes and she knew the truth of Josh's relationship with his father wasn't so easily defined.

"I'm not glad he's dead. I know I said that right after he was killed, but it's not true. I guess I didn't really want him dead, I just wanted him out of my life and my mom's life. It's weird that he's gone, you know? I keep expecting him to come slamming into the house and start picking on my mom for whatever thing bugged him most that day. Instead, it's only Ross there and he never says much of anything."

"It's natural for you to be conflicted, Josh. You're grieving for your father, or at least for the relationship you might have wanted to share with your father."

Josh shrugged. "I guess."

"Nobody can make that process any easier. We each have to walk our own path when it comes to learning to live with the things we can't have anymore. But one thing I've found that helps me when I'm sad is to focus not on the things that are missing in my life but instead on the many things I'm grateful to have."

"Glass-half-full kind of stuff, huh?"

"Exactly. You're in the middle of a crisis right now and many times it's hard to see beyond that. That's perfectly normal, Josh. But it can help ease a little of that turmoil to remember you've still got your uncle standing by your side. You've still got good friends who can help you through."

"I've got Lyndsey."

Josh had mentioned his girlfriend at least five or six times in their session. Julie hadn't met the girl but it was obvious Josh was enamored of her.

"You've got Lyndsey. Many people in your life care about you and are here to help you get through this."

"I know what I have. Just like I know what I have to protect."

Julie mulled over his statement, finding his choice of words a little unsettling.

"What do you need to protect? And from whom? Your mother? Lyndsey?"

He became inordinately fascinated with the upholstered buttons on the arm of the easy chair, tugging at the closest one. "The people I love. I should have acted sooner. I should have protected my mom from Lloyd a long time ago."

"How would you have done that? Your mother was a grown woman, making her own choices. What could you have done?"

After a long moment, he lifted his shoulders. "I don't know. I should have figured something out."

She pressed him on the point as much as she could before it became obvious he didn't want to talk anymore. He became more closed-mouthed and distant. Though they technically still had five minutes, she opted to end the session a little earlier.

"Thanks for…this," Josh said. "The talk and stuff. It helped a lot."

She had no idea what she had possibly been able to offer, but she smiled. "I'm glad. Will you come again?"

He hesitated just long enough to make the moment awkward. "I guess," he finally said. "I don't think I really need therapy or anything but I don't mind talking to you."

"Great."

She quickly wrote her cell number on a memo sheet from a dispenser on her desk. "I'm going to give you my mobile number. If you want to talk, I'm here, okay? Anytime."

"Even if I called you at three in the morning?"

She smiled a little at his cynicism, the natural adolescent desire to stretch every boundary to the limit. "Of course. I might be half asleep for a moment at first, but after I wake up a little, I'll be very happy you felt you could bother me at 3:00 a.m."

She wasn't sure he believed her, but at least he didn't openly argue.

Ross was thumbing through a magazine in the reception area when they opened Julie's office door. He rose to his feet and she was struck again by his height and the sheer solid strength of him.

With that tumble of dark hair brushing his collar and those deep brown eyes, he looked brooding and dark and dangerous, though she had come to see that was mostly illusion.

Mostly.

Her insides gave that funny little jolt they seemed to do whenever she saw him and she fought down a shiver. She had to get control of herself. Every time she was around the man, she forgot all the many reasons she shouldn't be attracted to him.

"Hey, Uncle Ross. I'm going to go see if Ricky is still shooting hoops out back," Josh said.

"Okay. I'll be out in a minute. I'd like to talk to Ms. Osterman."

Josh nodded, picked up his backpack and headed out the door. Josh had been her last appointment of the day and this was Susan's half day, so no other patients waited in the reception area.

She was suddenly acutely aware that she and Ross were alone and she ordered her nerves to settle.

"How did things go in there?" Ross asked.

She sent him a sidelong look as she closed and locked her office door. "Just fine. And that's all I can or will tell you."

"Did he tell you he insisted on going back to school today, over all my well-reasoned objections?"

"He did."

"Am I wrong in thinking he should take more time?"

She studied him, charmed despite all the warnings to herself by his earnest concern for his nephew's well-being. She knew Ross was trying to do the right thing for Josh and she could also tell by the note of uncertainty in his voice that he didn't feel up to the task.

She chose her words carefully, loath to give him any more reason to doubt himself. "I think Josh needs to set his own pace. He's supposed to graduate in two weeks. Right now it's important for him to go through the motions of regaining his life."

"He didn't say much about school today on the way over here, but I know it couldn't have been easy." His features seemed hard and tight for a moment. "I know how cruel kids can be, how they can talk, especially in small towns."

He spoke as if he had firsthand experience in such things and she had to wonder what cruelty he might have faced as a child. She wanted to ask, but she was quite certain he would brush off the question.

"Josh can handle the whispers around school," she answered. "He's a very strong young man."

"He shouldn't have to go through any of this," he muttered.

"But he does, unfortunately. Whether he should or shouldn't have to face it, this is his reality now."

"I wish I could make it easier for him."

"You are. Just by being there with him, caring for him, you're providing exactly what he needs right now."

He studied her for a long moment, a warm light in his brown eyes that sent those nerves ricocheting around her insides again. She wanted to stay right here in her reception area and just soak up that heat, but she knew it was far too dangerous. Her defenses were entirely too flimsy around Ross Fortune.

"Shall we go find Josh and Ricky?"

Could he hear that slight tremble in her voice? she wondered. Oh, she dearly hoped not.

"Right," he only said, and followed her outside into the warm May sunlight, where Josh was shooting baskets by himself on the hoop hanging in one corner of the parking lot of the Foundation.

"No Ricky?" Ross asked.

"Nope. He must have gone home while I was talking to Ms. O. Left the ball out here, though."

Josh shot a fifteen-foot jumper that swished cleanly through the basket.

"Wow. Great shot," Julie said.

"My turn," Ross said and Josh obliged by passing the ball to him. Ross dribbled a few times and went to the same spot on the half-court painted on the parking lot. He repeated Josh's shot, but his bounced off the rim.

Josh managed what was almost a smile. "Ha. You can never beat me at H-O-R-S-E. At least you haven't been able to in years."

"Never say never, kid." Heedless of his cowboy boots that weren't exactly intended for basketball, Ross rolled up the sleeves of his shirt. "Julie, you in?"

She laughed at the pair of them and the suddenly intent expression in two sets of eyes. "Do I look crazy? This appears to be a grudge match to me."

Her heart warmed when Josh grinned at her, looking

very different from the troubled teen she knew him to be. "There's always room for one more."

"You'll wipe the parking lot with me, I'm sure. But why not?"

She decided not to tell them she was the youngest girl in a family of five with four fiercely competitive older brothers. Sometimes the only time she could get any of them to notice her was out on the driveway with the basketball standard her father had nailed above the garage door.

H-O-R-S-E had always been her favorite game and she loved outshooting her brothers, finding innovative shots they couldn't match in the game of elimination.

It had been years since she played basketball with any real intent, though, and she knew she would be more than a little rusty.

The next half hour would live forever in her memory, especially the deepening shock on both Ross's and Josh's features when she was able to keep up with them, shot for shot, in the first five rounds of play.

After five more rounds, Josh and Ross each had earned H and O by missing two shots apiece, while she was still hitting all her shots, despite the handicap of her three-inch heels.

"Just who's wiping the parking lot with whom here?" Ross grumbled. "I'm beginning to think we've been hustled."

"I never said I couldn't play," Julie said with a grin, hitting a one-handed layup. "There was no deception involved whatsoever."

She had to admit, she was having the time of her life. And Josh seemed much lighter of heart than he had been during their session. She still sensed secrets in him, but for a few moments he seemed to be able to set them aside to enjoy the game, which she considered a good sign.

After another half hour, things had evened out a little. She had missed an easy free throw and then a left hook shot that she secretly blamed on Ross for standing too close to her and blasting away all her powers of concentration. But she was still ahead after she pulled off a trick bounce shot that neither Josh nor Ross could emulate.

"I'm starving," Ross said. "What do you say we finish this another night?"

"You're just saying that because you know I'm going to win," Julie said with a taunting smile.

Ross returned it and she considered the game a victory all the way around, especially if it could help him be more lighthearted than she had seen him since they had found his brother-in-law's body.

"Hey, Julie, why don't you come to the house and have dinner with us?" Josh asked suddenly. "We could finish the game there after we eat."

"Dinner?" She glanced at Ross and saw he didn't look exactly thrilled at the invitation. "I don't know," she said slowly.

"Please, Julie. We'd love you to come," Josh pressed her. "You don't have other plans, do you?"

"Not tonight, no," she had to admit.

"Then why not come for dinner? Uncle Ross said he was going to barbecue steaks and there's always an extra we can throw on the grill."

"Well, that's a bit of a problem," she answered. "I'm afraid I'm not really much of a meat eater."

"Really?" Josh said with interest. "Lyndsey is a vegetarian."

"I wouldn't say I'm a vegetarian. I just don't eat a lot of red meat."

"Those are fighting words here in cattle country," Ross drawled.

She laughed. "I know. That's why you won't hear me saying them very loudly. I would prefer if the two of you would just keep it to yourselves."

"Okay, we won't blab your horrible dark secret to everyone—" Josh gave her a mischievous smile "—as long as you have dinner with us."

She was delighted that he felt comfortable enough to tease her. "That sounds suspiciously like blackmail, young man."

"Whatever it takes."

She returned his smile, then shifted her gaze to see Ross watching both of them out of those brown eyes of his that sometimes revealed nothing.

"I suppose we could throw something else on the grill for you," Ross said. "You eat much fish? We've still got bass from the other day."

If she were wise, she would tell Josh 'thanks but no thanks' for his kind invitation. She already felt too tightly entangled with Ross and his nephew. But the boy was reaching out to her. She couldn't just slap him down, especially if it might help her reach him better and help him through this grief.

"In that case, I would love to have dinner with you, as long as you let me pick up a salad and dessert from the deli on the way over."

"You don't have to do that," Ross said.

She smiled and tossed the basketball at him. "I don't mind. It's a weird rule in my family. The winner always buys the loser's dessert. You can consider the salad just a bonus."

He was still laughing as she climbed into her car and drove away.

Chapter 6

By the time she left the deli with her favorite tomato salad and a Boston cream pie, her stomach jumped with nerves and she could barely concentrate on the drive across town to the Frederickses' luxurious home.

She let out a breath. It was only dinner. This jittery reaction was absurd in the extreme. It was only a simple dinner with a client and his uncle.

Nothing more than that.

Still, she couldn't deny that Ross affected her more than any man had in recent memory. It had been seven years since her husband's death. Seven long, lonely years. She had dated occasionally since then but only on a casual basis. She knew she was the one who always put roadblocks up to avoid things becoming more serious. The time and the person never felt right.

For a long time, she had been too busy trying to glue together the shattered pieces of her life. Then she had been too wrapped up in her new career as a child and family therapist and the new job at the Fortune Foundation to devote much time or energy to a relationship.

For the past year or so she had begun to think that she was finally in a good place to get serious about a man again, to try again at love. She had dated a few possibilities but nothing had ever come of them.

Ross Fortune was definitely not serious relationship material. Despite the attraction that simmered between them—and she knew she was not misreading those signs—Ross Fortune came with complications she wasn't prepared to deal with. Beyond his current family turmoil, she sensed he was a hard man, not very open to warmth and tenderness.

She tried to picture him being content spending a quiet evening at home with a child on his lap and couldn't quite manage it. But maybe she wasn't being fair to him. Maybe that restlessness she sensed was a result of his brother-in-law's murder and the subsequent fallout from it.

Julie sighed as she approached the Fredericks's large house that gleamed a pale coral in the fading sunlight. That unspoken attraction between them was real and intense, but for now that was all it could remain.

She wasn't sure she could afford to see what might come of it, not when she had the feeling Ross Fortune was the kind of man who could easily break her heart like a handful of twigs.

Josh, she reminded herself.

She was here only because he asked her, because she wanted to think they had formed a connection since his father's death and she wanted to help him sort through his jumbled mix of feelings.

Her own weren't important right now.

The evening was warm and pleasant as she closed her car door. In other neighborhoods, she might have heard the happy sounds of children playing in the last golden twilight hours before bedtime, but the Frederickses lived in Red Rock's most exclusive neighborhood. All she could manage to hear was the whir of air conditioners and a few well-mannered birds tweeting in the treetops.

Her own neighborhood near the elementary school was far different, an eclectic mix of old-timers who had lived in Red Rock forever and some of the new blood that had moved into the town, drawn by the quiet pace and friendly neighbors.

Moving here from Austin a year ago had been good for her, she thought as she rang the doorbell. She had made many new friends, she had a busy social life and she enjoyed a career where she felt she was affecting young lives.

Did she really need to snarl that up by yearning for a man who appeared unavailable?

At just that moment, Ross opened the door and she had to swallow hard. He was wearing Levi's and a navy blue shirt with the sleeves rolled up. He looked casual and relaxed and her traitorous body responded instantly.

She was staring at his mouth. She realized it a half second too late and jerked her gaze up, only to find him watching her with a strange, glittery light in his eyes that struck her as vaguely predatory.

"Hi," she murmured.

"Evening."

"It's a gorgeous one, isn't it?"

He glanced past her to the soft twilight and blinked a little as if he hadn't noticed it before. "You're right. It is. Come in."

She followed him inside. Though his sister had been in custody for less than a week, the grand house already felt a little neglected. A thin layer of dust covered the table in the foyer and several pairs of shoes were lined up by the door, something she was quite sure Frannie wouldn't have allowed.

"Where's Josh?" she asked.

"Holed up in his room, claiming homework. I'll let him know you're here in a minute. Actually, I'm glad to have a chance to talk to you alone first."

Her heart skipped a beat, despite her best efforts to control her reaction. "Oh?"

"About Josh, I mean."

She hoped he didn't notice her flushed features or the disappointment she told herself was ridiculous. "Of course."

"Do you mind coming out back with me? We can talk while I throw the steaks and your fish on the grill."

She nodded and followed him through the house, noticing a few more subtle signs of neglect in the house that weren't present when she was first here nearly a week ago. A few dirty dishes in the sink, a clutter of papers on the edge of the kitchen island, a jacket tossed casually over the back of a chair.

Ross grabbed a covered platter from the refrigerator, then opened the sliding doors to the vast patio that led to an elegantly landscaped pool. In the dusky light, the area looked quiet and restful. While she didn't much care for the style of the rest of the house, Julie very much admired the gardens around Lloyd and Frannie Frederickses' mansion.

She eased into a comfortable glider swing near the grill and watched while Ross transferred the meat from the plate to the grill with the ease of long practice. When he was done, he approached the swing and after a moment sat beside her, much to her dismay.

He was so big, so very masculine, and she was painfully aware of his proximity.

"What did you want to talk about?" she finally asked, hoping he didn't try prodding her again to reveal details about her counseling session with Josh earlier.

"I'm looking for an honest opinion here," he said. "What do you think about Josh's girlfriend?"

Okay, she hadn't been expecting that. "Lyndsey? I haven't met her."

"But Josh has mentioned her, right?"

"Yes. That first night when I stayed here with him while you were at the jail." She didn't want to breach Josh's confidences by mentioning all the times he had brought up her name during their therapy session. "Why do you ask? Don't you like her?"

Ross was quiet for a moment, a push of his boot sending the glider swaying slightly. "I've only met her briefly myself. Can't say whether I like her or not. But I know Frannie was concerned about how serious they seemed to be getting. Now that I've had a chance to take a closer look at the situation firsthand, I've got to admit, it worries me a little, too."

"In what way?"

"To me, it seems like they're together all the time. I mean, *all* the time! When he's not over at her place or she's not here, he's talking to her on the phone or texting her or talking to her online. I don't know how intense things were between them before Lloyd's death but I'm a little worried that he's becoming too wrapped up with her. He's only a kid, with his whole life ahead of him."

"Don't you remember your first love? They can be pretty intense."

"No," he said, his voice blunt. "I never had one."

She stared. "You never had a girlfriend?"

"No. Not in high school, anyway. I was too busy with…things."

"What kind of things? Sports?"

His mouth tightened. "Family stuff."

He didn't seem inclined to add any more, so Julie forced herself to clamp down on her curiosity to press him.

"Well, first love can be crazy for a teenager," she said instead. "Wonderful and terrible at the same time, full of raw emotions and all these fears and hopes and insecurities. I'm sure his emotional bond to Lyndsey is heightened by the chaos elsewhere in his life. She must seem like a sturdy rock he can hang on to."

"She strikes me as the clingy, needy sort, just from the little I've been able to see of her," Ross said.

She could barely think straight, sitting this close to him, but she did her best to rearrange her mind to gain a little clarity. "Well, that might be part of her appeal to him. Lyndsey is somebody who needs him. Look at things from Josh's perspective. His father is dead. His mother is in deep trouble, but not any kind of trouble he can solve for her. Aiding this girl with whatever troubles she's having might make Josh feel less helpless about the rest of the things going on in his world."

He pushed the swing again with his foot. "So you think I ought to let their little romance run its course?"

"Josh is almost eighteen. There's not really much you can do about it."

"I could lock him in his room and feed him only gruel," he muttered.

She laughed. "He's a teenage boy. I imagine he would figure out a way to sneak out and go for pizza."

He was quiet for a long moment. When she glanced over to gauge his expression and try to figure out what he was thinking about, she thought she detected a hint of color on his cheekbones.

"Should I take him to buy condoms, just to be on the safe side?" he asked, without looking at her.

The temperature between them seemed to heat up a dozen degrees and she knew it was not from the barbecue just a few feet away. She cleared her throat. "Maybe that's a conversation you ought to have with his mother."

"I can't discuss my nephew's sex life with my sister while she's in jail!"

She supposed she ought to be flattered that he felt he could discuss such a delicate subject with her, but she couldn't get past the trembling in her stomach just thinking about "Ross" and "condoms" in the same conversation.

"I can't tell you what to do," she said. "You're going to have to make that decision on your own. But I will say that if Josh were my son or in my care, it's certainly a conversation I would have with him, especially if he's becoming as serious with his girlfriend as you seem to believe."

He didn't look very thrilled by the prospect, but he nodded. "I guess I'll do that. Thanks for the advice. I can see why you make a good counselor. You're very easy to talk to."

She smiled. "You're welcome."

He gazed at her and she saw that heat flare in his eyes again. The world seemed to shiver to a stop and the night and the lovely gardens and the soft wind murmuring in the treetops seemed to disappear, leaving just the two of them alone with this powerful tug of attraction between them.

* * *

He was inches from kissing her.

Ross could feel the sweet warmth of her breath, could almost taste her on his mouth. He wanted her, with a fierce hunger that seemed to drive all common sense out of his head.

He tried to hang on to all the reasons he shouldn't kiss her. This was *not* supposed to be happening right now.

His life was in total chaos, he had far too many people depending on him and the last thing he needed was to find himself tangled up with someone like Julie Osterman, someone soft and generous and entirely too sweet for a man like him.

One kiss wouldn't hurt anything, though. Only a tiny little taste. He leaned forward and heard a seductive little catch of her breath, felt the brush of her breast against his arm as she shifted slightly closer.

His mouth was just a tantalizing inch away from hers when he suddenly heard the snick of the sliding door.

"Ross?" Josh called out.

Julie jerked away as if Ross had poked her with hot coals from the grill and the glider swayed crazily with the movement.

"Over here," Ross called.

He didn't like the way Josh skidded to a stop, his size-fourteen sneakers thudding against the tile patio, or the way his eyebrows climbed to find them sitting together so cozily on the glider.

He also didn't like the sudden speculative gleam in his nephew's eyes.

"Hi, Julie. I didn't hear you come in."

She was breathing just a hair too quickly, Ross

thought. "I only arrived a few moments ago. Your uncle and I were just…we were, um…"

"Julie was helping me with the steaks. And speaking of which, I'd better turn them before they're charred."

He definitely needed to get a grip on this attraction, he thought as he turned the steaks while Julie and Josh set the table out on the patio.

She was a nice woman who was doing him a huge favor by helping him figure out how to handle sudden, unexpected fatherhood. It would be a poor way to repay her by indulging his own whims when he had nothing to offer her in return.

"I think everything's ready," he said a few moments later.

"We're all set here," Julie said from the table, where she sat talking quietly with Josh about school. They had set out candles, he saw, and Frannie's nice china. It was a nice change from the paper plates he and Josh had been using while he was here.

He went inside for the russet potatoes he had thrown in the oven earlier while they were waiting for her to arrive, and he put the tomato salad Julie had brought into a bowl.

"Wow. I'm impressed," Julie exclaimed as he set the foil packet containing her fish on her plate and opened it for her. The smell of tarragon and lemon escaped.

"Better wait until you taste it before you say that," he warned her.

He knew only two ways to cook fish. Either battered and fried in tons of butter—something he tried not to do too often for obvious health reasons—or grilled in a packet with olive oil, lemon juice and a mix of easy spices.

He knew he shouldn't care so much what she thought

but he still found it immensely gratifying when she closed her eyes with sheer delight at the first forkful. "Ross, this is delicious!"

He was becoming like one of the teens she worked with, desperate for her approval. "Glad you like it. How's the steak, Josh?"

His nephew was still studying the two of them with entirely too much interest. "It's good. Same as always."

"Nothing like family to deflate the old ego," Ross said with a wry smile.

"Sorry," Josh amended. "What I meant to say is this is absolutely the best steak I have ever tasted. Every bite melts in my mouth. I think I could eat this every single day for the rest of my life. Is that better?"

Julie laughed and it warmed Ross to see Josh flash her a quick grin before he turned back to his dinner. He didn't know what it was about her, but when she was around, Josh seemed far more relaxed. More like the kid he used to be.

"What are your plans after the summer?" she asked.

Josh shrugged. "I'm not sure right now."

Ross looked up from dressing his potato and frowned. "What do you mean, you're not sure? You've got an academic scholarship to A&M. It's all you could talk about a few weeks ago."

His nephew looked down at his plate. "Yeah, well, things have changed a little since a few weeks ago."

"And in a few *more* weeks, this is all going to seem like a bad dream."

"Is it?" Josh asked quietly and the patio suddenly simmered with tension.

"Yes. You'll see. These ridiculous charges against your mom will be dropped and everything will be back to normal."

"My dad will still be dead."

He had no answer to that stark truth. "You're not giving up a full-ride academic scholarship out of concern for your mother or some kind of misguided guilt over your dad's death."

Josh's color rose and he set his utensils down carefully on his plate. "It's my scholarship, Uncle Ross. If I want to give it up, nobody else can stop me. You keep forgetting I'm not a kid anymore. I'll be eighteen in a week, remember?"

"I haven't forgotten. But I also know that you have opportunities ahead of you and it would be a crime to waste those. I won't let you do it."

"Good luck trying to stop me, if that's what I decide to do," Josh snapped.

Ross opened his mouth to answer just as hotly but Josh's cell phone suddenly bleated a sappy little tune he recognized as being the one Josh had programmed to alert him to Lyndsey's endless phone calls.

He didn't know whether to be annoyed or grateful for the interruption. He had dealt with his own stubborn younger brothers enough to know that yelling wasn't going to accomplish anything but would make Josh dig in his heels.

"Hey," Josh said into the phone. He shifted his body away and pitched his voice several decibels lower. "No. Not the best right now."

Ross's gaze met Julie's and the memory of their conversation earlier—and all his worries—came flooding back. Was it possible Lyndsey was part of the reason Josh was considering giving up his scholarship?

Josh held the phone away from his ear. "Uncle Ross, I'm done with dinner. Do you care if I take this inside, in my room? A friend of mine needs some help with, um, trig homework. I might be a while and I wouldn't want to bore you two with a one-sided conversation."

He and Julie both knew that wasn't true. He wondered if he should call Josh on the lie, but he wasn't eager to add to the tension over college.

"Did you get enough to eat?"

Josh made a face. "Yeah, Mom."

Ross supposed that was just what he sounded like. Not that he had much experience with maternal solicitude. "I guess you can go."

The teen was gone before the words were even out of his mouth. Only after the sliding door closed behind him did Ross suddenly realize his nephew's defection left him alone with Julie.

"You know, lots of parents establish a no-call zone during the dinner hour," Julie said mildly.

He bristled for about ten seconds before he sighed. Hardly anybody had a cell phone twenty years ago, the last time he'd been responsible for a teenager. The whole internet, email, cell phone thing presented entirely new challenges.

"Frannie always insisted he leave it in his room during dinner."

She opened her mouth to say something but quickly closed it again and returned her attention to her plate.

"What were you going to say?" he pressed.

"Nothing."

"You forget, I'm a trained investigator. I know when people are trying to hide things from me."

She gave him a sidelong look, then sighed. "Fine. But feel free to tell me to mind my own business."

"Believe me. I have no problem whatsoever telling people that."

She gave a slight smile, but quickly grew serious. "I

was only thinking that a little more consistency with the house rules he's always known might be exactly what Josh needs right now. He's in complete turmoil. He's struggling with his mother's arrest and his father's death. Despite their uneasy relationship, Lloyd was his father and having a parent die isn't easy for anyone. Perhaps a little more constancy in his life will help him feel not quite as fragmented."

"So many things have been ripped from his world right now. It's all chaos. I was just trying to cut him a little slack."

She stood and began clearing the dishes away. "Believe it or not, a little slack might very well be the last thing he needs right now. Rules provide structure and order amid the chaos, Ross."

He could definitely understand that. He had craved that very structure in his younger days and had found it at the Academy. Police work, with its regulations and discipline—its paperwork and routine—had given him guidance and direction at a time he desperately needed some.

Maybe she was right. Maybe Josh craved those same things.

"Here, I'll take those," he said to Julie when she had filled a tray with the remains of their dinner.

After he carried the tray into the kitchen, he returned to the patio to find Julie standing on the edge of the tile, gazing up at the night sky.

It was a clear night, with a bright sprawl of stars. Ross joined her, wondering if he could remember the last time he had taken a chance to stargaze.

"Pretty night," he said, though all he could think about was the lovely woman standing beside him with her face lifted up to the moonlight.

"It is," she murmured. "I can't believe I sometimes get so wrapped up in my life that I forget to enjoy it."

They were quiet for a long time, both lost in their respective thoughts while the sweet scents from Frannie's garden swirled around them.

"Can I ask you something?" Ross finally asked.

If he hadn't been watching her so closely, he might have missed the slight wariness that crept into her expression. "Sure."

"How do you know all this stuff? About grieving and discipline and how to help a kid who's hurting?"

"I'm a trained youth counselor with a master's degree in social work and child and family development."

She was silent for a long moment, the only sound in the night the distant hoot of an owl and the wind sighing in the treetops. "Beyond that," she finally said softly, "I know what it is to be lost and hurting. I've been there."

Her words shivered through him, to the dark and quiet place he didn't like to acknowledge, that place where he was still ten years old, scared and alone and responsible for his three younger siblings yet again after Cindy ran off with a new boyfriend for a night that turned into another and then another.

He knew lost and hurting. He had been there plenty of times before, but it didn't make him any better at intuitively sensing what was best for Josh.

He pushed those memories aside. It was much easier to focus on the mystery of Julie Osterman than on the past he preferred to forget.

"What are your secrets?" he asked.

"You mean you haven't run a background check on me yet, detective?"

He laughed a little at her arch tone. "I didn't think about it until just this moment. Good idea, though." He studied her for a long moment in the moonlight, noting the color that had crept along the delicate planes of her cheekbones. "If I did, what would I find?"

"Nothing criminal, I can assure you."

"I don't suppose you would have been hired at the Foundation if you had that sort of past."

"Probably not."

"Then what?" He paused. "You lost someone close to you, didn't you?"

She gazed at the moon, sparkling on the swimming pool. "That's a rather obvious guess, detective."

"But true."

Her sigh stirred the air between them.

"Yes. True," she answered. "It's a long, sad story that I'm sure would bore you senseless within minutes."

"I have a pretty high bore quotient. I've been known to sit perfectly motionless on stakeouts for hours."

She glanced at him, then away again. "A simple background check would tell you this in five seconds but I suppose I'll go ahead and spare you the trouble. I lost my husband seven years ago. I'm a widow, detective."

Chapter 7

For several moments, he could only stare at her, speechless.

She was a widow. He would never have guessed that, not in a million years, though he wasn't quite sure why he found the knowledge so astonishing—perhaps because she normally had such a sunny attitude for someone who must have lost her husband at a young age.

"I'm sorry. I shouldn't have pushed you to talk about something you obviously didn't want to discuss, especially after you've done nothing but help Josh and me."

"It's okay, Ross. I wouldn't have told you if I hadn't wanted you to know. I don't talk about it often, only because it was a really dark and difficult time in my past and I don't like to dwell on it. I prefer instead to enjoy the present and look ahead to the future. That's all."

"What happened?" he asked after a long moment.

He sensed it was something traumatic. That might

help explain her empathy and understanding of what Josh was dealing with. He braced himself for it but was completely unprepared for her quiet answer.

"He shot himself."

Ross stared, trying to make out her delicate features in the dim moonlight. "Was it a hunting accident?"

The noise she made couldn't be mistaken for a laugh. "No. It was no accident. Chris was…troubled. We were married for five years. The first two were wonderful. He was funny and smart and brilliantly creative. The kind of person who always seems to have a crowd around him.

"After those first two years, we bought a home in Austin," she went on. "I was working at a high school there and Chris was a photographer with an ad agency. Everything seemed so perfect. We were starting to talk about starting a family and then…everything started to change. *He* started to change."

"Drugs? Alcohol?"

"No. Nothing like that. He became moody and withdrawn at times and obsessively jealous, and then he would have periods where he would stay up for days at a time, would shoot roll after roll of film, of nothing really. The pattern on the sofa cushions, a single blade of grass. He once spent six hours straight trying to capture a doorknob in the perfect light. Eventually he was diagnosed as schizophrenic, with a little manic depression thrown in for added fun."

Ross frowned. He knew enough about mental illness to know it couldn't have been an easy road for either of them.

"You stayed with him?"

"He was my husband," she said simply. "I loved him."

"You must have been young."

"We married when I was twenty-four. I didn't feel young at the time but in retrospect, I was a baby. I suppose I must have been young enough, anyway, that I was certain I could fix anything."

"But you couldn't."

"Not this. It was bigger than either of us. That's still so hard for me to admit, even seven years later. For three years, he tried every possible combination of meds but nothing could keep the demons away for long. Finally Chris's condition started a downward spiral and no matter what we tried, we couldn't seem to slow the momentum. On his twenty-eighth birthday, he gave up the fight. He returned home early from work, set his camera on a tripod with an automatic timer, took out a Ruger he had bought illegally on the street a week earlier and shot himself in our bedroom."

Where Julie would be certain to find him, he realized grimly. Ross had seen enough self-inflicted gunshot wounds when he had been a cop to know exactly what kind of scene she must have walked into.

He knew her husband had been mentally ill and couldn't have been thinking clearly, but suddenly Ross was furious at the man for leaving behind such horror and anguish for his pretty, devoted young wife to remember the rest of her life. He hoped she could remember past that traumatic final scene and the three rough years preceding it to the few good ones they had together. "I'm so sorry, Julie."

He wanted to take it away, to make everything all better for her, but here was another person in his life whose pain he couldn't fix.

The unmistakable sincerity in Ross's voice warmed the small, frozen place inside Julie that would always grieve for the bright, creative light extinguished far too soon.

She lifted her gaze to his. "It was a terrible time in my life. I can't lie about that. The grief was so huge and so awful, I wasn't sure I could survive it. But I endured by hanging on to the things I still had that mattered—my faith, my family, my friends. I also reminded myself every single day, both before his death and in those terrible dark days after, that Chris wasn't responsible for the choices he made. I know he loved me and wouldn't have chosen that course, if he could have seen any other choice in his tormented mind."

He didn't say anything for a long time and she couldn't help wondering what he was thinking.

"Is that why you work with troubled kids?" he finally asked, his voice low. "To make sure none of them feels like that's the only way out for them?"

She sighed. "I suppose that's part of it. I started out working on a suicide hotline in the evenings and realized I was making an impact. It helped me move outside myself at a time I desperately needed that and I discovered I was good at listening. So I left teaching and went back to school to earn a graduate degree."

"Do you miss teaching?" he asked.

"Sometimes. But when I was teaching six different classes, with thirty kids each, I didn't have the chance for the one-on-one interaction I have now. I can always go back to teaching if I want. I still might someday, if that seems the right direction for me. I haven't ruled anything out yet."

"Do you ever wonder if anything you do really makes a difference?"

How in the world had he become so cynical? she

wondered. Was it his years as a police officer? Or some-thing before then? It saddened her, whatever the cause.

"I have to give back somehow. I've always thought of it as trying to shine as much light as I can, even if it only illuminates my own path."

He gazed at her, his dark eyes intense, and she was suddenly painfully aware of him, the hard strength of his shoulders beside her, the slight curl of his hair brush-ing his collar.

"You're a remarkable woman," he said softly. "I'm not sure I've ever known anyone quite like you."

He wanted to kiss her. She sensed it clearly again, as she had earlier in the evening. She could see the desire kindle in his eyes, the intention there.

This time he wouldn't stop—and she didn't want him to. She wanted to know if his kiss could possibly be as good as she imagined it. Anticipation fluttered through her, like the soft, fragile wings of a butterfly, and she caught her breath as he moved closer, surrounding her with his heat and his strength.

The night seemed magical. The vast glitter of stars and the breeze murmuring through the trees and the sweet scents of his sister's flower garden. Everything combined to make this moment seem unreal.

She closed her eyes as his mouth found hers, her heart pounding, her breath caught in her throat. His kiss was gentle at first, as slow and easy as the little creek running through her yard on a hot August afternoon. She leaned into it, into him, wondering how it was pos-sible for him to make her feel shattered with just a kiss.

She was vaguely aware of the slide of his arms around her, pulling her closer. She again had that vague sensation of being surrounded by him, encircled. It wasn't unpleasant. Far from it. She wanted to savor every moment, burn it all into her mind.

He deepened the kiss, his mouth a little more urgent. Some insistent warning voice in her head urged her to pull away and return to the safety of the other side of the patio, away from this temptation to lose her common sense—*herself*—but she decided to ignore it. Instead, she curled her arms around his neck and surrendered to the moment.

She had dated a few men in the seven years since Chris's suicide. A history teacher at the high school, a fellow grad student, an investment banker she met at the gym.

All of them had been perfectly nice, attractive men. So why hadn't their kisses made her blood churn, the lassitude seep into her muscles? She supposed it was a good thing he was supporting her weight with his arms around her because she wasn't at all sure she could stand on her own.

In seven years, she hadn't realized how truly much she had missed a man's touch until just this moment. Everything feminine inside her just seemed to give a deep, heartfelt sigh of welcome.

They kissed for a long time there in the moonlight. She learned the taste of him, of the wine they'd had with dinner and some sort of enticing mint and another essence she guessed was pure Ross. She learned his hair was soft and thick under her fingers and that he went a little crazy when she nipped gently on his bottom lip.

His tongue swept through her mouth, unfurling a wild hunger for more and she tightened her arms around him, her hands gripping him closely.

She didn't know how long the kiss lasted. It could have been hours, for all the awareness she had of time passing. She only knew that in Ross's arms, she felt safe and desirable, a heady combination.

They might have stayed there all night, but eventually some little spark of consciousness filtered through the soft hunger.

This was dangerous. Too dangerous. His nephew could come outside to the patio at any moment and discover them in a heated embrace.

Although Josh was almost eighteen, certainly old enough to understand about sexual attraction, she had a strong feeling Ross wouldn't be thrilled if his nephew caught them kissing.

She wasn't sure how, but she managed to summon the energy and sheer strength of will to pull her hands away and step back enough to allow room for her lungs to take in a full breath.

The kick of oxygen to her system pushed away some of the fuzzy, hormone-induced cobwebs in her brain but for perhaps an entire sixty seconds she could only stare at him, feeling raw and off balance. Her thoughts were a wild snarl in her head and she couldn't seem to untwist them.

An awkward silence seethed around them, replacing the seductive attraction with something taut and clumsy. She struggled for something to say but couldn't think of anything that didn't sound silly and girlish.

Ross was the first one to break the silence. "I swear, that wasn't on the agenda for the evening," he finally said.

His hair was a little tousled from her fingers and he looked rumpled and rough around the edges and rather dismayed at their kiss.

She found the entire package absolutely irresistible.

"I believe you."

"I'm not… I didn't intend—"

He raked a hand through his hair, messing it up even more. A muscle worked in his jaw and he seemed so uncomfortable that she finally took pity on him.

"Ross, don't worry. I'm not going to rush out and start looking at bridal books just because you kissed me."

His eyes widened with obvious panic at simply the word "bridal." Under other circumstances, Julie might have laughed but it was all rather humiliating in the moment. She was still reeling from the most sensuous kiss she thought she had ever experienced and he just looked at her with that stunned, slightly dazed look, as if she had just stripped down and started pole dancing around the patio umbrella.

"If I could take back the last ten minutes, I would," he said.

She refused to acknowledge the sharp sting of his words. "Don't give it another thought."

"Like that's possible," he muttered.

At least the kiss left him just as off balance as it had her. She found some small comfort that he hadn't been completely unaffected by it, though she still wasn't thrilled that he seemed so aghast.

"Look," he said after another long, awkward moment. "I'm very attracted to you. I guess that's pretty obvious by now and I'd be lying if I tried to pretend otherwise. But this is not a really good time for me to be…distracted."

She wasn't sure she'd ever been called a distraction before and she didn't quite know how to react. At least he had prefaced it by admitting he was attracted to her.

"Right now my focus has to be my family," he said. "Frannie, Josh. They need me and I can't afford to let my attention be diverted by anything, especially not, well, something as complicated as a relationship."

Just because of his family? she wondered. Somehow she doubted it. While she was quite certain he wasn't using his difficult situation as an excuse, she had a feeling even if his family wasn't having such a hard time right now, Ross wouldn't be quick to jump into any involvement with her.

He struck her as a man who shied away from anything deeper or more meaningful than a quick fling.

"I understand," she murmured.

"Do you?" His eyes were murky with regret in the moonlight. Because he had kissed her? she wondered. Or because he was determined not to repeat it?

"You've been thrust into a tough role here with Josh, trying to do the right thing for him at the same time you're deeply worried about your sister. I can see why you want to keep the rest of your life as uncomplicated as possible."

He frowned, shoving his hands in his pockets. "Tell me I haven't jeopardized your willingness to help with Josh?"

She certainly wouldn't be able to quickly forget the magic and heat they had shared. But that didn't mean she couldn't move on from here.

"It was just a kiss, Ross! Of course I'm still willing to help with Josh, if he's interested in more sessions. That's a completely separate issue. I would still want to help him any way I could, even if you and I had just gotten naked and rolled around on the living room carpet for the last two hours."

She wasn't quite sure if it was her imagination but his eyes seemed to glaze slightly and he made a sound that might have been a groan. Julie regretted her flippancy. The last thing she needed right now was that particular image in her head, not with the unfulfilled desire still pulsing through her insides.

Ross drew in a ragged breath. "I'm glad for that, at least. Josh responds to you. I don't want to lose that because I overstepped."

She held a hand up. "Ross, stop. Let it go. It was just a kiss. Just a momentary impulse that doesn't mean anything. You're attracted to me, I'm attracted right back at you, obviously, but that's all it is."

To her amazement, he opened his mouth as if he wanted to disagree—which she decided would make Ross Fortune just about the most contrary man she had ever met, if he intended to argue both sides of the issue.

She decided not to put the matter to the test. "I'd better go," she said. "It's been a long day and I have paperwork to finish tonight."

He still looked as if he had more to say but he only nodded. "Thanks for coming. I'm sorry again that Josh ditched on you. I'll have a talk with him about keeping the cell phone away from the dinner table."

"Excellent idea."

"Let me just go call him down to say goodbye to you."

"That's really not necessary."

Right now she just wanted to leave so that she could try to put a little distance between them in an effort to regain both her dignity and a little perspective.

"It *is* necessary," he said. "Josh is the one who invited you to dinner with us and then he just abandoned you for a phone call, which I should never have let him get away with. The least he can do is come down to tell you goodbye."

She didn't want to argue, she only wanted to leave,

but she decided to give in with good grace. He was right, Josh needed to hold onto civility and manners, even if his life had been turned upside down.

She waited in the ornate foyer of the Fredericses' home while Ross hurried up the stairs to his nephew's room. A moment later, he returned with Josh, who rubbed the back of his neck and looked embarrassed.

"Sorry about leaving, Julie. It was way rude of me and I shouldn't have done it. I wasn't thinking about what bad manners it was, I was just… I needed to talk to my friend."

"I understand. Next time, maybe you could wait until we've all finished eating to take your phone call."

"I'll try to remember to do that. Thanks for coming to dinner and for…everything else today."

"You're welcome. I enjoyed it." *Some parts more than others,* she added silently to herself, and she forced herself not to look at Ross even as she felt a blush steal over her cheeks.

"We never did get to finish playing H-O-R-S-E."

"We'll have to schedule a rematch next time we have a session. If you think you want another one, anyway."

He shrugged. "I guess. You're pretty easy to talk to."

"Thanks." She smiled. "How about Tuesday after school?"

"That should work, I think."

"I'll see you then. Be sure to bring your game for afterward. You wouldn't want me to whip your butt on the court again."

He laughed. "I'll see if I can find it," he said. "See you later."

He headed up the stairs again, leaving her alone with Ross. He looked rough-edged and darkly handsome amid the pale, elegant furnishings of the house and she had a tough time not stepping forward and tasting that hard mouth one last time.

"Thanks again for dinner, Ross," she forced herself to say. "It was delicious."

"You're welcome."

They exchanged one more awkward, tentative smile, then she opened the door and walked out into the Texas night.

As she hurried to her car, she couldn't help wondering how one kiss had managed to sear away seven years of restraint.

Ross stood on his sister's veranda and watched Julie drive away in a sensible silver sedan.

He still felt as if he'd been tied feetfirst to the back end of a mule and dragged through cactus for a few dozen miles.

That kiss. Damn it, he didn't need this right now. He had never known anything like it, that wild fire in his blood that still seemed to sizzle and burn.

He had wanted to make love to her, right there on Frannie's Italian tile patio table. Even now, he could remember the sweet, luscious taste of her, the smell of her, like juicy peaches ripened by the sun that he couldn't wait to sink his teeth into.

What was he supposed to do with a woman like Julie Osterman? She was far too sweet, far too centered for someone like him.

She had lost a husband.

Just thinking about it made his heart ache. He could picture her—younger, even more idealistic, certain she could fix everything wrong in the world. And then to come up against such a tough, thorny thing as mental illness in someone she loved. It would have broken a woman who wasn't as strong as Julie.

She was a lovely, courageous, compassionate woman.

And not for him.

Ross gazed out at the night. What the hell did a man like him have to offer someone like her? She needed softness, romance, tenderness, especially after the pain she had been forced to endure.

He didn't know if he was capable of any of those things. He was cynical and rough, more used to frozen pizza than candlelight dinners. He liked his life on his own and wasn't sure he had room inside it for a woman like Julie.

He couldn't let himself kiss her again, especially not after he'd told her what a mistake it had been. As much as he might want to hold her in his arms, it wouldn't be fair to her to give her any ideas that he might be open to starting something with her, not when he would only end up hurting and disillusioning her.

Like he did everybody else.

He let out a breath, wishing for a good, stiff drink. He needed something to push back the regret that he wouldn't have the chance to taste that delectable mouth again, to hear her soft little sigh of arousal, to feel her curves pressing against him. Frannie and Lloyd had a well-stocked liquor cabinet but he wasn't sure it was a good idea for Josh to see him turning to alcohol to escape the weight of his obligations.

He heard the creak of the door behind him and Ross turned to see his nephew standing in the lighted doorway, studying him with concern in his eyes.

"Everything okay?" Josh asked.

"Sure. Why wouldn't it be?"

His nephew shrugged. "I don't know. You've just

been standing out here without moving for at least half an hour. My bedroom window has a perfect view of the front door and I watched you while I was on the phone."

"Oh, right. Your study session."

Josh flashed him a quick, rueful grin but it faded quickly and those secrets took its place. He definitely needed to figure out what was going on with the kid.

"So what's up?" Josh asked. "Is something wrong?"

"No. I was just…thinking."

"About my dad's murder and the case against my mom?"

That was exactly what he *should* have been thinking about out here. The boy's words were a harsh reminder of yet another reason he needed to stay away from Julie—the most important one.

She distracted him at a time when he could least afford the inattention. He had a job to do—clearing his sister. It was quite possibly the most important case of his career, the one he had the most stake in, and he needed to focus.

"There are still a lot of inconsistencies," Ross said instead of answering his nephew directly. "The whole thing is making me crazy, if you want to know the truth. If your mom would only try to defend herself, things would go much easier for her. We just need to hear her side of the story."

Josh leaned against the pillar, his arms crossed over his chest. "Why do you think she's not talking?"

The question was just a little too casual. He searched Josh's features but his face was in shadows and Ross couldn't quite read him.

"It's a good question," he said. "One I sure wish I could answer. Why do *you* think she's staying quiet?"

Josh turned to look out at the quiet road in front of

his house and Ross couldn't help wondering if he was avoiding his gaze. "I don't know. Maybe she's blocked out what happened. Lyndsey said that can happen to people when they've been through a traumatic event or something."

What the hell did a sixteen-year-old girl know about disassociation? Ross frowned. "Maybe that's what happened. I don't know. But even if that's the case, I would still like to hear her say so. At this point, I'd like to hear anything—that she can't remember what happened or she's not sure or aliens abducted her and sucked out her memory with their proton beams. Anything at all. I wish she could see that her silence is as good as a confession."

"She didn't do it, though," Josh muttered. "You and I both *know* she didn't. I hate thinking of her in jail."

His voice broke a little on the last word but he quickly cleared his throat, embarrassed, and straightened from the pillar.

Ross rested an awkward hand on Josh's shoulder, wishing he was better at this whole parenting thing. "Your loyalty means the world to her, I know."

To his dismay, instead of taking his words as praise, as Ross intended, Josh seemed even more upset by them. He looked as if Ross had shoved a fist in his solar plexus.

"I'm going to bed," he said after a moment, his voice strangled and tight. "I'll see you later."

"'Night," Ross said and watched with concern as Josh went back inside the house.

These sessions with Julie were a good idea, he decided. He just hoped she could get to the bottom of the kid's odd behavior.

Chapter 8

"I appreciate you coming out here, son. I know you're busy and I hope it didn't mess up your schedule too much."

As Ross shook his uncle William's hand in the foyer of the Double Crown, he thought how much he respected him. His mother's brother was as unlike Cindy as he imagined two people who came from the same womb could possibly be.

William had always struck him as decent and honorable. Though Ross hadn't known him well growing up because William and his wife and five sons lived in Los Angeles and their respective spheres rarely intersected, his uncle had invariably been kind to him and his brothers and sister when they did.

His wife Molly had died a year ago, and William had temporarily moved from California to Texas and the family ranch just a few months earlier after a string of mysterious incidents threatened the family's security.

Ross thought of the word he had used the night of the dinner with Julie that had upset Josh so much—*loyalty.* William typified family loyalty. His uncle invariably thought first about the Fortunes and what was in the family's best interest, and Ross had to respect him all the more for it.

"Not a problem," he said now. "I'm staying in Red Rock with Josh anyway so it wasn't any trouble to come out here to the Double Crown."

Before William could answer him, Lily—William and Cindy's cousin by marriage—walked down the stairs.

At sixty-three, she was still exotically lovely from her Apache and Spanish heritage, with high cheekbones, tilt-tipped eyes framed by thick lashes and a wide, sultry mouth.

She was also one of his favorite Fortunes. He would have loved having a mother as warm and caring and maternal as Lily Fortune.

"Ross, my dear. You don't come to the Double Crown enough," she said, gripping his hands and squeezing them tightly.

"Sorry about that. I've been pretty busy lately."

"You've got your hands full right now, don't you? How is Frannie?"

He frowned. He had seen Frannie that morning at the jail—just another frustrating visit. How had he never guessed that such obstinance lurked inside his delicate sister? He had asked, begged and finally pleaded with her to tell him what had happened the night of Lloyd's death, but she remained stubbornly silent.

"I can't talk about it."

That was her only response, every single time he pushed her. Finally she had told him she would tell the guards she wouldn't take any more visits from him if he didn't stop haranguing her about it.

"She doesn't belong in prison. That's for damn sure."

He heard his own language and winced. "Sorry, Lily. For darn sure, I meant."

She rolled her eyes. "If a little colorful language ever sent me into a swoon, I wouldn't be much good on a working ranch, would I?"

Ross grinned. "I suppose not."

"For what it's worth, I completely agree with you. I can't believe that pip-squeak Bruce Gibson was able to get his way and have her held without bail. It's an outrage, that's what it is."

"I couldn't agree more," William put in. "Any word on appealing the judge's decision on bail?"

"The lawyers are working on it." Like everything else, they were in wait-and-see mode.

"Whatever you need, Ross," William said, his expression solemn and sincere. "The family is behind you a hundred percent on this. We can hire different attorneys to argue for a change of venue if that would help."

"I don't know what's going to help at this point. I just need to figure out who really killed Lloyd so I can get her out of there."

"Whatever you need," William repeated. "Just say the word and we'll do anything it takes to help you."

"Thanks, Uncle William. I appreciate that."

He did, though it wasn't an easy thing for him to admit. As much as he respected his Fortune relatives, they had all come to his immediate family's rescue far more often than he could ever find comfortable. Cindy would have sucked the Fortune financial well dry if she could have found a way.

"Come on back to the kitchen, why don't you?" Lily

said after a moment. "Rosita made cinnamon rolls this morning and I'm sure there are a few left."

His stomach rumbled, reminding him that breakfast had been coffee and a slice of burnt toast made from one of the last pieces of bread at the house. They were just about out of food. If he didn't want his nephew to starve, he was going to have to schedule a trip to the grocery store soon, as much as he heartily disliked the task.

He couldn't help comparing the big, warm kitchen at the Double Crown with Frannie's elegant, spare kitchen. *This* was the kitchen of his childhood dreams, something he didn't think was a coincidence. On his few trips to the Double Crown as a kid, this place had seemed like heaven on earth, from the horses to the swimming hole to the big rope swing in the barn that sent anyone brave enough for it sailing through the air into soft, clean-smelling hay.

Given a choice, he would much rather slide up to this table, with its scarred top and acres of mismatched chairs, than Frannie's perfect designer set.

Rosita, Lily's longtime friend and housekeeper, bustled around in the kitchen in an old-fashioned ruffled apron. She beamed when she saw Ross and ordered him to sit.

"You are too skinny. You need to come eat in my kitchen more often."

He raised an eyebrow. Only someone as comfortably round as Rosita could ever call him skinny. "If those cinnamon rolls taste as good as they smell, I might just have to kidnap you and take you back to Frannie's mausoleum to cook for Josh and me. We're getting a little tired of ordering pizza."

"You know you and Josh are welcome here anytime," Lily said.

"I wasn't hinting for an invitation," Ross said, embarrassed that his words might have been construed that way.

Lily smiled and squeezed his arm. It took him a moment to realize why the gesture seemed familiar. Julie had the same kind of mannerisms, that almost unconscious way of reinforcing her words with a physical touch.

He had come to crave those casual little brushes of her hands on him, though he would rather be hog-tied and left in a bull paddock than admit it.

They spoke of family news for a few moments while he savored divine mouthfuls of the gooey, yeasty cinnamon rolls. William caught him up on the upcoming wedding of his son Darr to Bethany Burdett, a receptionist at the Fortune Foundation, then Lily shared news about her family.

Ross had never quite figured out his place on the Fortune family tree. Sure, he shared the surname since Cindy had never bothered to change her name through any of her three marriages and had made sure each of her children carried it, as well. But he never quite felt a part of the family.

Cindy had been estranged from her siblings for years. Until Frannie's marriage to Lloyd eighteen years ago gave her more of an excuse, Cindy only popped into Red Rock once in a while, usually to hit somebody in her family up for money.

How many times had his uncle William and aunt Molly bailed Cindy out of some scrape or another? Even Lily and her late husband Ryan had taken a turn.

Ross felt keenly obligated to them all for it—which was exactly why he was here listening to family gossip he didn't really care about and enjoying Rosita's exquisite cinnamon rolls.

"I guess you know the reason we asked you here," William finally said when there was a lull in the conversation. "We're just looking for an update on your investigation."

"Which one?" Ross muttered ruefully, taking a sip of coffee. Right now he felt as if he were spinning three or four dozen plates and was quite sure each one was ready to crash to the ground.

"Finding out the truth behind whoever killed Lloyd has to be your priority right now, for Frannie and Josh's sake. We completely understand that." William paused, his expression serious. "But I hope you understand that my priority right now is keeping the rest of the family safe."

His gaze flickered briefly to Lily just long enough for Ross to wonder if something were going on between the two of them. *William and Lily?* As stunning as he found the idea, it made an odd sort of sense. They each had lost—and mourned—their respective spouses and they were both heavily involved with the Fortune Foundation.

He hadn't heard anything from any other family members about a burgeoning romance between the two of them, but maybe it was still in the early stages.

He had enough genuine mysteries to solve, he reminded himself. He didn't need to concern himself with any hypothetical romance between Lily and William— and it was none of his business anyway.

"Have you discovered anything new about the fires here and at Red or the mysterious notes we've received?" William asked.

In January, a fire nearly destroyed the local restaurant owned by good friends of the Fortunes, the Mendozas. At that same time, William and his brother Patrick each received a mysterious note that said simply "One of the Fortunes is not who you think."

Just a month later, another fire had destroyed a barn at the Double Crown, killing a favorite horse, and Lily had received a note of her own that read "This one wasn't an accident, either."

Ross had been brought in after that, when the family realized all these seemingly random events were connected.

He hadn't been very successful, though, much to his chagrin, both professionally and personally. Then in April, the mystery deepened and became even more sinister when his mother wrecked her car after a visit with Frannie and the Red Rock police discovered that her brakes had been tampered with.

Ross still couldn't completely convince himself Cindy hadn't done it herself for attention. That was a pretty pitiful suspicion for a son to have about his own mother, but he had learned during his forty years on the planet not to put much past her. Still, he was investigating the brake-tampering incident as part of the pattern.

"I'll be honest with you, Uncle William," he said now. "I'm hitting a wall. The private lab I sent the letters to was unable to find any legible fingerprints on either the notepaper itself or the envelopes used, and they were both very generic items that could have been purchased anywhere. Nothing distinctive at all that might help us identify who purchased them and sent them. The lab was able to collect a small amount of DNA from whoever licked the envelopes, but it's not in any of the databanks we can access."

"Which means what, exactly?" Lily asked.

He gave them both an apologetic look. "Until we have a suspect to compare the sample to, DNA doesn't do us much good."

"Where do you suggest we go from here?" William asked, his expression troubled. He slanted a look at Lily and the obvious worry in his eyes made Ross wonder again at their relationship.

"I've still got some leads I'm following on Cindy's brakes and the accelerant used in both fires. But I'll be honest, right now my focus has to be on Frannie."

"That's just as it should be," Lily assured him, her features sympathetic. "I worry so for her. She's such a quiet soul, one who certainly doesn't belong in jail. I hate that she has to go through this."

"What about Josh?" William asked. "In a way, he's lost both a mother and a father, hasn't he?"

"Only temporarily, until I can clear Frannie and get her home where she belongs." He spoke the words in a vow.

Lily touched his arm again, her hands cool and soft. "You're such a good brother, Ross. You always have been. I don't know what would have happened to Frannie or your brothers if not for you."

William made a face. "It was an outrage what you children had to endure. The rest of us should never have allowed it. It's one of my greatest regrets in life that we didn't realize just how bad things were and didn't sue for custody of all of you."

How different his life might have turned out, if that had happened. He might have grown up in California with William and Molly and their sons or here on the ranch with Ryan and his first wife. He might have had breakfast every morning in this big, comfortable kitchen, instead of in whatever dingy apartment Cindy found for them.

"I wish I could say my sister ever outgrew her irresponsibility," William went on, "but she's as flighty and self-destructive at seventy as she was when she was a girl. I'm only sorry she dragged the four of you with her."

The last thing Ross wanted to talk about right now was his mother and the chaos of his childhood and all the might-have-beens that seemed more painful in retrospect. He quickly changed the subject.

"I'll admit, I'm worried about how this is all affecting Josh. He went back to school last week but he won't talk about how things are going. I know how kids can talk and I'm sure a scandal like this is the hot topic at Red Rock High School."

As he hoped, the diversionary tactic did the trick. Lily's eyes grew soft with concern, as they did whenever she heard about a child or youth in need.

"Have you thought about grief counseling for him?" she asked. "Perhaps someone at the Foundation might be able to see him. Julie Osterman, for instance, specializes in helping teens who have suffered loss."

Okay, maybe changing the subject hadn't been the greatest idea. He didn't want to talk about Julie any more than he wanted to discuss Cindy.

He certainly hadn't been able to stop thinking about her since their dinner and the heated kiss they had shared nearly a week before. He had tried everything to get the blasted woman out of his system. He had worked like a maniac tracking down leads in Frannie's case, had taken Josh out fishing three more times, had swum so many laps in his sister's pool he thought he might just grow fins.

But he still dreamed of Julie every night and thoughts of her had a devious way of slithering into his mind at the most inconvenient time. Like, oh, just about every other minute.

"He's actually seeing Julie," Ross admitted. "He's been to a few sessions now. I can't say if they're helping yet."

"Julie is wonderful," Lily exclaimed. "Don't you just love her?"

Ross nearly choked on his coffee. "Um, she seems nice enough." Somehow he managed not to choke on the understatement, as well. "Josh likes her and that's the important thing."

"Julie is the perfect one to help him," Lily said. "She understands what it is to lose someone she loved."

"Yeah," Ross said, his voice gruff. "She told me about her husband."

Lily blinked a little at that. "Did she?"

Ross fiddled with his cup. "Yeah."

"What happened?" William asked. "I had no idea she was even married."

Lily touched his hand. "I'll tell you later," she said, then turned back to Ross. "I can't tell you how pleased and relieved I am that Josh is talking to someone. I've been so worried for him, especially since the last words between Josh and Lloyd were so harsh."

Ross frowned. "Harsh? Why do you say that?"

Lily shifted in her chair, looking as if she wished she hadn't said anything. "They were fighting, maybe a half hour before Lloyd was found dead. I'm sorry. I assumed you knew."

Fighting? Josh and Lloyd? This was the first he had heard anything about Josh even seeing his father the night of Lloyd's death. His nephew had never said a word about it.

Why hadn't he? Ross wondered.

"Did you hear them?" he asked.

"It wasn't my intention to eavesdrop. You have to understand that. But I left the dance for a moment and returned to the art booths, hoping to catch one of the vendors who was selling a particularly lovely plein air painting I had my eye on. I had talked myself out of it then decided at the last moment that it would be stunning in one of the guest bedrooms here. It *was* perfect, by the way. Would you like to see it?"

Lily was stalling, which wasn't at all like her.

"What did you hear?" he asked.

She sighed. "I was taking the painting to my car when I heard raised voices. I would have walked past, but then I recognized Josh's voice. They were some distance away, behind the exhibits, and I'm sure they didn't see me. I'm not sure they would have noticed anyway. They both sounded so furious."

His gut clenched. Why hadn't Josh mentioned any fight with his father? In the nearly two weeks since the murder, his nephew hadn't said a single word about any altercation. Why the hell not?

"Could you hear what they were saying?" Ross asked, unable to keep the harsh urgency out of his voice.

Lily glanced at William then back at Ross. "Not clearly. I'm sorry, Ross. They were some distance away from me. And though their voices were raised, I couldn't hear everything. Lloyd was mostly yelling at poor Josh about something or other. I heard him call him a careless idiot at one point and he said something else about Josh ruining his life."

"Did you hear Josh's response?" he asked. It suddenly seemed vitally important, for reasons Ross wasn't prepared to analyze.

Again Lily looked at William as if seeking moral support. His uncle looked as concerned as Ross was and he was quite certain this was the first his uncle had heard about an altercation between them, as well.

"He's just a boy," she said. "He didn't mean anything."

"What did he say, Lily?" William picked up her hand and curled his fingers around it. "Tell us."

She sighed. "He said he wouldn't let Lloyd get away with it. Whatever *it* might have been. I couldn't hear that part. And then he said something about how he—Josh—would stop Lloyd, no matter what it took."

The coffee and cinnamon rolls seemed to congeal in Ross's stomach. "Have you told anyone else about this?"

"No." She frowned, suddenly pensive. "But I think Frannie heard their argument, too. In fact, I'm almost certain of it. I saw her just a few moments later and she looked white and didn't even say hello, which was not at all like her."

What else had his family not bothered to tell him? His first instinct was to drive to the high school, yank Josh out of his chemistry final and rip into him for keeping these kinds of secrets.

What had Josh and his father been fighting about? And more importantly, why the hell hadn't Josh told him?

"I'm sorry, Ross. I can see you're upset. I would have told you earlier but I just assumed Josh or Frannie must have mentioned it to you."

"No," he said grimly. "Both of them are apparently keeping their mouths shut about any number of things. But I intend to find out what."

* * *

He had learned after more than a decade on the police force and two more years as a private investigator that sometimes he just needed to give his subconscious time and space to chew on things, to sort through all the pieces of a case and help him put them back together in the right order.

Sometimes mundane tasks helped the process, so Ross decided to stop at the grocery store on the way back from the Double Crown.

The wheels were spinning a hundred miles an hour as he pushed the cart through the cereal aisle, trying to remember which were Josh's favorites.

He disliked grocery shopping. Always had. He had a service in San Antonio that delivered the same things to him every week. Milk, eggs, cheese, a variety of frozen dinners. He still had to make the occasional trip to the store but most of the basics were covered by the delivery service.

Yeah, it made him feel like a pathetic old bachelor once in a while, but he figured it was all about time management. Why waste time with a task he disliked when he could pay someone else to take care of it?

He knew why shopping bothered him. He didn't need counseling to figure it out. It was a silly reaction, he knew, but somehow grocery shopping reminded him far too much of those frequent times when Cindy would take off when they were kids—of being nine years old again, pushing five-year-old Frannie in a shopping cart and nagging his six- and seven-year-old brothers to stay with them while he roamed through the aisle trying to figure out what they could afford from the emergency stash he always tried to stockpile with money he stole out of his mother's purse for just these moments.

He pushed back the image as he mechanically moved through the store, trying to remember what kind of food he liked when he was eighteen.

He passed the pharmacy at the front of the store and suddenly saw Jillian Fredericks standing at the counter.

Damn. He was in no mood for a confrontation with the woman right here in the middle of the Piggly Wiggly, for her sake or his own. She had been through enough and he didn't want to dredge up any more pain for her.

Sidestepping to a different aisle was simply the humane, decent thing to do, he told himself, though slinking through the store made him feel even more like that nine-year-old of his memory.

He was so intent on avoiding Jillian that he didn't notice anybody else in the aisle until someone called his name.

"Ross. Hello! How are you?"

He lifted his gaze from the detergent bottles and found Julie Osterman standing just across the aisle from him.

To his eternal chagrin, his heart did a crazy little tap dance at the sight of her.

She glanced at the few items in his cart. "Please tell me you and Josh are eating something besides cold cereal and potato chips."

He felt his face heat. "We had steak the other night with you. And we've gone to Red a few times. Tonight we're ordering pizza."

She didn't roll her eyes but he could tell she wanted to. Instead, she gave a rueful smile. "I won't nag."

He didn't want to think about the way her concern for their diet sent a traitorous warmth uncurling through him. "But you'd like to."

She opened her mouth to answer, but sighed instead. "Just remember, he's right in the middle of finals. A balanced meal here or there won't hurt."

"I'll have Mel down at the pizza parlor throw on extra vegetables, how about that?"

"Sounds perfect." She smiled, her lovely blue eyes bright and amused, and he suddenly couldn't think about anything but the heat and wonder of that blasted kiss. "You're not working today?" he asked.

"It's my afternoon off. Usually I try to catch up on my reports at home where it's quiet but I've been putting off grocery shopping and I decided to check that task off my list this afternoon."

"It's a pain in the neck, isn't it?"

She looked surprised. "I kind of like shopping. All those possibilities in front of me. I can walk out of the store with the makings of a gourmet supper or I can just run in for a glazed doughnut that's lousy for me but tastes divine. It all depends on my mood."

"Must be a girl thing."

She laughed and he realized how much brighter the world suddenly seemed than when he walked into the store. It was an uncomfortable discovery, that she could affect his entire mood just with her presence.

"How's Josh doing today?"

"That seems to be the question of the day. I wish I could tell people some answer other than 'fine.' He doesn't talk much to me about it."

He hadn't pushed the boy, but after his conversation with Lily, he was beginning to think that had been a mistake.

"That's completely normal, Ross," she answered. "Most seventeen-year-old boys would much prefer going outside and shooting hoops to sitting around discussing their emotional mood of the moment."

"I think it's probably fair to say most forty-year-old men aren't much different."

She laughed softly and he was suddenly consumed with the desire to taste that delectable mouth again, right there beside the fabric softeners. He even leaned forward slightly, then caught himself and jerked back.

Josh, he reminded himself. Focus on Josh. The conversation with Lily came back to him. Had Josh told Julie about his fight with his father the night of his death?

"Josh talks to you, though, right? I mean, you've had two sessions with him now."

"Yes," she said, somewhat warily.

"Did he mention anything about talking to his father the night of the Spring Fling?" he asked.

She sighed. "You know I can't tell you anything about my conversations with him, Ross. They're confidential. Right now Josh is still willing to talk to me and I don't want to do anything to jeopardize the trust he has in me. I'm sorry."

Sometimes he really hated when people were decent and honorable.

That didn't mean he always had to play by the same rules. A good investigator could read as much in what a person *didn't* say—in her body language and her facial expressions—as in her words. He had learned that sometimes offering information of his own could elicit the reaction he needed to verify his suspicions.

"I had an interesting conversation with someone today who said she overheard Josh and his father in a bitter argument shortly before Lloyd's death," he said with studied casualness. "I was just going to ask if he had said anything to you about it."

Julie was pretty adept at hiding her reaction to his words—but not quite good enough. He didn't miss how her eyes widened with surprise and the ever-so-slight way her lips parted just for an instant.

So Josh *hadn't* mentioned the fight to Julie in their sessions. *Why not?* he wondered, concerned all over again at what other secrets his nephew might be keeping.

"Do you think that's pertinent to investigating what might have happened that night?" she asked.

He shrugged. "I can't say. I just find it surprising that Josh hasn't bothered to mention it. He never even told me he saw his father at the Spring Fling. Even though he claimed to hate Lloyd, I imagine it's got to be tough on any kid to know the last words he had with his old man were angry ones."

Not that he would know. His own father had left Cindy when Ross was less than a year old. Riley Randolph hadn't exactly been the fatherly type. Big surprise there, that Cindy would pick that kind of husband.

"If you're trying to get me to divulge anything from our therapy sessions," Julie said with a frown, "I'm afraid I can't help you."

Sweetheart, you already have, he thought. While he wouldn't exactly call her transparent, she was far too open a person to keep all her reactions concealed.

"I just wanted to pass on information," he said, which wasn't completely a lie. "Thought it might help you to have a little more background on that night when you're talking to Josh. You could ask him in the next session why they fought."

And why he hasn't bothered to tell anyone, he added silently.

"Thank you, Ross. I appreciate the information, then."

They lapsed into silence and Ross thought he probably ought to be moving his cart along, but he was suddenly loath to leave. He searched for some excuse to prolong their conversation, even as some part of his mind was fully aware of how pathetic it was that he was so conflicted over her.

He told himself every time he was with her that he needed to keep his distance. But then the next time he saw her, he was drawn to her all over again.

He knew he shouldn't find it such a consolation that she didn't seem in a hurry to leave his company, either.

"Josh told me it is his eighteenth birthday this weekend. What are his plans?" she asked.

He seized on the question. "Actually, I'm glad you brought that up. While I have you here, I could use some advice."

"Sure."

"We have to do something to celebrate his birthday. I mean, a kid only turns eighteen once. But I'm wondering if you've got any suggestions about what might be appropriate. Before everything happened, Frannie had talked about throwing a big party for him, but that doesn't seem right now, given the circumstances."

"That's a really good question." Her brow furrowed. "What would make Josh happiest? What might help him forget for a few hours all that's happened in his world?"

"I think he got a kick out of going out to the lake last week. We could do that again." He paused. "And he has that girlfriend, Lyndsey. Maybe I could have a barbecue that night and invite her and a few of his other friends."

"That sounds like a wonderful idea, Ross. See, you're better at this whole parenthood thing than you give yourself credit for."

He wasn't, though. He had sucked at it when he was a kid forced to take care of his younger siblings and he didn't feel any more capable now.

"Will you help me?"

The question came out of nowhere, surprising him as much as it did her.

"Help you how?" she asked, that wariness in her eyes again.

So much for keeping his distance from her. Ross sighed. But now that he had asked her, it made sense. He really *could* use help. It would certainly be easier on his self-control if that help came from someone else, but it was too late to back down now.

"I'm not sure I can handle throwing a teenage party by myself, even a little one," he admitted. "Sure, I can grill steaks and maybe some burgers but other than that, I wouldn't know where to start."

He thought he caught a flash of reluctance in her eyes and he felt foolish for asking. He had already dragged her into their lives too much.

"Never mind," he said. "I'll just get some pop and open a few bags of chips. We should be fine."

She let out a long breath. "I can help you. I don't have any plans Saturday. Why don't you take care of the grill and I'll handle all the other details? The side dishes, the chips, the cake and ice cream."

"Are you sure?"

"No problem." She smiled, with no trace of that hesitation he thought he had seen and he wondered if he had been mistaken. "It will be fun."

* * *

Fun. Right.

She was an idiot.

Julie sat in her car in the parking lot of the grocery store for several moments after she had loaded her groceries into the trunk of her car.

She had absolutely no willpower when it came to Ross Fortune. Since that stunning kiss they had shared the week before, she had promised herself she would do her best to return things to a casual friendship.

For the sake of her psyche, she had no other choice. It was painfully obvious he wasn't available for anything else. He had made it quite clear that he only wanted her help with Josh, not for anything else.

She was happy to help with Josh. But she wasn't at all certain she could continue to do so when she was beginning to entertain all sorts of inappropriate thoughts about the teen's uncle.

She couldn't afford to let herself care for Ross, not when they obviously wanted far different things from life.

A woman came out of the store and pushed her cart to the minivan beside Julie's car. She had a preschool-aged boy hanging off her cart and a curly-haired baby in the cart. The baby was perhaps nine months old, in a pink outfit with bright flowers.

The boy said something to his mother that Julie couldn't hear but the mother laughed and kissed the child on the nose before she picked up the baby to settle her in her car seat.

As she watched them, Julie's heart turned over.

That was what she wanted. She was ready for children of her own, for a family. Seven years had passed since Chris's death and in all the ways that mattered, she had been alone for the last few years of their marriage before that.

She was tired of it. She was ready to move forward with her life. She had even talked to Linda Jamison, the Foundation director, about adopting an older child as a single mother. She had so much love inside her and she wanted somewhere to give it beyond her clients.

Allowing herself to become any more entangled with a man like Ross Fortune would jeopardize all that progress she had made these past seven years toward healing and peace. She sensed it with a certainty she couldn't deny.

Oh, they might have a brief affair that would probably be intense and passionate and wonderful while it lasted.

But Julie knew she would end up more alone than ever. Alone and heartbroken.

The mother beside her finished loading her groceries and her children and backed out of the parking lot. Julie watched them go with renewed determination.

She would help Ross with Josh's birthday party and that would be the end of it. If he asked for her help with his nephew again, she would politely tell him she was only available in a professional capacity for more counseling sessions.

It would hurt, she knew. She was already coming to care for him and Josh too much. But she didn't see she had any other choice.

She'd already lost too much to risk her heart again.

Chapter 9

Two days later, she was working on paperwork in her office when Susan Fortune Eldridge poked her head in the doorway.

"Hey," her friend and coworker exclaimed. "I haven't talked to you in ages. It seems like we're always running in different directions. How are things?"

"Good," Julie answered. "Busy, as usual. How about you?"

"Great. Wonderful, really. Listen, Ethan and I are throwing an impromptu dinner party this weekend. We thought maybe you could bring Sean or whatever is the name of that art teacher you're seeing."

Julie couldn't help but laugh. "I would certainly do that, but I'm not sure his fiancée would appreciate it."

Susan's green eyes opened wide and she moved fully into Julie's office and sat in the easy chair her clients usually took. "Fiancée? When did that happen?"

"A few weeks ago, from what I understand. I bumped into him the other day at the library and he told me about it. He started seeing her not long after we stopped dating, around New Year's."

Susan made a face. "Some friend I am. You broke up with someone five months ago and I'm only just hearing about it? Why didn't I know?"

"We didn't really break up. We just mutually decided that while we enjoyed each other's company, we didn't have that sizzle. We only dated a few times anyway. It was never anything serious."

Unfortunately, their brief relationship had coincided with the holiday party season and Sean had escorted her to several parties around town that Susan and her veterinarian husband Ethan had also attended. Julie could completely understand why she might have been under the impression they were more serious than they were.

"Well, bring whoever you're seeing now," Susan said. "It's obviously been too long since we socialized outside the office, since I apparently have no idea what's going on in your life."

Julie had a quick mental image of the heated kiss with Ross that she couldn't get out of her head. She had a feeling Susan would probably misunderstand if she mentioned that particular encounter.

"When is your party?" she asked.

"Tomorrow night. Around seven."

She winced. "I'm sorry, Susan, but I already have plans tomorrow."

"Oh? Hot date? Tell me all!"

"Nothing to tell, I'm afraid. Um, I told your cousin Ross I would help him throw a small party for Josh's eighteenth birthday."

"I completely forgot Josh's birthday was coming up."

She paused, an expression of concern on her petite features. "So tell me. How is Ross doing?"

"Fine, as far as I can tell. Why do you ask? Usually everyone seems to be most concerned with Frannie or Josh."

"I've been worrying about him. I've tried to call a few times to check on him and Josh and always get voice mail. We've been playing phone tag. I was planning on making time this weekend to go to the house to see how things are with them. This can't be an easy situation for Ross."

She frowned. "What can't?"

"The instant parenting thing landing in his lap so abruptly. I've always had the impression he wanted nothing to do with kids and parenting after his lousy childhood. He probably figured he did his share while practically raising his brothers and sister."

Julie suddenly realized how little she knew about Ross's past. She knew he had been a cop in San Antonio but his life before then was a mystery. "Where were his parents?"

"I don't know about his dad. I think he took off when Ross was just a baby. I don't know about him or the other fathers."

"Other…fathers?"

"Frannie's his half sister and he has two half brothers, Cooper and Flint. They all have different fathers, except the middle boys. None of the men stuck around for long, except Frannie's dad, I guess, who might have if he hadn't died first."

"How sad!"

"Yes, well, my aunt Cindy certainly knows how to pick them."

"That's Ross's mother?"

"She's the woman who gave birth to him, anyway," Susan answered. "Calling her a mother might be a bit of a stretch. She was sister to my father, Leonard, as well as Patrick and William."

Julie frowned. "I'm not sure I've met her."

"Believe me, you would remember if you had. Cindy is a real piece of work, let me tell you. She wears tons of makeup and still dresses like a hootchie-kootchie dancer, which I've heard rumors she was, in between stints as a showgirl in Vegas."

"Wow."

"Right. She's seventy years old and still dresses in tight pants and halter tops."

"Sounds like an interesting character," she said faintly.

"*Interesting* is one word for it. From family gossip, I've heard she ran off to Vegas to be a dancer when she was barely eighteen. She had a long string of lousy relationships and three marriages. During that time, she gave birth to Ross and his siblings but I don't think she had much to do with raising them. She was too busy shaking her booty in one club or another."

Julie tried to imagine Ross growing up under those circumstances and couldn't. No wonder he seemed so hard and cynical if that was the only example of a family he had.

"Ross was the oldest," Susan went on. "Frannie told me once that he was always the one who fixed her hair, packed her lunch and sent her off to school. Cindy was always either entertaining company or too tired from working into the night. He kept that family together, dysfunctional as it was."

Julie thought of her own family, warm and loving and completely supportive of whatever she had ever tried to do. During those dark and terrible times during Chris's illness and then after his suicide, she had moved back home with her parents in Austin and they had enfolded her with loving arms of support and comfort.

Her four brothers might drive her crazy sometimes with their overprotectiveness but she adored them all.

What must Ross's childhood have been like? She tried to picture a younger version of the hard, implacable man she knew trying to fix his little sister's hair and the image just about broke her heart.

"I've always wanted to see him happy," Susan went on. "Settled, you know, with a home and family. I don't know if I'd say he's really happy, but he seems content with his bachelor life. It's terribly sad, really, when you think about it. I wonder what scars he still carries from such an unstable childhood."

Julie knew it was ridiculous to feel this sudden urge to cry. She fought back the tears and hoped Susan didn't notice her reaction.

"I've worried that his temporary guardianship of Josh—again, someone else's child he's suddenly responsible for—must in a sense feel like he's reliving his own childhood," Susan said. "I've been worried about his head and wanted to make sure he's in an okay place about the whole thing."

"I had no idea," Julie said. "Ross never said anything."

Susan gave her a curious look, which quickly turned speculative. "Why would he have told you? I wasn't under the impression you knew Ross well, other than in your capacity as Josh's grief counselor."

Her eyes suddenly widened. "Which begs the question—why, again, are you helping with Josh's party?

That seems above and beyond the call of duty, no matter how wonderful a counselor you are."

Julie ordered herself not to blush. "Ross asked for my help. I couldn't say no."

Her friend was quiet for a long moment, then she tilted her head, giving Julie a searching look. "Is there something between you and my cousin?"

Did a heated kiss and a fierce attraction she couldn't seem to shove out of her head count as something? Her face felt hot and she couldn't meet Susan's gaze.

"We've become friends, I guess you could say."

"Only friends?"

"I don't think he's available for anything else right now."

She regretted the words as soon as she said them. As a psychologist, Susan was an expert at analyzing people's words, sifting through layers of nuances and meaning to help her have better clarity into their psyches. Julie realized too late how her words must have sounded—and she heard the echo of the ruefulness in her voice.

"If he were?" Susan asked, studying her closely.

She let out a breath. "Since that's a rhetorical question, I don't really have to answer it, do I?"

Susan was silent for a long time. When she finally spoke, her eyes were soft with concern. "I love Ross, Julie. If I could pick anyone in the world for him, she would be someone exactly like you. Someone nurturing and caring and generous. Someone who could help him heal."

Since Julie was also trained to listen carefully to her clients and parse through their words, she didn't miss how Susan had phrased her comment. "Someone exactly like me, but not me?"

"I love Ross," Susan repeated. "But I love you, too. You've been through so much pain. I ache just thinking about what you've had to survive. You deserve a man whose heart is healthy and strong, someone who is free to love you without reservation."

"And you don't think that's Ross."

Susan's silence was a harsh answer. Julie reminded herself she had known. Hadn't she promised herself she would give him one more night for Josh's birthday party and then try to extricate herself from his life so she could move forward?

Still, she couldn't deny the spasm of pain and regret twisting through her at having her own convictions reinforced.

"Then it's a good thing Ross and I are only friends, isn't it?" she said briskly. "I'm only helping him with a birthday party, Sus. That's all."

"Sure." Susan forced a smile. "Well, I'm sorry you can't come to our dinner party. We'll do it another time, then. Give Josh a big birthday kiss for me, okay? And tell Ross I'll keep trying to reach him."

Unexpectedly, Susan hugged her on the way out the door. She hugged her back, then returned to work, trying her best to shake the discontent pulling at her mood like heavy, intractable weights.

Ross pulled into the circular driveway in front of Frannie's house, fighting off the bleak mood that settled over him as he looked at it. There was no reason such a silly froth of a house should seem so ominous, but he had begun to dread coming back here each night.

Josh wasn't home. The boy's aging sports car wasn't in the driveway and Ross knew damn well he shouldn't have this vague feeling of relief that he didn't have to deal with his nephew right now.

He was going to have to talk to him sometime. A serious, blunt conversation between the two of them was long overdue. Ross rubbed his temples as the implication of all he had learned over the last two days centered there in a pounding headache that slithered down his spine to his tight shoulders until it became a cold, greasy ball in his gut.

He still didn't want to believe any of it, but it was becoming increasingly difficult to keep an open mind.

After his talk with Lily and William at the Double Crown, he had spent two days tracking down leads, trying to find anyone else who might have heard Josh fighting with his father and who might be able to shed more light on the content of their conversation. He wanted to be prepared with as much information as possible before he faced his nephew with what he had learned.

He finally found a potter whose stall had been not far from the scene of the argument. Reynaldo Velasquez had indeed heard the fight. He had recounted it much as Lily had—that he couldn't hear many of the words but he had heard raised voices, had heard Lloyd yelling at his son and then had heard Josh say he would stop him, no matter what it took.

And, more chilling than that confirmation, Reynaldo had added that he had been surprised to hear such harsh words coming from Josh. He'd seemed like a nice kid, the artist said, when he had come to his booth to pick up the large vase his mother had purchased earlier in the evening.

Ross closed his eyes, his hands tight on the steering wheel. Even now, remembering the conversation, his stomach felt slick with nausea. As far as he could tell, Josh had been the last one in possession of the vase.

Josh. Not Frannie.

Josh had fought with his father in front of witnesses. Josh had a rocky relationship with his father. Josh was a hotheaded teenager.

And most damning of all was Josh's behavior since his father's death. The furtive conversations, the obfuscations. Ross had sensed he was hiding something. He supposed it made him a pretty damn lousy investigator that he hadn't once suspected his nephew was capable of killing his own father.

Despite the witnesses and Josh's own dishonesty by omission in not saying anything about the fight with Lloyd, Ross still couldn't make himself believe it, any more than he had been able to contemplate the ridiculous notion that Frannie might have killed Lloyd.

Josh was a good kid. Yeah, he had a temper and his relationship with Lloyd was tense and strained and had been for some time now. But Ross couldn't accept that Josh might be able to commit patricide. And he absolutely couldn't see the boy he knew standing by and saying nothing while his own mother took the fall for it.

Ross would have to talk to him about what he had learned, no matter how difficult the conversation. He would have to walk a fine line between seeking the vital information he needed to put these pieces of the puzzle together without sounding accusatory. It would take every ounce of his investigative skills.

He didn't want to ruin Josh's birthday, but he had no choice. Josh would legally be an adult in just a few hours. Perhaps it was past time Ross started treating him like one.

With a sigh, he let himself into the house. The empty

foyer echoed with every sound he made, from the clink of his keys on the polished white table to the scrape of his boots on the tile floor.

He hated it here. He found the entire place depressing. He had never liked it, even when Frannie was here, but without her, the house seemed lifeless and cold.

He had a sudden, irrational, very Cindy-like desire to walk away from everything here, to escape back to his apartment in San Antonio where he had no responsibilities except to his agency clients. Where he was free to come and go at will, without this nagging worry for those he loved.

Ashamed of himself for indulging the impulse to flee, even for a moment, he walked through the house to the kitchen and flipped on the light switch.

The first thing he saw was a note from Josh on the memo board above the small kitchen desk that Frannie had always kept meticulously organized. It was written in Josh's careless scrawl on the back of a takeout menu for the pizza parlor.

Helping a friend. Don't wait up.

Ross frowned. Helping which friend do what, where? The kid was a few hours away from eighteen and now thought he could come and go as he pleased without any more explanation than one terse, say-nothing note?

Fighting down that instinctive relief again that he could put off the coming interrogation for a while longer, he pulled out his cell phone and hit Josh's number. The phone rang four times then went to voice mail.

Ross sighed. "Call me," he said after the beep, not unaware of the terseness of his own message.

He thought about dinner, but he didn't have much of an appetite anyway, he decided. A better expenditure of time would be to enter the field notes from his interview with Reynaldo into his case file.

He headed down the hall to the guest room he had taken over for his use since coming to stay at the house. Compared to the rest of the house, this room was simply decorated, with a double pine bed, dresser and a comfortable desk. He figured Lloyd hadn't bothered to come into it enough to insist on more of his atrocious taste.

Ross set his laptop case on the bed and pulled out the digital recorder and the small notebook he used on field interviews.

An hour later, he finished logging in his work for the day. Since the notebook was nearly full, he opened the desk drawer to find a new one and his gut suddenly clenched.

Something wasn't right.

He had a strict system of organization with his case files. He kept the field notebooks he used in numbered order, meticulously dated and filed so he could easily double-check information on any case when needed. No matter what else was going on, he always took the time to refile them in order.

The notebook on top of the stack was *not* the most recent. He frowned and flipped through the half-dozen books he had filled with various casework in the days since coming to stay with Josh.

None of them was in order, the way he was absolutely certain he had left them just that morning.

He stared at the stack as that greasy ball in his gut seemed to take a few more rotations. He might be haphazard and casual about some things—his clothing came to mind and, yeah, he needed a haircut—but not about work. Never about his cases and the interviews.

He couldn't afford to be careless as a private investigator. He had to be able to find information quickly and reliably. And while the computer was a great backup for storing data, he still depended on his own hand-written field notes.

Someone had rifled through his notes. He should have locked them up, but the thought had never even occurred to him.

His mind sorted through other possibilities. He wanted to think maybe he had just been sloppy the last time he was in here. That would be a much more palatable option than what he was beginning to suspect, but he couldn't lie to himself.

He knew without a doubt that he hadn't left his notebooks like this. Which meant someone else had rifled through them.

He only had one suspect and it was the very one he didn't want to believe capable of it. Josh. Who else could it have been? The boy had access to the notebooks and plenty of opportunity when Ross wasn't here. He never bothered to lock the desk drawer. That heedlessness on his part had obviously been a mistake, but Ross had never considered it, had never believed for a moment it might even be necessary.

But motive. Why would Josh want to know what Ross was digging into, unless he had reason to want that information to stay buried?

It was another good question. He now had several for his nephew—if only he could find the kid.

By 8:00 p.m., he still hadn't reached Josh.

Ross paced the living room of Frannie's house, not sure whether to be angry or worried about his nephew, especially when all his calls started going directly to voice mail.

He had been through this waiting game enough with his brothers. He couldn't count the number of nights he had sat up stewing while he waited for either Flint or Cooper to come home, hours later than they were supposed to. Of course, this was a little different situation, since he had never been preparing to question his brothers about a murder.

When his cell phone rang at eight-thirty, he lunged for it.

"Yeah?" he growled.

A slight pause met him then he heard Julie Osterman's voice. "Ross? Is that you?"

His hopes that he might be able to clear everything up quickly with Josh and get the kid home faded.

"Oh. Hi."

A slight pause met his response. "That's a bit of a disheartening reaction," Julie said, her voice suddenly tight. "I just needed to ask a question about tomorrow but I can call back later. Or not."

He cursed under his breath. "Sorry. It's not you, I swear. I'm always glad to talk to you." He probably shouldn't have said that, even though it wasn't a lie. "I was just hoping you were Josh."

She picked up his concern right away. "Josh? Is something wrong? What's going on? Where is he?"

"No idea. He's not answering his cell. He left a note saying he was helping a friend and that I wasn't to wait up."

"But of course you will."

"Oh, undoubtedly," he said grimly. "I have a few words to say to my nephew."

"When did you see him last?"

"This morning at breakfast. Everything seemed okay. Nothing out of the ordinary. He left for school to take his last final. We talked about the kids he had invited tomorrow and what movie they planned to watch after dinner. Nothing unusual."

"He didn't say anything about going anywhere after school?"

"Not a word."

But then Ross had kept secrets of his own. He hadn't mentioned anything about the direction he was taking in the investigation because he had wanted to be more certain of his information before confronting Josh about the fight with his father. "He took a call, said something about being on his way, then took off for school."

"Are you sure he went to school?"

"No. But the school's long closed. Unless I drag the principal in from home to go through the attendance records, I'm out of luck."

"What about his other friends? Did you try Lyndsey's cell phone?"

"I don't have her number. I called her home, though, and got no answer."

"What about Ricky or one of his extended cousins?"

"Good idea. I was planning to give him a little longer before I hit the phones."

He didn't tell Julie he would have done that before, but he had still been holding out the vague hope that Josh would walk through the door on his own.

She was quiet for a long moment. "You know, Ross, it's a natural human reaction when life becomes too stressful to seek escape. Perhaps he just needed a little time away from things here in Red Rock."

He hated to ask, in light of her own firsthand experience with suicide, but he had to know her professional opinion. "You're right. Things have been tough for him lately. You don't think he would do anything rash, do you?"

She was silent for a moment and he knew she guessed what he meant. "I couldn't say definitely, but in our two sessions, I didn't get any vibe like that from him, Ross. He wouldn't have any reason to, would he?"

A guilty conscience, maybe? Ross thought of those disordered notebooks and what he had learned the last two days. He hoped Josh didn't feel hopeless or cornered enough to do something drastic.

"I'm going to go look for him," he said suddenly. "I can't just sit here."

Chapter 10

Julie heard the desperate determination in Ross's voice and she ached for him, especially in light of her conversation with his cousin earlier in the day. He was a man who took his responsibilities seriously and right now he had far too many.

"I'll come with you," she said. "I can be there in fifteen minutes."

"You don't have to do that," he exclaimed, not bothering to hide his surprise that she would make the offer.

"I know I don't. But a second pair of eyes wouldn't hurt, don't you agree? And I have a few advantages."

"What are those?"

"From my clients at the Foundation, I happen to know the location of many of the local teen hangouts. I also have connections among the different teen groups, from the jocks to the druggies to the cowboys to the hackers. I can help you, Ross, if you let me."

She kept her fingers crossed even as she went to her closet and pulled out a jacket and sturdy walking shoes.

Silence met her assurances as he hesitated and she was certain he would refuse her offer of help. Ross was a man who liked to do things on his own, she was learning. He hated depending on anyone else for anything, even for assistance he might desperately need.

She was bracing to tell him she would go on her own looking for Josh when he surprised her.

"All right," he answered. "I probably *could* use your help, especially given your connections to the local teen scene. But stay at your place and I'll come pick you up."

Julie quickly changed out of her lounge-around-the-house sweats into jeans and a tailored blue shirt and sweater and pulled her hair into a ponytail.

While she waited, she went to work gathering a few provisions and compiling lists of any possible friends she might have ever heard Josh mention and several potential places they could look.

When Ross pulled into her driveway exactly sixteen minutes later, she was ready. She opened the door to her house before he could walk up the steps.

He drove a white SUV hybrid that she imagined was perfect for a private investigator—bland enough to be inconspicuous but sturdy enough to be taken seriously.

She opened the door to the backseat and set the large wicker basket inside before she opened the front passenger door and climbed inside.

In the pale glow from the dome light, she could see baffled consternation on his rugged features. "What's all this?" he asked, gesturing to the basket.

She shrugged, feeling slightly foolish. "A few supplies. A Thermos of coffee, some soda, a few snacks, sandwiches. I didn't know what might come in handy so I packed a little of everything."

He glanced at the overflowing basket in the backseat and then back at her as if he didn't quite know what to make of her. "We're not heading out on a cross-country trek here. We're only driving around town looking for one kid."

"It doesn't hurt to be prepared, does it? You never know what might come in handy." She swiveled in the front seat and reached back to pull a flowered tin off the top of the basket. "Here, have one of my caramel cashew bars. I made them for Josh's birthday tomorrow but I thought maybe we could use them for bribes or something."

"For bribes."

She shrugged. "You know, to get somebody to talk who doesn't want to."

He opened his mouth for a second, his eyes astonished, then closed it with a snap. "That good, are they?" he finally said.

She managed a smile, despite her worry for Josh. "See for yourself."

After a moment's hesitation, he picked one up and bit into it. As he chewed it slowly and then swallowed, his eyes glazed with sheer ecstasy.

"Okay. You win," he said after a few more bites. "Right now, I would tell you anything you want to know."

She laughed, though a hundred questions tumbled together in her mind she would have asked him if circumstances between them had been different.

She held out the tin. "I've got a dozen more in here. You're welcome to eat them all if you want."

He gave her a half smile as he put the SUV into gear

before backing out of her driveway. "Wrong thing to say to an ex-cop," he said. "We're like locusts. If there's food available, we eat it."

She had a sudden wild urge to make a hundred different home-baked treats for him. Dutch apple pie, jam thumbprint cookies, snickerdoodles.

It was a silly reaction but she couldn't help remembering all the bleak details Susan had told her about Ross's childhood. His mother didn't sound like the sort to cook up a batch of warm, gooey chocolate chip cookies for her kids after school and Julie wanted suddenly to make up for all those things Ross never had.

She sighed and pushed the impulse away. Right now they needed to concentrate on Josh, she reminded herself.

"Where to first?" she asked.

"Nobody answered at his girlfriend Lyndsey's house but I figured that's a logical place to start."

The small tract house was in a neighborhood with dozens more that looked just like it. The siding might be a little different color and a few details varied from house to house, but Julie would be hard-pressed to tell them all apart, if not for the house numbers.

No lights were on inside and only a low-wattage porch light glowed on the exterior.

"Doesn't look like anybody's home," he said.

"Her mom works nights," Julie said. "Josh told me that once in passing. I think she's a nurse or something."

"Well, it doesn't hurt to double-check since we're here."

Julie opted to stay in the SUV while Ross walked to the front door and rang the bell. Even with her vehicle window rolled up, she could hear a dog's deep-throated barks from somewhere in the backyard.

The neighborhood shouldn't have seemed ominous. It had obviously seen better days and some of the houses had peeling paint, with a few junk cars up on cinderblocks in the driveways, but it was equally obvious that families lived here. She spotted multiple bikes, trampolines, play sets.

Still, she was immensely grateful for Ross's solid presence. She wouldn't want to be here by herself.

She watched him ring the doorbell once more, then to her surprise, he reached down and tried to jiggle the doorknob, without success.

"Would you have gone in if the door hadn't been locked?" she asked when he returned to the SUV a moment later.

He shrugged and she didn't miss the gleam of his smile in the darkness. "Don't know," he admitted. "I'm always glad when the opportunity doesn't present itself to find out exactly how far I'm willing to push the law I've always tried to uphold. Any ideas where to try next?"

"Actually, yes. I made a list."

"Why doesn't that surprise me?" Ross asked, a rueful tone to his voice. "Something tells me I'm going to need another caramel cashew bar."

By midnight, they had run out of friends that either of them had ever heard Josh mention. They had hit all the usual hangouts—the quarry, the pizza place, the lover's lane that curved through a forested area south of town. They had even checked beneath the bleachers on the football field.

On a Friday night the week before graduation, they had interrupted a group of half-stoned skinny-dipping seniors, found a half-dozen cars with steamed up windows and nearly found themselves in the middle of a verbal altercation that looked to have been shaping up into one heck of a fistfight.

All the way around, it seemed an exciting night for Red Rock. But Josh was nowhere to be found.

In the parking lot of the high school—their last stop—Julie leaned against the hood of his SUV while Ross stood next to her and dialed the number to the police station.

It was a last resort, a call he didn't want to make, but he thought there might be a slim chance Josh might have tried to contact his mother.

To his surprise—and consternation—he was patched right through to the police chief and he had an instant's sinking fear that Josh might be in custody.

"Hey, Jimmy. It's Ross Fortune."

"Oh. Ross. Hello. This is a surprise. A little late for social calls, isn't it?"

"Yeah, it's late. Oddly enough, you're still there. I wouldn't have thought the Red Rock police chief would pull the graveyard shift. Is something up?"

Jimmy hesitated just long enough for Ross to figure out his guess was correct. He drew a deep breath. *Damn it, Josh. What have you done?*

"Just another wild Friday night in Red Rock. You know how it is. The high schoolers are done with finals so they're all a little nuts. We're busting 'em like crazy on underage drinking and some minor drug possessions."

Ross thought about narcing out the skinny dippers at the quarry, then figured he'd let Jimmy's officers find the party on their own.

"We're a little busy tonight," the police chief said after a moment. "What can I do for you?"

He picked his words delicately. "I'm looking for my sister's kid, Josh. Any chance he stopped in to visit her tonight?"

The police chief was silent for a long moment that seemed to last forever and Ross held his breath, aware of Julie watching the one-sided conversation carefully.

"Not today," Jimmy finally said. "Think he came by earlier in the week. Just a minute. I can call the visitor log up on my computer to double-check for you."

Ross could hear keys clicking and then a moment later, the police chief came back on. "Nope. He was here on Tuesday but hasn't been back. Why do you ask?"

Ross debated telling him the kid had taken off but decided that information could wait. Jimmy was too damn smart and just might look at the puzzle pieces and come up with the same picture Ross was beginning to find.

"Oh, Frannie just asked for some warm socks and I wondered if Josh had had a chance to take them to her. No big deal. I'll stop by with them tomorrow."

"You sure that's all it is?"

They were both circling around each other like a couple of mangy old junkyard dogs after the same bone. "Positive. That's it. You know women and their cold feet."

"Don't I ever!" He gave a jovial laugh that sounded false to Ross's ears, but he wondered if he was imagining things. "Christy Lee just about freezes me out every night. Her feet can be like two little popsicles on the end of her legs."

"Well, thanks for the information. Guess I'll see you tomorrow when I drop off the socks."

"You be sure to do that."

After Ross hung up, he gazed out at the night, replaying the conversation in his head. Something didn't fit with his usual interactions with the police chief.

"Josh hasn't been at the police station?"

"Not that the chief was willing to tell me, anyway."

"Maybe he didn't know."

"There's not much happens at the Red Rock police station that Jimmy doesn't keep an eye on."

It made no sense for the chief to be at the station this late at night unless something big was going down. But short of busting into the police station, Ross had no way of knowing if Josh was there confessing to a murder.

And he could only hope that Josh would have the presence of mind to make a lousy phone call first before he did anything so rash.

"I think we need to check back at the house and see if he came home," Ross said. "I left a big note for him to call me on my cell but maybe he didn't see it."

She looked doubtful and he didn't add that the police station was on the way and that maybe they would just casually take a little drive through the parking lot, looking for a beat-up yellow RX-7.

He didn't see Josh's car in the parking lot of the police station, though. Nor was it in the driveway of Frannie's house.

He must have cursed aloud because Julie reached a comforting hand to touch his forearm. "I'm sure he's fine, Ross. He'll probably turn up any minute, full of apologies and explanations."

"I hope so," he muttered. He led the way inside the house and went immediately to the answering machine. It was blinking to indicate a new message and he stabbed the button.

To his vast relief, Josh's tenor filled the kitchen.

"Hey, Uncle Ross. Sorry, I must have left my phone

somewhere in the…somewhere. It was almost out of juice anyway. Anyway, I can't find it right now so I'm calling from a pay phone. Since I couldn't remember your cell number, I'm leaving a message here and hoping you get it. Don't worry about me. I've got a few things I need to take care of. I don't know when I'll be back but I'm fine, I promise. Everything's fine. Don't worry about me! Just take care of my mom and I'll be back as soon as I can. Thanks, Ross. Sorry about the fishing trip in the morning. Tell Ms. O to forget about the dinner, too. I'll make it up to you both, I promise."

Ross looked at the time stamp on the message and growled a harsh curse. "We only missed his call by half an hour."

"He said he was calling from a pay phone," Julie said. "Did the number show up on the caller ID? I don't know how these things are done but maybe you could trace it and at least narrow down where he was a half hour ago."

"Great idea." He scrolled through the numbers, then stopped on the most recent, noting the San Antonio prefix. What in blazes was the kid up to? He didn't know whether to be angry or relieved that Josh wasn't calling from the Red Rock police department.

He could do a reverse lookup to find the number but it would be faster just to call it, he decided. He dialed and waited through six rings before somebody picked up.

"Yeah?" a smoker-rough, impatient-sounding female voice answered.

"Hey, my friend called me a little while ago from this pay phone and needed a ride but he forgot to give me an intersection to pick him up," he quickly lied. "Can you tell me where you're at?"

"Hang on. This ain't my usual stroll. I don't know

this neighborhood. Just a sec." She returned a second later. "My friend says we're on the corner of Floyd Curl and Breezy Hill."

"Near the hospital?"

"Yeah. That's it. Hey, man, I think your friend might have found another set of wheels. Ain't nobody else here but us. You could give me a ride, though. Me and my friend can wait right here for you."

"You two might be waiting a while, sugar. But thanks anyway."

He hung up on her protests and found Julie watching him with a curious look in her eyes.

"That was quick thinking, to say you were picking up a friend."

He shrugged. "Old cop trick. I've got a million of them."

"I'm beginning to figure that out," she said. "We're going to go check it out, aren't we? Maybe we can find Josh's car somewhere in the vicinity."

"That's exactly what I was thinking. But you don't have to do this, Julie. I can handle things on my own."

"I know you can, but I'm worried about him, too."

She paused, looking uncertain for the first time all night. "If you would rather not have me along for whatever reason, I certainly can understand but I would like the chance to help if you want me."

"It's not that. I want you."

He heard the echo of his words and wished he could yank them back, but they hovered between them.

She cleared her throat. "That's good."

"I want you along," he corrected, trying not to be too obvious about amending his statement. "It's only that it's already past midnight and I know an all-nighter trip to the city wasn't in your plans for the evening."

"I can be flexible, Ross. We can keep each other awake."

Inappropriate images popped into his head and refused to leave there. He could think of far more enticing ways for the two of them to stay awake than looking for his recalcitrant nephew, but he knew those kinds of thoughts about Julie were dangerous.

He wanted to tell her to forget it, that he was better off on his own. But she had been wonderful all evening, helping him get into teen hangouts that otherwise might have been off-limits to him.

"All right," he said. "Let's go to San Antonio. It's a good thing we've already got all your provisions, isn't it? Looks like it might be a long night."

Three hours later, they were no closer to finding his nephew and Ross was beginning to wonder if they should even be looking. The kid was now officially three hours past eighteen. He was an adult. If he wanted to take off for a night, was Ross really in a position to have any objection?

Or even to worry about him?

Maybe he should have left Julie at the house in case Josh tried to call again. He had taken the precaution of changing the message on the answering machine, leaving pointed instructions for Josh to call Ross's cell phone immediately if he happened to call home and got the message, and they had left scrawled messages all over the house saying the same thing.

As Ross drove through some of the rougher neighborhoods of San Antonio, he worried he was putting Julie through all this unnecessarily.

He glanced over at the passenger seat. She was hanging on, but just barely. For the last half hour, her lids had been drooping and her face was tight with fatigue.

"All right. I'd say we've tried long enough. We've covered a three-mile perimeter around the pay phone and come up empty. Let's get you back to Red Rock."

She scrambled up in the seat. "I'm sorry. No. I'm fine. Don't stop searching on my account."

"This is worse than looking for a needle in a haystack. We don't even know if the needle's here at all or in some other haystack altogether. You need a little rest. And to be honest, I could use some sleep myself."

She slanted him a look. "What would you do if I weren't here?"

"My apartment isn't far from here. Under other circumstances, I would probably catch a few hours of sleep there and head out again first thing."

"Let's do that, then. I can bunk on your couch. It's silly to drive all the way back to Red Rock if you're going to be here bright and early in the morning looking for Josh anyway."

Even for 3:00 a.m. logic, her words made sense. Beyond the time it would save in the morning, he wasn't sure she would make it all the way back to Red Rock.

And Josh was close. He sensed it somehow, with that cop's intuition that had never failed him yet. He had learned not to ignore it—even if that meant sharing his apartment for a few hours with Julie Osterman, the woman he had vowed to do his best to stay away from.

By the time they reached his place she was nearly asleep, but she managed to stumble out of his car and up the steps to his third-floor apartment.

He didn't know if it was the night air or the climb, but by the time they reached his door, a little color had returned to her cheeks and her eyes didn't look nearly as bleary.

As he unlocked the door and flipped on a light, he told himself the apprehension was completely his imagination.

She did a slow turn then walked to the window.

"Oh," she breathed.

"It's not much, I know."

"No, it's great! What an incredible view."

Though his apartment was only on the third floor, he overlooked the River Walk. His favorite evening activity was sitting out on the small terrace with a beer, enjoying the lights in the trees, the boats on the water and all the activity below.

He opened the sliding door and she walked out, lifting her face to the night air.

Though the lights of the city muted the stars much more than they did out in Red Rock, the heavens still offered an impressive display, a vast sea of tiny pinpricks of light against the black silk of the night sky.

Just a few hours before daylight, the River Walk was quiet now compared to how it probably had been even an hour or two ago.

"This is great. If I lived here, I would have a tough time wanting to do anything but sit here and enjoy."

She was beautiful, he thought. Lovely in that serene way that sometimes stole his breath.

And tougher than she looked, he admitted. She had stuck with him all evening, even through some of the rougher neighborhoods where he had looked for Josh. She hadn't shied away from situations that might have made her uncomfortable. Instead, she had been right there with him, keeping an eye out for his nephew.

And her provisions. He fought a smile all over again.

How adorable was it that she had packed everything from his favorite cola to bandages, just in case?

"Come on," he said after a moment. "Let's get you settled. You can take the bedroom. I'll show you where everything is. I might even have an extra toothbrush."

She arched an eyebrow. Though she didn't say anything, he could read the speculation in her eyes.

"Josh comes to stay with me sometimes and he always seems to forget his so I try to pick up a few extras when I'm at the store."

He had no idea why he was compelled to defend himself but he didn't want her thinking he was in the habit of bringing strange women back to his apartment. He rarely even brought women who *weren't* strange here. The last time had been further back than he cared to remember.

He led the way down the hall to his bedroom, grateful he had taken time to pop over and clean up a bit just a few days ago, when he was in town catching up on things at the office.

"I'm sure I've got a T-shirt or something you can sleep in."

"Thanks. That would be great."

He opened a drawer and pulled out one of his less disreputable T-shirts and tossed it at her. She caught it one-handed and clutched it to her chest.

"Thank you."

She looked so soft and rumpled, with her hair a little bit messed from dozing in the car and her eyes wide and impossibly blue. As he gazed at her, she swallowed and offered a tremulous smile and his body burned with sudden, insatiable hunger.

Her smile slid from her features though she didn't look away, and he wondered if he was imagining the sudden tension, the swirls of awareness that seemed to eddy around them.

"I'm sorry to take your bed," she murmured.

"No problem. I don't mind the couch." His voice sounded raspy and tight. He cleared his throat. "Good night, then."

"I...good night."

He watched her for a few seconds more, then swallowed a groan and stepped forward. One kiss. Surely they could both survive one little kiss. It seemed a small enough thing when he had spent all night with her and managed to keep his hands to himself, when his body was crying out for so much more.

Chapter 11

With a breathy, sexy little moan that scorched down every nerve ending, she slid into his kiss as if she had been waiting all night for his mouth to find hers.

She tasted of coffee and something sweet and cinnamony and he couldn't get enough. He pulled her closer, relishing the soft curves against his chest and the way she wrapped her arms around his neck as if she couldn't bear to let him go.

He wanted more. He wanted *everything,* all of her gasps and the inhaled breaths and those infinitely arousing little sounds she made.

Her mouth was soft and luscious and so welcoming that he lost track of time. For several delectable moments, all the stresses weighing on his shoulders lifted away and the only thing that mattered to him was this woman, this moment.

He deepened the kiss, his tongue tangling with hers,

and he felt the little tremor that shook her body as she responded, heard the little hitch in her breathing. His body was rock hard in an instant and a slow, unsteady ache spread through him.

He slid a hand to her back, under her shirt, and the sultry softness of her skin against his fingers was irresistible.

One kiss wouldn't be enough.

How could it be, when he found just the small brush of her skin against his hands so heady, so addictive?

If he didn't stop now, though, he wasn't sure he would be able to find the strength. Even now, it took all his control to wrench his mouth from hers.

"We have to stop, Julie."

"Why?" she murmured against his mouth. He groaned at the note of genuine confusion in her voice.

"We don't…it's not…"

She kissed the corner of his mouth before he could form a single coherent thought and his brain took a siesta when, with tiny, silky little darts of her tongue, she began licking her way across to the other side.

"What were you saying?" she murmured, her voice low and husky.

"No idea," he answered truthfully, and returned the kiss with all the fierce hunger raging through him.

When she had walked into his apartment earlier, Julie had been emotionally drained and physically exhausted from their futile all-night search for Josh. But his kiss was as invigorating as a straight shot of high-octane caffeine.

Her body buzzed with heat and energy, like she was standing in a desert windstorm, being buffeted from every direction.

She had enough energy right now to run a marathon without even working up a sweat.

Or to spend what was left of the night in his arms.

She shivered as he trailed kisses down her jawline to the sensitive skin of her throat and then down to the open collar of her blouse.

Desire surged through her, wild and potent, as he pressed kisses to the curve of her breast above her bra. His mouth tasted her, exploring every inch he could reach that wasn't covered by her clothing, but it still wasn't enough.

Not nearly enough.

Her gaze held his as she shrugged out of her sweater and reached trembling fingers to unbutton her shirt.

His brown eyes blazed with desire as he watched her and she saw a little muscle jump in his cheek.

"Are you sure about this?" he asked, his voice little more than a growl. "We can still stop now, though it just might kill me."

"Absolutely sure," she replied. To prove it, she pulled her arms through the sleeves of her shirt, quickly worked the front clasps of her bra and then stepped out of her jeans.

The raw hunger in his eyes did crazy little things to her insides. She wasn't sure a man had ever looked at her like this, as if she was every fantasy he had ever conjured up.

She shivered a little at the force of that look but she didn't back away. How could she?

"Your turn," she murmured, and her hands found the buttons of his shirt, then his pants. She wasn't sure where this eager response was coming from but she liked it.

She had always enjoyed the closeness of making love

with her husband in his better years, but it had been a long, long time for her. She couldn't remember this kind of urgent ache inside her, this insistent, undeniable need to be closer.

She had to touch him. All of him. He was masculine and tough and his lean strength beckoned her, seduced her. She trailed her fingers across the planes of his chest, relishing his hard muscles and the leashed strength beneath her hands.

His abdominal muscles contracted tightly when she gently dipped her thumbs into the hollow below his ribcage and he stood immobile under her exploring touch for only a little longer before he groaned under his breath and pulled her against him again.

She didn't mind. He was warm and solid against her bare skin. As he kissed her, he pulled her close enough that her breasts were pressed against that hard chest she had been exploring earlier and she couldn't breathe around the delicious friction of her skin against his.

At last he lowered her to his bed and she could see the lights of the city spread out beyond his window. He had angled his bed to take full advantage of the view through the wide windows and somehow she found the idea of him lying in his bed looking out at the night sweetly charming.

And then she forgot all about the city lights and everything else but Ross when his mouth covered hers for another long, drugging kiss at the same time his hand found her breast, his fingers clever and arousing on the peak.

She gasped, arching into him. His thumb teased her nipple, rolling it around and around until she thought she would implode from the tension and the heat inexorably building inside her.

When he slid his mouth away from hers and lowered his head to her breasts, she nearly came off the bed from the torrent of sensations pouring through her. He teased and tasted for a long time, until she was writhing beneath him, desperate and aching for so much more.

At last, those deft fingers headed lower, toward the core of her heat. She clutched him tightly, pressing her mouth to the warm column of his neck as his thumb danced across her thighs, coming close but not quite reaching the place she ached most for him to touch.

He circled around it and continued to tease until she finally growled with frustration and nipped at his shoulder.

His low laugh rang through the room. His gaze met hers and her heart seemed to swell at the lighthearted expression in his eyes, a side of Ross she rarely saw but which she was coming to adore.

"Very carnivorous of you, Ms. Osterman."

"I have my moments, when provoked," she answered, her voice husky.

"Remind me to provoke you more often, then," he murmured.

She smiled and he stared at her mouth for a long time, his expression unreadable and then he kissed her again, his mouth slow and unmistakably tender on hers.

Oh, she was in trouble here, she thought as heat began to build again, as he continued to tease her.

"Just touch me already," she all but begged.

He laughed roughly. "With pleasure. And I absolutely mean that."

His fingers finally found her and she cried out as she nearly climaxed with just one slight touch.

She thought she knew what to expect. She had been married for five years. Before her husband's illness, she had always considered their lovemaking fulfilling, an enriching, important part of their marriage.

This insatiable need for Ross was something completely out of her experience. She thought of that desert windstorm again, fierce and violent, ripping aside a lifetime of convention and restraint.

It frightened her more than a little, this lack of control, this urge to throw herself into the teeth of the maelstrom and let it carry her away.

She could feel herself begin to withdraw, to scramble back to the safety and security of that restraint, but Ross wasn't about to allow it.

"Let go," he whispered in her ear. "Let go for me, Julie."

His words were all it took to send her tumbling into the storm. He lifted her higher, higher, and then she cried out his name as she climaxed.

He quickly donned a condom from the bedside table and entered her even before the last tremor shook her body. His gaze locked with hers as his body joined hers, and she felt truly alive for the first time in forever.

She wanted to burn every sensation to memory—his scent, of cedar and sage and something citrusy she couldn't identify, the salty, masculine tang of his skin, his strength surrounding her, engulfing her. She wrapped her arms around him as tightly as she could manage.

He could hurt her.

The thought slithered into her mind out of nowhere and seemed to take hold, despite the hazy satisfaction still encompassing her.

She wasn't sure if she could treat this moment with the same casualness she knew Ross would. This meant something to her, something rare and precious and beautiful. She only hoped she could hold on to that and remember it as such after he pushed her away once more, as she was quite certain he would when the night was over.

That wild hunger began to climb inside her, insistent and demanding, and she pushed her concerns away. She would savor every moment with him. She wasn't going to ruin the magic and wonder of this moment with regret, with needless worry about the future.

With renewed enthusiasm, she threw herself into the kiss and after a surprised moment, he responded even more intensely.

His movements became more urgent, more demanding, and she arched to meet him, welcoming each joining of their bodies.

"Julie," he gasped after a long moment, and then he arched his back one more time as he found completion.

In the sweet, languid afterglow, she lay in his arms, trying to burn the memory into her mind. She couldn't regret this, even though she could already feel the tiny cracks in her heart expanding.

He would hurt her. She only hoped she was strong enough to endure it.

It was her last thought before she surrendered to the *other* demands of her body and finally slept.

Julie was beautiful in sleep. Her hair curled around her face in a filmy, sensuous cloud and long lashes fanned high cheekbones.

She looked delicate and lush at the same time and he couldn't seem to look away.

How could he ever have guessed a few short weeks ago that the prim and tight-lipped do-gooder he had thought her to be that night at the Spring Fling art fair would be so wildly passionate in bed?

He should have guessed it by the fierce way she defended the scruffy teenager he erroneously thought had been stealing her purse. He had been so busy snapping back at her that he hadn't allowed himself to see past her anger to the breathtakingly beautiful woman behind it.

She fell asleep as easily as a kitten in his bed and with the same liquid stretch of her limbs.

He pulled her closer and she purred and snuggled into him. It gave him the oddest feeling, this complete trust she had in him. He found it exhilarating and terrifying at the same time and wasn't quite sure how he should react.

Over her shoulder, he could see the lights in the trees outside on the River Walk. He watched them flicker and dance on the breeze, as he did many nights. This time his mind wasn't busy running through the details of a case. It was too occupied with Julie and the mass of contradictions she presented. She could be sweet one moment, fiery the next; pensive with one breath, then wildly passionate the next.

Everything about her fascinated him, from the courage she displayed after becoming a young widow under such tragic circumstances to the dedication she devoted to her job.

He thought of the huge basket of provisions she had packed earlier tonight and smiled all over again. It didn't last very long, though, when he suddenly remembered just why she had packed that basket.

Josh.

He hadn't thought of his nephew once in the last hour. Not once. Josh was out there somewhere, possibly in trouble, and Ross had forgotten all about him, simply because he found Julie so enticing.

He let out a breath, feeling chilled even though his bedroom was a comfortable temperature.

He needed to focus. He should never have given in to the hunger to kiss her. He was being pulled in too many different directions and right now his family needed him. He couldn't regret it, though. Not right now, with Julie warm and soft in his arms and this curiously appealing tightness in his chest.

He must have drifted asleep eventually. When he awoke, pale dawn sunlight was coyly peeking through the windows where he had forgotten to draw the curtains.

He stretched a little, struck by a curious feeling of contentment inside him. He wasn't used to it. In truth, the quiet peace of it left him a little unsettled and he didn't quite know how to react.

He gazed down at Julie, still sleeping beside him. If anything, she looked even lovelier than she had a few hours earlier.

Her mouth was slightly parted in sleep and she made a tiny, breathy little sound. He wanted to kiss her, with an acute, concentrated desperation.

He couldn't do it. It wouldn't be fair, not when she needed her sleep.

He tried to shift away but even his slight, barely perceptible movement must have disturbed her.

She blinked her eyes open and gazed at him for a moment, then she smiled softly and he had the random thought that the sun breaking across the city after weeks of rain couldn't be any more lovely or more welcome.

"Good morning," she murmured, her voice throaty and low.

"Hi."

"How long did we sleep?"

He glanced over at the digital readout on his alarm
clock. "Not long enough. Only a few hours. It's almost
six-thirty."

She reached her arms over her head and stretched
until her fingers touched the headboard. "That's funny.
I feel oddly invigorated."

He had the sudden, painful awareness that she was
naked beneath the sheet that barely covered her. She
was inches away from him, all that soft, glorious skin
and those delectable curves.

His body snapped brightly to attention.

"Invigorated. Yeah. I know what you mean," he muttered.

She smiled again, her eyes half-lidded and knowing, and he couldn't mistake the sultry invitation. He
held out as long as he could manage—oh, maybe a
second and a half—before he lowered his head to hers
and kissed her.

She responded just as sweetly as she had a few hours
earlier, her mouth warm, slick and eager against his.
Those arms she had just stretched out above her slid
around his neck now and she pulled him close.

He loved when she touched him. Whether it was a
casual hand on his arm in the middle of a conversation
or her lips brushing his or her body arching against him
in the sweet throes of passion, he couldn't seem to get
enough of her.

A weird feeling seemed to trickle through him as
that sensuous magic surrounded them again. It welled
in his chest, clogged in his throat. Something warm
and tender and terrifying. He wasn't sure what it might
be—and he wasn't sure he liked it.

He wanted to take care of her. To cherish her. To rub her feet at the end of a hard day and make sure her car was filled with gasoline when she needed it and cook her fish on the grill just the way she liked it.

What was happening to him? For one jittery, panicky minute, Ross wanted to jump out of bed and rush out of his apartment and not look back. He didn't want this. Any of it. He didn't need another soul to take care of in his life, especially not a woman whose heart was so huge and full of love.

Anyway, she didn't need somebody else to watch out for her. She was doing fine on her own. She especially didn't need a cynical ex-cop with more baggage than an airline lost and found.

"Something wrong?" she asked, watching him carefully out of those big blue eyes, and he realized he had wrenched his mouth away and was staring at her as if she had just sat up in the bed and started spouting pig latin.

He quickly forced his emotions under control. He'd had plenty of practice at that when he was a kid and again as a cop.

This weird feeling wasn't love. It couldn't be. He wouldn't *let* it be.

He liked her well enough and he was more grateful than he could ever say for her help with Josh. That's all it was.

"What is it?" she asked.

"Nothing. Nothing at all," he said.

He pushed away the jumpy feeling and turned his attention to that spot on her neck that he had discovered drove her crazy. She shivered and tightened her arms around him.

He might have thought their second time making

love wouldn't have been as intense, as shattering, as the first. He knew what to expect, after all. He had already had the exhilarating chance to explore all those delectable curves. He had already discovered that little mole above her hipbone and he knew she made those soft, sexy little sounds when she was close to finding release.

But if anything, the repeat performance was even more astonishing. It was slower-paced, sweeter somehow, as if they were moving through soft, warm honey. Every sensation seemed magnified a hundredfold. He had never known a woman to give herself so generously, without any reservations, and it stunned and humbled him.

Even more, she acted just as stunned by her own response, which only seemed to accentuate his own.

She cried out his name when she climaxed, then wrapped her arms tightly around him when he joined her with a groan, and Ross never wanted her to let go.

All those scary feelings crowded back as he held her afterward, her head nestled in the crook of his shoulder, but he forced himself to hold them all back.

He *wasn't* in love with her. No way, he told himself.

He was still trying to convince himself of that when his cell phone suddenly bleated from somewhere in the bedroom.

Chapter 12

He might have been tempted to ignore it, to dive back into the heat and magic they shared, if not for the sudden recollection of just why they were there in his apartment in San Antonio.

But who else would be calling him at 7:00 a.m., unless Josh had just bothered to return to the house and found all his strongly worded orders to do just that?

"Is it Josh?" Julie asked.

"It had better be," he muttered. He grabbed his phone from the bedside table.

"Where the hell are you?"

A long silence met his growled question and then a small female voice spoke. "Um, still at the jail. But my lawyer assures me that's only for another few hours. They're releasing me on my own recognizance."

"Frannie?" He scrambled up against the headboard and pulled the comforter up to his waist, as if his sister could see through the telephone.

"What are you talking about?" he demanded. "What's going on? Why are you calling me so early?"

She let out a strangled sound that was half sob, half laugh.

"You haven't heard, I guess. Nobody has picked up the story yet this morning since the police aren't releasing any details. They're letting me go."

"Dropping the charges?"

"The next best thing to it, my attorney says. They've dropped my bail to nothing. They're not holding me any longer. I'm going to be freed, Ross. Can you believe it? They've brought someone else in for questioning. I'm going home to Josh. It's like some kind of miracle, isn't it?"

His sister started crying in earnest but Ross felt as if his heart had jerked to an abrupt stop.

He couldn't believe it. He didn't *want* to believe it. But how could it possibly be a coincidence that Josh goes missing a few hours ago "helping out a friend" at the same time somebody gets hauled in for questioning about killing Lloyd?

Josh, what the hell have you done?

But, maybe he was way off base. If Josh had confessed and was now in custody, wouldn't Frannie be hysterical instead of reacting to the news with this sort of stunned jubilation?

"Who killed him?" he asked, unable to keep the wariness from his voice but hoping she didn't notice.

"I don't know. Nobody's telling me anything," she answered. "All I know is that they've got some 'person of interest' and they're ready to let me go. Oh, I can't wait to be home. Will you come get me?"

He slid out of the bed, already reaching for his khakis. "Of course. Stay in touch and call me the minute you hear from your attorney. I'll be there as soon as I can."

"Don't wake up Josh, okay? I want to surprise him."

Ross frowned. Somebody in the family was definitely in for a surprise. He could only hope it was indeed Josh who was surprised at learning his mother had been released and not him and Frannie when they found Josh already in custody.

"I'll see you in a little while," he said, instead of responding to his sister's plea about her son.

He hung up, his mind racing in a hundred different directions as he yanked on his socks and thrust his arms through the sleeves of his shirt.

"Ross, what's going on?"

He looked toward the bed and found Julie watching him with consternation. How could he have forgotten Julie? She looked soft and tousled, her hair messed and her lips swollen from his mouth. He gazed at her, wishing with everything inside him that things could be different, that he could stay with her, right here in this warm, cozy bed.

But his family needed him. And just like always, he had no choice but to help. Still, the choice had never seemed so damned hard before.

"I've got to hurry back to Red Rock. That was Frannie."

Her features tightened with concern. "What is it?"

"They're letting her go. They've brought someone else in for killing Lloyd Fredericks."

She stared at Ross, not quite sure she had heard him correctly. "Letting her go? Are you serious?"

"Completely." He started buttoning up his cotton shirt and it was only as she watched his grim features that Julie realized why all this seemed so discordant and unreal. He wasn't reacting like a man who had just learned his sister was about to be freed from jail.

"Okay, my brain obviously isn't working correctly yet this morning," she said. "Tell me again why you're not throwing the world's biggest party? Isn't this what you've wanted? What you've been working so hard to bring about for the last two weeks? Frannie's coming home, Ross! Why on earth do you look like you're heading to a funeral, instead of celebrating?"

He was silent as he started to slip on his boots, but his features looked even more austere than normal.

"Ross, tell me. What's wrong?"

At last he lifted his gaze to hers and she nearly gasped at the haunted expression in his brown eyes. Her mind sifted through the pieces, Frannie, Lloyd, the Spring Fling and the events of that awful night.

And Josh.

Josh was the missing piece, she realized, as everything clicked into place. She thought of his determined efforts to find his nephew the night before, and the odd phone call he had made to the police station, their seemingly casual route back to the Fredericks es' home that had led them right past the station house.

She gasped and stared at him. "You think it's Josh they've hauled in. You think he killed his father!"

He didn't respond for a long moment but his silence was answer enough. "I don't know what I think," he finally said. "All I know is that Josh fought bitterly with his father that night and uttered what could be taken as a direct threat. He was seen with the murder weapon, not long before his father's body was found. He knows something, something he's not saying. I told you that since the murder, he's been secretive. He takes these mysterious phone calls and I can tell he's troubled."

"He's had a rough few weeks, losing his father and his mother at once. You can't honestly think he had anything to do with killing Lloyd! That he would let his mother go to jail for his own crime!"

"Where is he then?"

She had no answer to give him, though she fervently wished she did.

"I'm sorry about this," Ross said, "but I've got to go back to Red Rock right away. I can drop you off at your house on the way."

"Okay. I only need a moment." She rose and quickly began to dress again, thinking with regret of the brief, stolen time they had shared together. Something told her those moments were as elusive and rare as a wildflower growing on a harsh, unforgiving rock face.

As she dressed, she listened to his one-sided conversation with the police station. She could have guessed the outcome, even before he hung up the phone in disgust.

"They're not saying anything until charges are officially filed, which might or might not happen any moment. I need to haul out of here."

"Of course." She threw on her blouse and sweater, doing her best to block out the dull ache of regret.

"I need to make some phone calls on the way back to Red Rock to see if I can find out what the hell is going on, just who it is who's confessed. How do you feel about taking the wheel so I'm not distracted by talking while I drive?"

"Anything I can do to help. You know I want to do whatever I can."

"Thanks."

Though gratitude flashed in his gaze, it was quickly gone, replaced by a deep anxiety. She wanted to soothe it but she knew nothing she said would help him right

now. But she could do as he asked and take at least one
responsibility from his wide shoulders by driving them
back to Red Rock.

He must have spoken with a half-dozen people as she
took the shortest route possible away from San Antonio. Listening to him probe each contact for information was fascinating. He seemed to know exactly the
right buttons to push with every person he spoke with.
He could be brash and abrasive when necessary, but he
could also pull out unexpected wiles that completely
charmed her—and whoever he was talking to.

As they neared the Red Rock town limits, she listened to him try to skillfully pry information out of a
source in the police department.

"You're not holding out on me, are you, Loraine?" he
asked after a short conversation where he had exhibited
a delicate finesse that surprised her.

He was quiet for a moment and Julie would have
given anything to know what the person on the other
end of the line was saying.

"How sure are you on that?" he asked after a long
moment, his features unreadable. "Ninety-nine. That's
good. And the other one percent?"

Loraine said something that made him laugh. When
the worry left his features, even for a moment, he looked
younger, lighter. Almost happy.

She jerked her gaze back to the road, her heart tumbling around in her chest like a bingo ball in the chute.

She was in love with him.

The knowledge burrowed into her heart, as clear as
the exit sign on the freeway. She wanted to push it away,
to deny and disclaim, but she couldn't. She knew exactly
what this dangerous tenderness curling through her meant.

She was in love with Ross Fortune, a hard and cynical man who seemed the last one on earth she ought to fall for, a man who was an expert at protecting himself from any deeper emotions.

She loved him. His deep core of decency, the care and concern he doled out to his family, his complete commitment to doing what was right.

She loved him—and he so desperately needed someone to love him, even if he would never admit it.

Why did that someone have to be her? she wondered with grim fatalism. She didn't want to love him. She wanted to go back to the way things had been just a few short weeks ago, before he had barreled into her life.

He would hurt her.

The knowledge hovered around her like the wavy mirages on the highway. Pain, harsh and unforgiving and unavoidable, waited for her. He would hurt her and she could do absolutely nothing to hold it back.

The time for protecting her heart might have been before that fateful night when he had accused poor Marcus Gallegos of stealing. She had been heading for this moment, for this inevitable pain, since then.

She might have been able to reduce its severity if she had walked away after that evening, if she had maintained all her careful defenses. Instead, she had let her life become entwined with his through Josh. Each time she saw Ross, she had allowed him to sneak a little further past her defenses.

Tears burned behind her eyes, blurring the road in front of her, but she blinked them away. He hadn't hurt her yet. She refused to waste this particular moment in anticipation of the future pain she knew was on the way.

He ended the call a moment later and Julie knew she wasn't mistaken that his mood seemed lighter. His eyes seemed brighter, his expression less anxious.

"That was a friend of mine who works in central booking at the jail. She said the guy they're holding is a 40-year-old male."

"So not Josh."

Her voice sounded like she'd just swallowed a handful of gravel but she hoped he didn't notice or that he would attribute it to emotional reaction to the news of his nephew's apparent reprieve.

"I won't be completely convinced of that until I find the little bugger and figure out where he's been all night. But no, at this point it looks like somebody else in Lloyd's legion of enemies had it in for him."

"How tragic, that so many people in Red Rock could have enough motive to want a man dead."

When he said nothing for several moments, she glanced away from the road just long enough to catch the quizzical look he threw at her.

She flushed, her hands tightening on the steering wheel. "Why are you looking at me like that?"

"You didn't even know Lloyd, did you?"

She shook her head.

"You didn't know the man but as far as I can tell, you're the only one besides his own mother and his mistress who finds anything to mourn in his death."

"I just think it's terribly sad that someone could take the precious gift of life and all the opportunities given him to make the world a better place and then twist them all so hideously that most of the world is glad he's gone."

He reached across the width of the seat and picked up her hand. Before she quite realized what he intended, he lifted her fingers and pressed his mouth to the back of her hand, in a very un-Ross-like gesture.

"Do you know what your greatest gift is?" he asked.

She let out a shaky breath, wondering how on earth

she was going to collect the tattered pieces of herself when this was over. "What?"

"You make everyone around you want to be better. To try harder to see the world through those same bright, optimistic eyes."

She loved the feel of his hand holding hers, the safety and warmth of him, even as she wanted to snatch her hand away, to protect herself from any more encroachment on her heart.

"You didn't get nearly enough sleep last night if you can wax philosophical this morning."

"No, I didn't."

Heat scorched through her at his words as she remembered all the ways they had kept each other awake in the night. She was almost positive she was able to keep her fingers from trembling in his.

"Do you mind if we swing by Frannie's house before I drop you off? I want to make sure Josh hasn't checked in. For all we know, he could be asleep in his own bed, not knowing that everything has suddenly changed."

"No problem," she answered, trying not to be too disappointed when he released her hand so she could use both of hers for driving.

Ross must have been listening to his cop's intuition again. The very moment she pulled into the Frederickses' driveway, a battered yellow sports car pulled up beside them and Josh climbed out.

He looked tired, Julie thought. Tired and worried and somehow older than he had appeared the last time she saw him.

She wondered how he would react to seeing them together so early at this time of the day but he didn't so much as raise an eyebrow.

"Hi," he said when they joined him outside their

respective vehicles. "You two are out and about early this morning."

Already the morning was shaping up to be a warm one. But the sun-warmed heat was nothing compared to the anger suddenly radiating from Ross.

"Well?" he snapped to his nephew. "Let's hear your explanation? I'll warn you, it better be good."

Josh looked genuinely bewildered and a bit wary. She also thought she saw a little guilt there, as well. "Explanation for what?"

"For what?" Ross's voice rose on the last word. "Let's start with where the hell you've been all night. Julie and I drove around Red Rock and San Antonio half the night looking for you!"

His eyes widened with shock. "Why? I left you a note and then I called and left a message on voice mail. Didn't you get it?"

"Sure we got your note," Ross answered tightly. "Do you think you could try to be a bit less cryptic next time? We didn't know *what* was going on. And then when you didn't answer your blasted phone all night long, what were we supposed to think?"

"I told you a friend of mine needed help." Josh suddenly seemed as taut and angry as his uncle and Julie wondered how much of his reaction was due to fatigue.

"Did it ever once occur to you that saying only 'a friend needs help' could mean anything from algebra homework to changing a flat tire to running drugs across the border? You said you were going to help this friend but you didn't say anything about it taking you the whole damn night."

"I didn't expect to take all night. It was a…routine thing. But there were…complications. But everything's okay now. She…everything's okay."

An echo of worry flickered in his eyes and Julie reached a hand to rest on his arm. "Are you sure everything's okay, Josh? You look tired."

Josh's gaze met hers and for an instant that illusion of maturity disappeared and he looked suddenly desperately young. He seemed to want to lean on someone. He opened his mouth and she held her breath, hoping he would choose to confide in her and his uncle, but then he changed his mind and closed it again.

He straightened his shoulders. "Yeah. It's been a long night. Sounds like for you guys, too. I'm really sorry you made an unnecessary trip to San Antonio, but you can't blame me for your own overreaction. I told you not to worry or wait up. And I left you a message, too. I told you not to worry about me."

"Easy for you to say!"

"I'm officially eighteen, Uncle Ross. An adult in the eyes of the law. You don't have to treat me like a baby and run off and look for me like some kind of bounty hunter."

Ross looked angry and uncomfortable at the same time. Julie cut him off before he could voice the angry words forming in his eyes and possibly say something he might come to regret after their respective tempers had cooled.

"We were worried about you," she said to Josh. "It seems uncharacteristic for you to just take off like this."

He suddenly seemed inordinately fascinated with the bluebells growing in his mother's flower garden. "It was an emergency. And that's all I can tell you right now."

Ross knew his nephew was holding out on him. The boy—no, not a boy anymore—had secrets in his eyes. Ross was an expert at extracting information from unwilling subjects and sifting through lies and subterfuge to the truth but somehow none of his techniques seemed to work on his nephew.

That was what happened when he let his emotions overrule his good sense. He ought to sit Josh in a room and make the kid tell him what was going on. But Josh was right, he was eighteen and Ross supposed he was entitled to a few secrets.

He was so relieved that Josh hadn't been involved with his father's murder that he supposed he could let the mystery of his whereabouts overnight remain just that for now—a mystery.

"If your cell phone had been working, I might have been able to call you to tell you the news," he said.

"What news?" Josh asked, his hand on the open doorframe of Ross's SUV.

He paused. "Your mom is being released from jail any minute now. I'm on my way to get her."

Josh stared at him as if he had just announced they were flying to Saturn later. "What?" he exclaimed. "Why didn't you say so?"

"You just got here. We haven't exactly had much time to chat."

"This is huge! What happened? Did the stupid district attorney finally agree to reduce her bail?"

"She's being let out on her own recognizance. According to my sources, they've got someone else they like for the murder."

He watched his nephew's reaction carefully and saw a mix of emotions chase across his features, everything from shock to disbelief and finally a deep, pure relief.

"Who did they bring in?"

"I'm still trying to get answers to that. Your mom called me a little while ago and said her attorney was working on getting the charges against her dropped but she didn't know many details. I've been able to find out a little but not a name or anything like that. I'm heading down to the police station right now to see what else I can find out."

Josh's hand tightened on the doorframe. "I'm coming with you."

His nephew had obviously been up all night, judging by the fatigue lining his eyes and the heavy sag of his shoulders. But he was young enough to survive an all-nighter. Ross had a feeling he wouldn't be able to keep Josh away.

"Get in, then. We can drop Julie off at her place on the way."

He took over behind the wheel from Julie and she slid into the passenger seat beside him. The three of them were mostly silent on the five-minute drive to her house. Ross found himself grateful for the buffer of Josh's presence, suddenly aware of the monumental shift in his relationship with Julie after the night they had shared.

He wasn't ready for things to change. He enjoyed her friendship too much to ruin things with sex but he was afraid that's exactly what he had done.

He didn't want things to get messy with her but he knew with brutal self-awareness that he sucked at relationships. He was much better at short-term flings, where women had few expectations beyond a few dates and a good time.

Julie wasn't like that. As he pulled up to her small, tidy house near the elementary school, he could see the proof of it.

He walked around and opened her door—manners instilled in him by his uncles. He walked her to the front door, past colorful terra-cotta containers full of bright flowers and a trio of birdhouses.

This was just the sort of house that made him nervous. The flower gardens spoke of settling in, of commitment and permanence, all the things that seemed so foreign to him. He couldn't remember a single plant his mother had tried to grow. They had never been in one place long enough to see a seedling sprout anyway, so why bother?

He had been in his condo for five years, though. Why hadn't he ever tried to grow anything on the patio? He had perfect light out there and it wouldn't be a big deal to plant some tomatoes and maybe a pepper plant or two.

At her door, he paused, feeling intensely awkward, in light of all they had shared together the last few hours. She seemed to sense it, too, and fiddled with her purse and the keys she had used to unlock the door.

He struggled for something to say but everything sounded lame. *Thanks for the most incredible night of my life* sounded like it came right off the pathetic bachelor's morning-after playlist.

"Let me know what happens with Frannie, okay?" Julie finally said.

"I'll be sure to do that," he answered. His chest ached a little as the morning sun lit a halo around her. She looked as pretty and bright as her flower gardens and he knew she wasn't for him.

He was going to have to break things off with her. She was digging in too deep and he couldn't let her. Not when she scared the hell out of him.

He hated being one of Those Guys, who slept with a woman and then brushed her off, especially when he had a feeling she expected more. But he also wasn't willing to string her along, not when he already was coming to care far too much for her.

Chapter 13

Ross's heart ached in his chest. He wanted nothing but to pull her against him and hold on forever, which was more than enough reason to push her away.

"Julie, I…"

She shook her head and for just a moment, he thought he saw something like sorrow flicker there before it was quickly gone. "Ross, don't say anything. What happened earlier was…wonderful. We both wanted it to happen. But I completely understand that it was only a one-time thing."

He scratched his cheek. "Twice, technically."

She laughed roughly, though again he thought he saw regret in those soft blue eyes. "Okay, twice. My point remains that I don't expect anything more than that. You can put your mind at ease. I promise, I'm not going to be clingy or throw a scene or rush inside my house and cry for hours. Don't worry about me, okay?"

He should be relieved. Wasn't this what he wanted? So why did his chest continue to ache like he'd been punched?

"I'm not the kind of man you need, Julie. I wish I could be. You have no idea how much I wish I could be. But I'm not."

"How did you become such an expert on what I need?"

"It's my job to understand people. I have to be able to read things about people that even they don't always see. I have to be able to understand their motivations, their triggers, their personality types."

"And what's my personality type?"

She asked the question with deceptive casualness but he heard the sudden tightness in her voice, in the way she compressed her lips just a little too hard on the last consonant so it popped. He was in quicksand here, he suddenly sensed.

He glanced at the car where Josh watched them curiously, too far away, thank the Lord, to hear their conversation.

He didn't want to get into all this right now. But he had started things and he owed it to her to finish.

"You're a nurturer. A natural healer. You take people who are hurting and broken and you try to fix them. It's what you do with the kids you work with at the Fortune Foundation but I've seen you put the same effort into everyone. I saw you slip more than a few bills to anybody who looked like they had a sob story last night while we were looking for Josh."

A tiny muscle flexed in her cheek. "And you don't want to be healed."

He bristled. "I'm not broken."

"Aren't you?"

Her psychoanalytical put-the-question-back-on-the-poor-patient crap suddenly bugged the hell out of him.

"I'm fine," he snapped. "Absolutely fine. I've got everything I need."

She said nothing, only continued to study him out of those eyes that saw entirely too much.

"Everything was going just great in my life until two weeks ago when somebody whacked my brother-in-law. Now that they've found whoever it was who did it and Frannie's coming home, I can return to the life I had before and everything will get back to normal."

"In my business, we call that self-delusion."

"Call *what* self-delusion?"

"You're supposed to be an expert on figuring out what makes everybody else tick. Their motivations, their triggers, their personality types. Isn't that what you said? Can you really be so blind to your own?"

"What's that supposed to mean?"

"Nothing. Never mind. Goodbye, Ross."

She opened the door and though he knew Josh and Frannie waited for him, he couldn't help himself. He followed her inside.

"Tell me what you meant," he growled.

She studied him for a long moment, then she sighed. "You keep everyone away, don't you? Because of the instability of your childhood, you're so determined not to count on anybody else, to be so completely self-sufficient now that you're an adult, that you close off everybody except your family. Frannie and Josh. And even then, you feel like you have to shoulder every burden for them, not share a single worry. As a result, you're probably the most lonely man I've ever met."

He stared at her, thunderstruck by the harsh analysis. Her words sliced at him with brutal efficiency. How did she know anything about his childhood? Fast on the heels of the shock and hurt came the sharp flare of anger. She had no right to think she could sum up his world in a few neat little sentences.

"I take back everything I said," he snapped. "You're not a nurturer. You're just plain crazy. I'm absolutely not lonely. Hell, I can't get people to leave me alone long enough for me to be lonely!"

"I guess we can both be wrong about each other, then," she said, sounding so damn calm and reasonable, he wanted to punch something.

"I guess so. Better to find out now than sometime in the future after we've invested more than just a night with each other."

"I'm sure you're right," she murmured. "You'd better go, hadn't you? Your sister's waiting for you."

He gazed at her for a moment, wondering how this whole thing had taken such a wrong turn, then he nodded. "Yeah. I guess I'll see you around, then."

She only smiled that impassive smile at him and opened the door, leaving him no choice but to stalk through it and down the sidewalk.

Julie watched Ross drive away, his white SUV suddenly anything *but* unobtrusive as its tires spit gravel and careened around the corner.

Apparently he couldn't wait to get away from her.

Drat the man. She swiped at a tear trickling down the side of her nose and then another and another, grateful at least that she had the strength of will to hold them back until he was out of sight.

She wanted to rant and rave at Ross Fortune's stubborn self-protectiveness, his apparent willingness to walk away from the magic and wonder they had shared, just so that he could guard his psyche.

A good tantrum would at least be an outlet for the wild torrent of emotions damming up inside her, but the hardest thing to accept was that none of this was Ross's fault.

She walked into bed with him with her eyes open. She might not have consciously admitted she was already in love with him but deep down she must have known, just as she had to have realized somewhere inside that Ross was completely unavailable to her, at least emotionally.

She had convinced herself she was strong enough to live in the moment, to seize the chance to be with him without regrets or recriminations later.

What a fool she was. And she called *him* self-deluded! How could she have ever believed she could share that intimacy with him, let him inside her soul and not feel battered and bruised when he walked away from all she was willing to offer?

This was goodbye then.

Their respective worlds weren't likely to intersect again. With his sister on her way to freedom, Ross had no reason to stick around Red Rock. Frannie would be able to care for Josh from now on and accompany him to the Fortune Foundation for counseling sessions if he still needed them.

Ross would return to San Antonio and his private investigation practice and that lovely, impersonal apartment and his self-contained life that struck her as immeasurably sad.

She pressed her hands to her face for just a moment then dropped them to her knees. She would survive a broken heart. She had no choice. As Ross said, she was a healer, a nurturer, and she couldn't do any of that if she turned inside herself and wallowed in her own pain.

He was an ass.

Ross sat in the reception area of the police station, replaying his conversation with Julie over and over in his head.

Had he really called her crazy? He burned with chagrin just thinking about it. He had reacted like some kind of little kid, lashing out first to protect himself from being wounded by her words.

She deserved better from him than that. Julie had always been nothing but warm and kind to him. She had just spent the entire night helping him look for Josh, for hell's sake. And then when she gave him an opinion that *he* had solicited, he snapped back at her like a cornered grizzly. It was unfair and unnecessarily hurtful.

He had to make it right, somehow, but he had no idea where to start.

He still didn't buy what she was selling. He had moved past his childhood a long time ago. Yeah, he might still have scars. The insecurity of growing up with Cindy Fortune would have been rough on any kid, he wouldn't deny that. But he didn't dwell on it anymore. He hadn't for a long time.

And lonely. She said he was lonely. He didn't buy that, either. He had plenty of friends, good ones. They went to basketball games together and had barbecues and fishing trips out on his boat.

Okay, he would admit she was right that he didn't let too many people close. But that didn't mean he was some kind of freaking hermit.

He thought of the nights alone in his apartment when he would stand at the window gazing down at the River

Walk, at the lights and the activity and the people walking together, content and happy in their tidy little family units.

More often than not, he would attribute the nameless ache inside him as he watched them to heartburn. It sure wasn't loneliness. Was it?

"Ross? You in there?"

He glanced up to find Josh staring at him with a quizzical look.

"Sorry. Did you say something?"

Josh rolled his eyes. "Only about a dozen times. I asked if I could borrow your cell phone to check on my friend."

The same friend whose troubles had occupied him all night? Ross wondered. He wanted to push his nephew to finally come clean and explain what was going on. But since he had screwed everything else up this morning, he decided maybe he ought to keep his mouth shut for now.

He handed over his phone and wasn't surprised when Josh walked outside to make his call. More secrets. He was getting pretty sick of them all.

Despite the fact that Frannie was to be released any moment now, Ross still didn't know much more than when she called him two hours before.

Try as he might, he couldn't manage to worm more information out of anyone in the department except what he already knew. A forty-year-old man was the new suspect in Lloyd's death.

He didn't understand why everyone was being so closedmouthed about the whole thing, but he could guess. They were no doubt engaged in the age-old police game of CYA. Cover Your Ass. No doubt they realized they had rushed to judgment with Frannie without looking around for any other suspects and wanted to avoid making the same mistake again and possibly jeopardizing their case.

He didn't care who killed Lloyd, as long as it meant his sister could return home where she belonged and he could go back to San Antonio where *he* belonged.

Josh returned a few moments later and handed his phone back.

"Everything okay with Lyndsey?" Ross hazarded a guess.

"Yeah, she's doing tons bet—" *Better.* Josh cut his word off but Ross completed the word for himself, even as his nephew frowned at being tricked into revealing more information than he wanted.

"What happened to her?" Ross asked. "Has she been sick?"

For an instant, he thought Josh would confide in him. He opened his mouth and Ross sensed he wanted to tell someone whatever was bothering him. Ross sat forward with an encouraging look, but before Josh could say anything, the door leading to the jail opened.

He and Josh both turned to look and found Frannie standing in the doorway, looking frail and exhausted, with no makeup and her blond hair scraped back in a ponytail.

Despite the outward signs of fatigue, her eyes glowed with joy.

"Josh. Oh sweetheart."

Josh rose from his seat, stumbled forward and then swept his mother into his arms. Both of them were crying a little, even his tough-guy, eighteen-year-old nephew. Ross watched their reunion, aware of a niggle of envy at the love the two of them shared, a love with no conditions or caveats.

Josh had probably never spent one moment wondering at his place in his mother's heart. Frannie loved him with everything she had.

Frannie touched Josh's face as if she couldn't quite believe he was there in front of her and then after a moment she remembered Ross and turned to hug him, as well. She felt like nothing more than fragile bones.

"You're fading away, Frannie," he growled. "Have you been on some kind of hunger strike in here?"

She shook her head. "I just… I haven't been very hungry. It was too hard to drum up an appetite when I could only think about how afraid I was."

If you were so blasted afraid, why didn't you defend yourself? Who were you covering for? Ross wanted to rail at his sister but he knew this wasn't the time. "We need to get you out of here and get some good cooking into you. What do you say we stop at Red on the way home for a huge brunch? We'll break out the champagne."

"That sounds delicious." She gave him a tremulous smile just as Loraine Fitzsimmons walked through.

"Hey, Ross." She smiled.

"Hi, Loraine. Thanks for the information earlier."

She looked around to make sure no one else could overhear them.

"Just thought I'd give you a heads-up. They're questioning him again."

"Who is it?"

She cast another furtive look at the doorway. "You're not going to believe this. It's one of Mendoza boys. Says here it's Roberto. Isn't he the one who's been living in Denver?"

Ross had just half a second to wonder why the man had hated Lloyd enough to kill him and to entertain the possibility of trying to post bail for the guy, whoever he might be, when suddenly he was aware of Frannie's small sound of distress. A moment later his sister's eyes fluttered back in her head and she started to fall.

"Mom!" Josh exclaimed. He dived for her and though he wasn't in time to catch her completely, he slowed the momentum of her fall.

Josh lowered her to the carpet and both he and Ross knelt over her.

Loraine hovered over them, her eyes wide with shock. "Do you want me to call a medic?" she asked.

"Give us a minute," Ross said. Frannie had looked so weak when she came out. Was it any wonder she had succumbed to exhaustion and nerves and fainted?

"Come on, Frannie. Come on back, sis."

"Come on, Mom," Josh added his voice. "You're scaring us."

She blinked her eyes open, then a moment later she scrambled to sit and looked around, trying to regain her bearings.

"Are you all right?" Ross asked. Her pulse seemed a little thready to him and he wondered if he ought to let Loraine go ahead and call a medic.

Frannie blinked a few more times, then her gaze met Loraine's and Ross saw full awareness come back in a rush. Frannie tried to stand but couldn't make it to her feet without his help.

"Take it easy," he said, but Frannie seemed to barely hear him.

"Who did you say they're holding?" she asked Loraine, and Ross couldn't miss the sudden urgency in her voice.

"Mendoza. Roberto Mendoza."

Frannie inhaled a ragged breath and, for a moment, Ross was afraid she would pass out again. "Do you know the guy?" he asked.

"I…no."

She was lying. No doubt about it. Frannie had always been a lousy liar. Maybe that was why she had opted instead to keep her mouth shut when she had been accused of killing her husband.

He knew most of the Mendozas on a casual basis, mostly because they were good friends with his family here in Red Rock. He tried to remember if he had ever met Roberto Mendoza and had a vague memory of bumping into the guy years ago on one of his visits to Red Rock.

What was his relationship with Frannie?

He was royally sick of all these Fortune family secrets. Though he wanted to drag his sister to one of the interview rooms in the police station until he got to the bottom of all this, he knew this wasn't the time. This should be a celebration for Frannie, a chance for her to start taking back her life.

As soon as things settled down for his sister, his own life could get back to normal. To stakeouts and paperwork and catching up on cases. He would be far too busy to pay any attention to those moments standing at his window in San Antonio, watching life go on below without him.

Chapter 14

He really disliked weddings, even when they were family obligations.

A week after Frannie's release from jail, Ross stood in the extensive gardens at the Double Crown watching his cousin Darr dance with his very pregnant bride of less than an hour, Bethany Burdett. Bethany Burdett Fortune, now, he supposed.

It was a lovely evening for a wedding. Little twinkly lights had been strung through all the trees and the garden smelled sweet, like flowers and springtime.

Darr beamed with pride and his new wife looked completely radiant. That was what they said about pregnant women and brides—and since she qualified on both counts, Ross figured *radiant* was an accurate description. She also couldn't seem to take her eyes off Darr.

The two of them seemed deliriously happy together, he would give them that. He hoped things would work out for the two of them and for Bethany's kid, which wasn't Darr's—and nobody was making a secret about it. The baby needed a dad and Darr appeared more than willing to step up and take responsibility. Ross just hoped he didn't grow to resent raising another man's kid.

They wouldn't have an easy road—a cynical thought to have just moments after their wedding, he knew, and he was slightly ashamed of himself for even entertaining it.

How did he get to be so pessimistic about happily-ever-afters? He couldn't really say he'd never seen a good marriage at work. His uncle William had adored his wife Molly before her death and they had been married for decades. Lily and Ryan had known several happy years, too, before Ryan's surprising death.

He couldn't deny there were many couples in his extended family who, by all appearances, had good, fulfilling marriages. He didn't begrudge any of them their joy, he just figured maybe Cindy's particular branch of the Fortune family tree had picked up some sort of withering disease that blighted their prospects of happy endings.

His mother had never stayed with any man for longer than a year or so. His brothers didn't seem capable of settling down, and God knows, his sister's marriage had been a farce from the beginning.

He glanced toward Frannie, sitting at a table with their cousin Nicholas and his fiancée Charlene. She looked as if she were only half-listening to their conversation and he wondered again why she didn't seem more ecstatic about being released from jail. She still seemed thin and withdrawn and she evaded and equivocated whenever he tried to probe about why she hadn't defended herself in Lloyd's murder and her strange re-

action to finding out one of the Mendozas had confessed to it.

Something was up with her and it bugged him that
she still refused to tell him what was going on, even
after all they had been through the past month. She was
a grown woman, though. If she didn't want to tell him
what was troubling her, he couldn't force her.

He glanced at his watch, wondering if twenty minutes into the reception counted as fulfilling his familial
obligation so he could go. When he looked up, his heart
seemed to catch his throat when he saw Julie Osterman
walk into the garden, wearing a soft yellow dress that
made her look as if she had brought all the sunshine
along with her.

In the week since he had left her at her house with
such heated words, he had forgotten how breathtaking
she was, with that soft brown hair shot through with
blond and those incredible blue eyes and delicate features. He suddenly realized with some vexation that
if he had the chance, he would be quite content just to
stand there and gawk at her all night.

As if she felt him watching her, she shifted her attention from her conversation with his cousin Susan and
looked up. For a long moment, the two of them just stared
at each other, their gazes locked. Emotions swelled up
inside him, thick and heavy and terrifying. He saw something in her eyes, something that made them look huge
and liquid and sad, and then she deliberately turned back
to answer something Susan said to her, though he knew
she was still aware of him, of this strange bond tugging
between them.

He wanted fiercely to go to her. His chest ached and
he actually lifted a hand to rub at it then caught himself and shoved it into the pocket of his dress slacks in-

stead. It still throbbed though, an actual physical ache that made him feel slightly ridiculous.

He had missed her. More than he had ever dreamed possible. In the week since he had seen her—since those stunning few hours they had shared at his apartment in San Antonio—she hadn't been out of his mind for long. Everything seemed to remind him of her, from shooting hoops with Josh to the starlit view from his bedroom window at night to—of all silly things—the scent of the particular brand of fabric softener he used, just because that day in the grocery store he had talked to her while they were standing in the laundry aisle.

It had to stop. He was miserable and he hated it. Surely this ache in his chest would eventually go away. He had to start sleeping again, instead of tossing and turning all night, reaching for someone who wasn't there.

Any day now, things would get back to normal. Or at least that's what he kept telling himself.

Lucky for him, he wasn't in love with her, he thought. Then he *really* would be miserable.

He told himself he wasn't staring at her but he couldn't help but notice when Ricky Farraday asked her to dance a few moments later. Ricky was slightly shorter than she was and only fourteen but she took the arm he held out for her with a shake of her head and a laugh he would swear he could hear clear on the other side of the plank dance floor set up in an open area of the garden.

"You're watching those dancers like you'd like to join them."

He jerked his gaze away to realize Frannie had joined him. "No. Not at all. You know I'm not much of a dancer."

"Neither am I. Why don't we trip all over the floor together?"

"I don't think so."

"Come on, Ross. Don't be a big chicken. We haven't danced together since I was twelve years old on my way to my first junior high school dance and you and Cooper and Flint put on some of Cindy's records and took turns trying to teach me a few steps."

He laughed at the memory of him and his brothers almost coming to blows about who could waltz better. Even though they had bickered their way through it, they had all had a great time that Saturday night. He'd forgotten the whole thing. It was so easy to focus only on the bad times that he often forgot how much fun they could all have together.

"Come on. I'd like to dance," Frannie pressed, showing more enthusiasm about this than she had toward much of anything since her release. How could he say no?

He shrugged. "Don't blame me if I ruin your fancy shoes with my clunky feet."

"I can buy more shoes," she said, and led him out to the dance floor. As he expected, he was rusty and awkward at first but Cindy had passed on at least some small degree of her natural ability and they quickly fell into something resembling dance steps.

The entire time, he was aware of Julie across the dance floor. She laughed at something Ricky said and his heart started to ache all over again.

"Okay, what's wrong?" Frannie asked. "Are you completely miserable to be out here dancing or is something else bothering you?"

He raised an eyebrow, finding her question the height of irony since he'd been hounding her to confide in him about one thing or another since the night her husband was killed.

"Nothing." He could equivocate with the best of them. "I'm just not a huge fan of weddings."

"I love them," she said promptly. "Bethany and Darr look so happy together, don't they?"

He stared at her. "How can you? Love weddings, I mean?"

She gave him an arch look. "Do you think I can't be a romantic, just because my own marriage wasn't the greatest?"

That was just about the biggest understatement of the decade, but he decided to let it slide. "I was thinking more about how tough it would be to love weddings when you grew up with a front-row seat to Cindy's messed-up version of relationships. That's enough to sour anybody on the idea of hearts and flowers and happily-ever-after, don't you think?"

"Oh, Ross." Sorrow flickered in her eyes and her fingers tightened around his. "Don't look to Cindy for an example of anything. Or at me, either."

"You don't think we've inherited her lousy relationship gene?"

"Oh, I hope not. I would hate to think you and Cooper and Flint could never find the same kind of happiness that Darr and Bethany share today."

Against his will, his gaze flickered to Julie, then he looked quickly back at Frannie, hoping she had missed that quick, instinctive look.

"Maybe Cooper and Flint might eventually settle down and you're still a young, beautiful woman," he said. "There's no reason you couldn't find someone someday, someone who will finally treat you like you deserve. But I think at this point, it's safe to say it's not in the cards for me."

She was silent for a long time and he hoped she

would let this awkward conversation die. Instead, when her gaze met his, Frannie's eyes were filled with sadness and regret.

"We have all treated you so poorly, haven't we?"

"What do you mean? Of course you haven't!"

"We all counted on you for too much, made you believe you were responsible for everything in our lives. Even Cindy. Maybe especially Cindy."

She squeezed his fingers. "You're not, you know. Not responsible for any of us. You're not responsible for Cindy's failed relationships or her lousy mothering or for my own mistakes or for anything but your own life, Ross, and what you make of it."

So far, he hadn't made much of it. Oh, he had a decent career that he enjoyed and had found success at. But what else did he have to show for forty years on the planet?

"Do you remember teaching me how to ride a two-wheeler without training wheels?" Frannie asked.

He blinked at what seemed an abrupt change of topic. "Not really."

"I do. I can remember it like it was yesterday. I remember exactly what you said to me. I was seven years old, far too old to still be riding a little-kid bike, which means you would have been about eleven. You worked with me for days trying to get me not to wobble. You were so patient, even though I'm sure there were a million other things you would rather have been doing than helping your stupid, clumsy baby sister. Finally one day, you just gave me a big push, let go of the bike frame and told me to forget my fears and just enjoy the ride."

He remembered they had been living in an apartment in Dallas and had gone to the park near their place every afternoon for two weeks. No matter what he tried, Frannie couldn't seem to get the hang of balancing on two wheels. Only after he gave her no other choice except to fall over on the sidewalk did she manage to figure it out. After that, there was no stopping her.

"Can I give the same advice back to you?" Frannie asked, her voice solemn.

"I know how to ride a bike," he muttered, trying to figure out where she was going with this.

"Yes. But do you know how to *live,* Ross?"

He bristled. "What's that supposed to mean?"

"Take it from somebody who feels like she's been one of those ice sculptures over at the bar for the last eighteen years—if a chance for happiness comes along, you have to take it. You can't be afraid because of our messed-up childhood, because of what Cindy did to all of us. Don't give her that much power, Ross. You deserve so much more."

Her words seemed to sear through him, resonating through his entire body. He was doing exactly that. He was still letting Cindy control his life, with her whims and her capriciousness and her instability. He was so convinced he was just like her, that he would mess up everything good and decent that ever came his way, that he was deathly afraid to let go of those fears and take a chance.

Frannie was exactly right. Just as Julie had been right a week before in everything she said to him.

He was afraid to count on anyone else, afraid to open his life to even the possibility of someone else touching his heart.

"I didn't mean to leave you speechless," Frannie said.

He blinked and realized the song had ended—a good thing, since he had stopped stock-still on the edge of the dance floor.

"Think about it, Ross. I just want you to be happy."
Frannie kissed his cheek, then slipped away.

The music started up again and somehow Ross managed to make his way off the dance floor before somebody collided with him. He needed a drink, he decided, even if it meant he had to stick around a little longer to give the alcohol time to wear off before he drove home.

Before he could reach the open bar and those ice sculptures Frannie had been talking about, Julie twirled by on the arm of his nephew, who must have asked her to dance the moment Ricky led her off the floor. Her gaze met his over Josh's shoulder and this time he was certain he saw something like sorrow there.

His chest ached again and he had no choice but to rub it as the truth seemed to soak through him.

He couldn't lie to himself anymore. He was in love with Julie Osterman. With her smile and her gentleness and her compassion for everyone around her. He loved the way she touched his arm to make a point and her enthusiasm and dedication to the rough-edged kids she helped and the way she always had everyone else's interests at heart.

He let out a shaky breath, feeling as if a dozen ice sculptures had just collapsed on his head. He *couldn't* be in love with her. He didn't know the first damn thing about being in love.

His instinct was to run, to climb into his SUV and head back to San Antonio, where he was safe. But he had supposedly been safe all week from Julie and these terrifying emotions she churned up in him and he had been miserable.

Just let go and enjoy the ride.

Frannie's words echoed in his mind. Did he have the courage? Could he let go of the past and seize this incredible chance for happiness that had been handed to him?

He watched Julie twirl around the dance floor with Josh and knew he had to try.

Ross was staring at her.

Julie tried to keep her attention on the dance steps, on not tripping all over her partner and making a complete fool of herself, but she was painfully aware of Ross's hard gaze scorching her all over. But why did he bother looking?

He had made it abundantly plain he wasn't interested in anything more than the one night they had together. She had spent all week trying to get over him, to convince herself her heart wasn't broken, and then he had to show up at her friend Bethany's wedding looking rough and masculine and gorgeous in a Western-cut dark suit and tie.

If he didn't want her, why was he looking at her like she was a big plate of caramel cashew bars he couldn't wait to gobble up?

She drew in a shaky breath and tried to answer something Josh said, though she wasn't sure if she made any sense. She barely heard what he said in reply, but his next words suddenly penetrated through the haze around her brain.

"What happened between you and Ross?" Josh asked.

She stumbled and nearly stepped on his foot but quickly tried to recover. "What do you mean? Why do you ask?"

His shoulder moved beneath her hand as he shrugged. "I just thought you two were getting along so well. I'm not blind. I could see the vibe between the two of you the night we had dinner. And suddenly it's like you're nowhere to be found and Uncle Ross is acting like a grizzly bear who needs a root canal. What happened between you two?"

She knew it was petty of her to find some satisfaction that Ross was acting cranky but she couldn't seem to help it. "Nothing happened," she lied. Other than they shared one incredible night together and then he broke her heart. "We're just friends."

"Are you sure? He really seemed to like you, more than anyone else I've ever seen him with."

She let out a breath and pasted on something she hoped would pass for a smile. "I'm positive. Just friends."

"Too bad. I think you would have been good for Uncle Ross. He needs somebody like you."

Though she knew Josh didn't realize it, his words poured like acid on her already raw wounds. She was still reeling when the music ended. One of Josh's extended cousins called to him and he excused himself with a smile.

She stood for a moment, aware of Ross across the dance floor talking to his cousin J.R. and J.R.'s lovely fiancée, Isabella Mendoza, who was Roberto's cousin. His gaze met hers one more time, his dark eyes unreadable, and she let out a shaky breath.

Julie couldn't take anymore. She had done her duty by her friend Bethany and had told her how thrilled she was for her and for Darr. There was no reason to stick around for more of this torture.

Quickly, she made her way toward the grassy field that was serving as a parking lot for the wedding, pausing only long enough to say a hasty goodbye to a few friends. Just as she reached the outskirts of the crowd, she heard Ross calling her name.

She briefly entertained the idea of pretending she

didn't hear him, but that would be the coward's way out. Besides, as quickly as he moved, he would catch up to her before she could reach her car anyway.

As he approached, she turned slowly, cursing him all over again for making her heart flip in her chest. His features wore an odd, unreadable expression and his eyes were gazing at her with an intensity that made her suddenly breathless.

"Hi, Ross," she managed.

"I thought I saw you leave. I'm glad I caught you. I…needed to talk to you."

"Oh?" She did her best to hide the tremble of her hands by folding them tightly in front of her.

For a long moment, he didn't seem inclined to say anything, he just continued to watch her out of those deep brown eyes. She wasn't used to seeing him at a loss for words and she didn't quite know how to respond.

Finally he let out a long breath. "Do you…would you like to take a walk with me?"

She ought to tell him no. She wasn't at all in the mood to dredge everything up again and she wasn't sure her fragile emotions could handle another encounter with him. But she was curious enough about what he wanted to talk about that she finally nodded. They walked side by side on the gravel pathway around the house in the gathering twilight, through more gardens, their shoulders barely brushing.

The silence between them was jagged, awkward. As a trained therapist, she certainly knew the value of a good silence to allow for thoughts to be gathered, but she couldn't endure this one.

"What did you want to talk to me about?"

He sighed. "I said I *needed* to talk to you. Not that I *wanted* to."

His words stabbed at her already-tender nerves and she stopped abruptly, then turned on her heel and headed back the direction she had come. "Fine," she said over her shoulder. "Let's forget the whole thing. I can find my own way back to my car, thanks all the same."

He grabbed her arm to stop her departure but quickly released her again when she turned back around. "Ah, hell. That didn't come out right. I do want to talk to you."

He was silent for a long moment. When he spoke, his voice was low and rough. "The truth is, I want to do more than talk to you. You're all I've been able to think about for a week."

Her stomach shivered at his words and she folded her arms tightly across it, as if he could see her tremble. "What am I supposed to say to that?"

He looked so uncomfortable that her heart tumbled around all over again in her chest. "I don't know. That maybe you missed me, too."

Only every moment, with every single breath. She swallowed and looked away. "What did you want to talk to me about, Ross? I was just on my way home."

He didn't answer, only started walking again and curiosity gave her no choice but to follow him. He finally stopped near a small, burbling creek that cut through a small copse of trees near one of the outbuildings.

They found a bench there, a weathered iron and wood creation that looked as if it had been there as long as the hills around the ranch. He must have known it was here, she realized, since he had led her directly to this spot. She sat, her emotions in turmoil. After a moment, he sat beside her.

"I love this place," he finally said, his voice low. "It was always my favorite spot whenever we came to the ranch when I was a kid. We didn't do it very often.

Come here, I mean. Maybe only two or three times I can remember, but I loved it. I cherished those times because I always felt...*safe* here."

She held her breath, more touched than she knew she ought to be that he had shared this secret place with her, though she still didn't understand why.

He gazed out at the creek, without meeting her gaze. "I didn't feel safe in very many places," he said after another long silence. "You were absolutely right, Julie. Everything you said to me the other morning at your house was right on the money. I keep everyone away because it's easier than letting myself count on people who let me down."

He finally looked at her. "I spent my entire childhood with nothing solid to hold on to but a few fragmented memories of this place."

She couldn't help herself—she reached out to touch his forearm. He looked down at her hand on his sleeve, his eyes deep with emotions she couldn't begin to name, then he covered her hand with his tightly to keep her fingers in place on his arm, to keep the two of them connected.

She could feel the heat of him through the fabric of his suit jacket, feel the muscle tensing beneath her hand. If he found some comfort from her touch, she wasn't about to move.

"My mother should never have had kids," he said hoarsely. "I don't think she wanted any of us and she didn't know what to do with us when we arrived. I was the oldest and it was left to me to take care of everybody else."

"And you did."

"I didn't have a choice. There was no one else. What you said, about keeping everybody out, counting only on myself. You were exactly right. I had to at the time for survival, and it just became a habit, I guess. I de-

nied what you said at first because I didn't want to believe I could be giving my childhood, my *mother,* that
much power to control my life. I'm forty years old. It
shouldn't still be so much a part of me."

"We can never completely lose our childhoods," she
said softly. "It's part of what shapes us. We just have to
learn as adults to accept that we don't have the power
to change it. All we can do is try to move forward and
make the rest of our lives the best we can."

"You also called me the loneliest man you ever met."

Her eyes stung with tears at the bleakness in his voice.
"I'm so sorry, Ross. I should never have said that."

"No. Don't apologize."

He was quiet. In the distance she could hear the
music from the wedding, muted and slow. "You were
right about that, too," he finally said. "I have been. I
never wanted to admit it before. I think I was afraid
to face that. I told myself I was perfectly happy, that
I liked being on my own, making my own decisions,
not having to be responsible for anyone else. But it was
only an illusion."

"Oh, Ross."

He let out a shaky breath. "I don't want to be lonely
anymore."

Hope fluttered inside her chest like fragile butterfly
wings but she was afraid to acknowledge it, afraid to
even look at it for fear of crushing it.

He shifted and before she quite realized what he intended, he grabbed both of her hands in his. Her heart
began to pound and she couldn't seem to catch her breath.

"This scares the hell out of me," he said, "but I had
some good advice thrown back in my face tonight and
I'm going to take it. It's time for me to let go of my fears
and enjoy the ride."

"I don't know what you're talking about," she murmured. "I'm sorry."

He laughed a little, but his features quickly grew solemn. "I'm in love with you, Julie. That's what I'm talking about."

"What?" Her fingers clenched in his and she would have jerked them away but he held on tightly.

"It's true. I think I've been in love with you probably since you just about whacked me over the head with that silly flowered purse I thought had been stolen."

"You can't be!" The delicate little butterfly of hope inside her became a fierce, joyful dragon, flapping furiously to take flight.

"That's exactly what I've been telling myself for the last week. I've never been in love before. I thought I would get over it, get over you. But seeing you tonight just made me realize this is too big, too deep, for me to just forget about. I can't pretend anymore."

"Ross, I…" her voice faltered and she couldn't seem to string two coherent words together.

"You told me first love was wonderful and terrible at the same time. Do you remember that?"

She nodded, vaguely remembering their conversation about Josh and Lyndsey.

"I've had the terrible part this week, without you. I'm ready for the wonderful part to kick in any time now."

She gazed at him there in the gathering dusk, looking so big and gorgeous and dear. She gave a sound that was half laugh, half sob and crossed the brief distance to throw herself into his waiting arms and press her trembling mouth to his.

He gave an exultant laugh and gripped her tightly, returning her kiss with all the passion and heat and wonder she had dreamed about for the past week.

"I love you, Ross," she murmured against his mouth. "I love you so much. I've been completely miserable this week."

"I probably shouldn't be happy about that, should I? You know what they say about misery loving company."

She laughed. "You could show a little compassion for my suffering."

"That's something you'll have to help me work on. That whole compassion thing you do so well."

"I'll do my best," she promised.

His features grew serious and he drew away a little. "I'm not the greatest bargain out there, Julie. I can't lie about that. I've still got some things to work through that might take some time. You and I both know you could probably do a whole lot better."

"No, I couldn't. There is no one better." She pressed her mouth to his again and poured every ounce of the love flowing through her into the kiss.

When she drew away, they were both breathing hard. "You are a wonderful man, Ross Fortune. The best man I know. I think I fell in love with you that first night, too, when I saw how concerned you were for everyone else around you but yourself. For Frannie, for Josh. You were even worried about me, and you didn't even know me then. You're good and decent and honorable, Ross. The kind of man a woman knows in her heart will watch out for her and protect her and do everything he can to make her happy."

"You make me want to be all those things and more."

He lifted her until she was sitting on his lap, her arms still wrapped tightly around the strong column of his neck.

"And just so you know," he said, his voice just a whisper against her skin, "you're it for me, Julie. This might be my first time falling in love but it's also my *only* time."

She fought back the sting of tears again and kissed him softly in the pale, lavender light, wondering how she had been blessed enough to love and be loved by two such completely different men.

A tiny part of her heart would always mourn Chris and all the possibilities that had been extinguished too soon. But she was more than ready to move forward, to take this incredible chance she had been given for happiness.

She had a sudden vision of a future with Ross, one that was bright and beautiful and shining with promise. She saw them taking on challenges and causes, opening their lives and their hearts to wounded children, filling their world with joy and laughter. A place where both of them would always feel safe and cherished and loved.

The image was as clear and as real as the huge, round moon beginning to gleam over the treetops. Only this was better.

Worlds better.

As beautiful as it might be, that moon was always just beyond their grasp. But Julie suddenly knew without a doubt that together, she and Ross would grab hold of their future and make it perfect.

* * * * *

Kristin Hardy has always wanted to write, starting her first novel while still in grade school. Although she became a laser engineer by training, she never gave up her dream of being an author. Her first completed manuscript, *My Sexiest Mistake*, debuted in Harlequin's Blaze line; it was subsequently made into a movie by the Oxygen network. Visit Kristin at kristinhardy.com.

Books by Kristin Hardy

Harlequin Special Edition

Her Christmas Surprise
A Fortune Wedding
Where There's Smoke
Under the Mistletoe
Vermont Valentine

Harlequin Blaze

My Sexiest Mistake
Caught
Bad Influence

Visit the Author Profile page
at Harlequin.com for more titles.

Kristin Hardy

A Fortune Wedding

To Susan, for her patience and careful editing.

To the other Fortunes of Texas authors
for being great collaborators.

And to Stephen,
who's been my best fortune yet.

Acknowledgments

Thanks go to William Hartley of the Hartley Law Firm
and Lt. Ron Marquis of the Boerne, Texas,
Police Department for helping bring this story to life.

Any errors are mine.

Prologue

Red Rock, Texas
July 1991

"Come on, boy, come on," Roberto Mendoza muttered, crouching over the withers of Cisco, his big bay gelding, as they raced up the tree-studded grassy slope. The speed was intoxicating. The wind rushed over his skin. A kaleidoscope of sound filled his ears—the thud of hoofbeats, the rush of his own breath.

The silvery sound of laughter ahead of him.

And then they burst up onto the hilltop, the great blue bowl of the sky arching overhead.

"Hah! We beat you!" Frannie Fortune whooped, reining in her little chestnut mare and wheeling around. "Who says the girls can't outdo the boys?" With her short, sunbeam-blond hair and tilted eyes, she looked like a pixie, ready for mischief.

Life, Roberto thought, just didn't get any better than this.

"You girls only won because you took a shortcut," he told her.

"Don't blame us because we're smarter. We just took a faster way."

"Yeah, like straight up the side of the hill."

"Admit it, you're impressed."

He grinned. "I am, but next time you decide to take your shortcut, leave me with a suicide note for your uncle. I'm supposed to be watching out for you."

Her cheeks were still flushed with the excitement of the race. "I keep telling Uncle Ryan I don't need looking after. So I got thrown once. It can happen to anyone. You try staying in the saddle when a killdeer flies up between the feet of that monster you're on," she challenged. "See how you feel when your fanny hits the ground."

Roberto's lips twitched as he slid off Cisco. "I guess you'll have to come to my rescue."

"If you're lucky." She gave him an arch look.

How had he ever thought her standoffish? It hadn't been that, but simple shyness that had kept her quiet and to herself when she'd first arrived at the Double Crown Ranch where he worked. As the weeks had passed, she'd blossomed, quiet diffidence giving way to a sly humor that perpetually hovered around that delicate mouth, the surprisingly bawdy laughter that burst out of her more and more often as the days went by.

Maybe it was just being here, out on the ranch, amid the rolling terrain of Texas hill country. It could make anybody happy, although he might be biased. No matter where his life took him, Roberto thought, no place would ever feel as right as this patch of territory where he knew nearly every tree, bush and bird by name. It was in his blood, as much a part of him as his brown eyes.

Frannie walked over to stand next to him. "You think you'll ever leave here?" she asked, as if she knew what he'd been thinking.

He watched as she bent down to pick a long stalk of grass. "I'd have to have a real good reason. I figure I'll save my money, buy a place of my own someday."

Living and working out on the land, he couldn't imagine anything better. Certainly not sitting all day in a college classroom, no matter how much his father wanted him to. José Mendoza hadn't taken the news of his twenty-year-old son dropping out well. To avoid skull fractures from the two of them butting heads in the family's restaurant, Red, Roberto had come to work at the Double Crown, where his uncle Ruben Mendoza ran operations for the Fortune family.

And where the lovely, coltish Frannie had appeared for a visit just days later.

Too bad she'd somehow gotten snowed into dating Lloyd Fredericks, the original self-important, silver-spoon guy. But she was a Fortune and he was a Fredericks, so maybe they did belong together. It still set Roberto's teeth on edge every time he saw Fredericks drive in to pick her up. The jerk didn't deserve a woman like Frannie.

"So, what are you going to call your ranch?" Frannie interrupted his thoughts. "The Rocking RM? The Double R?"

"I was thinking Red Oaks."

"How about the Slowpoke?" she offered.

His eyes narrowed. "Remind me again who won when we raced last week?"

"That's because you had an unfair advantage," she argued. "Cisco's two hands taller than Peaches. We had to outsmart you."

What she'd done was about stop his heart when he'd seen her tearing up the side of the hill. She might have started out quiet and shy, but she was fearless now.

"You just got lucky this time," he said.

"No, I was prepared," Frannie corrected him, twirling her grass. "Lloyd says that's what luck is, just opportunity meeting preparation."

"That sounds like your boyfriend. Always looking for an angle."

She rolled her eyes. "He's not my boyfriend. We're just going out. Anyway, I don't want to talk about Lloyd. You buy Red Oaks and I'll come to visit." She gave him an impish look. "And Peaches and I will beat you then, too."

He reached out and swiped the blade of grass from her hand.

"Hey," she protested.

"You need to learn some respect for your elders."

"My elders?" She snorted. "You think a fancy new hat makes you all grown-up?" That all-too-delectable mouth of hers curved.

Roberto eyed her. "You got a problem with my hat?"

"I don't know, but maybe you do." And quick as a flash, she swiped the black Stetson and dashed away, squealing.

He sprinted after her. "Oh, you're gonna be sorry."

"Big talk," she scoffed, clapping the hat on top of her head. She was willow thin and fleet, feinting one direction and dashing the other, making him give chase until both of them were laughing and out of breath, circling the red oak that crowned the top of the hill.

"Give it up," he told her as they faced off on either side of a stand of piñon.

She glanced over to Peaches as though judging her distance. "Not a chance." She faked one way and he mirrored her, faked the other. And then she went just a fraction too far and he whipped around the tree and caught her, snaking an arm around her waist to draw her in.

"That's it, *chica,* you're in for it now," he growled.

"Oh, yeah? What are you going to do to me?" There was humor in those soft blue eyes, and mischief and glee. And under it all, something else, something that started the blood rushing in his veins. He caught a hint of scent that made him think of spring and sunshine. He could feel every breath she took. His pulse thundered in his ears.

She wasn't even out of school yet, he reminded himself. He worked for her uncle. He had no business kissing her. Even as his lips hovered over hers, he made himself release her.

And then Frannie leaned in to press her sweet, warm mouth to his.

Chapter 1

Red Rock, Texas May 2009
Three days after the Spring Fling...

How in the name of God had it happened? Frannie Fredericks wondered as she stared through the visitor's window in the Red Rock County Jail. One minute she'd been riding horses that golden summer, the next she'd been pregnant, the next, married.

And the next, she'd been bent over her husband's dead body at the town's Spring Fling, the blood on her hands black in the moonlight.

Suspicion had slid into interrogation, and, impossibly, arrest, the giddy shrieks of the kids on the carnival rides fifty yards away still ringing in her ears. And now, she was here in the county jail on the wrong side of the barrier, accused of Lloyd Fredericks' murder.

* * *

Lily Fortune, Frannie's sort-of aunt, sat as calm and poised as an aristocrat, her dark hair up in a twist, her hand holding the black telephone receiver that linked them. From the rows of windows to either side they heard angry accusations, plaintive whispers, false bravado as people visited sons and daughters, spouses, lovers, friends. The temperature in the room rose with the closely packed bodies.

"You really don't have to come here," Frannie said into the handset.

Lily gave a serene smile. "Of course I do. You forget, I know what it's like."

Almost ten years before, Lily had been the one behind bars, wrongly accused of the murder of Ryan Fortune's then wife. She'd been freed, though, freed to finally marry Ryan, her lifelong love, freed to find happiness.

Frannie could barely remember what happiness felt like. "How did you make it through?" she asked, her voice barely audible.

"I knew I was innocent. The same way you're innocent. Of course, it would help matters if you told that to someone. Or if you told them anything else that you know."

Anything else that you know. Frannie looked down at the floor. "My lawyer said we shouldn't talk about the case."

Lily was silent for a long moment, then let out a quiet sigh. "All right. We're behind you, Frannie, whatever you decide. And we're doing our best to get you out of here. That DA makes me so mad, holding you without bail as a campaign stunt. We'll have you out of here soon, though. William's working on it."

William Fortune, Frannie's uncle. Something flickered in Lily's eyes when she said his name, a light that had been missing in the four years since she'd lost Ryan to cancer. Frannie's life might have been in turmoil, the lives of all of the Fortunes of late, but at least one good thing had come of it.

"You like him, don't you?"

"Well, of course," Lily answered too quickly. "He's been very helpful since he came out from California."

"I don't think it has anything to do with being helpful," Frannie countered. "And you're blushing."

Lily straightened. "I am not. It's just warm in here."

For the first time since that nightmare moment of discovering Lloyd's body, Frannie found herself smiling. "You've always been so good to me," she said.

"You make it easy."

The two women had hit it off from the day they'd met, despite the twenty-five-year difference in their ages. Maybe it was that they were both outsiders of a sort—Lily because she'd just married into the Fortune family and Frannie because, well, the children of a family's black sheep always were.

Growing up, all Frannie had ever wanted was a normal life—a home instead of a succession of apartments and hotels, a father instead of a parade of uncles. She would have traded anything she had for a stable, loving mother. Instead, she and her brothers had been stuck with the brash, temperamental, self-destructive Cindy Fortune, which had been better than being raised by wolves, but only marginally. Cindy operated on three levels: derision, manipulation and indifference.

She'd been working on husband number five when a few too many drinks and some ill-advised behavior had wrecked it. Short on money—her trust fund was long gone—she'd had to go to plan B. For housing, a stay on a yacht in the Mediterranean with some of her jet-setting friends. And if she couldn't marry for money herself, she'd marry her daughter off, instead. So she'd dumped seventeen-year-old Frannie with Ryan and the rest of the Fortunes at the Double Crown, taking care to introduce her to the wealthy Fredericks family and their eligible son before heading out to Santorini.

How strange it had been to be with people who didn't make a lifestyle of making scenes, Frannie remembered. Adults who were responsible. Cindy might have infuriated and appalled them, but they never gave a hint of it to Frannie, just loved her and encouraged her and gave her the space to discover who she really was.

"Cindy dropped me at the ranch like extra baggage." Frannie shook her head. "No one ever said anything, not Uncle Kingston, not Uncle Ryan."

Lily frowned. "You weren't extra baggage, you were family. Kingston offered to let you stay from the time you were a toddler, you know."

"What?" Startled, Frannie stared at her.

"Every time Cindy showed up angling for money and talking about what a burden motherhood was, he'd offer to take you, all of you kids. When you were about five, Kingston demanded that she let him adopt the lot of you." Lily looked down. "She said no, of course. Ryan said it was the worst fight they'd ever had."

"I had no idea. She never said…"

"She wouldn't, would she?" Lily put her hand to the clear barrier between them. "Frannie, you're dear to all of us and we all want you out of here. Whatever you think it's doing to help your case by staying quiet, you're wrong. Don't make a mistake that you're going to pay for forever."

But she already had—that long-ago summer when Lloyd Fredericks had come around flirting. Lloyd had been a junior at Rice University, sophisticated and handsome and initially irresistible.

Until she'd gotten to know Roberto Mendoza, the dark-eyed ranch hand with the smile that flashed like hidden treasure. She'd lost her heart. He'd walked away.

And then things had changed shockingly quickly. One moment she'd had all the possibilities in the world. The next, only a single option had remained—a night's misjudgment becoming a life choice. The years had gone by, her world shrinking around her until she no longer recognized that girl she'd been. And now she was here, accused of Lloyd's murder, unable to deny it.

Unable to even bring herself to think about the alternative—that the one who really belonged in the cell might be Josh, their son.

Roberto Mendoza stood in the afternoon sunlight of the empty field, watching a line of ants weave a path through the grass. Ticket stubs and bits of litter fluttered in the breeze, scudding along to catch around the bottoms of the row of honey mesquite that lined the field's edge. They were almost finished blooming now, showering the grass with their pale yellow petals and infusing the air with a faint hint of sweetness. It was the scent that always made him think of home.

He shook his head. How the hell had he wound up back in Red Rock? Eighteen years before, he'd started walking away and just kept going. Time was, he'd figured it would take an act of God or a funeral to get him home. In the end, it had only taken one phone call, a call he'd been powerless to ignore. His family needed him, it had been that simple. And he, who had resisted all ties for so long, started the long drive back.

He'd figured it would be quick and over; he'd hit

town planning on it. He'd figure out who was threatening his family and put an end to it. He'd never expected to be sucked into the middle of someone else's mess.

Or that he'd be powerless to walk away.

At the sound of an engine, Roberto turned to see a dark blue sedan pull off the highway and crunch down the gravel road to park beside his truck. The doors opened and two men got out. He didn't move, just watched as they adjusted their jackets and walked over to him, taking their time. They came to a stop before him.

"I guess you'd be Roberto Mendoza," said the older of the two. He was heavyset with thinning, brownish hair, but the man who made the mistake of thinking he was soft was the one who'd wind up on the losing end of the fight.

Roberto nodded. "And you'd be…?"

He flipped out his badge in a practiced motion. "Lieutenant Len Wheeler, Red Rock PD. This here's Investigator Bobby McCaskill. How about you show us some ID?"

Roberto's brow rose as he brought out his wallet. "You always card citizens offering information?"

Wheeler glanced up from the driver's license. "The job's about paying attention to details," he said mildly, and handed Roberto's license back. "Now, how about you tell us why we're here?"

"There's something I think you need to see."

Wheeler's washed-out blue eyes studied him. "I checked the files. The units on the scene interviewed you the night of Fredericks' murder. Said you reported an unspecified person dressed in a black hoodie walking away from the scene."

"Black and red. Maybe."

"Whatever this thing is, why didn't you tell the on-site officers then, when the scene was fresh?"

"It wasn't until I was running it over in my mind later that I realized there was something else that might have mattered."

"And you couldn't just call it into the hotline?" McCaskill asked sourly.

Roberto shot him a glance. "I left a message on the hotline a week and a half ago." A week and a half. A week and a half that Frannie had been sitting in the county jail for Lloyd Fredericks' murder when he knew damned well she was innocent.

And no matter how little he thought of the faithless woman she'd proven to be, he couldn't leave the golden, laughing girl from the hilltop to that. "You didn't do anything about the tip. I figured I needed to take things into my own hands," he said aloud. Clear his conscience and be done with it.

Wheeler shook his head. "We got ourselves a good two hundred pages of notes from that fool hotline. Something about the murder of a guy like Fredericks brings out all the bedbugs."

Like you, was the unspoken subtext. Roberto's jaw tightened. "Do you want to solve this case?"

"Already have." Wheeler smiled. "We got us a guy calls every day swearing Ronald Reagan appeared in his bedroom to tell him Dr. Phil did it. Another one who says it was all a plot by the arugula-eating elitists." Abruptly, the smile vanished. "You live in Denver. Long way from Red Rock. You mind telling us what you were doing in town and all the way down here that night?"

It shouldn't have taken him by surprise. It did. "I was at the Spring Fling."

"Spring Fling was going on a good twenty, thirty

yards away from here." Wheeler glanced around. "This area would have been back away from the booths, out in the dark. So maybe you want to explain just how it was you happened to be around to see your mysterious person. And there was a whole line of outhouses over by the dance, and in the opinion of our officers you were stone-cold sober when they talked to you, so if I was you, I'd think twice about wasting our time with any stories about needing a bathroom." And that quickly, the affable exterior fell away to show the cop beneath.

Whether or not to tell the truth was an easy decision. Figuring out how much to tell was harder. "I came back from Denver for family reasons."

"That's right, someone burned up your dad's restaurant." That was McCaskill, reaching down to pluck a ticket stub off the ground. "I guess they didn't like their combination platter."

It was a clumsy attempt to provoke a reaction. Roberto wasn't about to rise to it. "You've been doing your homework."

"Yep, we've done a lot of studying." Wheeler squinted at the trees. "Funny thing, the Fortunes have been having their share of fire trouble, too. What was that note Lily Fortune got? 'This one wasn't an accident, either'? You know anything about that?"

"Why would you think I would?" Or about the other cryptic notes—*One of the Fortunes is not who you think*.

"Oh, maybe on account of you worked at the ranch about twenty years back."

Roberto shot him a look. "You investigating the murder of Lloyd Fredericks or you investigating me?"

"Lloyd Fredericks. Although you're becoming an

interesting sideline. So what were you doing creeping around back here, Mendoza?"

Funny how sometimes your entire life could hinge on chance. He hadn't planned to attend the Spring Fling, wouldn't have.

Except for the message.

"I got a call to meet someone. They said they had some information for me."

"What was it?"

Roberto shrugged. "I never saw them." The caller hadn't bothered to show up. Instead, Lloyd Fredericks had.

McCaskill flipped the ticket stub away. "No mystery caller, just you standing here when Lloyd Fredericks got his head staved in twenty yards away. Oh, and your imaginary hooded avenger running away—"

"Walking."

"Yeah, sure, walking away. Except no one else around here saw them. You really expect us to buy that?"

"Take it easy, Bobby," Wheeler said. "Who was it you were supposed to meet?"

"I don't know."

"Man? Woman?"

"I don't know," Roberto repeated. "It was a cell phone message, a bad connection with a lot of noise in the background. Look," he snapped, patience finally evaporating. "I came here to show you something that could be important to your investigation, not get grilled. You got any more questions to ask, I want a lawyer."

Wheeler looked mild again. "No need to lawyer up, we're just talking here. Why don't you show us whatever it is that's got you so excited?"

"Over there." Roberto pointed over at the line of bushes at the field's edge. "I told your officers about the

guy hurrying off a couple of minutes before the screaming started. I wasn't watching all that close, just figured
he was swinging his arms, but the way he was swinging them was funny. I got to thinking maybe he tossed
something away. That's why I called the hotline. I figured you'd check it out, but you all seemed a lot more
interested in railroading Frannie Fredericks."

Wheeler looked interested. "You got some kind of
acquaintance with Miz Fredericks? Or the deceased?"

Roberto cursed himself silently. "I told you, no more
questions without a lawyer. And if you don't look in
that honey mesquite over there in the next two minutes, I'm going to fish the damned thing out and haul
it to the lab myself."

"Now you just take it easy, Mr. Mendoza." Even as
Wheeler said the words, McCaskill crossed to where
Roberto pointed.

Roberto could tell the minute he saw it, see the sudden attention in the line of his body. "Hey, Len, you
might want to come on over here."

Wheeler had been on the job too long to show obvious interest in anything, but he moved with purpose to
stare at what Roberto had found.

It had been tossed back into the center of a thicket of
branches, a thick metal bar maybe the length of a man's
forearm, but far more deadly. And Roberto knew what
they'd see if they looked closer—the dark residue, the
clots of matter. And hair.

"Bobby, get the forensics team out here," Wheeler
said without looking up.

"Already got 'em on the line." He spoke into the
phone as Wheeler bent back the twigs under the end of
the bar with a pen.

"When did you find this, Mr. Mendoza?"

"This morning, after I got sick and tired of waiting for one of you people to call me back or at least get your asses out here."

"And you haven't touched it?"

The mildness was gone, the gaze flat and assessing.

"I think I want that lawyer, now," Roberto said.

"We'll set you up with your phone call as soon as we get back to the station," Wheeler said as he and Mc-Caskill fell in on either side of Roberto.

He felt a thread of disquiet. "Are you arresting me?"

"Just taking you in for some questions. Because I've got a lot more of them for you. Starting with why we found pictures of someone who looks a whole lot like you on Lloyd Fredericks' cell phone."

Wrought-iron chandeliers cast golden light over the tiled floor. Antique serapes hung on pale ocher walls next to antique maps of Texas. In three or four hours, the main room of Red would be filled with diners, noise and the savory scents of the restaurant's Tex-Mex specialties. At this hour, though, it was still peaceful and empty.

Sort of. "It's a good thing you own a restaurant, otherwise the rehearsal dinner would break you," Jane Gilliam commented, glancing around the polished wood table at the people who had become a kind of second family to her in a matter of months.

And at the man who'd come to mean everything.

Jorge Mendoza had the knife-edged cheekbones and the rogue's grin of a heartbreaker, but when he looked at her, there was something more, something deep and true for her alone. Impossible to think that mere months before she'd barely been aware of his existence. Now, he was her first thought upon rising and her last before going to sleep.

And soon, he would be her husband.

Catching her gaze, he leaned over to kiss her thoroughly.

For a moment, Jane just sank into it before realizing the impropriety. "Hey," she said. "There are people here."

"They're not people, they're family," he corrected, giving her another kiss for good measure. "Besides, they're used to it."

"He's right, you know," José Mendoza said, planting a kiss on his wife, Maria.

"Pay attention, you." Maria pushed him away, round cheeks tinting.

He stroked his graying mustache. "I am paying attention."

"We have a rehearsal dinner to plan," she scolded. "We barely have two months until the wedding."

"It's all right, I know the owner," said José.

"Who is going to be very embarrassed if his son's rehearsal dinner is a failure," she responded starchily.

"Women," José said to Jorge, shaking his head.

"They never have their priorities straight," Jorge agreed.

"Listen to Mama," admonished his sister Christina. "We have to get your dinner planned."

"And the wedding planned and the honeymoon planned. Plan, plan plan. Life doesn't always have to be serious," Jorge reminded her.

"Trust me, I know." Her mouth curved as she watched a girl run past, followed by a giggling boy of about four. "That's why you plan, so you can afford to not be serious. Bowie, stop barging around after Elsa or you'll break something," she ordered.

"Like your head," added Sierra, Jorge's youngest sister, as she tied up her waist-length, curly brown hair. "Come on, Jorge, let's get the planning done so we can go out into the courtyard and have some dinner."

"You've gotten bossier since you've become a mother," he observed, watching her pull her daughter onto her lap.

"I was always bossy," she countered. "Anyway, think of Jane."

"Oh, trust me, I do," he assured her. "In fact I—" A snatch of electronic music played and he pulled out his cell phone, glancing at the display before opening it up. "About time you called. Everybody's here, you're the only one missing. Now get your lazy—what?" He stopped. "You're *where?*" The grin disappeared in an instant, replaced by shock and then a taut anxiety. "Whoa. Wait a minute, hold on. Run through it from the beginning." Jorge listened, then cursed. "They're out of their minds. How can they—all right, all right. Don't worry about it, I'll take care of it. Give me fifteen minutes, thirty tops." He ended the call and lowered the phone slowly to the table.

"What? What is it?" Jane asked.

Jorge stared into space for a moment, then stirred. "That was Roberto."

"Where is he?" Worry infused Maria's voice. "He's more than an hour late."

"He's at the police department." Jorge looked at them all helplessly. "They're holding him for questioning in the murder of Lloyd Fredericks."

Chapter 2

"Cordell Fredericks conducted the reading of the will last week, but the bulk of Lloyd's property is held in your living trust. That means it's all yours." Royce Gahan glanced up from the papers on his polished mahogany desk to Frannie, sitting across from him.

It was all faintly unreal, going from orange jumpsuits at the county jail to a plush leather client chair at the office of their lawyer. Her lawyer, now. One minute she'd been in a cell, the next she'd been released on her own recognizance.

At least until the police changed their minds.

"Was there anything in the will I should know about?"

"I don't think so. Just the disposal of some Fredericks family heirlooms. There's a copy of the document in the folder I've given you. It's...unfortunate you couldn't be there."

Frannie didn't think so. She was happy to have missed it. Even without the suspicion cast on her, the reading would have been unpleasant. Jillian Fredericks had never made any secret of the fact that she thought Frannie had trapped Lloyd. Never mind that Frannie's trust fund had largely supported them, that he was just as much at fault as she for the unplanned pregnancy.

Or more.

When Frannie had turned up pregnant after leaving Texas, Cindy had dragged her back to Red Rock to face Lloyd. It had taken a DNA test to convince the Fredericks family. By that time, Frannie had been so emotionally shell-shocked that she'd been in no shape to decide anything. Lloyd will take care of you, Cindy had told her, and she'd obeyed.

Why he'd married her, Frannie couldn't say. Not for his son; he'd scarcely been any kinder to Josh than to her. And yet he'd refused to divorce her. He'd liked having a beautiful wife, the same way he'd liked having a luxury automobile. In a way, his affairs had been a relief, better than those cold couplings in the dark when, despising herself, she'd pretended to enjoy it in the hope it would be over more quickly.

She'd played the part of society matron, loved her son and endured her days trying not to remember that she'd once hoped for more. That for one golden afternoon she'd held everything in her hands. Still, she had her health and a wonderful son she loved, and maybe that was all she could expect. Maybe there were some mistakes that you paid for forever.

Or not quite forever because now Lloyd was gone, killed, possibly by Roberto Mendoza, the man she'd thought for a few hours she'd loved.

The man who'd walked away without a backward glance.

Ridiculous to think it was impossible that he was behind the murder. She needed to believe it, needed, for Josh's sake, for it to be true. Lloyd had certainly had no shortage of enemies and Roberto Mendoza was maybe just one more.

She glanced up to see Gahan watching her. "Where do Josh and I stand?"

"Everything that you owned previously, you still own. For now, anyway."

She felt a little flutter of disquiet. "What do you mean, for now?"

"Well, it all comes down to what you can bring in." He made a dismissive gesture at the papers before him. "Your debt load is considerable."

"You mean Lloyd's debt load is—"

"*Your* debt load," he corrected pointedly. "You're responsible for all debts held by you as a couple and as I'm sure you know, you owe quite a lot."

But she hadn't known. She hadn't known at all. "What do you mean we owe quite a lot? There's the house and a few years left to pay on Lloyd's car, but that should be it. We own my car outright and we bought Josh's car used."

"I'm not talking about those kind of debts, although your second mortgage is certainly hurting you. It's the credit card debt that's the worst, the commercial properties that you've borrowed against."

"Second mortgage? Commercial properties?" Her head was spinning. "But we paid off our credit card every month."

"Credit cards," he emphasized. "Several of them are maxed out, particularly the airline miles card."

"That wasn't our account, that was for Lloyd's business," she protested.

"He may have used it for business expenses, but it's a private card, Mrs. Fredericks. It was never transferred to Fredericks Financial. And you're responsible for it."

She resisted the urge to put her hands over her ears. Lloyd had never let her be involved in their personal finances, had become hostile and abusive any time she'd ever asked. Now, she understood why.

Consciously seeking calm, she let out a breath. "All right, how do I go about getting a draw from the trust fund to cover it?"

"Trust fund?" Gahan looked at her as though she'd just announced she was flying to the moon. "Your trust fund is gone."

"Gone?" She stared. "It can't be gone. It was twenty-five million dollars, for God's sakes. The income alone was more than a million dollars a year."

"I guess a million doesn't go as far as it used to," he said. "You spent down the capital about three years ago."

There was a roaring in her ears. "I didn't spend anything. I didn't…good Lord, it's gone? *All* of it?" Even she could hear the faint note of panic in her voice.

"The right investments—or the wrong ones—can eat up that kind of money pretty quick. Lloyd wasn't nearly as smart about finance as he liked to think he was. He wanted to be a player. Sometimes when you play, you win," Gahan said, "and sometimes you lose. Lloyd lost more than most."

"But he had money of his own."

Gahan studied her for a long moment, seeming to go through an internal debate. Finally, he let out a quiet breath. "The Fredericks family has been broke for years.

Fredericks Financial has been struggling—the credit crunch hit it hard and it was significantly overextended. You and Lloyd would have been broke, but he was good at arranging loans. He guaranteed the last one through your son."

Disbelief gave way to anger. "That's impossible. Josh only inherited his money a week ago. Lloyd would never have used Josh's trust fund to secure anything."

"Lloyd did," Gahan said simply. His intercom buzzed and he pressed a button on his console. "Give me five minutes, Colleen," he said, and turned back to Frannie. "Mrs. Fredericks, I'm sorry that all of this has come as such a shock, but there's really nothing I can do. My advice to you is that you talk to your family, arrange a loan. If they can secure your debts, you have as good a chance of moving forward as anyone." He rose and put out his hand. "I wish you luck."

Frannie left the office in a daze, scarcely feeling her feet as they slid along the carpet. It didn't feel real, nothing felt real.

Twenty-five million dollars, gone. Her father had left it to her when she was born, then died mere months later. She had no memory of him. But he'd loved her and wanted to provide for her, leaving the trust for her care, with the bulk to be awarded upon the birth of her first child. It was, she realized now, probably the real reason Lloyd had married her.

And now the money was gone, and so was Lloyd.

She touched her cheek, remembering the times he'd lashed out with his tongue. And, less frequently, his hands. He was gone and only she and Josh remained, trying to move forward through the morass he'd left behind. She pressed the elevator call button, the sound ringing in her ears.

* * *

"They grilled you for two days without pressing charges?" Jorge glanced over at Roberto as they walked through the police station parking lot to his car. "That's some lawyer you got. Or, excuse me, some lawyer I got you."

Roberto barely registered the joke. He glanced around, squinting at the sun and despising himself as he realized that he was looking for Frannie. "No charges— at least that's what they tell me right now. Of course, that could change."

"Why would they let you out if they were going to charge you?"

He shrugged. "Maybe they're waiting to get more information. Maybe they want to watch what I do."

"That could be a little paranoid, big brother." Jorge pulled out his keys.

"And it could be reality. It doesn't seem like they know much at this point."

"Well, they'll have to watch for a long time, because there's nothing to find unless you did it. Which I'm assuming you didn't."

Roberto opened the door and slid into Jorge's glossy black Jaguar. "You ever think about putting your money into your business instead of pricey toys?"

"We're in different industries. In your line of work, a ride is just to get you to the lumberyard. In my part of the world, it's a branding statement." Jorge started the engine. "You didn't answer the question."

"I wasn't aware I was being asked one."

Jorge studied him a moment, then smiled faintly. He backed out of the parking slot and headed for the exit.

And for the first time in two days, Roberto felt like he could draw a real breath.

"You want to tell me again how you landed yourself in the hot seat? I mean, didn't you think we had enough trouble going already? You don't even know Frannie Fredericks." Jorge flicked a glance at Roberto. "Do you?"

There had been a time he'd thought he'd known her, but he'd found out he was wrong. He'd left her behind long ago—she wasn't why he'd returned to Red Rock. So why had he been idiot enough to go charging to the rescue? "I met her the summer I worked at the ranch."

And that quickly he was back to that day all those years ago, watching Fredericks stomp off and Frannie ride out like the wind, fury in every line of her body. When Roberto had caught up to her, he'd seen the tears. Somehow, comfort had turned to something more, to connection, to revelation. They'd lain down together in the soft grass under one of the spreading red oaks. And he'd shown her what making love was truly like, learned it for the first time himself.

"You knew her at the ranch? Is that why they held you? For chrissakes, Roberto, that was what, twenty years ago?"

"Close enough."

He stopped at a traffic light. "What makes them think that's remotely relevant? She wasn't even the one who got dead, he was."

"And he had pictures of me on his cell phone."

Jorge stared at him. "What the hell? Why would he do that?"

Roberto smiled faintly. "Maybe he thought I was cute."

"Even if there were pictures of you, anyone could have taken them. He could have taken them by accident.

There's no way they can say that means anything. Any decent lawyer would shred that."

Jorge's lawyer had. But there'd been no explanation for the text message sent to Cindy Fortune: "Is this who I think it is?"

"What I want to know is what you thought you were doing by barging into the middle of this," Jorge said. "They're cops, they know their jobs. You should have left it up to them instead of trying to be some kind of hero—"

"What if she didn't do it, Jorge?" Roberto demanded. "What if it had been Sierra or Gloria or Christina sitting in that jail and I knew something that could get them off the hook? Would you still be pushing me to stay out of it?"

There was a beat of silence. "What happened between you and Frannie Fredericks?" Jorge asked quietly.

"Nothing," Roberto snapped.

Jorge drove in silence for a few minutes. "You know, even if a lot of nothing went on between you two, you don't need to take the fall for her."

Roberto turned to stare out the window. "I appreciate you helping line up the lawyer."

"You never have been any good at taking advice."

"You'd think you would have figured that out by now." Faint amusement replaced the irritation in Roberto's words.

Jorge grinned. "I'm what you call an optimist."

"How are Mama and Papa?" Roberto asked.

Jorge's grin faded. "Not good, especially when the cops showed up asking questions. I thought Pop was going to throw one of them through the window."

"Blond guy, brush cut?" Roberto asked.

Jorge nodded.

"McCaskill. Too bad he didn't, the guy could have used it. Hey, pull in at the bank, will you? I need some cash."

He was quick in the ATM. The enclosed space felt way too much like the cell he'd called home for the past two days. He just needed to be out; he needed to be moving. The hours of police interrogation had been bad enough; given Jorge's behavior, it didn't appear that the questions were likely to stop anytime soon.

Impatiently, Roberto pushed open the door that led out to the street. And came to an abrupt stop.

The recognition was instantaneous. It didn't matter that nearly two decades had passed since they'd stood in each other's presence. It was Frannie, he was as certain of that as he was of his own name.

She'd been striding down the sidewalk, not paying attention, but she was paying attention now, eyes wide, lips parted. They studied one another, taking a measure of what the years had wrought.

He tried not to let the shock show. "Frannie." It was her and yet not her. She'd changed so much, the vibrant young girl washed away. Once, she'd been laughing and mischievous, riding along beside him, playing jokes, teasing. Now, she was pale, cool and sophisticated to the point of almost not being there. There was a brittleness to her, a vulnerability hovering around her mouth that about broke his heart.

"Roberto." It was shock that had snatched the breath from her lungs, Frannie told herself, adrenaline that had her heart hammering. Surprise, nothing more, but still she kept staring, drinking in the sight of him, unable to look away.

And unable to keep from remembering that long-ago afternoon.

It was Roberto as she had known him and yet not: more lines, a wariness about the eyes. His dark hair was cropped short now, not long as it had been. Something about him had always made her think of a nineteenth-century bandit riding the border, tough and reckless. There was a strength, an uncompromising hardness in his face, yet in the Roberto she had known, that could soften into easy approachability when a smile curved his mouth, a mouth she knew was capable of passion and tenderness.

Frannie gave herself a mental shake. Hadn't she thought about this moment over and over again across the years, the dismissive glance, the cutting comment, the artful put-down? There had been a time she'd hated him. There had been a time he'd deserved it. Any sane person would think he deserved it now. Now, when he'd possibly murdered her husband. Now, when he'd possibly been the one to set her free. She straightened her shoulders. "I didn't know you were out."

"For now," he said briefly. "And you? They dropped the charges?"

"Not quite. They released me on my own recognizance."

"That's only because they don't want to admit they were wrong without another suspect. You've got nothing to worry about. You'll be all right."

"Of course. Everything's going to be fine." It was a lie. Everything was falling down around her ears, she could be back in jail any minute; someone, maybe the man before her, had murdered her husband. Yet she stood there in the sunshine as though she was just having an afternoon chat with an old acquaintance, mouthing platitudes, conditioned so well over the years not to feel that she'd maybe forgotten how.

And yet she couldn't stop herself from reacting to him, no matter how little sense it made. Maybe you never really forgot the first man who moved you.

Even if it had all been an illusion.

She swallowed. "Are you back to stay?"

"For now. The cops have me on the same leash as you. We're still trying to figure out who set the fires, I've got to finish some renovations on Red, and there are my parents to take care of, and Frannie—"

"What?"

He stared down at her. "I'm sorry about your husband."

How was it she wasn't?

Frannie shook her head like a dog shaking off water. "I have to go." She moved blindly past him toward where Josh had pulled up to the curb, his car idling as he waited for her, coming to pick her up after a visit to his girlfriend.

She got into the car, consciously not looking back.

Josh wasn't so subtle. He shot a glance over his shoulder at Roberto. "Who is that guy?"

"Someone I used to know a long, long time ago," she said.

And only then did she begin to tremble.

Chapter 3

The sun had long since set when Roberto stretched out on the couch, a Scotch at his elbow, a magazine propped up on his knees. He could hear the rush of the wind outside, the restless tapping of branches against the windows. He looked at the page, not registering the words, thinking only of Frannie. How many times over the years had he imagined her face? How many times had he thought he'd heard her voice?

He was grateful he was staying in the mother-in-law's addition to his parents' adobe, a separate space with its own entrance, affording him privacy where he could at last think about what had come to pass.

Funny how the two days he'd spent in police custody seemed like a flash, but the time he'd stood talking to Frannie—a minute? Two?—stretched out to become all-consuming. And yet he couldn't for the life of him figure out what he felt.

For a time after he'd left Red Rock all those years ago, he'd drifted, picking up work when he ran out of money. Picking up women, too. But time after time, night after night, he'd filled his hands with warm, willing female flesh, and found it wanting because it wasn't the right flesh, because it wasn't the right female.

Because it wasn't Frannie.

And he'd grown to hate her because he could never get away from the shadow of memory. All it would take was a whiff of scent, the sound of some stranger's laughter on the breeze to bring it all back. Because she was there, always there in the back of his mind, like a splinter that had worked its way so deep that the body could only form scar tissue around it. And part of him knew that no matter how much he might curse her inconstancy, her fickleness, her betrayal, that splinter of her would always remain somewhere inside him.

He'd settled, finally, in Denver, thrown himself into building a successful construction business. A man could make a million, then more when work was all he focused on. There had been women, of course, women whose laughter brought a smile to his eyes. But they never shared his house. And they never lasted, because eventually they ran into that scar tissue, that place inside him that could never be theirs.

He'd seen enough of the world since he'd left Red Rock to know that disappointment lay around every corner. He'd just learned it a little younger than most, and for that, perhaps, he should've thanked her. She'd helped him grow a skin of hardness and cynicism that had served him well over the ensuing years.

And he was full of crap, because all he could do was remember her face and feel an impotent fury at the thought of what might have been. But then what was he supposed to have expected from a young girl who'd grown up with wealth and privilege? A young girl who'd never been tested, a young girl who took the easy way because the easy way was all she'd ever known?

Except that was crap, too. He knew some of what she'd been through; he knew it hadn't been easy. So why, why had she thrown everything he'd given her of himself back in his face? Why had she cast aside everything they might have been together for a lifetime of unhappiness with an SOB like Lloyd Fredericks?

And why, after all of it, did he still want her?

In a burst of fury, he sat up and slapped the magazine down on the coffee table.

In time with the sound of the impact came a sharp rap on the outside door. Roberto frowned. Almost eleven o'clock. Jorge had taken to assuming he could come by whenever he liked, but this was taking it too far. Roberto wasn't in the mood for any more questions and it was time to tell Jorge so.

He crossed to the door and yanked it open. Only to see Frannie standing there.

"What the…"

She pushed past him, striding into the room without waiting for an invitation, a little gust swirling in after her. "What are you doing here?" she demanded, whirling on him. "Why did you come back?" Her eyes blazed blue, her hair flew around, full of static electricity from the wind. There was something of the witch in her then, something wild and uncontrolled. And her energy and agitation whipped up his own.

He closed the door. "You always just blast into people's homes?"

"You left. Why didn't you just stay gone?"

"What makes you think that's any of your business?" he countered.

"I don't need you here. I don't want you."

"And I don't want you. I came back because my family needed me here. It doesn't all revolve around you, you know."

"I learned a long time ago that nothing about you revolved around me," she retorted. "But what I don't understand is why you decided to get mixed up with Lloyd. All these fires, these cryptic notes floating around? Is that you?" she demanded, taking a step closer with each word until she was just inches away from him.

"Me?" He stared at her incredulously. "You think I'm behind all of this? Setting a fire at my parents' restaurant?"

"I don't know what you're capable of. I obviously never did. A man's been murdered and they had you in jail over it."

He turned away and reached for his glass of Scotch. "In case you've forgotten, *chica,* they had you in jail, too."

"You can't possibly think I killed him."

"You make a better suspect than I do."

"You know I didn't do it," Frannie snapped.

"I've been wrong about you before. But yes, I do." He took a swallow of the Scotch and set the glass down. "And just for the record, I didn't kill Lloyd, either. But I may have seen who did."

Was it his imagination or did she tense? "Is that why they arrested you?"

"They never put me under arrest. They were just asking questions because I came across what appears to be the murder weapon. Which is what got you out. You ought to be thanking me."

She raised her chin. "I didn't need you. They would have let me out eventually."

"They had you in jail for two weeks. When, exactly, were they going to let you loose? Especially when you wouldn't even deny it."

"I couldn't," she burst out.

"Why the hell not?"

She didn't answer him; instead she paced away, shaking her head.

"Why did all of this have to happen? Everything was going to be better, I had it all planned. Josh was going to go off to college, I was going to leave Lloyd. Everything was going to be okay, finally. But then it all started flying apart, and on top of everything else, you have to come back." Frannie rounded on him. "Why are you here?" she cried, pushing at his chest. "It was done, it was over. Why didn't you just stay gone?"

He caught her wrists. "You would've liked that, wouldn't you? After all, I don't have a multimillion-dollar trust fund or belong to the country club. You wanted me gone practically as soon as we got together."

"How can you say that? You lied to me. My God, one minute you were talking about how much you loved me and what you wanted for the future, and the next you broke and ran—without even telling me, without even a note. What happened, Roberto, did it get too real for you?" Her voice rose. "Did you get scared when you realized you might have to stand behind all the pretty talk?"

"I ran?" He echoed incredulously. "What the hell are you talking about? I would have done anything for you. Anything," he repeated, his face a fraction of an inch from hers.

"Then why didn't you?"

"Because you sent your mother out to run me off." He'd been more naive than he'd had a right to be, thinking their feelings for each other would be enough. They'd ridden back to the ranch house that long ago evening, suffused with quiet happiness.

Or at least he had.

But they'd come back to a house lit up and a strange car in the courtyard, and the next night instead of Frannie coming to meet him as she'd promised, there had been Cindy.

Love, a life together. To Roberto, it had been simple but Cindy had made it simpler—clear out or get thrown in jail for statutory rape, with Frannie's testimony. He'd been a mistake. Frannie was done with him. The words had stirred only defiance—until he'd looked up from the dark barnyard to see Frannie staring down at them from an upstairs window.

"You sat up there and watched," he said furiously. "Don't act like you didn't know about it. I told her I wanted to marry you and she laughed and said you'd never marry me in a million years. You watched the whole thing."

And worst of all, she'd turned away.

Frannie's mouth fell open. "I watched the whole thing? Roberto, she gave me a note that said you weren't coming. I was inside with the lights on, I didn't see anything except my own reflection. And by the time I got out, you were gone."

"What was I supposed to do?" he demanded. "What was there for me here? Jail? I left because you gave me no reason to stay. And I stayed gone because…because I couldn't take seeing you again."

They stood, staring at each other as the enormity of their words sank in. The ticks of the clock on the mantle sounded very loud in the silence.

"That's it?" Frannie whispered. "It was all my *mother?* This is nuts, Roberto. This kind of thing happens in soap operas, not real life. Do you hear me?" Her voice rose, flirting with hysteria. "You're trying to tell me that it was all just a misunderstanding, that she played us for almost twenty years? Sweet Jesus." She dropped down onto the couch and buried her face in her hands.

Beside her, the cushions gave as Roberto sat next to her. "I don't know what's sane or insane at this point," he said softly. "I know what I was told, and I know what I did. And maybe we were too young, maybe it wouldn't have lasted, but I do know I meant everything I said to you that day, and I was ready to tell the whole world."

Frannie raised her face from her hands and turned to look at him. "Don't tell me that. I don't want to hear that." Because she couldn't bear to think of how different her life could have been.

Roberto reached out, his fingertips as gentle against her chin as a butterfly landing, and turned her to face him. "I never stopped thinking about you, Frannie. Never once. And I guess that makes me an idiot, because you married another guy and had a kid with him."

"We were so young," she whispered. "What we were feeling wasn't real. It would never have worked."

"Maybe, maybe not. Maybe this is all about another chance."

"How can we have another chance? Time changes people. I'm not the same person I was. Neither are you. That Frannie and Roberto are gone. What they felt is gone."

"You think so?" he murmured. "Let's find out."

And he leaned in to press his mouth to hers.

So many years had passed, each exacting its toll, changing the body, slowing the mind. How was it, then, that this was so familiar, so true? Nearly two decades had passed and she'd forgotten a million and one things in that time. But she remembered his kisses, oh, she remembered his kisses.

Even before his mouth settled on hers, her lips knew the touch of his—the softness, the warmth, the gentleness that he always brought. Lloyd might have said words of love in the beginning, but Roberto had made her feel them. With every touch, she felt cherished, wanted, enveloped in warmth. As though she were a sunflower turning toward the light, she felt herself blossoming.

How many times had he thought of this? How many times had he imagined the sweet scent of her, the soft coolness of her fingertips stroking his cheek? There had been other women, but always, inevitably, he'd found himself comparing them to his memories of Frannie.

And always, inevitably, he'd found them wanting.

He'd told himself that it was all his imagination, that no one woman could possibly feel so right. He'd told himself he was an idiot to even think it. He'd just gotten caught up in the same memory, month after month, year after year, and year after year it changed, like some internal game of telephone until memory transformed into a fantasy impossible for any reality to match.

That was what he'd told himself.

And in the moment his lips touched hers, he knew that he'd been wrong.

She was all that he remembered and more—soft and fragrant and sweet. They fit, purely and simply. Her mouth felt so utterly right against his, every touch, every move. Her hair spilled over his hand. And as he heard his pulse roaring in his ears, he understood afresh how the twenty-year-old boy he'd been could have returned from that afternoon under the red oaks utterly and completely thunderstruck with love for her.

He raised his head. Frannie stared up at him, her eyes huge and dark.

He slipped his arm around her. "I guess we've got our answer."

"No." She shook her head to clear away the haze. Her heart hammered in her ears. Life with Lloyd had been a battle for survival, but she had just about started to find the strength to start again. And now, to find herself so utterly taken with the barest brush of Roberto's lips over hers was terrifying. "No," she said again. "I don't think we've got any answer at all. Just more questions and complications."

"You're trembling." He held up her hand. "You call that a complication?"

"Yes." She shifted away from him. "Right now everything is crazy. I can't keep up. There's too much going on. The fires, the notes, Cindy's crash, Lloyd getting killed, I'm in jail, you're in jail, I'm broke, we're—"

"Wait a minute, back up. You're broke? I thought Lloyd was rich."

"So did I." She closed her eyes a moment and let out a long breath. "It's been a day for surprises. I met with my lawyer this morning and found out that my trust fund has been cleaned out, courtesy of Lloyd. I'm in debt up to my eyeballs."

"How did he manage that?"

She shrugged. "My fault, I guess. I was seventeen when we married, I didn't know much of anything about anything. I knew that I got the main bequest of my trust fund when I had my first child, but Lloyd managed our finances."

"And later?"

"He ran everything. If I ever asked him for details, even to see a stock statement or a tax return, he got furious. I gave up control without even a fight. And I guess once that happens, you can never really get it back."

"The best defense is a good offense. He didn't want you to know what he was up to."

"And it worked. I sat there in that office today listening to the lawyer talk about mortgages on office buildings and rental properties I didn't even know we owned."

"Don't beat yourself up. It's understandable."

"It's pathetic," she burst out, rising to pace. "I'm a grown woman and I barely even know my bank balance. He kept me in the dark, cleaned me out, and *I* let him do it."

"You're not to blame for it, he is. But he's gone now. Everything's going to be all right." Roberto came up behind her. "You and Josh will get through this, you'll see."

Frannie sighed. "Yes, I'll get through this. But I'm not taking money from Josh. His trust fund is for college, to get him started on life. I'm not going to siphon it off like Lloyd and my mother did to me." And she burned at the thought of asking anyone in the Fortune family for money. After a lifetime of watching Cindy beg, the idea of coming to them with her hand out made Frannie cringe. "I'll get through this," she said again. And maybe if she repeated it enough times, a miracle would happen and it would be true.

"*We'll* get through this." Roberto slipped his arms around her. "Whatever help you need, you've got it."

She turned to look at him. "I can't take your money."

"Sure you can."

"You don't understand. It's more than two million dollars."

To her surprise, he laughed. "Frannie, you don't know what I do for a living, do you? I own the second-biggest commercial construction and real-estate development company in Denver. I've got plenty of money, enough to help you take care of whatever problems you've got. More to the point, I can probably figure out how to make you a profit on those commercial properties that Lloyd's stuck you with. Don't worry. Leave it to me, I can fix it."

She moved away from him with a frown. "Haven't you been listening at all?"

"Enough to know we can take care of the details later."

"No."

"What?"

"No," she said again, her words stronger now.

"You mind telling me why, exactly, you're turning down help?" He kept his voice even, but she saw the little flare of temper in his eyes.

"Roberto, I appreciate the offer, I truly do. But I just found out that the man I've been married to for the past nineteen years took me for everything I was worth while I just sat idly by."

"I'm not going to con you."

"That's not the point. Or maybe it is. I haven't seen you for decades, I don't know you at all. And I don't know what we're doing here right now. We were kids when we were together before. Being in love at seventeen isn't real."

His eyes were hot and dark. "It felt pretty damned real to me."

"But that was at the time. I'm not that girl anymore

and you're not that boy. For all we know, we could spend another hour together and start driving each other nuts."

"Judging by that kiss, I'd say that's a given."

"You know what I mean." She threw him an impatient look. "I just got out of a horror of a marriage. I can't turn around and dive into something else with you. With anyone. There's just too much going on."

"So that's it?"

"I don't know." Her voice rose in frustration. "I can't decide this right now. I'm not made of stone, I felt something here when we kissed, but what does that signify? Maybe what happened tonight just means that we got back that afternoon we spent together. Maybe it means a whole lot more, I can't say." She shook her head. "If anything's going to happen between us, we have to get to know each other all over again, don't you see? I can't just throw up my hands and turn the reins over to you. First it was my mom controlling me, and then Lloyd. I'm on my own now for the first time in my life and I'm going to take care of myself. I've got to."

"I'm not Lloyd Fredericks."

"I know that, believe me, but it doesn't matter. I've spent so much of my life reacting to him, following his orders, living within his boundaries." She brushed back her hair. She'd worn it long because Lloyd had preferred it that way. "He didn't want me to go to college, so I didn't go. He didn't want me to work, so now I'm thirty-six and I don't have a clue how to make a living. For all these years I've had nothing but Josh. There were days that I felt like I wasn't even there at all and *I can't live like that anymore.*" Her voice rose in a passionate torrent.

"I've got to figure out who I am. I've got to learn to stand on my own two feet, and I can't do that if

I'm leaning on you. And if it means that working off Lloyd's debts takes me the rest of my life, then that's what that means. I have to do it myself. I can't let you take care of me."

"I didn't make the offer with strings attached."

"I know you didn't. But you have to understand, I need to get past this on my own." She blinked. "Before I can possibly be of any use to you or to myself, I have to figure things out. I need to know what I'm capable of. And I need to get Lloyd out of my head."

"I thought you didn't love him," Roberto said flatly.

Frannie gave a ragged laugh. "Are you kidding? I spent most of our marriage hating him—when I wasn't hating myself. And you. It's all a mess, Roberto. I'm a mess. You deserve better."

"Let me decide that."

"I just… I need some time, can you understand that? I just need time." She stepped in and pressed her lips to his cheek, then turned to the door.

Roberto followed. "You're going to leave, just like that?"

Frannie's eyes softened. "Not just like that. What happened here has changed everything. And even if there's nothing left once this is done, I'll always be grateful to you."

"It's not gratitude I'm looking for."

"Will you take friendship, instead?" She tipped her head. "Look at it as kind of a lease-to-buy program."

And as she'd hoped, he smiled.

"Whatever you need right now, you've got. And I'll take friendship." He caught her hand in his. "For now."

Chapter 4

"What the hell is going on here?" Hands on her hips, Cindy Fortune surveyed the confusion of boxes scattered around Frannie's living room and foyer.

Frannie went back to the box she'd been packing with books when Cindy had knocked on the front door. "Getting the place ready to sell."

"In this market? You'll lose your shirt, and this is way too sweet a house to give away. You and Josh could get lost in here. Hell, I could move in for a month and you'd never notice." A speculative look entered her eyes. "Maybe I will."

She kicked a box out of the way and sprawled on the couch, her brassy blond hair spilling over the back, long legs stretched over the coffee table. The ravages of time didn't stand a chance against the determination of Cindy Fortune, teased, Botoxed, lifted and liposuctioned to within an inch of her life. Seventy was the new forty, she was fond of saying, and she considered herself living proof.

As long as you didn't look too close into her eyes. Something hid there behind the false cheer—something that veered perilously between weariness and despair. But Cindy didn't like to think about that too often. Easier on the whole to toss down a drink or three and forget.

Frannie sealed her box and thumped down the tape dispenser. "Mother, what are you doing here?" Frannie had never even seen Cindy out of bed before ten, let alone ambulatory.

Cindy blinked. "Well, to congratulate you on getting out. I told those idiots at the police department that you couldn't have murdered Lloyd Fredericks, even if the pipsqueak did have it coming."

"I'm sure that was a lot of help." Cindy Fortune making a scene at the police station. No wonder they'd held Frannie so long.

"Anyway, I haven't seen you in a while so I wanted to stop by."

"That's right, you never did come to see me the whole time I was in jail, did you?" Frannie's voice was cool.

Cindy coughed. "Hey, well, you know me, kid. Jails aren't my style."

"Except for your DUIs," Frannie agreed, ignoring Cindy's sharp stare. Instead, she brought a group of framed photos over to the coffee table and set them on a stack of packing paper. Pushing her hair back behind her ears, she picked up the top picture to wrap it. It was Josh at his first Christmas, surrounded by gaily colored holiday paper and ribbons, laughing against her.

"I don't see why you have to put all that stuff away," Cindy groused, but Frannie noticed she didn't offer to help.

"Photographs are distracting. They make the buyers think of the current owners rather than imagining themselves happy in the home." She set the wrapped picture in the box and reached for the next. Times changed, she thought, glancing at the shot of her and Lloyd and a ten-year-old Josh on horses at a dude ranch in Montana. The smiles had all become a little strained, with a distinct hint of annoyance in Lloyd's eyes.

But it was on the next photo that Frannie's hands faltered. It was from a luau on a Hawaiian vacation taken just a few years before. Lloyd's eyes were focused off to the side—at the hula dancer he'd been flirting with, no doubt—Josh stood between them with a bored, sulky pout and Frannie...

Frannie looked lost, even in paradise.

How was it that she hadn't seen it before? Had she just lived with unhappiness for so long that she'd grown numb to it?

Her hands tightened on the frame.

"Anyway, if the place is too big, get another one," Cindy was going on. "No reason to unload this one."

"Yes, there is. I'm broke."

"Because you could just get another—*what?*"

"I'm broke, Mother, thanks to Lloyd. Remember Lloyd? The man I was supposed to marry because he'd take care of me? Instead of Roberto Mendoza?"

"Roberto who?"

The words came out a beat too late, a shade too innocent, and if she'd had any last doubt, Frannie knew now that it was all true. "How dare you," she said in a low voice.

"What?" Cindy asked weakly.

"I said how dare you." She stood. "Don't try to pretend you don't know what I'm talking about. I loved him and he wanted to marry me and you knew it." Her voice rose. "You ran him off like he was trash, and you made him think I was a part of it."

Cindy swallowed. "I... I did what was best for you."

"What was best? Look at this picture. Look at it," Frannie demanded. "Do I look happy to you? Do I look like I've had a good life?"

Cindy's gaze skated away. "That Mendoza boy would never have stood by you or been able to take care of you, especially when you were—"

"When I was what? Pregnant with another man's child?"

"Yes," Cindy whispered. "I did what I had to. You needed someone to provide for you. You were in trouble and Lloyd had a promising future."

"So promising he bankrupted me," Frannie said bitterly. "The Fredericks have been broke for years, apparently. I guess I was the last to know. Or you were. Lloyd blew through my trust fund and left me with more debt than you can imagine. So if you came here to hit me up for a loan or a place to stay, you're barking up the wrong tree." The words dripped with scorn. "The two of you were quite a pair. You bled off all the initial money when I was growing up and then he took care of the rest. And don't even think for a minute you'll get a penny from Josh. I'll make sure of it."

"Frannie—"

"Get out of here, Mother." She rounded on her. "I mean it. I can't even look at you right now."

"But…" Cindy protested. "Roberto Mendoza was just a man. He didn't matter. And it was so long ago. It would never have lasted."

"You made sure of that, didn't you?" Frannie's voice shook with anger. "Why leave it up to chance when you can lie? Especially when you'll never have to live with the consequences."

"It was for your own good," Cindy defended.

"For my own good?" Frannie repeated incredulously.

"It was for your good, it always is." Whirling, she flung the Hawaiian picture into the fireplace, the glass shattering into shards.

Cindy jumped. "Frannie. I… I only…"

Abruptly, Frannie's fury was gone and in its place was only exhaustion. "Just go, Mother. Now." And she turned to the kitchen, leaving Cindy standing there.

Frannie had never been any good at fights. Part, she supposed, of why Lloyd had kept the upper hand. He'd relished them, going for blood every time. She'd always felt faintly sick from the roiling emotion, as though anger and hostility were toxic fumes that could overwhelm.

So she drifted from room to room after Cindy left, feeling shaky and unsettled, not finishing anything. Instead of continuing with the books and knickknacks, she found herself stopping at the long refectory table in the kitchen to pack up some of the dozens of albums of photographs she'd taken. But packing them turned into leafing through them, losing herself in the images the same way she lost herself behind the lens.

Next to riding her quarterhorse mare Daisy, photography had always been Frannie's truest escape. Lloyd might have done everything he could to block her from getting an education, but in this area alone, he hadn't managed to stop her. She'd joined a local darkroom co-op to perfect her processing skills, quietly taken what he'd ridiculed as hobby classes. She hadn't minded; she'd welcomed his derision—as long as he was making fun of her, he wasn't paying attention.

He'd never registered that she carried a camera with her nearly everywhere she went. He'd never heard about the handful of local exhibitions she'd been involved in. And he wouldn't have dreamed of escorting her to any event given by her friends, so he'd never discovered that she'd begun to photograph weddings and christenings. Outside of Josh, it was one of the few aspects of her life that brought her joy.

Too bad she couldn't make a living at it.

Or could she?

Eyes narrowed, Frannie began sifting through the images afresh, this time looking at them with an independent eye. She had a substantial body of work and a large amount of amateur experience. Could she turn that into a portfolio, put the word around to get work? Was it worth trying?

Could she afford not to?

A sound had her glancing over to see Josh walk into the kitchen. He was growing up, his once blond hair darkening, the face of the man he would become beginning to emerge. Somehow, when she hadn't been paying attention, the days had turned into months, the months into years and he'd become an adult. Just days before, she'd photographed his graduation. In another month or two, she'd be seeing him off to college.

Frannie swallowed against the sudden tightness in her throat. "Did you sleep all right?" He looked tired now, she realized as she asked, drawn somehow, thinner in his jeans and muscle shirt.

He shrugged. "Something woke me up. Anyway, it doesn't matter. Lyndsey and I are going to the lake today."

"Again?"

Ignoring her, he walked over to study the photos she'd laid out. "Hey, those are my graduation shots." Interested now, he sat. "Man, you caught it," he said, pointing to a shot of the class flinging their mortarboards into the air. "And I like this one of everybody lined up in their robes with no one's faces showing. It looks kind of like abstract art or something."

And then he fell silent.

Frannie didn't have to ask what picture he was looking at—she knew. It was a shot of him with his girlfriend, Lyndsey Pollack. Waiflike and blond, Lyndsey clutched Josh's hands in hers and gazed up into his face with that singular intensity that always made Frannie a little uneasy. Granted, teenage girls tended toward the dramatic, but Lyndsey seemed more prone to it than most. Never in all the time the two had been dating, as far as Frannie knew, had a day gone by without the girl calling Josh at least two or three times.

He pulled out his phone, and Frannie suppressed a sigh as she heard the simulated click of the device's camera, followed by the tap of his fingers on the keyboard.

"Isn't it a little early to start texting?"

She heard the bleat his phone made for an incoming message, followed by more tapping. Then he glanced over. "Sorry, Mom, what did you say?"

She shook her head. "Never mind."

"Lyndsey's coming by in a few." He went over to the counter to pour himself some coffee, doctoring it liberally with cream and sugar. "She wants to know if you've got any more pictures of us at graduation. She's making a collage."

"I'll look." Frannie watched him walk back over to sit at the table. "You're going to the lake. This is the third time this week, isn't it?"

"Yeah."

"Don't you think you're spending a little too much time together? She's only seventeen. And you're going off to college next year."

"Maybe." He took a swallow of his coffee.

"Maybe what?"

"Maybe I'm going to college. Or maybe not. I've been thinking about sticking around here, instead. Take some classes at Red Rock Tech."

Frannie stared. "You're talking about giving up a full-ride scholarship to Texas A&M for a community college? And just when did you decide this?"

He flushed. "A couple of weeks ago."

"With Lyndsey."

"Yeah."

"It's not Lyndsey's decision."

A stubborn light entered his eyes. "Maybe it is. We're together."

"Josh…" Frannie bit back a sigh. "You're only eighteen."

"That's right," he shot back. "I am eighteen. That means I'm an adult. You're still treating me like I'm some middle-schooler with a crush."

Frannie blinked at her usually easygoing son, the tension in his face, the sharpness in his voice. "Take it easy. I know you're an adult. But trust me, I was eighteen, too, and I can tell you for a fact that you don't know nearly as much right now as you think you do. Going to college will open up your whole life—change it in so many ways."

"Yeah, like taking me away from Lyndsey," he retorted. "That's what this is all about, isn't it? You and Dad have been trying to break us up since practically the day we got together. You don't take us seriously. You've never taken us seriously."

For the hundredth time, Frannie cursed Lloyd. They'd shared misgivings over Lyndsey's intensity, but true to form, Lloyd had tackled Josh head-on. And not surprisingly, the more he pressured Josh to give up Lyndsey, the more hell-bent Josh was on sticking with her.

Frannie's instinct had been to gamble that Josh would eventually begin to chafe at Lyndsey's neediness. Now, though, with him threatening to give up his plans for a four-year college program—and she knew how quickly plans for community college could turn into dropping out—she had to say something.

"I'm not trying to break you and Lyndsey up, Josh. I'm just trying to get you to think about your future."

Josh's expression turned stormy. "This isn't about my future, it's about you not liking Lyndsey."

"I think Lyndsey is a lovely person," Frannie said carefully. But there was something about the girl that had made her uncomfortable from the beginning, an almost desperate drive to intertwine herself with Josh. Maybe Lyndsey was just an insecure high-school girl, but her expression in the photo had less a flavor of love than desperation. "Think about it, Josh. College Station is only a couple of hours away. If you go to A&M you can still be home on weekends and holidays and during the summer break. And who knows what happens after?"

He thumped down his coffee cup. "I've got a better idea. I start here and go to Red Rock Tech. Lyndsey and I can be together all the time and then we can go to Texas A&M later if we want to."

"But you'll lose your scholarship," Frannie protested.

"Who cares about the scholarship? I inherited my trust fund. I've got all the money I need."

All the money I need. "You're right," she responded. "You do have a lot of money now. And that means being more careful. You're going to have all sorts of people wanting a piece of you, coming to you with all kinds of deals to invest in. Or wanting to get involved."

He flushed an angry red. "Are you saying that Lyndsey's after me for my money? You're out of your mind. She didn't even know about it when we met."

"I'm just trying to get you to think about—"

"You're treating me like a little kid," he shouted, jolting to his feet. "Everything's changed, now. But you don't know what I'm dealing with, you don't know the spot I'm in and I've got to—"

The doorbell rang, interrupting the tirade. The silence rang.

Frannie's lips felt cold. "What have you done, Josh?" she whispered.

For a moment he stood, jaw working, and then he turned away. "I have to get this," he muttered. "Be there in a sec, Lyns," he called.

It couldn't be, Frannie thought numbly. He couldn't mean what it sounded like, he couldn't. She heard the snick of the dead bolt unfastening.

"Boy, you sure got here in a hurr—" Josh stopped. "Can I help you?" The words were flat and unfriendly.

"Is your mother here?"

Not the police again, Frannie prayed. She just didn't think she could take any more, not right now, not after all that had happened. She forced down the roil of emotions and headed toward the front door where Josh stood. It tugged her heart to see how protective he looked, holding it nearly closed, standing in the gap. He couldn't have done what she feared, not the boy she'd raised.

She stepped up behind him. "Who is it, Josh?"

And over his shoulder she saw Roberto Mendoza.

Nerves, pleasure and above all reassurance surged through her. It wasn't fair, not when she was still struggling to stand on her own feet. She couldn't afford to start leaning on someone. No matter how much she was tempted to.

Roberto wore jeans and boots and a snap-button denim shirt with the sleeves rolled up. With his black Stetson and his five o'clock shadow, he carried a flavor of, if not danger, then power and unpredictability, an ability to dominate any situation that came up.

No wonder Josh had gotten protective.

"You're the guy who was downtown yesterday," Josh asked, "weren't you? What do you want?"

"Josh," Frannie protested.

"You're not the only one who has to be careful," he shot back at her, then turned to Roberto. "In case you haven't heard, there's a lot going on around here right now. My mom and I are busy."

"Roberto, this is Josh, my son," Frannie said with a glare at Josh.

Roberto nodded. "He's right, you know. You do have to be careful." He stuck out his hand. "I'm Roberto Mendoza. My father runs Red and my uncle Ruben used to run the Double Crown. Your mom and I are old friends."

"Roberto Mendoza? The guy who—"

"Was helping out the police," Frannie interjected.

Josh gave him a swift, uneasy look. Behind them a horn sounded as Lyndsey drove up in her little red Toyota. "Josh," she called. "Come on."

Josh glanced between Roberto and Frannie, then grabbed his hat and backpack from the table by the door. "I've got to go."

"Josh, we have to finish this," Frannie began, but he was already bounding down the steps.

She let out a long breath and watched him get into the car.

Roberto studied her. "You okay?" he asked.

Frannie sighed. "I could use a cup of coffee. How about you?"

Chapter 5

Roberto knew he had no business coming over. She'd asked for space; by all rights, he should have given it to her. And he'd tried. He'd waited as many days as he could, but somehow that morning, he'd left the house to go to Red and instead found himself turning into her driveway.

"How did you find me?" Frannie asked as she stood back to let him in.

"Red Rock is a pretty small town. I made a good guess." Based on what he knew of Lloyd Fredericks, not Frannie. Certainly, the neighborhood wasn't the Frannie he remembered, this gated community of sprawling, pretentious, badly designed homes with security even a child could get around. In his case, he hadn't even needed a child. "A guy I went to high school with works the gate, so he let me in."

She was looking calmer, the high color fading from her cheeks.

"What's going on?" he asked.

She gestured at the packing mess. "I'm getting ready to put the house on the market. With luck, I'll make enough to pay down some of my debt."

"I wasn't talking about the boxes," he said quietly.

She shot him a hunted look. "Coffee first."

He trailed her into a kitchen that looked more like an operating theater with its glossy white cabinets and brushed-steel appliances. Hard, cold and soulless. Not Frannie, not even close. Then he glanced over the breakfront to see the photographs strewn over the kitchen table.

"Yours?"

At her nod, he walked over to get a closer look. There was a picture of a row of blooming cacti before a deep orange wall, a study in color and geometry and serenity. Underneath was a shot of groomsmen at a wedding. Instead of lining up stiffly, they'd gathered in a couple of pews of the church, some sprawling in the front row, some leaning over from behind, one standing. It felt like a moment captured in time rather than a staged picture. "Hey, some of these are pretty good."

"Gee, thanks." Her voice was dry as she reached into a cabinet to pull out a pair of mugs.

"No, I mean really good. You've got an eye for it."

She gave him a speculative look. "You think?"

"Yeah. Don't you?"

"Maybe," she said as she picked up the coffeepot. "I'm toying around with the idea of maybe trying to get a business going. You know, weddings, birthdays?"

"And graduations?" He held up the picture of Josh and Lyndsey.

She flushed. "I'm sorry you had to overhear that spat with Josh."

"I just caught the tail end. It happens. I remember having it out with my folks a few times at that age myself. Black," he added when she raised a mug with a questioning glance.

Frannie carried the coffee to the table. "Can you believe he's talking about giving up a full scholarship to Texas A&M for community college here so he can be close to his girlfriend?"

Based on what he'd felt for Frannie all those years ago, he could. "I guess you're not thrilled with the idea. Or with her."

Frannie sighed. "She wants to be with him every waking minute, share his every thought, even wear his clothes. Sometimes I feel like she just wants to, I don't know, absorb him."

"Sounds like high school to me."

"It's hard to explain. I just think they're too involved. They're still young. And don't look at me like that," she defended. "I'm fully aware of the irony. It's a different situation."

"But not to Josh."

"Of course not. It's part of what we were fighting about."

"Only part? You looked pretty upset when I got here."

She added sugar to her cup and stirred. "It's just all so crazy and it never stops coming. Every time I turn around it's something else. I was a widow, then a jailbird, then bankrupt and now I'm a single parent. Who knows what's next? I couldn't hear your voice clearly at the door. All I heard was someone asking for me. My first thought was that it was the police."

"Not likely."

"How can you say for sure?" she challenged. "Lloyd's murderer is still out there. They're still looking for him. What if they haul me back in? What if they decide to arrest you? What if they decide to arrest—"

"Who?"

She closed up. "Anyone. It doesn't matter."

"*Chica,* if there's anybody on earth it matters more to right now than you and me, I'd be hard-pressed to name them." Roberto reached out for her hand. "You never came out and told them you were innocent, even though you are. Why?"

She pulled away. "How did you know that?"

"Not much stays secret in Red Rock for long. Tell me."

"I can't. What if I'm wrong?"

"What if you're right?"

"I can't be," she said passionately.

"Frannie." His gaze was unwavering. "For both of our sakes, I need to know what you know."

She shook her head mutely. Her eyes swam in despair.

"Tell me," he said softly.

"Josh." She swallowed. "I'm afraid it's Josh."

But you don't know what's happened, you don't know the spot I'm in—

"You think Josh had something to do with Lloyd's murder?"

"No," she said too quickly. "It's impossible. There's no way he could kill his own father. It's just that…"

"What?" He kept his voice gentle.

"He and Lloyd have been—were—at each other's throats the last couple of months. They fought at the Spring Fling."

"That doesn't necessarily mean anything."

"It was right before Lloyd was killed. Roberto, he could have been the last person to see him alive."

"Do the police know this?"

She turned to look back at him, eyes shimmering with tears. "How could I tell them? He's my son."

"Just because they fought doesn't mean anything happened. Did anybody else hear it?"

"A potter at the Spring Fling named Reynaldo Velasquez. And Lily. My brother Ross talked to her about it. He's a private investigator." Frannie dashed away the tears impatiently. "I was working the raffle tent for the Fortune Foundation. I went to the back to get more tickets and I heard them."

"What were they fighting about?" Roberto asked, getting to his feet.

"They were a ways away, but they sounded absolutely furious. Josh told Lloyd he'd be sorry, that he'd make him sorry, and there was something in his voice, something I've never heard before…hard, almost violent." She shivered.

He crossed to her. "What happened?"

She shook her head. "There was so much noise from the dance and the carnival and people walking by. And I got called away to help some customers. By the time I got done, I couldn't hear the fight anymore. When I went around to the back to look for them, I found—" Her mouth moved, but no words came out.

Roberto reached out and gathered her to him, stroking her hair.

"I dream about it almost every night," she whispered, her breath hitching. "I'm leaning over him and there's moonlight and I can see his blood. There's so much of it. I can't get away from it, I can't get it off. It's everywhere, all over my face, and my clothes…my hands… everywhere." And she wept then, giving in to the horror.

Roberto swung her up into his arms and carried her over to the couch, holding her, aching for her, hating the fact that he couldn't protect her from what she'd been through, that he couldn't wipe it all away. But he was here now and he'd do his damnedest to take care of her from now on.

The moments slid by and finally the cataclysm passed, leaving her wrung out and quiet against him. Finally, she stirred. "I'm sorry."

He stroked her hair lightly. "There's no reason to be."

"It's all just been such a nightmare. I've been numb. Until now." Frannie sighed. "I don't know what to do. How can I talk to the police about Josh?"

"The only thing that makes you suspicious is the fight?"

This time the sigh was longer. "That's not the worst of it. The night of the murder, the police found a pottery vase that had blood on it. They found it pushed under the flap of a tent." She swallowed. "I bought that vase. It was part of what made them suspect me. But I wasn't the last one who had it."

"Josh?"

She nodded. "He was supposed to take it to my car. Somehow, he never did. Instead, it wound up under the edge of the Fortune Foundation tent, at the back."

"But it's not the weapon."

She blinked. "It's not?"

"I don't think so. If it was, they wouldn't have been so curious about the bar that I found."

"The bar? What bar?"

"I saw someone leave the area where Lloyd was found, in a hurry, right around the time all the noise started. They tossed something away. Turned out to be a kind of a blue-gray crowbar thing, with stuff on it that looked a hell of a lot like…evidence."

She paled. "Oh my God."

"What?"

"That came from the Fortune Foundation tent. The table supports got jammed and we used it to pry them loose. The guys who were helping with setup dropped it at the back of the tent before they draped the tarps over." She stared at him, eyes filled with anguish. "Roberto, what if he really did it? What if he was trying to tell me today and he just couldn't say the words?"

"Do you honestly think Josh could kill anyone? Especially his father?"

"I don't know," she burst out. "I can't imagine it, but he was there at the right time. He could have swapped the vase for the bar. He made threats. And he's been acting so strange. He looks like he hasn't slept right in weeks and he's so on edge. He's never blown up at me like he did today, never."

"It just doesn't add up," Roberto said. "I can't see how the kid who was standing there protecting you killed Lloyd. Someone else did it, we just need to find out who."

"How are you going to do that?" she demanded. "My brother Ross still hasn't figured it out after almost three weeks on the case. What makes you think you can?"

"I have what you call a vested interest. Take me to see Ross and we can compare notes, set up a game plan."

"Roberto, you can't just take over here."

"And you can't be so dead-set on turning down help from anyone, especially me, that you put us all at risk," he shot back.

She opened her mouth then closed it. "All right, fine. I'll call Ross and see what he says."

"Good," Roberto said. "Keep me posted. Now where did we leave that coffee?"

They skirted the boxes and Roberto looked around the room. Lloyd Fredericks was dead and no one knew why. The killer was still at large, and maybe it was Josh, but maybe it wasn't. In which case, it wouldn't be a bad idea to stick close to Frannie, just to be sure she was safe.

"All right, that's one of your problems taken care of," he said aloud, following her back to the kitchen table. "Next is getting your house sold. It shouldn't stay on the market long. It's a nice-enough place."

"It's not a nice house, it's a horrible house," she countered, her spirit back, he was relieved to see. "Lloyd picked it out. It's so big it echoes, and the rooms are all at weird angles to each other, and it's in a Stepford neighborhood. It's true," she defended when one corner of his mouth curved up. "You look when you drive out. They're all alike. It's a good thing he didn't drive me to drink or else I'd have come home some night and pulled up at the wrong house and crawled into someone else's bed."

And before he could stop it, the image flashed in Roberto's mind of Frannie, silky and fragrant and wrapped around him. He suppressed it ruthlessly.

But not before he saw her eyes darken.

Roberto cleared his throat. "Well, you've got a guard. Some people like that."

"I wouldn't want to bet on our security team to take down anyone much more dangerous than a kindergartner." She picked up the mugs.

"At least you're safe from preschool gangs. Thanks,"

he added, taking his cup from her. "What kind of house would you have picked if you'd had the chance?"

"Something older, quirkier. Cozier," she added as she leaned a hip against the counter. "Wood and wallpaper, not marble and chrome. I'm going to look for something small. With Josh going off...to college, I won't need much space." There was a beat of silence. "But I've got to sell this one first before I can go looking. There's no way the bank would give me another mortgage at this point—I don't have quite Lloyd's gift for the con."

"You want me to take a look at those commercial properties you were talking about and give you my opinion?"

"Roberto," she said in exasperation. "How many times do we have to have this discussion? I can take care of my own business. I'm not going to turn around and let somebody else run the show again, including you. Especially you," she added.

The walls were back up, he realized with a pulse of frustration. All the years they'd lost, the life she'd had without him. If she'd at least been happy, it would have been easier to accept, but she hadn't and he hadn't been there to help. And now she was pushing him away, again.

But this time, he wasn't going anywhere.

"I told you, I do property development for a living. It wouldn't be free. I'd take a commission. I could assess what you've got, give you my advice on which ones to unload, which ones to keep, which ones to invest money in."

"No, okay? You can't come in here and fix everything. I'll get to it."

"Will you get to it in time?"

She raised her chin. "We'll find out, won't we? Right now, I've got to focus on two things—getting some kind of paid work, and selling this place. Assuming it'll move."

"It'll move." From ingrained habit, he'd been evaluating the house since he'd walked through the door, studying the ceilings and walls for clues to the bones underneath. Expensive, it might have been, but it wasn't well built by anyone's standards. With a little repair work, though, it would probably attract a buyer. "How long have you been here?"

"Five years. We moved in when they were first built."

He traced a crack in the plaster next to what he presumed was the pantry door. "You've had some settling. It happens a lot when developments are built on construction fill, especially if they don't compact it right."

Frannie followed him out to the foyer. "They must not have because we've got cracks all over. And half the doors won't stay closed—the latches don't catch."

"That's easy enough to fix." He nudged a loose floor tile. "You'll need to reset this. And once you get the cracks fixed, the whole place could probably do with a coat of paint."

She sighed. "I should start making a list. I'm going to need to get someone in to do an estimate."

"You know, I could do this work for you."

"Roberto—" she began.

Frustration rippled in his voice. "I rebuilt my parents' restaurant after the fire, but since then I've either been helping tend bar at Red or sitting on my hands, neither of which I'm good at. If you gave me this job—and I do mean job—I'd estimate it and give you a payment schedule. A payment schedule," he repeated firmly, when she would have interrupted. "There are a lot of

clients I do that for. You'd be able to concentrate on getting your business going, and in return, you'd be doing
me a favor. What do you say?"

She crossed her arms and looked at him.

"Look, I'm not trying to compromise your all-fired
independence. This would be purely a business arrange-
ment, customer and vendor."

There was a moment of silence.

"It'll sell faster." He gave her his best guileless look
and was rewarded by a twitch at the corners of her
mouth.

"Do you by any chance sell as part of your real-
estate work?" she asked.

He raised his brows. "Sometimes. Why?"

"I bet you're good at it." And she put out her hand.
"It's a deal."

"I still can't believe the police had the nerve to lock
up Roberto just to grill him," Isabella complained. "I'd
like to give those Red Rock detectives a swift kick
somewhere painful."

"Tell that to Roberto," Jorge invited. "I'm sure he'd
appreciate it."

They sat at a table in Red with Isabella's fiancé, J.
R. Fortune, and Jorge's fiancée, Jane.

"I've barely ever spoken to Roberto," Isabella said.
"What are we, third cousins twice removed?"

"Well, if you haven't much talked to him, that puts
you in good company. He's not too chatty except with
people he knows well," Jorge said.

"Unlike you." Jane reached for a chip.

"Is that your way of telling me I'm a silver-tongued
devil?" He gave her a leer.

"Hey, enough of the tongue talk, you two." J.R. took a swallow of his beer.

"So, if Frannie didn't do it and Roberto didn't, then who did?" Jane asked.

"I don't think the police know," Jorge said. "They're still looking for information."

"I wonder…" Isabella stopped.

The others looked at her. "Yes?" Jane said.

"Well, I don't know." Isabella nibbled on her thumbnail.

"Oh, come on, you can't stop there," J.R. complained.

"It probably means nothing, but remember when we had that fight?"

"You mean a couple days before you promised to fight exclusively with me for the rest your life?" he asked, his eyes glimmering.

She blushed. "That night. It was about a week and a half before Lloyd Fredericks got killed. I went out for a drink, like I told you, and there was a guy in there." The other three at the table all raised their brows.

"Now she tells me," J.R. said.

"Oh, it wasn't like that." She frowned impatiently. "I barely talked to him, although he was definitely looking to hook up. But the thing was, he had a fight with someone on his cell phone while I was there, and it sounded like…well, like he was being threatened." She hesitated. "I'm pretty sure the guy in the bar was Lloyd Fredericks."

It got their attention. "Did you tell the cops?" Jorge demanded.

"Not yet. I didn't know 'til now. I don't read the papers a lot or watch the news," she confessed. "I didn't see his picture until this whole thing came up about Roberto. The bar was pretty dark, and the guy didn't look just like the shots they showed of Lloyd Fredericks, but the more I think about it, the more I'm sure it was him."

"We need to get Roberto over here. He needs to know about this," Jorge said.

"I suppose. It's been almost a month, though. I'm not sure what I can tell him. The weird thing was, after he hung up, he looked all flushed and angry, but he said something about it being a telemarketer. That was what made it stick in my memory. You don't know the names of telemarketers, and he called this guy by name."

"What was it?"

She ran her hands through her hair. "I've been racking my brain trying to remember. It was kind of unusual, started with a *J.* Jonas, Jo Jo…"

"J.R.?" Jorge put in helpfully.

Jane swatted at him. "This is serious."

"See this, J.R.? Less than two months to the wedding and she's already beating me," Jorge said. "Don't say you weren't warned."

"You're so abused," Jane said, giving him a quick kiss. "So, let's see, unusual *J* names. Um, Jasper? Julius? Jonah? Jocelyn?"

"Josh," Isabella said triumphantly. "That was it. He was talking to someone named Josh."

Chapter 6

The gray rock felt smooth and warm against Josh's fingers. With a hard snap of his arm, he sent it flying over the water to skip once, twice, thrice before it disappeared. A stone on water, out of its element and sinking.

The same way he felt.

"Hey, Josh, stop messing around and come sit with me."

He looked back over his shoulder to see Lyndsey sitting on the sand in her beach chair, his hat clapped on her head. He bent to search out another rock, adding a little more juice to get four flat, hard bounces before it went under. Out of its element, in an impossible situation.

There were lessons to be learned. Keep moving, first and foremost. If you kept moving, you wouldn't go under—if you kept moving and didn't let yourself touch anything for too long.

He wished he'd been smarter.

"Josh."

He sighed and turned back up the beach.

"Stealing my hat?" he asked.

She adjusted the brim. "I needed some shade. And black's my color. Anyway, who cares? You're more interested in rocks than me," she pouted. "Maybe I should be worried."

"Nah." He gave her a quick kiss and sat next to her on the sand. "I was just thinking."

"About what?"

He shrugged. "Stuff."

"Don't be such a worrywart. Things are going to be fine."

He studied her, her uncreased brow, her guileless blue eyes staring back at him—happy and untroubled. "How can you be so sure? What if my mom finds out that I—"

"That you're what? Going to be a dad?" She reached out for his hand and laid it over the still-slight curve of her belly. "She ought to be excited and proud of you. Everybody should. Anyone who's not, well, they can take a flying leap. We're not going to let anybody stop us, right? No way, no how."

A baby. As if everything else wasn't enough, there was this. "It might not be as easy as that, Lyns."

"Worry, worry, worry. You know what they say, if you worry you die, if you don't worry you die, so why worry?"

Josh gave her a tight smile. "Can we not talk about people dying, please?"

There was a flash of temper in her eyes. "Okay, let's talk about names. How do you feel about Cheyenne if it's a boy, and Piper if it's a girl?"

Josh leaned back on his hands and stared out over

the lake. He remembered going to Six Flags on a class trip back when he was in fourth grade. All week, he and his friends had been daring each other to ride the great white knuckler. But it was so big when they had gotten there, so high, and maybe his mother had seen something in his face because she'd told him he couldn't go, he was too young. That had been all it took. Anger had made him heedless and he'd found himself fighting back until finally she'd relented.

And then he'd been in the train ratcheting its way up the hill and all of a sudden he'd realized what he'd done—acting without thinking, hotheaded—to wind up in the middle of something he'd never really wanted. But by then they had been at the top of the hill and it had been too late to do anything but ride it out. Sometimes that was all you could do. You made your choices, whether you meant to or not, and then you figured out a way to live with them.

Lyndsey, oblivious, was still talking about names. "What about Veronica? Or Cissy? That's the name of the nurse at the obstetric center. I think it's cute. Speaking of the center, I got my checkup and the doctor said everything's going just great with my pregnancy. There's absolutely nothing to worry about."

And with her smiling at him, how could he tell her that she was wrong, that there was everything to worry about? That when he thought about the future, what he saw were obstacles and chaos. To her, though, the path forward was crystal clear—they'd marry, move out, start a family and everything would be wonderful.

"I still think we should tell my mom," he said.

"And we will, when the time's right, but think about what she's been through, Josh. Why give her one more thing to worry about?" Lyndsey argued, twining her fingers around his. "If we hold off, it's not going to affect us. We're set for money now that you've inherited, so let a couple months go by. I'll look around for a nice place to buy, and you can tell her when we're ready to move out. She's not going to stand in our way now that your dad's gone. Anyway, you're eighteen, you're an adult."

He sure didn't feel like one, though. What he felt like was that little kid on the roller coaster, sick about what he'd done and scared stiff about what lay ahead.

"Thanks for driving," Frannie told Roberto as he helped her into the cab of his truck.

"No problem."

It was strange, she thought, as he circled around the front of the truck, but it felt for all the world like a date, with him coming to pick her up and opening the door for her and driving. Except that instead of going out to a movie or dinner, they were headed to San Antonio to compare notes with her brother Ross on a murder investigation.

Too much to think about. In the weeks that had passed since the Spring Fling, she'd discovered that the only way to stay sane was to simply not look at too much at any one time. Focus on the details, worry about what was directly ahead of her.

Except that what was directly ahead of her just then was Roberto.

"All set?" he asked as he opened the door and got in.

Focus on what was directly ahead of her, not the look of his lean, long-fingered hands on the wheel, not on the jitters that ran through her stomach every time he got just a little too close. Because letting him get closer would be dangerous. If he could dominate her thoughts so effortlessly without even a touch, if she ever let him get truly in she'd be lost. She'd already had a taste of it that night at his apartment, that mindless, drugging wonder. Anything more could be fatal.

Roberto snapped on his seat belt. "You know where we're going, right?"

Straight toward the hazard signs, if she didn't watch out. "East," she said. "Straight to San Antonio."

Don't think, she reminded herself, instead focusing on the glossy blue hood of his truck. "So why did you drive all the way out from Denver? Why not fly?"

"I figured the truck would come in handy for hauling materials when I was working on Red." He started the engine. "Plus, I hate being crammed into airplanes."

"I can imagine." It wasn't just his height. He'd grown into a man since she'd known him before, with solid width of shoulder, heft of muscle. Even the cab of the truck seemed too small for him, though perhaps it was more force of personality than mere physical size that made her think so. There was a power to him, an assurance that he hadn't had at twenty. And underlying all of it, a smoldering sexuality that was fueled by confidence and intensity as much as by looks. She hadn't noticed it back when she'd been seventeen—maybe it hadn't existed yet—but it was there now, and as a woman, she found it impossible to ignore.

Focus on what was directly ahead.

"Anyway, the drive here from Denver isn't bad," Roberto was saying. "It took maybe seventeen hours, counting stops."

"You drove straight through?"

He coasted past the guard shack, raising a hand to his friend. "I like to get where I'm going."

"I'll say. I guess you're one of those goal-oriented types."

"I tend to stay pretty focused on what I want." He flicked a glance at her. "Don't say you weren't warned."

There was heat in those dark eyes, heat that ran through her and took her by surprise. She swallowed. "Seventeen hours is a long time to spend in a car on your own."

"I didn't mind," Roberto said. "It gave me time to think."

"About what?"

"Lots of things. Coming back, for one. What's going on with my family. Projects at work." He accelerated onto the highway. "Seeing you."

Less than a week had passed since they'd reconnected. It seemed more like a decade. Frannie turned to study his profile. "Would you ever have looked me up if we hadn't run into each other?"

"I doubt it. As far as I was concerned, things were still status quo. But Red Rock isn't that big and I figured that if I came back, there was a better-than-average chance I'd run into you."

From the time she'd heard he was in town, she'd simultaneously dreaded seeing him and wondered what it would be like. "Was it what you expected?"

"Not even close. I thought that after all this time, it just wouldn't matter anymore. But it did. You did. It felt like we'd just been out riding half an hour before."

"I know. It's so strange. It's been almost twenty years, but it feels like yesterday. I have to keep reminding myself that we don't know each other anymore."

"You know me."

"How can I?" Her throat tightened. "I don't even know what happened to you last month, let alone a decade ago."

"Ask," he invited. "You said it yourself, we have to get to know each other again."

Nerves skittered in her stomach. "I also said there was too much going on."

"Nothing's going on right now. We're just driving." He nodded at the passing hills. "Ask and I'll tell you whatever you want to know."

With so long a time, it was hard to even figure out where to start. "What do you do with yourself? How do you spend your time?"

"I've got a horse. I ride some."

"What kind?"

"A big bay quarterhorse. I call him Rocky."

"For the mountains?"

"For his attitude, mostly." His voice was amused. "He's a good match for me when I'm in a mood."

"I've got a little chestnut mare named Daisy that I keep out at the Double Crown," she said. "Too bad Rocky isn't here, we could race."

He was already shaking his head before she got the words out. "No way, I remember how you race."

"How long are you going to hold that against me?"

"How long you got?"

"Sore loser," she said, smiling. "So what do you do when you're not riding?"

"Mostly, I work."

"That's right, building your empire. Why construction? What made you go there?"

Roberto shrugged. "It was easy to find a job and I was good at it. Besides, I'm not all that crazy about being stuck inside all day."

He never had been, Frannie thought. There was something reassuring about the notion that a part of him she had once known hadn't changed.

"You must be good at it to have made such a success of yourself."

His teeth flashed. "I guess you'll find out, won't you?"

She'd taken him on without question to do the work on her house. For a person who was trying to take control of her own life, she hadn't done the best job with her first decision out of the gate. "I suppose if I were smart, I'd have gotten a couple more estimates for the work at my house," she mused aloud. "Compare prices and pick the middle one. Isn't that what you're supposed to do?"

"Depends. If you want it done right, forget price and pick the person who's going to do the best job."

"And are you the best?"

His grin widened. "Give me a couple of weeks and you'll see for yourself."

This time, the heat was definite. Frannie reached out for the air-conditioning vent.

"So that's it, Rocky and work?"

"Uh-huh."

"Nothing else? Nothing personal?"

His lips twitched. "What are you asking?"

Odd that she would find it so difficult. "Did you ever... Are you—"

"No," he cut in. "Never married, no kids."

She'd noticed the lack of rings, but it was a relief, even so. "Nothing?"

"I had girlfriends, but they were never permanent."

"I'm sorry."

"I wasn't," he said frankly. "It was always kind of a relief when things blew up and I found myself back on my own. I guess I'm like a junkyard dog, too territorial. Or maybe I'm just a self-absorbed son of a bitch."

"I doubt that that's true, otherwise you wouldn't be

here. Anyway, it takes two people to make a relationship fail."

"Yeah? Is that how it went with you and Lloyd?"

With her and Lloyd, none of the usual rules applied. Except one. "We never should have gotten married in the first place. I knew it from the start. I never should've agreed."

"Why did you?"

"Because I—" The words caught in her throat. "Because I was pregnant."

He didn't reply right away, letting the silence be a balm. "I'm sorry," he said finally, his voice quiet.

Her chin went up. "I'm not. How could I be? Otherwise, I wouldn't have Josh."

"That's not what I'm talking about and you know it."

She shook her head, warding off his pity. "Things happen. I figured it out about a month after we left Red Rock. I told Cindy, just because I didn't know what else to do. She brought me back to confront Lloyd."

A moment passed. "And you're sure it was his?" The words were a little too careful.

"Oh, yes," Frannie said aridly. "He and his parents insisted on a DNA test after he accused me of sleeping around with everyone in town. But he knew it wasn't true and there wasn't much he could say once we got the results."

"It must have been hell for you."

She looked out the window, flashing back to that long ago chaotic fall. "I remember being twisted inside out, waiting to hear the answer. And even though I thought you'd run away, even though I hated you, I still kept thinking and hoping the baby would be yours. But it wasn't. And the next thing I knew I had Lloyd's ring on my finger."

She wrapped her arms around herself, cold now. "It's funny, I used to imagine sometimes that everything had turned out differently, that you and I were together, that Josh was ours. But then I'd remember how it ended between us." She swallowed. "It was like having a bruise that never healed. I'd get really good at not touching it, but every so often I'd forget and…"

The pain would be there, just as sharp as it had always been.

"It's history now." Roberto's voice was soft. "It doesn't matter. What matters is what we do from here on out."

But what she did from there on out could possibly be as perilous for her as anything that had come before. She didn't want to go from one man to another, dependent physically, emotionally, financially. It would be so easy to fall under Roberto's sway, like she had with Lloyd. And what would be left of her when it was over? She'd been through it once and she didn't think she could survive it again.

And so she turned to the window and watched the hills roll by.

"I'm not sure what to tell you," Ross Fortune said as he led Frannie and Roberto across his living room to the couch.

He was prickly, Roberto diagnosed—not happy about what he no doubt interpreted as somebody questioning his work. "Anything you can tell me is probably more than I know," he replied.

"It's not a territorial thing, Ross. There's a lot at stake. It would be good for us to know the details." Frannie's voice was firm, her expression soft.

Ross gave Roberto the kind of assessing look any

brother would recognize. "Lloyd was a guy with plenty of enemies, I'm sorry to say, Frannie. How many of them disliked him enough to want him dead is another matter. So far, I've got no traction in working it out, and neither have the cops." He paused as they sat. "Can I get you something to drink? I can't offer you a whole lot— I haven't been spending a lot of time here lately."

"Anything," Frannie said.

Roberto watched Ross walk into the kitchen. The guy was rangy, solid enough to look like he could take care of himself if he had to mix it up. Darker hair than Roberto would have expected from Frannie's brother, and long enough to show he didn't give much of a hang about looks, which also netted him points in Roberto's book.

"I gotta say, you got my hopes up when they hauled you in, Roberto," Ross called over from the kitchen. "I figured that got Frannie and Josh off the hook. Too bad it was a washout."

"Sorry to disappoint you," Roberto said drily.

There was a hint of humor in Ross' voice. "Glad to have you out, but I'd be even more glad if they'd find out who really did it."

Frannie looked out at the lights of the Riverwalk outside the window, her fingers twisted together in her lap. Roberto reached out and put his hand on hers.

"The problem is, I still can't put together a picture that means anything." Ross walked in with a glass of water for Frannie along with beers for Roberto and himself. "I've been asking questions, and nobody—" he stopped for a beat, eyes on their hands "—seems to know anything."

"Even the cops?" Roberto asked, amused when Ross

handed him the beer from the side that made him take his hand from Frannie's to grasp it.

"Well, that's the question, isn't it? I've got a source in the department." He took a chair facing them.

"Right."

"I'm going to assume I can trust that whatever I tell you won't be passed along," Ross said, eyes on Roberto. When Roberto gave a fractional nod, he continued. "First of all, Frannie's vase wasn't the murder weapon at all. Right blood type, wrong DNA."

Roberto nodded. "I kind of figured that was the case. And the crowbar I found?"

"A match across the board—tissue, hair DNA," he said over the sharp intake of breath from Frannie. "It was the weapon that killed Lloyd. They pulled a couple of latent prints from it, a finger and a partial thumb, but they don't match anyone in the database. And they can't figure out where the damned thing came from."

"From the back of the Fortune Foundation booth," Frannie said, a look of strain about her mouth. "We used it when we put up the tent. I think they dropped it at the back before they draped the tarps over the frame."

Ross sat up. "The cops found the vase under the table at the very back of the booth, half-under the tarp. Somebody behind the tents could have shoved the vase out of the way and grabbed the bar as a better weapon."

Frannie's fingers clenched the couch cushions until her knuckles turned white. "Not Josh," she whispered. "Please."

"We don't even know if his fingerprints are on the bar," Ross reassured her. "All we really have is a fight between him and Lloyd and witnesses who could place him with the vase."

Roberto stirred. "There's something else you should

know. About a week and a half before the murder, my cousin Isabella was talking to a guy in a bar." He exhaled. "She's pretty sure it was Lloyd."

Frannie turned to stare at him and he ached for her. "It was just a short conversation in a bar, Frannie, nothing more. But the thing is Lloyd got a call while she was there, a call that turned into a pretty nasty fight. She says Lloyd called the person he was talking to Josh."

Ross leaned forward to rest his elbows on his knees, fingertips together. "Hearsay. It wouldn't stand up in court. But cases are made of details and right now there are a lot of them adding up against Josh."

"He can't have done it, Ross." There was a note of entreaty in Frannie's voice.

"I don't want to think it, either, but we're starting to get a lot of information and sooner or later we've got to do something with it. Eventually, Lily and Roberto's cousin are going to have to talk to the cops. Eventually, you are."

"Ross, he's my son." Her voice shook.

"I know. That's why I've been holding off and I'll keep doing that. But I can't do it forever, Fran."

"Which means we've got to start finding some answers," Roberto said. Beside him, Frannie's breath sounded unsteady. "Hey," he said softly, "it's going to be okay."

"How can it be?"

He took her hands in his. "It will be. Trust me."

He held her gaze and suddenly everything fell away and it was just the two of them, bound together. The moment spun out and he let her fear dissipate through him, gave her back all the hope he had. "Trust me," he whispered again.

She blinked and shook her head, then rose. "I'll be right back."

If he'd ever seen courage, it was in the set of those fragile shoulders, Roberto thought, watching her walk away. He turned to see Ross Fortune studying him.

"You were at the Double Crown the summer before Frannie married Lloyd, weren't you?"

Roberto nodded. "For a while."

"And then you lit out and stayed gone."

"I had my reasons."

"Lloyd Fredericks made Frannie's life hell, and it hasn't gotten any better with him dead. She doesn't need any more trouble."

"I'm not planning on giving her any." Roberto kept his voice even.

"She also doesn't need a hit-and-run."

Irritation pricked at him. "You're making some pretty big assumptions based on zero data."

"I'm watching out for her."

"So am I."

"She's under duress right now. And vulnerable."

"Don't underestimate her," Roberto returned. "She's stronger than you think. And smart."

"Smart enough to know what she needs?"

"One of the things she needs, and I hope she's got," Roberto said tightly, "is a brother who believes in her." He let out a breath. "Look, I know where you're coming from. If it was one of my sisters, I'd be doing the same thing. So even though it's none of your business, I'll tell you that she matters to me, a lot. I'm here and I'm not going anywhere. Whatever she needs from me, she's got it. And if there's anything that I can do to take care of her, it's done."

Ross studied him. "She was the reason you came forward about the crowbar, wasn't she?"

"What do you think?"

"That you took a hell of a chance, as it turned out."

Roberto smiled faintly. "I didn't know they'd react quite that way."

"Would it have mattered?"

"No."

Ross was silent for a long time and finally nodded. "All right. Good to know where we stand." He picked up his beer.

Roberto clinked his bottle against Ross'. "Now that that's done, let's figure out what the hell I can do to help you find Lloyd's killer and get Frannie and Josh off the hook."

Chapter 7

Roberto wedged the pry bar between the cover board and the stack of two-by-fours that formed the frame around Frannie's garage door. Between rain, sun and chipmunks, the wood was cracked, gnawed and peeling—damage that couldn't be covered by a coat of paint. Better to replace them altogether, he'd judged.

He set himself and pulled until the nails creaked. It was satisfying to feel the resistance, satisfying to do something with his muscles for a change. It gave him an outlet for the tension that seemed to run through him perpetually now, the ceaseless companion of his days and his nights. It was more than the unsolved murder and the arson at Red. It was the wanting, the need for Frannie.

Just being around her again was more than he'd ever hoped for and yet, with every day that went by, it was further and further from enough. Seeing her walk by, catching the elusive hint of her scent, hearing the laughter that came more and more often as the days passed only combined to make him want her more.

The hell of it was, he understood why she needed space. He couldn't imagine what she'd been through. Lloyd Fredericks, damn his soul, had very nearly extinguished hers. But he hadn't; the spark had survived and it was coming back.

And seeing it just sunk Roberto deeper than ever. She needed to figure out her life, though, and she wanted to do it alone. He'd agreed to give her the time to do it.

He just hoped he could keep to his word.

Dropping the bar, Roberto reached back to slide the claw hammer out of his tool belt.

He needed a bigger job, that was the thing, something he could lose himself in. A few hours and the current repairs would be done, leaving him once again to be sitting around jumping out of his skin. He needed a project that lasted for days, weeks, something that kept him working hard, hammering, sawing, lifting, carrying. He was built for effort and strain, not sitting around and getting soft.

Not for endless waiting.

He'd been working with Ross Fortune, asking questions, building up pictures, trying to find out anything he could about the fires at Red and the Double Crown, about the Spring Fling and Lloyd. And about a person in a hoodie that only he had seen. It wasn't enough to keep his mind off Frannie, though. None of it was enough.

Behind him, he heard a car pull up into the driveway. The rush of adrenaline had him shaking his head at himself. That was how pathetic he was. She'd been gone five minutes and he already missed her. Five minutes? Shoot, he'd begun to miss her before she'd even left.

Truly lame, he told himself, and yet all he could do

was turn to see her with a ridiculous smile plastered over his face.

But the vehicle wasn't Frannie's tidy silver Volvo, and the person getting out of it wasn't Frannie, he saw.

Cindy Fortune slammed the door of the fire-engine-red Viper, adjusting the skirt of the white sleeveless sheath she wore. She took her time sauntering up, taking a long, slow survey of the work underway. And of him. "Well, about time she got this place fixed up a little. You get done here, I've got a few things you can do for me, sugar." She winked.

Then recognition hit. It was almost comical the way her expression cycled from seduction through shock, dismay and alarm before settling on livid. "You," she breathed.

And that quickly he was back in that dark barnyard, staring at her with impotent fury as she tore his dreams to shreds.

She looked now as though she'd be happier tearing him apart instead. "What the hell do you think you're doing here?" she demanded.

Roberto turned back to the door frame and set the hammer claw against a projecting nail. "Fixing the garage."

"That's not all you're fixing, I bet."

He ignored the comment. "If you're looking for Frannie, she's gone. It's her morning to work at the Fortune Foundation." With one swift move, he wrenched the nail out.

"Well, listen to that," Cindy said nastily. "He even knows her schedule. You didn't waste a minute moving in on her, did you? I guess you think you're pretty cute."

"I'm not moving in on anything." In quick sequence, he ripped out the other nails and tossed the loose board aside on the grass nearby. "I'm just helping her get the house ready to sell."

"Oh, sure, helping out the poor little widow."

"Someone should be a help to her." He set the crowbar to pry off the next two-by-four in the stack.

"She doesn't need your kind of help."

He turned to her. "With you around? I think she can use all the help she can get."

"What do you think you're going to do, cozy up to her and take her for all she's got?"

"I think you and Lloyd already took care of that."

"Oh, you've got an angle." The words dripped with scorn. "Your type always does."

"You don't know what my type is. You never bothered to find out." He dropped the crowbar. "You were too busy sticking your daughter with that miserable excuse for a human being."

"Lloyd Fredericks was worth ten of you."

"Doesn't look that way now, does it? But I guess at the time, you were hoping the two of you would become good friends. Maybe good enough that he texted you just before he was killed." Roberto strode into the garage to his toolbox.

She followed him. "What are you talking about?"

"He sent you my picture from the Spring Fling. What else did he send? Who was he meeting there?" He rounded on her. "Help your daughter."

"I don't know what you're talking about."

"And maybe you know a whole lot more than you're saying."

Her eyes narrowed. "Don't you point the finger at me. You're the one they had in jail."

"But Frannie's the one they filed charges against and they haven't dropped them. It could be her freedom at stake. For once in your life, look past your own nose and do something to help her."

"I always took care of her," she said hotly.

"Who are you trying to kid?" His voice was incredulous. "Do you have any idea what her life was like with that creep?"

"I did what was best for her."

"You did what was best for *you*," he shot back. "I'm not sure what you got out of it—maybe Lloyd threw a few checks your way—but don't ever think you can fool anyone into thinking you did any of it for Frannie's benefit."

"I suppose that's what you're telling her. You're trying to turn her against me, aren't you? Well, it won't work," Cindy snarled. "I know all about trash like you. I ran you off once before and I'll run you off again."

"Try it," he invited. "Go ahead, take me on. We're not kids anymore and I'm more than a match for you. Give it up, Cindy."

"Don't you tell me what to do, you parasite," she shouted, pure fury distorting her features.

A clank behind them had them both spinning. Josh stood at the edge of the garage where sunlight met shadow. "Hey," he said weakly.

Alarm flashed over Cindy's face. "Josh, my God, where did you come from? You scared the life out of me."

"Lyndsey dropped me off. What's going on?"

"Oh, nothing," she said, her gaze jumping nervously between Roberto and Josh. "Isn't that right, Mr. Mendoza?"

Roberto wasn't particularly crazy about jumping in on Cindy's side, but there was no sense in dragging the kid into her histrionics. That said, Josh had grown up with Cindy as his grandmother. He probably had a pretty good idea what she was like. He certainly didn't look convinced by her attempts to gloss things over.

Roberto cleared his throat. "I need to get back to work," he said, fishing a chisel out of his toolbox.

"Give me a hug, baby." Cindy crossed over to kiss Josh.

"I didn't know you were around."

"I couldn't miss my best boy's graduation, could I?"

Josh gave her a cynical look. "That was a week ago."

"Oh...of course," she floundered. "I, uh, meant I couldn't miss celebrating it with you. Sorry I wasn't at the ceremony. Something came up."

"It usually does," Josh said.

"I'll make it up to you. We'll go out to the mall, buy you something."

Josh shook his head. "Don't worry about it, there's nothing I need." He turned to watch Roberto.

Cindy just stood a moment, ill at ease, glancing between the two of them. She was clearly dying to ask when Frannie would be back, Roberto realized in sour amusement, but she wasn't about to give him the satisfaction. Finally, she turned toward her car.

"Well, I can't stay around all afternoon. Tell your mom..." She hesitated. "Tell her I stopped by," she said to Josh.

"Okay." He watched her get into her car and drive away.

Roberto, meanwhile, was stripping out the rest of the nails from the last board. He felt, more than saw, Josh staring at him.

"What were y'all fighting about?"

Roberto pulled the board loose and tossed it onto the grass near the other. "I'd say that's between us."

"It sounded like it had something to do with my mom. That makes it my business."

"No, that makes it your mom's business."

"Yeah? You going to tell her about it?"

"Not if I don't have to. She doesn't need any more grief right now." Roberto picked up one of the replacement boards and got out his tape measure to check the length.

Josh let his backpack drop to the ground. "So, what's the deal with you and my mom?"

"That's also your mom's business."

"She's not here. I'm asking you." He raised his chin. "I've never seen you before, my dad gets killed, and all of a sudden you're showing up around the place. You got something going on with her?" There was an edge to the kid's voice made up as much of anxiety as challenge.

He'd stood at the door to protect his mother, Roberto remembered. And maybe he deserved a little straight talk.

He leaned the board up against the door frame. "You mean are we having an affair? No. Until last week, I hadn't seen your mother for almost twenty years."

The cynical look returned. "And now you just happen to be here. You expect me to buy that?"

"I don't expect you to buy anything," Roberto said evenly. "You asked, I answered. I happened to be here to see family and your mother and I ran into each other."

"They arrested you for my father's murder, didn't they?" Something flickered in Josh's expression, something that Roberto couldn't quite identify.

"No, they just asked me some questions."

"Then why'd they lock you up?"

"They thought I knew some things that I didn't."

"What?" Josh's gaze skated away, over to the crowbar lying on the driveway.

Roberto watched him. "Legally, I can't tell you. All you need to know is that it got your mom out."

"Is that why you went to the cops, so they'd let her go? Whatever happened with you guys must have been a big deal for you to do that after all this time."

"We were…friends, for a little while."

"More than friends."

"Definitely not your business."

"Definitely more than friends," Josh said, nodding to himself. "But I guess it didn't last. I heard what my grandmother said about running you off. Is that what she did? You and my mom hooked up twenty years ago and she didn't like it? She wrecked things?"

There was an intensity in the kid's eyes that went far beyond curiosity. "There's more to it than that, but yeah, basically."

Josh glared upward, shaking his head. "I don't freakin' believe it," he exploded, spinning to slam his palm against the garage-door frame.

"Hey," Roberto said.

"Man, parents are so full of it. For the whole last year, almost since Lyndsey and I got together, all my mom and dad could do was try to break us up. And now you tell me that she went through the same thing with you?" He cursed. "You'd think she would've remembered what it was like and gotten my dad off my back. I mean, he was always on me, you know? It was like I was eight instead of almost eighteen, and he's ordering me around and yelling and talking all this trash about Lyndsey, I mean trash, and telling me what I can and can't do and getting in my face until I swear I just wanted to knock his damned head—" He stopped abruptly.

"Yeah?" Roberto stayed absolutely still.

Josh looked down, reddening. "I'm just saying that. I didn't mean for real."

"Sure." Roberto studied him, the high color, the agitation, the fear that came off him in waves. "But it doesn't matter how your dad acted now, does it? He can't stand in your way anymore."

"He sucked," Josh muttered. "I hated the way he treated my mom. I hated him. But I didn't want him dead."

"No?"

"No."

"Who did?"

"I don't know." Josh shifted his feet and looked away.

"They could still take your mom in at any time. You want that to happen?"

"No! I never wanted that. That was the worst."

"Well, she's out for now and I want to keep it that way. If you know anything about the murder, you'd better tell me."

"I don't," Josh said, staring at the crowbar. "I don't know anything at all."

"Well?" Lily looked expectantly at Frannie. "How did it go?"

The café was a little slice of Europe on Red Rock's Main Street, with snowy-white linen, wrought-iron chairs and baskets of crimson geraniums hanging from the glossy green lampposts along the curb. It was unseasonably cool for June, which in Texas meant it was just right for lunch outdoors.

Frannie sat down, propping her portfolio case against the chair. "How did it go? I was a nervous wreck. My hands are still shaking," she confessed, holding them up. "See?"

"How can you be nervous? Nick Fortune is your cousin. You see him every week at the Fortune Foundation when you volunteer. And Emmett and Linda. They don't bite."

"But they do run the Foundation. It's one thing to see them when I'm helping out. It's another to be looking at them across a conference table, trying to convince them to hire me." The breeze pushed a lock of hair into her face and Frannie tucked it behind her ear impatiently.

"I don't see what the problem is," Lily said, signaling to the waiter inside the café. "You have something to offer, a service that they need."

"I'm sure they have their choice of fancy marketing agencies to do the photographs for the new Foundation brochure. They don't need me."

But it was worth taking a chance to see if they might. If nothing else, it was good practice. All things considered, the meeting had gone better than Frannie had expected. She hadn't detected any signs of surprise when they looked at the portfolio, which gave her confidence that she hadn't done anything wildly wrong. For the pitch, she'd gone with her instincts. Now, she just had to wait for their decision.

"So, what did they say?"

"They're still interviewing photographers. They expect to decide next week." It was a long shot, but if she came through it would be a big win—her first professional job, one that would lead to others.

She hoped.

"Why the big rush to start a business?" Lily asked as the waiter filled Frannie's water glass. "I mean, I can understand that you'd want something to do now that Lloyd's gone, but with everything that's going on right now, wouldn't it be better to wait?"

"I can't wait." The words were too quick, the desperation in her voice a little too naked. "I mean, I want to get it going," she said more moderately. "You know, take my mind off things."

"I can appreciate that, but isn't there a better way? One that doesn't give you more stress to deal with?"

"I need to do this, Lily." She kept her voice low, for the pedestrians walking beside their table.

"Why?" Lily stared at her. "What's going on, Frannie?"

She let out a breath. "This is for you and you alone to know, all right?"

Lily nodded.

"Lloyd left me with a lot of debt, Lily, a lot. And he never bothered to get life insurance."

"He always seemed like one of those guys who figured he'd live forever."

"Yeah, but he was wrong. He left me in a deep hole and I've got to figure out a way to get out of it."

Lily turned for her purse. "Well, that's easy," she said briskly. "How much do you need?"

"None, Lily. I don't want your money. I need to do this myself."

"Fine, we'll make it a loan."

"Put the checkbook away," Frannie told her. "Please. I'm not Cindy, I can't come to you with my hand out."

Lily's eyes softened. "Sweetheart, you could never be like Cindy in a million years. And money isn't an issue. We've got scads of it, we can get you whatever you need."

"What I need, for once in my life, is to take care of myself." Frannie looked at her, eyes pleading. "Everybody wants to help—you, Ross, William, Roberto—but I need to do this alone. I've been depending on other people for way too long."

"Roberto? Roberto Mendoza? What's he got to do

with all of this?" Lily frowned. "Frannie, the police were questioning him about the murder. You shouldn't even be talking to him. It'll just make things worse."

Frannie smoothed her hair back. "I'm still charged with Lloyd's murder, Lily. They could haul me back in at any time. How can it possibly be any worse?"

"How dare you show your face here?" a voice hissed venomously.

Frannie jolted and glanced up to see a cadaverously thin blond woman stopped on the sidewalk, staring at them. Lloyd's mother, Jillian Fredericks. Frannie had been wrong. Things could get worse.

A whole lot worse.

Chapter 8

"How did you get them to let you out?" Jillian's voice was low and hostile.

Frannie raised her chin. "They finally realized they didn't have enough evidence to hold me."

"Oh, I'm sure. After all, you're related to Ryan Fortune," she sneered. "Nothing that goes on with you people in this town should surprise me. But we all know how you really got out."

"The way I got out was by having nothing to do with Lloyd's murder."

"You're lying. You have been from the beginning. You trapped him into marrying you."

"*I* trapped *him?*" Anger began a slow burn in her. "You have no idea what you're talking about, Jillian. If anyone set a trap, it was Lloyd."

"I doubt that very much."

Frannie's gaze was very direct. "Do you?"

She remembered that night, the one that had changed her life forever. A party thrown by some of Lloyd's fraternity brothers. He'd shown her off, introduced her to Long Island iced teas and taken her, stumbling, to a back room. He'd been insistent and she'd been in no condition to protest. *It'll be good,* he'd said, *I promise.* But it hadn't been. He'd been too rough, too eager, too focused on his own pleasure to have a care for hers as he'd stripped her of her innocence.

She'd sworn she would never allow Lloyd to touch her again. But when she'd told him the next day, he'd railed at her, accusing her of sleeping with Roberto. "You think you can throw me aside for some hired hand?" he'd demanded. "I'll make you sorry."

She'd fled on horseback, but Roberto had followed. And heartache had come on their heels.

I'll make you sorry, Lloyd had promised.

And he'd spent nineteen years doing just that.

"You're lying." Jillian's eyes glittered. "You've always lied."

"You know it's the truth."

"Don't you talk about my Lloyd." Her voice rose. "You held him back. You were never good enough for him, ever. He could have married anyone and he settled for you, you little round-heeled piece of trash. You're nothing, Frannie Fortune, nothing," she spat. "I hope they send you to jail to rot."

Lily shot to her feet. "That's enough, Jillian."

Jillian turned her malevolent gaze to Lily. "That's enough, all right, enough of you Fortunes."

Frannie raised her hand. "Lily, let me handle this. Jillian, I'm sorry about Lloyd," she said evenly. "No mother should lose her child, and maybe that kind of pain can make a person say anything. But you're out of line and this is no place for a scene."

Jillian shook off the friends who were trying to draw her away. "You want a scene? Just wait. Everyone knows you killed him. There's blood on your hands. I don't care who you bribed to let you out, everyone knows you did it. And I'll make sure you pay for it."

And she turned away, leaving Frannie shaking.

"Are you all right?" Lily asked.

Frannie took a deep breath and let it out. "I should be. You'd think I'd be used to her after all this time."

Lily frowned. "I don't like to be unkind about anyone, but I really think Jillian is not right in the head. I think the strain of Lloyd's murder has sent her off. I hope Cordell gets her some help."

"She's always been that way, Lily. You can't imagine how awful she was to live with." Frannie remembered the weekly visits, the phone calls, the steady drip of poison in Lloyd's ear every time he talked to his mother. "Nothing was ever good enough for her, nothing I said, nothing I did. Anything nice I ever tried to do she threw back in my face. If it wasn't Lloyd ordering me around, it was Jillian, always trying to butt in with Josh and Lloyd, telling me how to decorate the house, what to do, what to wear, how to move, how to think, how to breathe." She took a deep breath. "I was a doormat, but I'm done with that now, it's over."

And it was as she said the words that she realized it really was. Lloyd's hatefulness, Jillian's hostility weren't a part of her life anymore. She didn't have to swallow her frustrations, put aside her desires, turn the other cheek to keep the peace, accept an unacceptable situation. She could live her life without compromise.

She turned to Lily with shining eyes. "Things are going to change."

Lily raised her water glass for a toast. "To your new life. To no more Jillian."

They clinked glasses. "No more sitting home all day waiting for something bad to happen," Frannie marveled.

"No more Stepford house."

"No more parties with people I hate."

Lily toasted her again. "No more mean people," she said.

"No more spending three days cooking Thanksgiving dinner, only to spend eight hours listening to Jillian tear it apart," Frannie countered.

"Oh, double toast on that one," Lily said.

Frannie's laughter turned into a sputter as the breeze blew a lock of hair into her open mouth. "Gack," she said, pulling out the strands. "No more eating my own hair. No more—" She broke off, staring across the street.

Lily raised a brow. "No more…whatever it is you're staring at?"

Frannie turned to her, mouth curving. "Would you mind if I skip out on lunch?"

"Skip out on lunch? Not a chance. Wherever you're going with that look in your eye, I'm going with you." Lily threw a bill on the table and rose to follow Frannie. "And just where are we going, anyway?"

Frannie laughed. "To do something I should have done a long time ago."

The glossy blue bulk of Roberto's truck blocked Frannie's driveway, forcing her to stop partway up the concrete apron. She got out to the sharp reports of hammer blows. Roberto was at work on the garage, she saw, craning her neck to glimpse the top of his head over the truck. She headed toward the front of the truck to find him.

And stopped in her tracks.

Roberto wore jeans and a plain T-shirt, his tanned skin dark against the white cotton. A leather tool belt was slung about his hips, making them look very narrow. A nail dangled from his lips like a cigarette. As she watched, he picked it out and positioned it against the board with one hand. With the other, he brought the hammer around in a sweeping arc and with a single blow drove the nail all the way into the wood.

Her lips parted.

He shifted and slammed in nail after nail, smoothly, rhythmically and with deceptive speed. There was an assurance, an insouciant grace in his every motion. Muscle flexed in his back, rippled in his forearms. She'd never seen a man who inhabited his body so completely. It made her think of some lithe, powerful animal like a jungle cat. She stared, transfixed.

He'd finished and was turning to pick up his tools when he saw her.

Time went by—seconds? Minutes?—she couldn't say because for just that time they didn't speak, didn't move, only locked eyes with each other. And then he was walking toward her, slipping his hammer into the tool belt without a glance. His eyes looked black, even in the sun. Her lungs snatched a breath of their own accord.

"You cut your hair."

She swallowed. "It was getting in my way."

"I like it."

There was something in his voice, some vibration that set up an answering thrum deep within her.

Straight toward the hazard signs.

You shouldn't even be talking to him.

The breeze caught up the strands of her hair and tossed them around. In his eyes, there was desire, but also something far more seductive—delight. "I remember the first time I saw you," he said softly, reaching out to brush her bangs off her forehead. "You'd just gotten out of the car. You were wearing this little white skirt and a pale green shirt with no sleeves. You reminded me of one of those pixies in the Disney movies."

It took her a moment to find her voice. "I didn't think you noticed me."

"I noticed you. Maybe you wouldn't say boo to a goose when you got there, but even then you had this look like you were fixing to make some kind of trouble."

"What trouble did I ever cause?"

"Besides distracting me every minute of every day?"

"You can't blame me for that," she said, moistening her lips.

"What about the fact that I haven't gotten a decent night's sleep since I hit town?"

He was too close, she thought, close enough that she could feel the heat radiating off of him.

"Show me what you're working on," she said with effort.

He studied her. "I think you know what I'm working on."

The seconds stretched out. She could feel each individual thud of her heart.

His teeth gleamed and he turned. "But if you want to see what you're paying for, I just finished putting in the new frames around the garage doors. It's supposed to rain tonight and tomorrow, so I'll have to wait to paint them until the weather cooperates."

"Nice job," she said, but she wasn't focusing on the wood. She was remembering the first time she'd ever seen him. He'd been lankier then, his hair longer, flowing thick down to his collar. He'd seemed so serious that she'd been afraid to talk to him. But she'd discovered that what she'd taken for brooding had been simple thoughtfulness, that he was also capable of laughter. He'd been genuinely interested in what she had to say instead of talking over her the way Lloyd had. Lloyd's idea of wooing her had been concerts and rides in his sports car. He'd never understood that the truest seduction was simply listening.

But then, he'd never understood her, period.

Roberto walked into the garage and picked up his toolbox. "I'm done out here. Why don't you show me those doors that don't latch and I can get to work on them?"

The interior of the house was cool and dim after the bright sunlight of the outdoors. "Do you want something to drink?" Frannie asked as they walked into the kitchen.

Roberto set down the toolbox. "Water would be great."

She reached into a cupboard and pulled out a glass, conscious of the way his eyes followed her as she went to the refrigerator to fill it. Such a simple thing, and yet there was something oddly intimate about the act of setting it down before him and watching him drink, his throat moving as he swallowed.

"Thanks," he said when he'd finished, handing her the glass. For a fraction of a second, their fingers brushed and she felt the heat bloom up her arm. "All right, where are those doors?"

Frannie set down the glass by the sink. "The pantry door right here, the door to the hall bathroom, the den, the—"

"Hold on. That's enough for starters. When you said half the doors in the house didn't close, I thought you were joking."

"Trust me, there are more."

"I'll let you know when I'm ready for them." He set down his toolbox by the pantry door and set to work.

She'd been wary of having him work on the house because she'd feared him getting too involved in her life. She hadn't considered the hazard of simply having him around for hours at a time, watching him make repairs with those clever, capable hands.

And being unable to forget what they'd felt like on her skin.

So she tried to distract herself by going back to packing. It didn't help, though. It was impossible to forget he was there. Over and over she found herself stopping to listen for the click of the tools on his belt when he shifted, the curses he muttered under his breath when he hit a snag, the whisper of his clothing as he walked. Somehow, the fact that they were in different rooms only made her more aware of him.

And she knew when he walked in even before he spoke.

"Okay, those are done. Where are the others?"

She rose to meet him. "There's the door on the guest room."

"Where's that?"

"Upstairs. And Josh's bathroom door."

"Upstairs?"

"Yes."

"Anything else on this floor?"

She hesitated. "The closet."

"The closet where?"

"My bedroom. The master bedroom," she corrected, feeling her cheeks warm.

A slow smile spread across Roberto's face. "Is that so? Does that mean I get the tour?"

She scowled at him. "I thought you were a professional."

"At some things." He eyed her. "At others, I like to think of myself as a dedicated amateur."

Her pulse beat a little harder. "The other two rooms are right next to each other."

"Might as well take care of this one first, since it's close." He picked up his toolbox. "Show me where it's at."

"You'll find it at the end of the hall."

"Oh, I think you'd better show me. A door that important, you'll want to get it done just right."

When she still hesitated, he grinned. "Relax, *chica.* It might shock you, but at thirty-nine I think I can just about manage to keep from tearing your clothes off and having my way with you at the sight of a bed. Not that the idea doesn't have its appeal," he added softly, the smile fading.

Frannie started down the hall, vividly aware of Roberto just behind her. Naked, on the bed, twined together. Would it be so hard to block the image if she hadn't been with him before? If she didn't remember the feel of his bare skin pressed to hers? They hadn't made love in a bed, but on the soft grass beneath the red oaks, with the rolling hills all around. And when he'd parted the front of her shirt to find her, he'd shown her just how electric touch could be.

The rooms opening onto the hallway were all closed off, leaving it dim, intimate. The door to her bedroom seemed very far away. And when they finally reached it, her hand on the knob was slippery with nerves. She opened it and they walked into a flood of light.

Soft blue walls, a cathedral ceiling, French doors leading to the pool deck. A half acre of pale gold carpet.

And a bed the size of Rhode Island.

He was being punished for boasting, Roberto thought. He was being made to suffer, because when it came down to it, he wasn't so far above it after all. What he was was full of it, because when he stood next to that wide swath of coverlet and pillows, all he could think about was having her naked beneath him, pressing her into the soft mattress and taking them both where he knew they could go.

"This is the door," Frannie said.

It was her hair that was the problem. He'd about flipped when he'd seen her come walking up with that sunbeam hair cut away into a little cap that made her look about sixteen and lighthearted and happy. All of a sudden, those delicate features weren't weighed down by the heavy spill of hair anymore. He could really see her again, chin and cheekbones, that delicious mouth that always spoke to him of mischief.

And tempted him to the point of madness.

Roberto set down the toolbox and pulled open the closet door.

It was his second mistake.

The closet was hers, he could tell the minute the door started to swing back and her scent flowed out to envelop him. The ranks of clothing whispered of her. There was a robe hanging from a hook on the back of the door. Red silk.

He swore he could smell his synapses frying.

Don't think about it, he told himself as he knelt next to the doorjamb and unscrewed the strike plate.

It was a simple repair that should have taken five minutes, but it seemed like it took him three or four times that because he couldn't focus. His eyes were on the wood and metal, but his attention was on Frannie.

She moved restlessly around the room, the way he imagined she might at night as she was getting undressed, slipping out of her shoes, unzipping her dress, sliding into that silky robe. Maybe she'd sit on the padded bench in her dressing area as she took off her jewelry. And he'd come up behind her and slide the robe off her shoulders to find her warm and naked and—

"How do you do that?"

The words brought him back to reality with a jolt. He blinked. "How do I..."

"How do you fix the door?"

He gave a sigh of relief. "Oh, that. See this hole?" He held up the strike plate, waggling his thumb in the gap. "The spring latch on the door is supposed to fit into it. In your doors, the strike plate's set too far into the jamb so that the latch never makes it that far."

"So how do you fix it?"

"Take it off and use a file to take away enough metal that the spring latch can make it in." He rose. "Where's your trash can?"

"In the dressing area," she said.

He walked through the threshold and in a flash took in the first room in the house that seemed truly hers. With its half wall of mirrors, deeply female furnishings and sense of luxurious disorder, it evoked the feel of a harem. On the polished wood counter, a hairbrush lay next to a bin of lipsticks and eye color. Within a wooden box with the top askew, he glimpsed the flash of gold. A deep blue silk scarf had been tossed over the padded stool as though she'd just taken it off. Her scent hovered in the air.

He saw painted porcelain sinks and gleaming fixtures. And in the far corner, next to a wall of glass brick, an enormous, unabashedly decadent tub big enough for two.

Soap, wet bodies, skin sliding over slippery skin.

That was it, Roberto thought. He gave in. A man could only take so much temptation, no matter how adult he was, and if he didn't get outside quick, his brain was going to go on overload. Forget the wastebasket, he'd file the strike plate in the garage. Better yet, he'd take it back to his place. He wheeled around abruptly.

It was his third mistake.

Because she was there, just behind him. They collided, and in the confusion he reached out to clutch her arms to keep her from falling.

Too bad he already had.

And with a low curse, he dragged her to him, crushed her lips to his and plunged them both into a hot madness.

It was nothing like their previous kiss. This time, there was no quiet exploration, no gentleness. This kiss was about heat and urgency. It was about the accumulated frustration of the past days, the need that pounded through him until it became all he was about. Her mouth was hot and avid against his and he drove her lips apart to taste her. Her body was lithe and he learned it anew with his hands. It was urgent, it was heedless and she matched him demand for demand. When he slid his hand up over her breast, the low moan in her throat very nearly drove him over the edge.

He was like a junkie getting his first taste after being on the wagon. He could feel the rush of her buzzing through his veins, intoxicating him, making him almost dizzy with it.

And like a junkie mainlining again, all he wanted was more.

The bed was there, mere feet away. All he had to do was walk over to it and lay her down. It was meant to happen. Why else would they have wound up together in this room if not for this? They were adults, they were both free. With all they had gone through, didn't they deserve it? Didn't they deserve the pleasure that they could give each other?

He heard her moan again and his body tightened. He felt her fingers slide up into his hair and he dragged them both deeper. He savored her mouth, let his lips press a tortured line down the smooth column of her throat, inhaled her scent. It had gone beyond want, now, beyond need, beyond choice and into the realm of compulsion.

Frannie couldn't catch a breath, didn't care. For that moment, she let the rush of sensation sweep her away into the heat and thunder, flash and fire. Twenty years before, she'd given him a playful kiss one afternoon at the end of a game of tag. It had sent little fizzes of excitement bubbling through her, but nothing compared to the way she'd felt days later when they'd finally made love. And now, history was repeating itself. That first brushing kiss at his place had ignited a slow burn in her that she couldn't ignore. But this, this was like gasoline thrown on fire.

She could feel the urgency, taste it even as she tasted him. His hands ran down her back, molding them together. Their mouths fused and she reveled in his touch, his scent, his taste, gloried in the pleasure that he drew forth from her with hands and lips and tongue. For years, she'd been deadened, but now under his touch she'd come alive.

It wasn't enough, Roberto knew it. It wasn't enough and yet he couldn't let himself take more. He heard Frannie's soft sigh of surrender, knew the exact moment that he could have taken her further, slipping off her dress, pressing her back on the bed. And maybe, caught up in the moment, she wouldn't have blamed him.

But he would have blamed himself.

So he stayed put, fought to pull back, fought to regain control. Fought finally to release her.

And watched as her eyes cleared.

They stared at each other, wordless.

She dragged her hands through her hair. "I must be out of my mind."

"Try to tell me that's just a complication," he challenged.

Frannie tried to slow her breath. "Try to tell me it's not."

"Don't pretend you haven't been thinking about it, because I don't buy it."

"Of course I've been thinking about it. But that doesn't mean I'm ready for it." She stepped away and whirled around to him. "What do you want from me, Roberto? I'm still trying to figure out how the pieces all fit together. I keep telling you I can't deal with this right now, and you won't listen."

"Yeah? That's because I didn't exactly notice you fighting me off just now." He clasped his hands together on top of his head, squeezed his eyes closed briefly and let out a long breath. "I shouldn't have said that. I'm sorry. I didn't intend for this to happen any more than you did. But there's something there between us or it wouldn't have."

She nodded slowly. "Then maybe we should stay away from each other so it doesn't happen again."

"Do you really think that's possible?"

It was her turn to be frustrated. "I don't know. Right now, I'm making this up as I go along. I do want you, Roberto, I admit it. I want you so much sometimes that I can't breathe. And it scares the hell out of me."

He didn't reply right away. "*Querida*," he said finally. "I can only imagine what you went through with that man. I'm not ignoring you. I get that you don't want to be involved right now after everything you've been through, but like I said before, I'm not Lloyd. At some point you're going to have to trust that. At some point you're going to have to trust yourself and listen to your heart."

"How am I supposed to listen to my heart if all I can hear is you telling me what you want me to do?" she fired back. "Give me—"

There was the sound of the door and giggling at the front of the house. "Anybody home?"

Frannie jerked away as though she'd been electrified. "Josh and Lyndsey," she hissed. "Be right out, honey," she said more loudly, smoothing down her dress and moving toward the door.

"Frannie." He waited until she turned. "You can hold back all you want, but we both know that's not going to make it go away. It's still there between us. Sooner or later you're going to have to deal with it."

"I know," she whispered.

And she walked out the door.

Chapter 9

Roberto put a coin into the self-serve car wash. In Denver, he had a car wash at his company's facility to serve their fleet, as well as a gas pump. At least last time he'd checked. A man couldn't run a business for long when he was a thousand miles away. So far, between the Internet, his cell phone and his job-site managers pitching in, he'd done okay, but that wasn't likely to last too much longer. Especially with the economy, he needed to be there in person.

But how could he leave Red Rock now with everything that was going on with his family, Lloyd's murder, the fires and Frannie?

Above all, with Frannie.

He hadn't come so close to winning her back only to walk away, especially when she was still in peril. Until things settled down with her, he wasn't going anywhere.

He twisted the knob on the dial to wash and squeezed

the trigger on the wand. Instantly, a jet of soap sprayed out over the dusty side of his truck, dripping onto the wet concrete below. It didn't seem to matter where in Texas he was, the dust just naturally found him. He moved around in a slow circle, from back to front, until soap was running down the paint.

And suddenly the water turned off.

"What the…" He looked behind him to see McCaskill with his hand on the control box and Wheeler just standing there, studying him with those washed-out blue eyes.

"Now you're going to tell me I'm not allowed to wash my car?" Roberto asked.

McCaskill propped one hand on the cinder block wall. "Nope, we just saw you here as we were driving by—thought you looked lonely."

"Feel free to grab a rag and pitch in."

"Pitch in. Hey, that's a good one, huh, Len?"

Wheeler didn't look amused. "I hear you been asking questions."

"No law against that."

"When it comes to police work, yeah, actually, there is. It's called obstructing an investigation."

"I'm not obstructing anything. I'm just having conversations with people."

"Oh, yeah? Cindy Fortune didn't seem to think so. I believe she used the word interrogation."

Roberto closed his eyes and gave a mental curse. "And you and I both know just how trustworthy Cindy Fortune's word about anything is."

"In this case, I'm inclined to believe her," Wheeler drawled. "We're in the middle of an investigation here, Mendoza. We don't need you interfering and getting citizens all riled up."

Roberto leaned the wand up against the cinder block wall. "And here I thought you were worried about finding out who killed Lloyd Fredericks, not keeping the citizens calm."

"Actually, Mr. Mendoza, we worry about both."

"I'll keep that in mind."

"Good. Because if you keep on having any more of those conversations, we might just wind up having a conversation with you—in a jail cell."

McCaskill leaned forward and smiled. "Right next to your girlfriend."

Roberto felt a flare of anxiety go through him. "My girlfriend?"

"Frannie Fredericks," Wheeler clarified. "The woman still officially charged with the murder of Lloyd Fredericks. You two been spending a lot of time together, haven't you? For a couple of people who just knew one another casually twenty years ago, I mean."

"She hired me to repair her house."

"From what I can see, you been fixing an awful lot for her. Garage doors, roof, walls, finding the murder weapon dropped by some mysterious figure no one else seems to have seen…" Those pale blue eyes studied him. "You help her fix anything else, Mendoza? Like her husband?"

It felt like ice going down his spine. Ignore it, Roberto told himself. They were fishing, nothing more. "Give me a break, Wheeler. You took my fingerprints and my blood when I was in for questioning. If that had matched up with any other forensic evidence, you'd have slapped me in a cell in a heartbeat. Same thing with Frannie. You don't have anything and we both know it."

"Until we do, we're happy to go with obstructing an investigation," McCaskill put in.

"Only if you can prove I was obstructing."

"I'm not going to dance around with you anymore on this, Mendoza," Wheeler interrupted. "Stay out of this investigation or we'll have both you and Frannie Fredericks back in."

"Based on what? She hasn't been asking questions, I have."

Wheeler's eyes chilled. "Stay out of it. And if you're smart, you'll keep your distance from her, too. I don't like having an open homicide in my town. I want this cleaned up, and the quicker you get out of it, the quicker it will be."

McCaskill swiped a finger down the side of the truck. "You'd better get to rinsing," he said over his shoulder as they walked away. "You let the soap dry on your paint, it'll wreck the finish."

Frannie had always loved weddings. Maybe it was irrational, given how miserably her own marriage had turned out, but there was something about the optimism of two people pledging their lives to each other that had always made it easier for her to get through the day. And the next day. And the next.

White satin, lily of the valley, flower girls meandering down the aisle. Even watching the bride and groom wandering around the reception never failed to make her smile.

At least most days.

"Congratulations, you two," she told her cousin Nicholas Fortune and his bride as they stopped at her table. "Or congratulations to you, Nick. The bride's supposed to get best wishes."

"Forget that." Charlene Fortune, née London, threaded her arm through her husband's. "I deserve congratulations for bagging the confirmed bachelor."

"Hey, who proposed to who?" Nick countered. "Give me some credit for knowing a good thing when I see it. Or see her." He grinned.

"You do look kind of like you won the lottery," Frannie observed. "Both of you."

Clad in a flowing white gown with a garland of flowers in her auburn hair, Charlene had a glow that could have lit Manhattan. Around them, guests began tapping knives against their water glasses to create an everlouder chorus of clinking.

"Listen to your guests and kiss the bride, Nicholas," Frannie told him.

"My pleasure," he replied, taking Charlene in his arms and dipping her back with a flourish to kiss her until everyone whooped.

Charlene was laughing as she came back up. "You loon," she said.

"You'd better get used to it," Nick told her. "You're stuck with me now."

"I think I can handle that. Kiss me again, just so I can make sure." When he did, she beamed. "Oh, I wish I could bottle this feeling and give some to everyone I know."

Maybe that was the allure of weddings, Frannie thought as they walked off, the hope that some of that giddy magic would rub off. Then again, what would she do if it did? Would she really have the courage to step out and take it?

Sooner or later you're going to have to deal with it.

Roberto made it sound so simple. He was so certain of what he wanted. That didn't mean that she was ready for it. It felt so right with him, but what if that was just sentiment talking, a mix of the excitement of their reunion and feelings from long ago?

Worse, what if it wasn't? What if it was real and she ruined it by diving in before she was emotionally ready to be a partner to anyone? Frannie sighed. When she sat down and thought about it, there were a whole host of good reasons to stay away from Roberto Mendoza.

And deep down inside, she knew it didn't matter. Over a week had passed since they'd kissed in her bedroom, over a week since she'd seen him. And every moment of every hour of every day in between, she'd wanted him. She'd tried to keep him at a distance, she'd tried to keep him out of her head. She should've realized at the start that it was impossible. And now, she didn't know what to do.

To distract herself, she brought out her camera and began to snap pictures: a little girl standing on her grandfather's feet, giggling as he sidestepped her around the dance floor, Nick's three black-haired goddaughters solemnly trading different-colored Jordan almonds from the favors, William Fortune sending Lily out for a twirl as they danced to Glenn Miller.

Frannie turned to frame up another shot and felt someone tap her on the shoulder.

"You're Frannie Fredericks, aren't you?" asked a stocky woman in heavy face makeup and a lime-green silk dress.

In the two weeks since her release from jail, Frannie had become an expert at recognizing the varying reactions of strangers to Lloyd's murder. There were the sympathetic ones, the ones who looked at her with pity, the curious, the sincere. And the ones like this woman, the emotional vultures who just wanted a story to tell.

"It must have been horrible to have your husband murdered like that." The woman eyed her avidly. "And for it to be one of those Mendozas. After everything your family has done for them."

Frannie felt a stir of anger at the presumption. "If you're talking about Roberto Mendoza, he hasn't even been charged." She rose. "Excuse me."

As much as she was thrilled to see Nick and Charlene so happy, she was sick to death of the stares, the comments, the hissing whispers that cut off when she approached. She didn't feel like a guest so much as a target. The good thing about the camera was that it gave her both a shield and a reason to leave.

She snapped a picture of Ricky Faraday holding hands with his girlfriend while a couple of younger boys wrinkled their noses. Nearer by, Josh and Lyndsey worked their way through the tables. He was introducing her to the relatives, Frannie saw. And Lyndsey was taking pains to shake hands and talk with each and every one of them. First Josh's clothes, now his family.

"It's so nice to meet you," Frannie heard her say to Emmett Jamison, who with his wife, Linda, ran the Fortune Foundation. "Everyone speaks so highly of the work the Foundation does. I hope that someday I might be able to come to work there." She paused expectantly.

"Uh, yes, well, stop in sometime." Emmett cleared his throat. "See what we're doing."

Lyndsey blushed becomingly. "Oh, could I?"

Maybe she was just being an overprotective mother, Frannie thought resignedly. Maybe it came from having only one child. Everyone else seemed to like Lyndsey; Josh thought he loved her. Frannie focused and squeezed off a sequence of shots of Josh leading Lyndsey onto the dance floor. It would make a good gift for the girl. A peace offering, perhaps. It was looking more and more like Lyndsey was going to be around for the long term. And Frannie supposed as she skirted a table at the edge of the room, it was past time for her to get used to it.

"She had blood all over her, I heard," someone said nearby, *sotto voce*. Frannie glanced over to see an older woman with short, gray hair leaning over to her companion. "And that Roberto Mendoza just walking the streets as big as life."

Frannie felt the flare of anger.

"You know, everything was fine until he came back," the woman's friend said. "Now we've got fires and murder and all sorts of things."

"I heard he left in the first place because he had to," the gray-haired woman replied.

Her friend nodded sagely. "Trouble with the law, someone said. I just hope they hurry up with the trial and put that murderer away for good."

Lies, complete fabrications, character assassination, Frannie thought as she walked past. An image of Roberto filled her mind—his strength, his unquestioning acceptance—and she stopped and spun back to the pair.

"Well, since I'm the only one who's been charged with the murder so far, I'm personally hoping the trial doesn't happen for a long, long time. Of course, maybe you have evidence the police don't. Smile." The pair gaped at her and she snapped a picture of them. "What a lovely photo of your fillings. Thank you," she sang, and turned away.

She was instantly sorry. "Frannie, Frannie, Frannie, you ought to be ashamed of yourself," she muttered under her breath, shaking her head.

"You think so?" a voice asked. "Here I was just about to applaud you."

Frannie turned to see Gloria Fortune, the wife of her cousin Jack. And the sister of Roberto. "Oh, Gloria, they're driving me crazy."

"You? Five more minutes of this and *I'm* going to be the one in jail for homicide."

"Oh, take down the one in the lime-green," Frannie begged. "I want to watch."

Gloria rolled her eyes, her honey-brown hair rippling. "I don't know whether to laugh or cry. But what am I doing complaining to you?"

"Who better?"

"You know he didn't do it, Frannie, right?"

"Of course I know it. What drives me crazy is that no one else in town seems to. They never even arrested him and everyone's got him convicted. It's not fair," she said in frustration. "He deserves better."

She glanced up and caught Gloria looking at her searchingly.

"You seem to have thought about this," Gloria commented. "I didn't realize you were such a fan of Roberto."

"He and I—I just don't think it's right," she said lamely.

And for no reason she could figure, Gloria suddenly gave a broad smile. "Me, either," she said, reaching out to tuck Frannie's arm through hers. "Tell me more about yourself, Frannie. I think it's time we get to know each other better."

"The young stock looks good."

Roberto and his uncle Ruben walked along the paddock behind the barn at the Double Crown. Roberto had come out to the ranch because he'd been too restless to sit still. There was anger at McCaskill and Wheeler, frustration that after two weeks of asking questions, he knew no more than when he'd started. But most of all, there was Frannie.

"Five colts and seven fillies," Ruben Mendoza said in satisfaction. "They're coming along. We're going to start gentling them." He glanced at Roberto. "You could come out and help with the halter training and getting them used to grooming. I'm too old to lean over and pick up their feet."

"*Tío* Ruben, when are you going to retire?" Roberto stopped to lean on the white railing. A brown mare and her filly walked over, ears pricked.

"I tried retiring," Ruben said, pulling out his pocket knife to quarter one of the apples he habitually carried in his pockets. "Your *Tía* Rosita threatened to brain me with a frying pan."

Roberto watched his uncle feed the mare some apple and reached out for one of the pieces. "That didn't have anything to do with you sneaking her fresh *churros,* did it? You know how she gets about those."

"I have made foolish mistakes in my time, but none so foolish as that. She said I was underfoot. The truth is, I was happy to retire from being retired. And now she has her days at the house, I have my days out here, and all is pleasant." He clapped a hand on Roberto's shoulder. "I will tell you a secret, Robertito. A man can only be as happy as the woman in his life."

Didn't he know it. He hadn't talked to Frannie since the afternoon he'd held her in his arms. And he hadn't stopped thinking about her once. He'd had everything in that moment, all he wanted, heated and gasping against him, and he'd pulled back. He'd been crazy, Roberto thought. Except that deep down he'd known he hadn't had everything. He'd had her body, not her mind.

There were parts of him that didn't seem to get it, though. Morning after morning, he awoke from tumultuous dreams of her, tense from arousal with no outlet, desire settled in his belly like a load of rocks.

He hadn't stopped wanting her once.

"The question is, how do you make them happy?" he asked aloud. The filly poked her muzzle through the slats in the fence, and Roberto held out the apple on the flat of his palm for her to lip up and crunch.

Ruben eyed him. "A young *caballero* like you, I think you would know."

Roberto snorted. "The more I know about women, the more I realize I don't know anything at all."

"Ahh, I understand. The question is not how do you make women happy, the question is how do you make *a* woman happy. A special woman, no?" Ruben turned toward the bar with a half smile on his face. "For that, we must go to my office."

Roberto gave him a dubious look. "Why, do you have a handbook there?"

"Better, *caballero*. A bottle of tequila."

"Now that might just—" Roberto began and stopped short. Frannie rode around the corner from the barnyard on a chestnut mare. She pulled up when she saw him.

He stared at her. The breeze tossed her hair a bit. There was about her a flavor of wildness he couldn't identify. Something kinetic surged between them then, something he had no words for, but that sent the adrenaline rocketing through his veins. The seconds stretched out.

And then she wheeled the mare around and rode out of the barnyard like the hounds of hell were behind her.

Roberto stood, watching without moving, barely registering the fact that his uncle was speaking as the hoofbeats faded. He stirred, and shook his head. "I'm sorry, *Tío* Ruben, what?"

Ruben gave him a shrewd glance. "I asked if you wanted to borrow a horse."

Chapter 10

Frannie crouched over Daisy's withers. She'd had enough. She'd had enough of the sudden silences, the false condolences and outrage of strangers who assumed Roberto had killed Lloyd. She'd given up trying to explain, sick of the way they looked at her, perplexed, as though understanding the facts wasn't nearly as important as having a target to blame. It had taken every last bit of her patience to stay to the end of the wedding.

And now, she wanted to wipe it all away.

She needed speed, she needed the wind in her hair, the vibration of hooves on the ground.

She needed Roberto.

"Come on, girl," she urged Daisy as the mare galloped along. Frannie knew where they were going. Even two decades hadn't wiped the memory away. Out through the rolling countryside toward the afternoon sun that hung low in the sky. Daisy picked her way down an embankment to cross the little stream that wound through the Double Crown, then Frannie urged her on, faster, to the place that lay waiting. They followed the trail straight up the side of the hill to the red oaks, the trail she hadn't used in years. Nineteen of them. And then they were at the top, out of breath.

Blue sky, a soft breeze and the almost-liquid rippling of the grass over the hillsides. This was what she'd needed—this sense that she'd escaped from all that dogged her, that she'd left it all behind back at the ranch house. Here, she was just Frannie, with no fears, no responsibilities, no threats—just open space and silence.

And then she heard the sound of hooves.

She'd been certain he would come, from the moment she'd seen him in the barnyard. She hadn't come to the ranch expecting him to be there, and yet the sight of his truck had come as no surprise. In some strange way, it was as though she'd known in her bones she would see him. And she'd known in her bones that he'd follow.

Roberto rode up over the edge of the escarpment. There were no words spoken, no smile, as he reined his horse in. Intensity shimmered around him. He slid out of the saddle, and Frannie began walking toward him. He took a step, then two, and then they were running toward each other across the gap.

The next instant, they were in each other's arms, pressed together so tightly she almost couldn't breathe, and yet she didn't want him to stop because it meant giving up this reality, this contact, this connection, the utter rightness of the two of them together in this place at this moment.

His mouth on hers was like a benediction and the words for what she felt were "now," and "finally," and "yes." She feasted on him like a woman starving. Her hands cradled his face. And then she was sliding her arms around him, tugging his shirt out of his jeans so that she could run her hands up underneath and feel his skin, finally, his skin against her palms.

It was unimaginable that she'd waited, impossible now to understand how or why she'd held back, when all she wanted was to devour him. The world reduced to touch and taste and sound: the feel of his hands roaming over her body, the dark male flavor of him, the rapid-fire clatter of snaps as she ripped his shirt open. Pleasure layered upon pleasure, touch upon touch.

With a sound of impatience, Roberto shrugged off his shirt. He caught the bottom of her tank top in his hands, stripping it off over her head with a suddenness that took her breath. For an instant, she stood before him, bare breasted. Then they came together, and the heat and the feel of his naked chest against the sensitive skin of her breasts made her moan aloud. How could they have spent so many years apart when the thought of separating for even a moment to pull off their boots seemed unendurable? They divided, they rejoined. And open mouth to open mouth, they lowered down to the grass as one.

Roberto unsnapped her jeans and tugged them down her thighs. She lay back on the grass and their discarded shirts, hair tousled, eyes slumberous, wearing only a scrap of black lace around her hips. He trailed fingers down over the long line of her body. "Frannie," he whispered in something close to awe.

And she was long and lovely and luminous, the unformed lines of girlhood turned to the sweeping curves of woman. And she was more beautiful, more desirable as an adult than she'd ever been as a girl. There was magic to her and mystery and a sort of hypnotic secret that came only from woman.

How many times had he dreamed of this, how many nights had he woken alone in the darkness, body soaked with sweat, lips still heated from the memory of hers, knowing, knowing above all else that they belonged together, that she was the only one?

And knowing that it was impossible.

To have her now in his arms, warm and willing, silky and fragrant against him, was more than he could ever have dreamed. It took him beyond simple desire into a kind of delirious joy. And when he stripped off the rest of his clothes and lay down next to her again, it was as though some tone had been sounded in his deepest soul, as pure as the ringing of a crystal goblet, a sound for which the words were "yes" and "this is it," the certainty that he'd found the one true thing.

Frannie gasped at the feel of his hands sliding over her body. How many times over the years had she wondered? How many times had she told herself that she just wasn't made for sex, that Lloyd was right—she was frigid? It was her, always something wrong with her that she couldn't respond to the impatient gropings of his hands, the awkward explorations that never worked because he never bothered to understand how it felt, and what she liked and what aroused her.

All that was gone because he didn't matter, none of it mattered. It wasn't about thinking when Roberto touched her. It was only about sensation, reaction, the same way a flame burned without knowing how or why.

He slid his hand up over her breasts and she arched against him, moaning incoherently as sensation ricocheted through her. And all she wanted was more because it wasn't enough, could never be enough. There weren't enough hours in her life for her to feel the roughness of his palm slip over her breasts, to feel those clever, clever fingers turn her nipples to hard peaks. And yet this was just the beginning; she knew there was more.

She remembered.

He traced his tongue down her throat to her breasts. The teasing trail dragged a moan from her. When he fastened his mouth over her nipple, coherent thought simply deserted her. She jolted, crying out, pressing against him, wanting, needing to move, to explore, yet utterly overwhelmed by the overlapping sensations of mouth and lips and tongue, by his hand tormenting her other breast. It was too much, but not enough. She burned for more.

As though he'd heard her thoughts, Roberto shifted to press kisses over the quivering flat of her belly. And Frannie was aware of precisely this: the soft grass beneath her, the warm trail of his tongue, the tension forming between her thighs, a slow curl of heat she barely recognized because it had been so long since she'd felt it.

With a sound of impatience, he hooked his fingers in the sides of her briefs, dragging them down and leaving her open to the heat of his breath. A shiver ran through her. Anticipation had her moving restlessly against him, clutching at the grass, his shoulders, anything.

Then he laid his mouth on her and she cried out. There was heat, the softness of his lips, the maddening swirl of his tongue as he caressed her and took her somewhere she hadn't been in so many years it should have been alien, and yet it was instantly familiar, this tension, this pressure, this bursting need. He took her to a world she'd soared in once, back before she'd known fear or defeat, a flight of ecstasy fueled by touch, her hips bucking against him until she was flung into free fall, shuddering and quaking, spiraling down from a great height into laughter and pure joy.

"Oh my, where have you been?" She kissed him wherever she could reach, half-giddy as he moved up over her.

"It doesn't matter. I'm here now."

But the tension had only been banked back, not vanquished. With his hands and his mouth he set her to trembling. When he moved up and over her, she wanted, she needed in a way she'd never dreamed possible. The setting sun behind him lit his hair with a penumbra of fire, shadowing his eyes, making him look like some primitive warrior.

"I need to be inside you," he ground out in what was half plea, half demand, and when he moved himself through that slick cleft between her thighs, searching for the spot, she held her breath in anticipation, shivering, feeling the ache, the need, the emptiness waiting to be filled.

"Please," she whispered.

Then he shifted and drove himself into her, and in one hot, slick rush they were coupled.

Her cry echoed his groan. For an instant they were poised, staring into each other's eyes, their gazes locked together as intimately as their bodies. Roberto leaned in and pressed a kiss on her. *"Querida,"* he breathed against her lips.

And slowly, slowly he began to move.

There was no rush, no furious pounding. Instead, his strokes were measured, almost leisurely, taking him nearly all the way out of her, then back in slow and deep. But there was a sense of power banked back in each thrust, a sense of breathless expectation. His eyes burned black with arousal. His body trembled with the effort of control.

And it drove her mad with need.

Each slide of his flesh against hers made her shudder. Each slide took her higher. She clutched at his back, feeling the muscles clench and flow under her fingers as he moved faster. And gradually, gradually, he reached a rhythm, that rhythm, that ancient, timeless rhythm that was love and hope and renewal all in one.

And it was impossible—the tension, the exquisite rush of pleasure that swept through her with every stroke—impossible for her to bear it one more instant, impossible for it to end. She gasped for air, twisted against him, wrapped her legs around his waist. She cried out for more. And then the tension compressed all that need, and arousal and desire down into a single point, a single point that held for a shuddering instant before it suddenly exploded, bursting through her entire body, sending her jolting and crying out, clenching around him in mindless ecstasy.

And she heard his helpless groan as it put him over the edge, as he drove into her one final time and spilled himself, pulling her hard against him.

Above them, one by one, the stars came out in the darkening sky.

He wasn't naive enough to think that perfect happiness existed, but if it did, it would have to feel something like this, Roberto thought as he lay beside Frannie, waiting for his heart rate to level.

She stirred. "If we stay out here too much longer, we're not going to be able to find our way back."

"Relax, there's a full moon tonight. Besides, the horses know how to find the barn."

She shifted to look at him. "How did you find this place again? It's been almost twenty years."

"I don't know. I didn't think about it." He hadn't, just mounted Barnabus, the gelding Ruben had given him, and gone on instinct. Or maybe it wasn't instinct. Maybe some part of him had a special sense for her and where she was. Maybe they were connected. It was a ridiculous thought, he knew it was ridiculous, but maybe a man was allowed to be ridiculous at a time like this.

Roberto laughed aloud.

Frannie turned her head toward him. "What's the joke?"

He shook his head a little. "Nothing. Life is good." He leaned over and pressed a kiss to her nose, and figured he'd kiss her cheek while he was there. And since her mouth was nearby, he might as well do that, and…

Long moments slipped away as hand smoothed over flesh, needs long denied built afresh. They touched, they demanded. Again they rose, again they fell. And this time when they finished, they stayed linked together and let themselves slip further into slumber.

The full moon overhead shone down, silvering the path before them as they rode up to the barn. Triggered by their motion, the flood lamps flicked on in the stable yard.

"Finally, light," Frannie said.

"I thought moonlight was supposed to be romantic."

"There's romantic and there's not being able to see where you're going." She stopped beyond the mounting block and slid down from the saddle, feeling the sweet ache between her thighs. "Lucky thing we found the road. Otherwise, we'd have been stuck out there all night."

Roberto gave her a lazy smile. "I can think of worse things than being left with nothing to do but make love with you until sunrise."

A shiver ran through her stomach. Still… "What would your uncle think if we'd come traipsing in tomorrow morning?"

"I doubt *Tío* Ruben would have been all that surprised. Hell, he was the one who gave me Barnabus to ride."

"He knew?"

"*Querida,* at this point, I'd say anyone who looks at us together for long will have a pretty good idea something's going on."

Like Lily, she thought. "Lily already warned me about being seen with you."

"Really?" His gaze sharpened. "When?"

Frannie led Daisy into the railed, U-shaped enclosure of the cross ties and turned the mare to face the front. "Last week, when I met her for lunch. Your name slipped out." She concentrated on swapping Daisy's bridle for her halter and clipping the lead lines onto either side.

"And she said stay away from that awful Mendoza boy?" His voice held not humor, but flickers of irritation.

"Lily isn't Cindy, Roberto. It's not about you as a person, it's the situation. My husband's dead, we've both been in jail for his murder, and now the two of us are involved? If that seems fast to me, how do you think it's going to look to everyone else?"

He ducked out of Barnabus' adjacent cross tie to face her. "If it was too fast, why did you come to the Double Crown?"

"I didn't know I'd find you here."

"But you rode out knowing I'd follow."

"Yes."

"Why?"

She turned to unfasten Daisy's cinch. "I'd think that would be obvious."

"Nothing's obvious here, Frannie, and nothing's simple. Are you getting cold feet about what we just did?"

"Yes. No. I don't know," she burst out. "How can I when all I want is for you to touch me again?"

His gaze heated. Electricity snapped between the two of them as he pulled her into his arms to fuse his mouth to hers. Desire and frustration, longing and hope. And fear. The emotions swirled around in the kiss, overlaying that always-present flare of arousal.

He released her. "Wheeler and McCaskill stopped by to see me today."

"What?" Head still spinning from the kiss, Frannie stared at him.

"It's all right. It wasn't about bringing either of us in. But it's gotten back to them that I'm asking questions and they don't like it."

Daisy shifted impatiently. Focus on the details, Frannie reminded herself. She needed to focus on getting Daisy untacked and groomed and bedded down, not on things she couldn't change. She moved away from Roberto to pull off the saddle and set it on the rail. "I don't know why they care. It's not like they're coming up with any answers."

"No, but they take a dim view of people they think are interfering with their investigation." Roberto walked back to where Barnabus was crosstied.

"You're not interfering with anything."

"That's not how they see it."

Frannie picked up the dandy brush and began sweeping the dirt out of Daisy's coat in long strokes. "You talked to a few people, that's all." She stopped. "Isn't it?"

"Yes, and I told them that. I also told them that you weren't a part of any of it."

Her stomach tightened with anxiety. "Me? How did I come into it?"

"Either they're watching us or your mother told them. Or both."

"Cindy? I don't understand."

He let out a breath. "She stopped by when I was at your house, working on the garage door."

"She stopped by? When?" Irritation pricked her. "And when, exactly, were you planning to tell me about it?"

"I didn't think I had to. She told Josh to tell you—I assumed he had."

"He didn't." And there was too much going on all together. "What did she want?"

"I don't know. But she wasn't thrilled to see me. She apparently went to the cops and told them I was asking questions and got them all riled up."

Focus on the details. Frannie went back to brushing Daisy. "What did the detectives say?"

"They tried to threaten me with arrest, but they don't have any cause." Roberto hesitated. "When that didn't work, they made noises about bringing you in for violating the conditions of your release by talking to people involved in the case."

The brush dropped out of her suddenly nerveless fingers. "But I—"

"You haven't talked to anybody, Frannie, I know." He bent down to retrieve it. "And they know, too. It's an empty threat. They're just trying to scare us."

"They're doing a good job." It was starting again,

that sense that everything was coming down at once, and she couldn't control any of it.

Swiftly, Roberto moved to her, put a hand to her cheek. "It's okay. They don't have anything on either of us or we'd be back in jail already."

"But that could change at any moment."

"Until they solve the murder, yes. The problem is, they also don't have anything on the case that we haven't given to them."

"What does that mean, we just wait?"

"We could. I can stop what I'm doing if you say so and leave it to your brother Ross. Or he and I could both stay out of it, which is what the cops want. I don't know that that's going to help us, though. The other possibility is that I keep asking questions and see if something bubbles up. It's your call—what do you want?"

"I want this done," she burst out, grabbing the saddle and bridle. "I want to stop worrying. I want to stop thinking about Josh and you and me being in trouble. I want to get on with my life." She strode toward the barn and the tack room.

He grabbed Barnabus' tack and followed. "That's the same thing I want."

"And do you really think what you're doing is likely to make that happen?"

"I don't know, to be honest. I'm not an investigator, I don't have experience to go by. But I do know people, and sometimes putting pressure in the right place can break something loose. To me, it's a chance worth taking. It's not just about me, though. I'm not going to do anything that might put you at risk unless you say it's okay."

It was too much, Frannie thought. It made her want to clap her hands over her ears, to run, to get far, far away from everyone and everything. And yet she knew that wasn't possible. Defiance stirred. "They could come get me at any time—I've known that from the day I got out. And I want it to stop. We've got to end this." She slapped on the barn lights and turned to him. "If you think there's even a chance that what you're doing will help, then keep at it."

"I think that's the right choice."

"There's a bigger issue here, though," she continued, "and that's the two of us. Lily was right, you and me being involved right now is a bad move. How do you think it's going to look to people if we start showing up around town together with Lloyd dead?"

"The police asked me about that, too," Roberto said. "The problem is, we are involved."

Frannie stepped into the tack room without responding and hung up the bridle.

He followed her inside. "Or are you talking about more than just staying out of the public eye?" he said.

"I think we need to keep our distance."

"This isn't about how it looks, is it?" Roberto asked, eyes steady on her. "It's about you backing away."

Temper flared. "I wanted what happened tonight. I still do—but it's not just about me, it's about this whole situation. We're not kids anymore. We have to do what's smart, Roberto. We have to be grown-ups. And right now, that means keeping this under wraps."

His jaw tightened. "And after?"

She took two swift steps toward him and pressed her mouth to his. The seconds went by and he felt the saddle slipping out of his hands.

She stepped back. "After, we'll see what happens."

Chapter 11

"What can I get for you?" Roberto asked, tossing down a couple of bar mats before the blonde in the red dress. Appropriate, he supposed, since she was here at Red.

She tossed her hair back. "My friends are going to have a margarita and a blueberry peach cobbler martini, and I'm going to try your PB&J martini."

A peanut butter and jelly martini. Roberto resisted the urge to roll his eyes as he reached for bottles and started mixing. Why people sucked down syrupy-sweet stuff and called it a cocktail was beyond him. If they didn't like the taste of alcohol, then why the hell drink it? And why try to pretend one of these concoctions was a martini when the only thing it had in common with the classic vodka and vermouth version was the shape of the glass?

But he didn't figure he had any business saying that

to a customer, especially not one buying ten-dollar cocktails. It wasn't her fault he'd been a cranky SOB for the past week. To compensate, he dredged up a smile.

"Are you good?" purred the blonde.

"What?" Roberto blinked, his hands freezing in the midst of pouring the contents of the shaker into the martini glass.

"Are you good? At mixing drinks," the blonde added with a throaty laugh.

It took him a minute to realize she was coming on to him. Of course. And meanwhile, the one woman he wanted, the woman who made it impossible for him to think, to sleep, he couldn't get near.

"I don't know, you tell me." Roberto set the martini on the bar mat before the blonde.

"It sounds like an invitation," she said, lifting up the glass to take a drink. "Mmm. Well, if you're this good at cocktails, I can hardly wait to see more."

The door from the outside opened. "—just have one drink and go," said a female voice. He glanced up out of habit to see two or three women walking in. And then everything seemed to stop for a moment.

Because with them was Frannie.

Adrenaline surged through his veins. Seven days had passed since they'd been together, seven days during which he hadn't touched her, hadn't seen her, hadn't even talked to her. Seven days during which all he'd done was want. And now, she was here, just across the room from him, so close and yet achingly far away.

"—you think?" The blonde was staring at him, obviously looking for an answer.

Roberto brought himself back. "What?"

She slid her fingers down the stem of her glass. "I

said, maybe I ought to come back near closing time and order myself another martini."

He put the other two drinks up on the bar and cashed out her tab. "Yeah, sure, there will be someone tending bar until eleven. Excuse me."

He moved to fill orders for one of the waitresses, but he was really only watching Frannie and her friends walk across the bar to cluster around a small table. Mechanically, he mixed drinks, grateful for the practice he'd gotten over the previous three months. It allowed his hands to keep moving while every bit of his attention was bent on her.

She slid onto one of the high bar chairs, shrugging off her purse and catching the strap as it hit her wrist so that she could hook it over the chair back. There was something unconsciously graceful and innately feminine about the gesture. Roberto snorted at himself as he opened a beer. This was how bad he'd gotten—even watching her take off her purse knocked him over.

And then she glanced up and caught his eye and it took him a second or two to remember how to breathe.

Fate's timing sucked. It had taken years, but they'd finally found each other again. They'd reconnected, slowly, but surely. For one incredible night, Frannie had overcome her fears and they'd glimpsed what they could be together.

Then the specter of Lloyd's murder had arisen and now the only thing more impossible than staying away from her was going to her. Silently, he damned Lloyd Fredericks. But damning him wasn't going to help anything. What was going to help was finding the murderer and putting this whole mess to rest.

Roberto caught Frannie's eye again. Putting a shot

glass on the counter, he poured in some tequila then cut his gaze and focused on the glass.

He didn't have to do it twice. "I'll get the drinks," he heard her tell her friends.

Then she was walking over to him and all he could do was watch and imagine for just that moment how it would be if she were coming to him for real. She wore a dress that swirled around her calves and left her arms bare, a dress the exact blue of her eyes. Her sunbeam hair gleamed.

She stopped before him and rested her hands on the polished wood of the bar. He found himself fascinated by the beat of her pulse in her throat. "How are you?" he asked.

"I'm good. How about you?"

"Just now? Perfect." A wisp of her scent reached him and that quickly he was catapulted back to those moments under the red oaks when he'd held her in his arms. He could taste her lips, feel her soft skin, hear the whisper of the grass in the breeze.

Her fingers were right there, inches from his as he tossed down the bar napkins. His mouth went dry with want. What was the harm in touching her? It would take so little to reach out, lay his hand over hers just for a second. Instead, he rested it on the edge of the wood and looked his fill.

"You're beautiful," he said.

She flushed. "I want to order drinks."

"I want you."

The quiet words vibrated in the air. For a beat, neither moved. Desire surged between them like a physical thing.

Frannie moistened her lips. "You should be careful. Someone could hear you."

There was a burst of laughter from a group farther down the bar. "Unlikely, but never mind. What can I get you?"

"I'll have a mojito, plus a Dos Equis and two frozen margaritas for my friends."

"Salt?"

"One with, one without."

"Coming up." He added margarita mix, tequila and ice to a blender and flipped it on.

"Have you found anything out?" she asked.

"Nothing noteworthy so far. I'm going to go see Lyndsey tomorrow." He poured the margaritas into glasses. "She might know something about what Josh did at the Spring Fling. I'll let you know what I find out."

"Good luck."

"I need it. It's driving me crazy that I can't find someone else, anyone else, who saw that guy who tossed away the crowbar. I need a way to convince the cops he's real. If I only had—" He stopped, staring down at the mint leaves he was muddling for Frannie's mojito. Like he'd been muddled, he realized suddenly. "We've been missing a bet."

"What do you mean?"

"Your camera. You always take it with you places. Did you have it with you at the Spring Fling?"

"Of course. I took three or four rolls of film before everything happened."

"Have you gone through them?"

"No." She smiled faintly. "I've been busy. I did get them developed, though."

"Good. We should go through them, see if we notice anything unusual. Maybe we'll find a picture of the guy, or catch Lloyd talking to someone."

"It's kind of a long shot."

"True. Then again, what have we got to lose? Let's at least go through them." He placed her mojito before her and set the other drinks beside it. "I could come over to your house."

"Do you think that's smart?"

"Do you care?"

Her eyes darkened. "No."

"Good. Then when?"

"Tomorrow night after it gets dark, maybe nine or ten. Josh is going to the ball game with Lyndsey. His curfew isn't until midnight. We should have plenty of time."

"To having plenty of time." Roberto picked up the shot of tequila, clicked it unobtrusively on her mojito glass and downed it.

"I'll see you there." She filled her hands with drinks.

"I'll see you in my dreams."

Lyndsey Pollack lived with her mother on the north side of town in a tired-looking neighborhood that had probably been old already when Eisenhower was president. There was no guard shack here, just sidewalks cracked by tree roots and lawns sporting foreclosure signs.

The Pollackses' small ranch could have used a few gallons of paint, Roberto thought as he studied the flaking stucco around the doorbell. There was no response when he pressed the button.

The red car he'd seen his first day at Frannie's was in the drive, but the shades on the house were still drawn. He checked his watch. Ten-thirty. He rang the bell again and waited. He'd hoped to stop by early enough to catch Lyndsey before she lit out for the day, but maybe he'd missed her. Or maybe she was just a late sleeper.

He was reaching out for the bell one last time when

he heard the noise of a dead bolt being drawn and the door opened a few inches.

"Jeez, chill out, already. There are people sleeping." Lyndsey peered out at him. "Who are you?"

"Roberto Mendoza. I was the guy working on the doors over at Josh Fredericks' house last week."

"Oh, yeah." She hesitated. "What do you want?"

"I was hoping we could talk for a couple minutes."

"About what?"

"About Josh and the Spring Fling."

She was already shaking her head before he even finished. "No thank—"

He put out his hand to block the closing door. "Wait."

Something in her eyes hardened. "Look, mister, I don't know you. You keep up like this, I'm going to call the cops." She reached in her pocket and pulled out a cell phone.

"The cops are precisely what I'm trying to avoid. Hear me out for five minutes. For Josh's sake."

It stopped her, as he'd intended. "What are you talking about?"

"Let me in and I'll tell you."

She studied him a minute, chewing on her lip. Even though she was seventeen, her face still held some of the unformed roundness of childhood. "Okay," she said finally, "but we'll have to keep it down. My mom's sleeping. She works the night shift."

"Whatever you say."

The house was smaller than it looked from the outside. Over the fireplace directly opposite the door hung a convex mirror with metallic rays coming off it. The sunlight streaming in through the back windows showed the worn spots on the carpet.

"Let's go into the kitchen," Lyndsey said, turning through a swinging door. "We'll make less noise there."

If the neighborhood looked like it was from the fifties, the kitchen was more a relic of the seventies with avocado appliances and maple veneer cabinets.

"You can sit over there." She nodded at a vintage dinette set. It was another seventies relic with a faux woodgrain top and a quartet of swiveling vinyl chairs. A stack of mail and a dirty cereal bowl sat to one side; a sweatshirt draped over the back of one of the chairs. Or not a sweatshirt, Roberto realized, looking closer. A black hoodie.

"Isn't it a little warm for sweatshirts?"

"What? Oh, that's Josh's," she said dismissively, digging a Coke out of the refrigerator. "He left it last time he was here." She cracked open the can and took a swallow. "All right, so talk. That's what you wanted, right?"

What he wanted was to take a good close look at the hoodie, but he supposed it would be a useless exercise. If it had been the one Josh had worn the night of the Spring Fling, he would have washed it. Assuming he'd gotten anything on it. Pure speculation, Roberto told himself. Then again...

"You were at the Spring Fling with Josh, right?"

"Yeah."

"What did you do?"

"Walked around, went on some rides. Ate corndogs." Lyndsey didn't bother to sit, but leaned against the counter.

"How did he seem? Did he act funny?"

"What do you mean, funny?" She tucked a strand of hair behind her ear. "You said something about Josh and the cops. What, is he in trouble? Like he had something to do with his dad getting killed?"

"Did he?"

"No way. Why would he have done that?"

"Things happen. Besides, from what I hear Lloyd Fredericks was putting up a pretty stiff fight to split the two of you up."

"Yeah? So? It made Josh mad—it made me mad—but you don't kill a guy over that."

"Someone killed him over something."

"Well, it wasn't Josh," she flared, thumping her Coke down angrily.

"How do you know?"

"Because I know Josh. Besides, I was with him."

"The whole night? Were you there when he fought with Lloyd?"

She opened her mouth, then closed it. "I had to go home a little early. I had this sinus thing."

"When did you leave?"

"Nine-thirty, ten. But I don't know anything about a fight."

She was lying, he thought. "That's funny, because it happened around nine. There were witnesses. People heard it."

A trapped look flashed over her face. "Maybe I had the time wrong. I don't remember."

"If you saw anything at all, if he said anything, you need to tell me."

"Josh wouldn't…you don't… I can't talk to you about this." Abruptly she seemed near tears. "You have to go."

"If you care about Josh, you'll tell me what you know."

Wordlessly, she walked to the door.

Roberto waited a moment, then followed. At the threshold, he stopped. "Here's one of my cards. It's got my cell phone number on it. If you change your mind and want to talk, call me."

She took the card, but didn't look at it. Instead, she

watched him walk out the door and step to the edge of the porch.

"Hey, mister."

Roberto turned back to her.

Lyndsey hesitated. "Lloyd Fredericks was a bad person. Whoever killed him did us all a favor."

Half a loaf was better than none. It was the mantra that had helped Frannie survive. Every time life with Lloyd had become intolerable over the years, she'd looked at Josh and reminded herself that maybe she couldn't have it all, but she had a lot. And it had gotten her through.

But it hadn't helped the previous evening at Red. It hadn't helped at all. She'd been with Roberto and yet not. She'd spoken to him, but only briefly, unable to say anything she really wanted to. She'd seen him, but only in carefully rationed glances, cautious not to give herself away. And she'd stood for an excruciating few moments with her hand mere inches from his, almost vibrating with the need to touch.

Walking out that door after only half a loaf had been one of the hardest things she'd ever done.

Over a week had passed since they'd been truly together. She knew all the reasons they had to stay apart. She knew they had to do it to defray suspicion; she knew she had to do it for her own preservation. In the past five weeks she'd been buffeted by crises and change on all sides. She was hanging on by a thread.

But if she had to wait any longer to see Roberto, she was going to die.

Frannie blinked. A faint pulse of alarm shivered through her. How had this happened? How had she come to need him so much? How, when she'd done her best to keep him at a distance? She'd let him sneak under her guard, she'd let him become a part of her life. She was dependent yet again. And what in God's name was she going to do now?

In time with that thought, she heard his knock and suddenly it all ceased to matter. One moment she was opening the door. The next, she was in Roberto's arms, crushed against him, his mouth sealed to hers. His hands roved over her body, taking ownership, making her shiver. She gloried in the reality of being able to touch him at last.

Roberto made an impatient noise and swung her up in his arms. He carried her down the hall to the room they'd been in two weeks before, this time not to fix the door, but to lay her down on that bed he'd fantasized about.

And do all the things he'd fantasized about next.

She sat up, her legs dangling over the edge. Her fingers raced down the buttons of his shirt and unbuckled his belt. "Now," she said, freeing him.

And stepping up close to the high bed, flipping up her little skirt, he obeyed.

It was hard and deep, fast and furious. There was no patience for undressing, no time for finesse, only an urgent need to come together. He felt her wrap her legs around his waist. He heard her cry out with every surge. He drove them both, recklessly, heedlessly, into that carnal haze where only pleasure had meaning. Control was precarious; the edge was too close.

And then they were there. He felt her tense, saw her throw her head back, heard her cries crescendo. Then she was quaking about him even as she dragged him past the point of no return.

And he knew as they lay after, hearts still racing together, that there was no point of return from her.

Chapter 12

Frannie pulled a floral box of photographs out of a cabinet and put it on the kitchen table where she and Roberto were sitting.

"I haven't even gotten them into an album yet," she said apologetically. "There's been a lot going on."

"You don't say," Roberto drawled.

"Anyway, here they are." She spilled them out onto the table. "What did you find out at Lyndsey's?"

"A whole lot and nothing at all," he said.

"What does that mean?"

"She knows something. She didn't want to let me in at first, until I mentioned Josh. I asked her about the Spring Fling and she couldn't keep her stories straight."

"What do you mean?"

"She swears he couldn't possibly have done it, but then she got all upset when I asked her about the fight with Lloyd, which she also swears she didn't know anything about. She said she was with Josh all the time, except later she said she left early, but the time she gave me was after the fight. When I pointed that out, she told me to leave. I think she was there." Roberto locked eyes with her. "And she had his hoodie."

"She's always wearing his shirts and things. Anyway, what's the importance of the hoodie?"

"I thought I told you about this. The guy I saw throw away the crowbar was wearing some kind of black hoodie, just like the one I saw today."

"What?" She stared at him. "You're sure?"

"Positive."

Relief made her lightheaded. "But Josh wasn't wearing a hoodie at the Spring Fling. Look, I'll show you." She shifted through the pictures, hands shaking with barely suppressed excitement. "He was wearing a blue snap-button shirt and his black cowboy hat."

"He could've changed, Frannie."

"When? Before the murder or after? If you saw him running off in a hoodie, he would have to have left his hat somewhere once he put the sweatshirt on. I can tell you for a fact that he didn't have it. Here," she said triumphantly, sliding a photograph across to him. "See? Western shirt and Stetson. Not a hoodie in sight. It wasn't him."

"This doesn't prove anything. He could have put his hat anywhere. He could have put the hoodie on before he met Lloyd to be less obvious, then run off in it, ditched it and come back. Anyway, where's his hat now? Have you seen it since the Spring Fling?"

"Of course," she responded. "It's here. He wore his ball cap to the game tonight."

She took the stairs two at a time to Josh's bedroom, then stopped short at the sight of one of his gray hoodies thrown over the back of his desk chair. It didn't matter, she reminded herself. It wasn't possible that he'd murdered Lloyd, let alone murdered him and brought the blood-soaked clothing home. Roberto was imagining things.

She stepped back into the kitchen to find him still studying the photograph.

"Here it is." She dropped the hat on the table triumphantly.

Roberto didn't look up from the picture.

"Hello? Earth to Roberto."

His eyes flicked from her to the hat, then back to the photograph. A muscle jumped in his jaw.

"Admit it, we were wrong. It's not Josh."

"It's not Josh." He slapped the photo down on the table. "It's me."

For an instant, the words simply refused to register. When they did, it snatched her breath away. Roberto, the killer? "That's not possible," she whispered. "You couldn't have murdered Lloyd. You couldn't have."

Roberto shook his head. "I don't mean the murder. I mean this." He held up the photograph. "This isn't Josh. It's a picture of me."

Relief made her weak, then angry. "Funny," she said shortly, reaching out for the photo.

"No," he said. "I'm serious. Look at it."

It was one of the many crowd shots she'd taken that night, showing people milling about not far from the carnival. Josh was in profile, his hat pulled down low, collar high, the gaudy wash of color from the rides turning his skin rainbow. "I am looking at it. It's Josh. I know my son."

But as the seconds passed, she wasn't so sure. Did the hair look darker, or was it simply the lighting?

"Look at the hat, Frannie," Roberto said softly. "Look at the hatband."

Silver medallions, shining in the lights. But the hat she'd brought downstairs from Josh's room had a band of tiny cobalt-blue beads, a birthday gift to Josh from Lyndsey the year before.

"The band in that picture is made of hand-tooled conchas from a Navajo reservation." Roberto reached over to the chair next to him and lifted up his black Stetson. The silver medallions gleamed. "I bought it about fifteen years ago out in Arizona from the guy who made it. It's one of a kind."

Frannie stared at the photo. And as though it were a game of hidden pictures, she saw what she'd missed—the stronger nose, the shorter hair, the broader shoulders. It was Josh, and yet not him. An older brother, maybe, or— And for an instant she felt the room tilt around her. "I must… I must be tired," she said aloud.

There was a buzzing in her ears. The profile in the photo looked like Josh, the way he held his shoulders looked like Josh. She glanced up at the framed picture of him on the étagère opposite the table. And suddenly it was like dominoes falling. "You stand the same way," she said slowly. "Your eyes are set the same. You walk the same way, you— No," she broke off, shaking her head. "No, that's—"

"What? Ridiculous? Is it so far off?"

She shot to her feet, raking her hair back off her face with both hands. "It's late and I'm getting punchy. We both are. There is no way that—"

"What?"

She shook her head. "It's impossible."

"What? Say it," he demanded, striding over to her.

"It can't be."

"Say it." He caught at her shoulders, forcing her to face him. "Say it. Josh is my son."

"No."

"He's my son, Frannie. He's ours."

"No," she cried out, slapping at his chest, and then her hands turned to fists and she was pummeling him, "No, no, no," she repeated, tears sliding crazily down her cheeks, her voice half-hysterical.

He folded his arms around her, trapping her against him until she quieted.

"My whole life..." she whispered brokenly against his chest.

And in that moment, looking down at her stricken face he understood Lloyd's assailant because for the first time in his life, he truly wanted to hurt someone.

And if Cindy Fortune had been there in that moment, he wouldn't have been responsible for what he would have done.

"Sit." He folded Frannie into a chair and one after another, yanked open the cabinet doors. "Do you have any liquor? Whiskey?" He found the bottles and poured them both a couple of fingers of tequila. He thumped Frannie's tumbler down before her. "Here, drink."

"I don't—"

"Drink it," he ordered.

He knocked back his own shot, but it didn't do much to calm him. Instead, he paced. "You and I had sex the night after you were with Lloyd."

"But the results of the DNA test—"

"I don't give a damn about the DNA test. It's true. You and I both know it. And I have a pretty good idea who did it."

"My...mother?"

"Who else would have had reason? Not Lloyd's family, not you. It had to be her."

"But how?" Frannie stood. "It's a lab test. She couldn't just magically change it."

"She wanted me out of your life and she wanted

Lloyd in. And she was ready to do whatever it took, including recruiting help."

"So everything I've lived through in the last nineteen years is because of a lie?" Frannie's voice rose. "Because of *her?*" She snatched up a porcelain figurine from the étagère, whirling to fling it against the wall. It burst into fragments.

"Hey, easy."

"Don't tell me easy," she rounded on him. "She lied to me. She gave me to Lloyd like I was chattel." She flung her hands up. "My *God.*"

Roberto welcomed the bright flare of anger, something to take away that terrifying fragility. He watched as she strode back and forth.

"This is crazy. Half of me can't understand how I could have missed it. The other half says there's no way it could be true or I would have figured it out years ago. Josh was blond when he was younger, explain that," she challenged.

"So are you. So was my grandmother. Why are you fighting this? Do you not want to believe it because you can't accept that your mother did this to you? Or because you don't want him to be mine?"

"I don't want to believe it because I can't accept that half my life has been built on a lie."

"And mine, too." He caught at her hands. "But Josh is real. I'm real. What you and I feel for each other is real. The lies that kept us apart are in the past now. What matters is right here."

"It's not that easy, Roberto."

"Easy? You think this is easy?" he asked, spinning away in frustration. "I don't even have words for how I feel right now. We've been robbed, Frannie, all of us, years taken away, just stolen. And if I think about it too long I'm going to lose it." He strode back and forth, eyes on her. "So I'd rather focus on what I can change, and what I can do and what comes next. You tell me, what do we do now?"

She stared at him. "What do we do now?"

"There's Josh. What do we say to him? How do we get the test redone? How do we deal with Cindy?"

Even the thought of her mother generated a wave of fury so powerful it made Frannie feel vaguely sick. "I can't handle dealing with her right now."

"Josh, then. What do we tell him? How do we confirm the results? How do we become a family?"

"A family?" What she'd always longed for and yet it seemed like an illusion, something to be snatched away the instant she began to believe in it. Happiness wasn't a part of her life. Reality had never been so kind.

But Roberto believed in it. "He's our son. We belong together, we always have. Cindy did her best to keep us apart, but it didn't work. And maybe it's late, but there's still time."

Cindy. Her stomach roiled. "You're going too fast," Frannie said sharply. "Stop." There were too many changes all at once, too many emotions buffeting her. Jet fighters trying to turn too quickly broke apart under the strain, she thought, the way she felt like things were breaking apart. Everything she'd experienced for nineteen years was a lie, every nightmare moment she'd endured had occurred in a prison of her mother's making. She'd nearly been destroyed, and now to discover that it should never have happened made her almost dizzy.

"I love you, Frannie," Roberto said. "I want us to be together. Didn't you tell me how you used to imagine that Josh was mine? Now it's real. We can make it real."

"It's too fast," she said again, circling around the table. "You don't understand. My entire life has been turned upside down. Lloyd wasn't just verbally abusive, Roberto. He hit me. Not often, but he made it count when he did."

"That bas—"

"But I survived it," she cut him off. "I survived it, and I lived through it day after day because I told myself that Josh needed his father, however poor a specimen he was. I told myself that it was a bed of my own making, that I'd made my choice long ago and that if anybody had to suffer for it, it would be me.

"And now you're telling me that it wasn't so at all? I can't just shrug it off, don't you see? I can't just say okay, good on me, and march ahead without a thought," she said, the words tumbling out. "You want to make up for lost time? I'm just trying to keep up. Five weeks ago, Lloyd was murdered. Three weeks ago, I was still in jail." She pressed her fingertips against her eyelids. "It's been one thing after another and it just keeps coming. I care about you, Roberto, I truly do, but I feel like I'm in a cement mixer that just keeps turning. I've got to find some way to make it stop before I can figure out what to do next. The only thing that hasn't been taken from me in the last five weeks is my son."

"Our son, who's been kept from me for eighteen years. Don't you understand, Frannie? It's time to set everything right. I love you and I want us all to be a family together, the way we were supposed to be."

"That's what Mom said about Lloyd…"

He slammed his fist down on the table. "Goddammit, I am not Lloyd Fredericks."

"But you're pushing me to do what you want me to do regardless of whether I'm ready or not," she flung at him. "Is that how life would be with you after the sweet talk went away, Roberto? Everything by your rules, everything on your schedule? I keep telling you I need more time, and *you don't listen*."

"I want to be there for you," he exploded. "With you. Josh is my son. We should have been married years ago. We should be married now."

"This isn't a square dance. I don't just belong to whoever Josh's father happens to be this week. We aren't a package deal."

"Is that what you think this is about?" Roberto demanded. "Dammit, Frannie, it's not just about Josh, it's you. I love you. I always have. I never stopped, not once. Even when I thought you had sent me away."

He linked his fingers together on top of his head and looked at the ceiling. "Frannie, you're not the only one who got robbed. I got robbed, too. We all did. Josh was robbed by not knowing who he was his entire life, by having to deal with a man like Lloyd Fredericks. I was robbed of watching my son grow. You and I were robbed of a life together. And I'm really angry and want to make it right. I want to get something redeemable out of it—we all deserve that. And the only way I can think that can happen is doing what we both want—to be together."

"I couldn't do that right now even if I wanted to, Roberto," she blazed. "And I don't want to, not while you're pushing."

"I'm pushing because we've already lost too much time. We've already waited too long."

"You won't wait? You want an answer now? It's no, okay?"

"You don't mean that. You know it's right with us, you know it. You can't walk away from this."

"Are you forgetting why we decided to stay apart in the first place? The murder, the police? There's too much going on with that and Cindy's accident, and the notes and the fires and—"

The notes...

One of the Fortunes is not who you think.

"Oh my God," she started. "'One of the Fortunes—'"

"'—is not who you think.' Josh," Roberto added grimly.

"They know. Whoever's behind the notes and the fires and all of it, they *know*. It's all connected." She turned for the wall phone. "We've got to call Ross. Cindy has to have some idea about this, she has to."

"What we've got to do is go to the cops."

"Are you out of your mind?" Frannie asked. "Go to the police? Tell them all of this?"

"Frannie, we have to. It's gone past us, now, don't you understand? Don't you remember that note after the second fire, 'This one wasn't an accident, either'? Someone set those fires and maybe that same person cut Cindy's brake lines. She could've been killed. If this keeps going, someone will be, someone—" He stopped.

"Lloyd." Frannie's voice was barely audible.

They locked eyes with each other, the ticking of the clock very loud in the silence.

"We've got to find out what really happened at the Spring Fling," Roberto said. "We've got to find out what Josh knows."

"He doesn't know anything," she shot back. "He wasn't your hoodie-wearing murderer."

Roberto caught her arms in his hands. "Even if he's not, we still need to know what he knows. We can't just keep dancing around this. It's got to end, Frannie. We've got to talk to Josh."

"Talk to Josh about what?" a voice asked.

And heart pounding, Frannie turned to see her son standing at the door that led in from the garage.

Chapter 13

Frannie swallowed. "Oh. Honey, hi." She turned to sit on one of the chairs at the breakfast bar. "How was the baseball game?"

"Fine." Josh gave Roberto a hard look, shutting the garage door. "What's going on? What did you want to talk to me about?"

"What happened at the Spring Fling."

"Roberto, this isn't the time," Frannie cut in, an edge in her voice.

He shook his head. "We can't just keep pretending there isn't a problem, not anymore. You spent two weeks in jail because you were afraid to mention it." He turned to Josh. "We need to know whatever you can tell us about your...father at the Spring Fling."

Josh glanced down. "What do you mean?"

"You had an argument with him."

He shrugged. "So we fought. We always fought. It

was no big deal." He walked to the refrigerator and got out a soft drink.

"It didn't sound that way to the people who heard you."

"Who heard?" he asked a little too quickly.

"I did," Frannie said. "You were right behind the tent I was working in."

Roberto watched Josh take a seat at the table, stretching out his legs, trying a little too hard to look at ease. The kid—his kid, he thought with inward amazement—concentrated on his Mountain Dew. An attempt to avoid eye contact or garden-variety teenager?

Josh took a swallow of his drink. "Why the third degree all of a sudden?"

"We just want your help, Josh," Frannie told him. "We need to find the killer."

"It sounds like Sherlock Holmes here thinks I'm the killer."

Roberto walked closer. "I'm just trying to get information. Right now, your mother's still the only one charged for the murder. That means until they catch the person who did it, she's still at risk."

Josh's faux relaxation vanished. "They can't bring her back in, can they?"

"Yes, actually, they can. There's a big difference between being released on her own recognizance and having the charges dropped," Roberto commented. "Maybe now you understand why I'm asking questions. And sooner or later, the cops are going to be asking questions about you because someone's going to tell them about your fight. Not your mom, but other people. You were too close to the tents, too loud." Roberto watched him closely. "And you threatened him."

"It wasn't any big deal. It was just trash talk."

"Lyndsey got upset when I asked her about it."

He gave Roberto a sharp look. "You had no right to go over and grill her."

Interesting that that was what provoked a reaction. "She told you, then. I thought she might."

"Leave her alone. You got questions, ask me."

"Gladly. Do you know anything about your father's murder?"

"No." The answer came out almost before Roberto finished the question.

"Does Lyndsey?"

He glanced away. "No."

"What does she know, Josh?"

"Nothing." Pulling off his ball cap, he scraped his hair back. He wasn't sprawled out now, but hunched over the table tensely.

"She's hiding something. It's pretty clear."

"Forget about Lyndsey, already, will you? She didn't do anything."

And suddenly all the vague disquiet coalesced and Roberto knew. "It was her, wasn't it?"

"What?"

"You didn't kill Lloyd Fredericks. It was Lyndsey."

Josh shot to his feet. "That's nuts," he said angrily.

"It's also true."

"Josh?" Frannie stood. "Is it?"

His eyes skated to one side. "No way. She had nothing to do with it."

"She was there for the fight, wasn't she?" Roberto probed.

"I'm not saying anything." Josh crossed his arms stubbornly, jaw set exactly like Jorge's did when he was in trouble.

"Stop taking care of her."

"I can't," he flared. "You of all people should get that. You protect the people you care about."

"Yeah? Then how about protecting your mother and stopping lying for the person who killed your father?" Roberto snapped.

The words hung in the air. The minutes stretched out in a humming silence. Roberto held his breath.

"It was an accident." Josh's voice was barely audible. He looked from the tabletop to Frannie. "She only told me tonight. I swear I didn't know when you were locked up, Mom. She's been a little weird lately, moody sometimes, but I figured it was just…"

"What?"

Josh stared up at the ceiling and blew out a breath. "She's pregnant," he said flatly, staring from one to the other.

"Pregnant?" Frannie croaked.

"We tried to be careful. She was supposed to be on the pill, it's just, you know…stuff happens."

"Why didn't you say something?"

"Say something?" An edge entered his voice. "After you and Dad spent the whole last year trying to get me to break up with her? If I'd told you she was pregnant, all you would have done was say I told you so."

"No, I wouldn't have," Frannie said vehemently. "My God, don't you think I know what it's like? I've been there, Josh. I know how scary and overwhelming it feels. I just wish you'd told me so you didn't have to go through it alone."

"I wasn't alone." Josh raised his chin. "I had Lyndsey. We were together."

We were together.

Roberto felt like he'd been punched in the stomach. He hadn't been able to be there for Frannie all those

years ago. They hadn't been together. The reason why
didn't matter; the fact was that she'd endured it without him.

The first of many things.

He shook his mind loose from the thought. "What
happened at the Spring Fling, Josh?"

Josh sighed. "I was taking that vase out to your car,
Mom, like you asked. Lyndsey was with me. We were
talking about the baby, and all of a sudden Dad was
there. He went ballistic, yelling and saying stuff about
Lyndsey—really bad stuff—and I don't know, I just
kind of lost it myself." Defiance flashed in his eyes.

"I know," Frannie said gently. "I've never heard you
sound like that before."

"I didn't want him around Lyndsey—he was acting
crazy—so I put the vase in her hands and told her to
leave and meet me at the dance. But I guess she got worried and came back…." He raised his hands helplessly.

"Anyway, I finally told Dad to go to hell and walked
away, but Lyndsey was still back there. She said the
vase was too heavy. She put it down under a tarp where
it would be safe, but she saw Dad coming toward her
and she got scared. There was this crowbar sticking out
from under the tarp, and…she grabbed it.

"All she wanted to do was walk past him, get back to
where people were, but he wouldn't leave her alone." A
muscle jumped in Josh's jaw. "He was talking all kinds
of trash about how he knew girls like her, girls who
trapped guys, girls who spread their legs for money,
just evil stuff, Mom, evil."

But it hadn't been Lyndsey Lloyd had been talking
to that night, Frannie understood. She closed her eyes
a moment. "What happened then?"

"He said he wasn't going to let her trap me with the

baby, so he grabbed her and put his hands around her neck and started to strangle her." Josh looked at them both, misery in his eyes. "She hit him with the bar because she had to, Mom, she had to. He was going to kill her. She was blacking out. And when she woke up, he was dead and there was blood all over. So she ran away." He put his head in his hands. Frannie walked over and put her arms around his shoulders.

"If she and Lloyd fought, why didn't anyone hear?" Roberto asked.

"Are you trying to say she's lying?" Josh raised his head to glare at him. "She's telling the truth. He tried to kill her. And now she's scared to death that they'll find out and she'll go to jail."

Roberto folded his arms. "Your mom can tell her what it's like."

"Roberto." Frannie shot him a look of warning, then turned to Josh. "Honey, if it happened the way she said, there's no jury in the world that would convict her. It would be self-defense."

"Are you telling me to call the cops on her?" he asked incredulously. "I can't turn her in. She's going to have my kid. And I... I love her."

"Nobody's talking about calling the cops." Roberto took a seat. "The best thing for her to do is turn herself in."

Josh shook his head. "No way. She's never going to do that. She's too scared."

"What about if we go talk to her?" Frannie said. "The three of us. We'll convince her and then we'll go to the police together."

"She won't listen."

Roberto rested his elbows on the table. "She's got to, Josh, or else we have to call the cops. Unless you want to chance your mom going to trial for a murder she didn't commit. We need to talk to Lyndsey. Now."

"Tomorrow," Frannie corrected. "It's after midnight. It's too late."

"The sooner she turns herself in, the better it's going to be for her," Roberto countered. "And as long as we know and don't act, we're accessories. Her mother works the night shift, we can catch her alone. Let's just go do it."

"She's going to hate me for telling," Josh said miserably.

Frannie touched his cheek. "You're trying to help her, honey. Eventually, she'll see that. Sometimes you have to make difficult choices in life. That's what you do for people you care about."

The minutes stretched out. Josh sat in silence, staring at his hands. Finally, he raised his head. "Being an adult sucks."

"It has its moments," Roberto agreed. "So what do you say?"

Josh nodded. "Okay." He swallowed. "Let's roll."

The yellow bug light at Lyndsey's house cast a faint amber glow over the uneven boards of the porch. Josh had given Lyndsey a call on the way over. Now, he gave Frannie and Roberto a sickly smile and knocked on the door.

It opened immediately. "Come in, quick," Lyndsey demanded, "or old lady Quinson across the street will—" She stopped, staring at Frannie and Roberto. "What are they doing here?"

There was none of the indecision of earlier that day, Roberto noticed. The look in her eyes was downright hostile. And she wore the black hoodie.

"Let us in, Lyns," Josh said. "We need to talk to you."

"My mom's going to be really mad if she gets wind of this. I'm not supposed to have people over when she's working."

"I'll talk to her," Frannie promised. "We'll only be here for a few minutes."

She'd been watching television, Roberto saw as they walked into the living room, *Romeo and Juliet* reset in what looked like modern-day Miami. An open soda sat on the coffee table by the couch. In what looked to be long-standing habit, Lyndsey and Josh sat next to each other. Frannie chose the remaining chair; Roberto just leaned against the wall by the entryway.

Lyndsey muted the television. "Why are you back here?" she asked Roberto.

"Same thing as this morning—the murder of Lloyd Fredericks," Roberto said.

"And like I said to you this morning, I don't know anything about it."

"It's okay, Lyns," Josh said gently. "I told them."

She blinked. "Told them? You told them what?"

"What happened between you and Dad."

For a moment her expression turned absolutely livid, then it relaxed, so quickly Roberto couldn't be sure he'd seen it. "Nothing happened with me and your dad."

"Lyndsey, it was self-defense," Frannie said gently. "If you turn yourself in to the police, that's what they'll say. You won't have to go to jail."

"Of course I won't. I didn't do anything."

"It's not that easy. They have forensic evidence," Roberto gambled. "Your blood on the vase, your fingerprints on the murder weapon. The best thing you can do is turn yourself in. It'll work in your favor, especially if the self-defense angle holds up."

"Of course it will hold up." Josh's voice held equal

parts anger and protectiveness. "You didn't see my dad that night. He lost it completely. She's lucky she's alive."

At that, Lyndsey's eyes filled with tears. "I didn't mean to. I thought he was going to kill me."

Josh slipped his arms around her. "It's going to be okay."

"I'm afraid," she whispered. "What if they put me in jail?"

"They won't."

"Lyndsey, you can't live with this hanging over your head forever," Frannie said. "You have to confess. It's for the best. There will be a trial, but we'll all testify for you."

Lyndsey chewed on her lip. "Do I have to decide now?"

"The sooner you do it, the better," Roberto said. "We all know now, Lyndsey, and there's no way we can cover it up. Just turn yourself in. Everything will be fine."

Lyndsey swallowed. "All right," she whispered. "Just let me go call my mom and tell her."

She walked past Roberto and through the swinging door that led to the kitchen. And he could hear her let loose the tears she'd been holding back. They all could.

Josh stared down at his hands, looking sick. "I did this. It's my fault."

"You didn't do anything." Roberto wanted to squeeze the kid's shoulder, do something, but it wasn't his place. Yet.

Instead, Frannie rose to go sit by him. "Sometimes things just happen." Her voice was soft, reassuring. "It's going to be okay, you'll see. It'll all work out."

"You bet it will," There was a click and they all turned to see Lyndsey standing at the kitchen door, a gun in her hand.

Chapter 14

For a frozen instant, no one moved. *A gun,* Frannie thought numbly. A quick squeeze of the trigger and any one of them would be gone instantly.

Josh blinked as though he couldn't make sense of what he was seeing. "Lyns, what are you doing?"

"Move away from her, Josh," Lyndsey ordered.

Frannie felt the quick rush of adrenaline. Not her son, she vowed, the numbness gone. If she had to physically throw herself in front of the bullet, she was going to make sure Josh came out of this whole.

"I'm not going anywhere," Josh returned. "This isn't the way. Don't hurt my family."

"It's not like I want to." She strode over to stand opposite them. "They're making me. No way am I going down to the police department and turning myself in."

"Lyndsey, you've got to. It's going to be okay. You'll get off with self-defense."

She laughed. "Is that what they told you? Of course they did," she answered her own question. "What else are they going to say? They want me to take the fall so that your mother gets off. But no way in hell is that ever going to happen."

This matter-of-fact calculation was far more dangerous than fear or anger, Frannie realized.

And maybe Roberto did, too, because he stepped forward a pace. Lyndsey whirled to face him. "Don't move or I'll shoot you right now," she threatened.

"No!" Frannie burst out in horror, starting up from the couch. Time broke into a series of images: flickering actors fighting on the television screen, Roberto standing, tension coiled in him like a spring, Lyndsey's face pale, the gun in her shaking hands.

The gun.

And in that moment of fear, Frannie realized what she'd tried so hard to block.

She was in love with Roberto.

"Lyndsey, you can't do this," she protested. "What about your baby?"

The round circle of the barrel swung toward her. "Shut up," Lyndsey snapped. "I should have killed you, too."

Frannie felt rather than saw Roberto tense. "Don't," she said under her breath. He couldn't put himself at risk, not now that she'd finally understood how much he truly mattered.

And what a desert her life would be without him.

"What are you doing?" Josh demanded.

"Don't distract me, Josh. I'm doing what I have to."

There was something in Lyndsey's eyes, Frannie realized, not panic precisely, but more the wary look of some sharp-toothed creature that hid in its burrow and only came out at night. For the first time, she understood that they weren't dealing with an entirely rational individual.

And her head became oddly clear. "We can work this out." Frannie kept her voice even. "We'll get lawyers. It wasn't your fault."

Say whatever it takes to get out of the room, whatever it takes to survive this so that you can tell him.

But Lyndsey wasn't buying it. "There's no way they'd let me go. Not after everything I've done."

"What's that?" Roberto asked.

She laughed. "Oh, we've been having fun." She took a few restless steps across the living room. "I liked seeing you Fortunes worried. For once, you weren't in control. For once, you were the ones who were scared. Like you're scared now."

"You were the one behind the fires and the notes, weren't you?" Frannie asked.

Lyndsey laughed. "Give the lady an A plus." Her face relaxed into the benign expression of a high-schooler talking about the latest download for her iPod. "I only did it for Josh and me. And for the baby. I'm going to call her Sarah, after my grandmother."

"For the baby?" Roberto brought her back to the subject.

"Of course." Impatient, she paced a few more steps. "Don't look at me like that, Josh. You've got to take the big-picture view. I mean, how could we get married and start a family if your dad and your mom—" she shot a look of silky dislike at Frannie "—were in the way? I had to stop that somehow."

"Josh is eighteen. He's gotten his inheritance. What could his parents have done anyway?"

She looked at Roberto pityingly. "You don't get it,

do you? The Fortunes own this town. We didn't have a choice. We had to put the screws to Lloyd. We had to scare him."

"Who's we?"

Roberto was pumping the girl gently, making her give details, keeping her going each time she stopped. If they ever got out of the room alive, Frannie thought, there would be enough to convict her for her crimes.

If they ever got out alive.

"*We* was my mom and me. We had it all planned out."

"It didn't work, though, did it?"

"I thought he'd be smarter," she complained, beginning to cross the room again like an erratic pendulum. "The fires and the notes were to soften him up, but it took him a while to get it. And it was so simple. All he had to do was stop making a fuss about us, and Mom and I would keep our mouths shut. If he kept it up, we'd see that he lost everything."

Josh frowned, looking from Lyndsey to Roberto. "What the hell are you talking about?"

"Lloyd loved being a Fortune." Lyndsey had an almost dreamy look in her eyes. "See, you guys are born with it. You don't know what it's like on the outside."

"But you and I do, don't we, Lyndsey?" Roberto said. *Say whatever it takes to get out of the room.*

"I guess you would," Lyndsey nodded to herself. "They say your families are friends, but you Mendozas get the short end of the stick every time, don't you? Anybody who deals with the Fortunes does. They have everything." Her voice filled with sudden venom as she glared at Frannie.

"But Lloyd was a Fredericks," Roberto reminded her.

Lyndsey gave him a scornful look. "We both know that doesn't count for anything anymore. But being a part of the Fortunes sure does. We had to threaten to take that away so that he'd behave."

"But that would affect Josh, too."

"You think I wanted to do this? I did it because I had to. I did it for us, Josh."

"For us?" Josh repeated. "That's why you burned my aunt's barn down?"

"Of course, silly," she said affectionately, missing his rancor. "Lloyd was in the way. And he was going to try to con money out of you, money that belonged to us and to Sarah. So I told him if he didn't watch out, we were going to tell everybody the truth."

"Tell everybody what?" Josh asked.

She made an impatient noise. "Jeez, Josh, how can you be so dense? He wasn't your real dad."

How do we tell him, Roberto had asked. Frannie had never in a million years imagined this would be the way.

Josh shook his head. "That's nuts."

"How can you be so sure, Lyndsey?" The question was out before Frannie knew she was going to ask it. Josh snapped his head around to stare at her.

"My mom's a nurse. She worked in the clinic that did the testing. Cindy brought money, lots of it. When the test results came in, Mom just switched them. It was easy, she said."

"I don't believe it." Frowning, Josh looked at Frannie. And then he seemed to realize that she wasn't surprised.

"My mom used part of the money to buy this house," Lyndsey continued, making another of her now-regular swings across the room. "Then my dad left. It got harder. I mean, look at this place. It's a dump, now. You Fortunes all live in palaces. And here's Cindy Fortune living the good life while Mom and I are scraping to get by."

For an instant, pure hatred flashed in her eyes. And then, unnervingly quickly, she returned to sunny and serene. "My mom went back a couple years ago and asked her for some more money. Really reasonable, just asking one person to another, can you help?"

Blackmail, Frannie thought. *Really reasonable.*

"You would have thought that Mom was asking her to open a vein. Cindy threatened to tell everybody. She said she'd make sure Mom lost her license if she tried anything. But we got her back good." Lyndsey smiled in satisfaction. "A little snip here, a little snip there."

"You cut Cindy Fortune's brake lines?" Roberto asked.

Lyndsey looked positively beatific. "It was hard not to laugh, seeing her walk around all banged up after her accident. It's too bad it didn't work. That's because you Fortunes always wind up on top. But not this time. It was fun to see you all afraid. You didn't feel so important then, did you?"

"You're talking about my family," Josh ground out.

"Oh, honey, I don't mean you. I love you. I can't wait to marry you and get our own place and raise our baby together. Lots of babies," she said smiling. "With your inheritance, we'll be able to afford them.

"That's all I ever wanted," she explained. "But Lloyd tried to mess everything up. Lloyd and you." Her mouth twisted as she stopped pacing and pointed the gun at Frannie. "You're why we had to go after Lloyd. It's your fault I had to be at the Spring Fling, telling him how it was going to go. I was going to fill you in as insurance," she added to Roberto, "but Lloyd sort of changed my plans."

"You were the one who called about the meet."

"Fooled you, huh?"

"Not really. The phone booth you called from was in this neighborhood, I looked up the number. What did Lloyd say after you told him his choices? Is that why you hit him?"

"He deserved it." She paced faster, agitated. "He said I was lying, he called me all kinds of names. And then he knocked me over and I hit my nose on your danged vase." She threw Frannie a malevolent look. "I thought I broke it. It bled like a stuck pig. But I showed him. It's like my daddy always said, 'you knock me down you'd better kill me because I'll make you sorry.' He never even heard me coming," she added with relish. "I whapped him a good one."

Frannie felt a chill.

"With the bar?" Roberto shifted his weight a bit. "That must have been hard. He was a lot taller than you. And stronger."

"I got him from behind as he was walking away. There was so much blood," Lyndsey said wonderingly, looking down so that she missed Roberto sliding one foot back to brace himself. "I didn't think I hit him that hard. It hurt my hand." She rubbed it against her jeans absently. "I had blood all over me, but I put on Josh's hoodie and threw away the crowbar. I got a ride into town with a trucker."

"It wasn't self-defense at all," Frannie said. "It was murder."

"You think I wanted to do that? He made me," Lyndsey snarled.

"Of course he did," Roberto said. "I know how it is, having people tell you you're not good enough for their family. It wasn't your fault. You were only doing what you had to." He eyed the arc of Lyndsey's steps, calculating. "They don't understand what it does to you to know that's what they think, every day, every night, every time you look in the mirror. And what it's like to not have enough. You and I, we know what that's like, Lyndsey."

"Yes," she whispered, walking closer.

"It eats at you. And to be pulled into Cindy Fortune's schemes and hardly get anything out of it?" He flicked a glance back at Frannie. "I'd have done just what you did. I would have been so mad. And that kind of mad makes you want to hurt someone, doesn't it?"

"Yes."

"Lots of people get mad," Frannie interrupted, praying she'd read Roberto's look right. "You don't see them murdering people."

"You bitch!" Eyes narrowed with fury, Lyndsey pivoted toward Frannie, bringing the gun up. And in that moment, Roberto sprang at her.

Noise and confusion, the tangle of limbs. Lyndsey fought Roberto for the gun with the adrenaline-soaked strength of the unbalanced. They rolled and wrestled on the floor as she screamed in fury, as Josh leapt over the coffee table to try to help pin the girl.

Frannie snatched up the telephone receiver on the side table.

"Nine-one-one operator, can I help you?"

There was the roar of a gunshot, the muzzle flash, the scent of cordite. And a choking fear as Frannie looked to see blood spreading on the rug.

"Come quickly," she whispered. "Someone's been shot."

Roberto punched the button on the vending machine, watching the cup fall down and the stream of coffee begin. There was something about hospitals that seemed to exist outside of time. It seemed that he had always been here, waiting for word, that it was endless, like those nightmare moments in Lyndsey's living room when she'd pointed the gun at Frannie and he'd felt his heart stop in fear.

"I thought I might find you here."

Roberto turned to see Len Wheeler. He turned back. "Where's your sidekick?"

"Writing up the initial reports. Don't worry about him."

"Wheeler, right now I can't say I give a damn about either of you." Roberto opened the little window and pulled out his coffee.

"I guess you have a right to feel like that."

Roberto's brows lowered. "Is that the best you can do? You lock Frannie up for two weeks, you sweat me down, the only way you find out anything is when we deliver it to you and all you can say is I have a right to feel like that?"

"I won't apologize for being skeptical because that's the nature of our business, but I saw the hoodie. You were telling the truth."

"For all the good it did me."

"For everybody who tells us the truth, there are twice as many lying."

"Isn't it your job to be able to tell the difference?"

"Yeah, the day I get to be perfect at it, I'll let you know." Wheeler fished in his pocket for change and stepped over to the machine.

"How about you skip that and just tell me what the hell is going on? I saw you hauling somebody out in handcuffs when we were in the E.R."

"Donna Pollack. Lyndsey's mother. McCaskill questioned her." Wheeler smiled faintly. "She takes a dim view of the Fortunes."

"Not nearly as dim a view as the Fortunes take of her. How's the daughter? Josh will want to know."

The coins jingled as Wheeler fed them into the slot. "I talked to the doc. They're still closing up, but he said the surgery to remove the bullet is done. Her leg should heal up with no problem."

"And the baby?"

"They think it's going to be fine."

"Tell Josh."

"Already did. Stopped in to see him and Miz Fredericks just before I came to find you. He still wants to stay until the girl's out. Not that the staff is allowed to tell him anything because of privacy laws."

"But you're going to keep him posted, aren't you, Wheeler?" Roberto asked with an edge to his voice. "Don't forget, we handed this case to you gift-wrapped."

Wheeler pulled his coffee out of the machine and walked to the little ledge that held sugar and creamer. "We had to wake up a judge to sign the search warrant, but McCaskill went through the Pollacks' garage. Found the same accelerants used for the arson fires and a pair of clippers with what looks like brake fluid on them. 'Pears that everything Lyndsey Pollack told you is true, maybe down to Josh Fredericks' parentage. Hell of a thing." He shook his head. "Hell of a thing."

"Yeah. Enjoy your coffee." Roberto turned for the door. Time to get back up to the O.R. waiting room and back to Frannie.

"Hey, Mendoza," Wheeler said. When Roberto glanced back, he gave him a level look. "I'm sorry everything worked out so crappy."

"You and me both."

Hell of a thing, Roberto thought as he rode the elevator to the surgical unit. The words weren't adequate to the occasion, but then again, he couldn't think of any that were. It seemed unimaginably long ago that he and Frannie had discovered Cindy's initial machinations to keep them apart. The shock of that seemed like nothing compared to what this day had brought.

If he let himself stop and think, he'd be reeling over it, and he was an adult. What was it like for a kid like Josh to discover that everything he believed about himself was a lie? Eighteen wasn't old enough to deal with that; hell, thirty-nine wasn't.

Roberto stepped out of the elevator car and turned toward the little waiting area at the end of the hall where windows looked out at a landscape now coming gradually into view with the approach of the day.

Josh sat in one of the chairs before the window, bent over his thighs, staring at his hands dangling between his knees. Next to him, Frannie leaned in to smooth back his hair and murmur something. Everything about her posture spoke of exhaustion, and yet still she found the strength to reassure, to support.

I feel like I'm in a cement mixer that just keeps turning, she'd told Roberto in a conversation that seemed like it had taken place a million years before. But right now, she wasn't paying attention to her own turmoil. She was focusing on taking care of her son. Their son. It was something he should have been a part of, Roberto thought in frustration, something they should have done together.

As he moved to go to her, Josh suddenly turned to lean his head into Frannie's shoulder. She slipped her arms around him in a gesture of such tenderness that it brought an ache to Roberto's throat.

And suddenly, he understood what she'd been trying to tell him all along. It didn't matter about him. Maybe it didn't even matter about them. What mattered was her taking care of Josh.

Give me time and space to deal with everything, she'd begged, but Roberto hadn't listened. He'd wanted, needed to make something happen between the two of them, to change what had gone before. But that wasn't important right now.

Despite how shattered she had to be, right now Frannie's only thoughts were of their son. That was the thing he'd missed, that loving someone meant putting aside your own wants to give them what they needed—even if what you wanted was to take care of them. In some alternative universe, he and Frannie and Josh might have been the perfect family. In this one, Roberto had to accept that here was maybe something he couldn't help. His steps slowed to a stop. Maybe here was something he finally needed to let go.

In the window behind where Frannie and Josh sat, he could just glimpse the first rays of the rising sun. Frannie turned to look out at the rose-stained horizon, and the light turned her hair into a glowing nimbus.

And as he had done on a dawn nineteen years before, Roberto Mendoza turned away and started walking.

Chapter 15

"All rise." The bailiff stood at the front of the courtroom. "Court is now in session, the Honorable Justice Constance Hamel presiding."

The Red Rock County Courthouse had been built in the 1920s, with the soaring ceilings and marble floors of the days before air-conditioning. There was a grandeur to the oaken paneling and bronze light fixtures, the burgundy velvet drapes that bracketed the tall windows. Over the course of the trial, Frannie had come to know them all well.

It seemed like a lifetime since that frozen tableau in Lyndsey's living room, but in reality only three months had passed, half of that spent waiting for Lyndsey to heal. By the standards of a city like Los Angeles or New York, perhaps, to go from crime to sentencing in the remaining six weeks was blindingly quick. To Frannie, it felt like forever that her life had been bounded by these four walls, bracketed by the morning announcements of the bailiff and the smack of the gavel at the end of the day.

It felt like forever since Roberto had been gone from her life.

"In case number eight-oh-eight, the State of Texas versus Pollack, Lyndsey, we are ready for sentencing," announced Judge Hamel, a brisk, no-nonsense woman who'd nonetheless shown surprising compassion in dealing with both Josh and Lyndsey. "We've already heard opening statements and character evidence. Prosecution, would you like to make your closing statement?"

"We would, Your Honor."

Had Frannie once told Roberto that her life made her feel like she was in a cement mixer? It didn't, it felt more like being trapped in an avalanche, taking blow after blow while never knowing precisely where she was. There had been a moment of the gunshot, followed by the blind gratitude of knowing that both Josh and Roberto were safe. And then the police and the EMTs had descended.

And somewhere during the endless hours in the hospital, Roberto had slipped away. He sat now, farther down the row from her in a blue suit and burgundy tie, looking heartbreakingly handsome. And all it did was hurt.

"Would the defense like to make a closing statement?" Judge Hamel asked.

"Yes, Your Honor." The public defender, a pretty brunette in a sober gray suit, rose to her feet.

Frannie had heard through the grapevine that Roberto was back in Denver. Oh, sure, he'd shown up for court dates, but he'd always managed to keep his distance and always managed to slip away without speaking to her. As the weeks had gone by, it had become increasingly difficult for her to convince herself it was anything but intentional.

She supposed she could have picked up the phone and called him. If she'd been a different kind of person, perhaps she would've flown to Denver. But she'd done neither.

Maybe he blamed her for what Cindy had done. Maybe Frannie had driven him off with what she'd said the night they discovered the truth about Josh. Maybe he'd just decided it was all too much. Or maybe he'd simply lost interest. He'd always been a man who knew what he wanted, and maybe, after the excitement of the reunion had faded, what he wanted was no longer her.

What was hardest was that she'd never had a chance to tell him how she felt. And now sentencing was here, perhaps the last day that she would see him. Even though they shared a son, Josh was an adult and perfectly capable of pursuing his own relationship with his father.

And so she sat and concentrated on the closing statements and tried not to let the misery well up.

Judge Hamel cleared her throat. "In the case of the state versus Pollack, Lyndsey, we are ready to pronounce sentence. Will the defendant please stand?"

In the end, it came out perhaps better than they could've anticipated. Donna Pollack was sentenced to a total of sixteen years in prison and thirty-thousand dollars in fines for her counts of arson, and attempted murder in the case of Cindy Fortune's car accident. For Lyndsey, though, there would be no prison. Instead, she would see the inside of a psychiatric hospital, and Josh and Frannie would have custody of the child after it was born.

Frannie sighed, rising. It was done.

She didn't think she could bear it.

She rose and began to walk toward the aisle then stopped. Roberto stood there, his eyes steady on hers. "Frannie, how are you?"

It hurt to even look at him. "I'm fine, how are you?"

"Better now, I think. How's it going, Josh? You okay with the verdicts?"

Josh shrugged. "Yeah, I guess so."

They waited for long minutes in silence as the courtroom emptied out. There had been a time they'd talked for hours. How was it possible that now she could think of nothing except the words she couldn't say?

Roberto glanced down at her as they started to move up the aisle to the door. "Are you going to need help with the reporters?" he asked.

"We're parked out back. We should be fine."

"I guess you've gotten good at avoiding the media circus."

She let Josh walk a little way ahead of her. "We've learned a few tricks. None as good as leaving town, but they work."

There was a beat of silence. "I guess maybe I deserve that," Roberto said quietly.

Frannie shook her head. "I'm sorry. I shouldn't have said it. It's just been a long trial. There were times it seemed like it was never going to end."

"Everything does, sometime."

Everything does.

"Look, maybe you and I need to go talk, get things settled," he said.

It had the sound of a close. Frannie sped up, suddenly desperate to get out of the room and into the open air and away from all the mistakes she'd made in her life. She shoved open the doors and strode out into the hall. And for the second time, came to an abrupt stop.

"Hello, Frances."

Cindy Fortune wore a demure black suit, probably a first for her. Next to her stood Josh, white-faced.

"Need some help?" a voice asked quietly behind her.

Frannie turned to see Roberto. He seemed so solid and reassuring, but this wasn't his fight. "I'm fine. Maybe…maybe you and Josh could go to the back doors and wait for me. This won't take long."

She watched for a minute to see them go and then turned back to Cindy. "What do you want, Mother?"

"The trial's over. I thought we could at least talk. Try to mend fences."

"Why would I want to talk to you?" Frannie asked. "You lied to me for nineteen years. Worse than lied. There aren't even words for what you did. You manipulated everyone."

"I don't want to fight," Cindy protested, "not over some stupid mistake I made a long time ago."

"You make it sound like you forgot to pack my lunch," Frannie said incredulously. "You stole from us, you stole our lives. Josh could have had a father who loved him, Roberto could have had a son. And they didn't, because you took that from them, you took it because in your twisted mind somehow it would benefit you."

"But I—"

"In your own way you're just as deluded as Lyndsey. She thought that whatever she did was okay as long as it gave her what she wanted. The end justified the means.

Well, you know what, Mother? Some means can't be justified. What you did was unforgivable."

Cindy's defiance wobbled. "What do you want from me?"

"I want you to admit it. Just once I want to hear you take responsibility, to say 'I was wrong, I blew it, I screwed up. I wrecked your life and never lost a single night's sleep over it.'"

Cindy stared. "That's not true," she whispered. "Give me a chance."

"I gave you a chance," Frannie flared, "over and over again when I was a kid, every time you'd come back from disappearing, making promises about how wonderful everything was going to be. I always believed you because I couldn't imagine that you wouldn't be there if I just gave you one more chance. And every single time you broke my heart."

Frannie turned to walk away.

"Wait."

Frannie kept walking.

"Frannie stop, please."

Frannie turned around. "What?" she asked wearily.

"I was wrong." Cindy swallowed. "I screwed up. I thought I was… I thought of me," she said simply. She paused a long time. "There's no excuse, and the hell of it is, there's not a thing in the world I can do to fix it. All I can do is say I'm sorry and I'll be here for you, if you let me."

Frannie stared at her, feeling the familiar mix of emotions. Words had deserted her.

Cindy moistened her lips. "What can I do?"

"Right now? Leave it be for now. Go away for a while—you've always been good at that. Go to your friends in L.A. or London or wherever it is. Let some time go by." Frannie let out a long breath. "And maybe when you get back, we can try it all again."

"Are you relieved to have the trial over?" Roberto asked Josh.

They stood in the echoing marble hallway around the corner from the back doors of the building. Above them, the high ceiling threw down echoes. A few yards away were the closed doors of a courtroom; Roberto couldn't help wondering whose fate was being decided inside.

Like his fate was going to be decided now.

"Yeah," Josh said. "It's good to have it over."

"Good for everyone. Lyndsey included."

Josh bit his lip and focused on the floor. "You know, the hard thing was seeing her day after day, looking at me like it was all pretend, like we could go home and have pizza and laugh about it. But we're not going to laugh about it, are we?"

"I think you know the answer to that." Roberto studied Josh. The boy—man—had lost more weight over the course of the trial and his skin had turned sallow as he'd stayed inside to avoid the media. "Did you decide what you're doing about school?"

Josh shrugged. "I figure I'll take a couple years off. If I go to A&M now, people are going to be after me all the time with all the stuff about the trial. And there's the baby." He hesitated. "I was thinking maybe I'd volunteer for one of those charity groups that builds houses and schools and stuff. You know, do some good. Get the bad taste out of my mouth."

"This has been hell for you, hasn't it?" Roberto asked quietly.

"It's been kind of weird. It's like nothing's what I thought it was, not me and Lyndsey, not anything. My whole life I have a dad and now I find out he wasn't my dad after all."

Roberto was shaking his head before Josh even finished. "He was your dad, for better or worse. You had a life with him. Just because you don't have his blood doesn't negate it. There had to be some good times, some decent things he did. Remember that and let all the other stuff go."

"Yeah." Josh watched him. "So what happens with you and me?"

The $64,000 question that he'd been wrestling with for three months. When he wasn't wrestling with himself to keep from jumping on a plane and coming to find Frannie. "I guess that depends on you. I know what I want. I'd like to get a chance to know you. I'd like for you to get a chance to know me and my family. They're a good bunch of people."

"That so?"

Roberto nodded. "The first thing you should know is that no matter what, even if we never talk again, if you ever need anything, all you have to do is call. That goes for me or anyone in my family. Although I have to warn you, if you call and my mother answers, you're liable as not to get a lecture, depending on why you're calling."

Josh's lips twitched. "So, it's kind of like Mendoza AAA? With a twenty-four-hour hotline I can call?"

Roberto grinned. "Something like that. You'll be getting your membership card in the mail. It's also good for dinner on the house any time you want to stop by Red. Of course, I should also warn you that as a member of the family, any time you stop by Red you also run the risk of being press-ganged into busing tables."

"Live by the fajitas, die by the fajitas?"

Roberto clapped a hand on Josh's shoulder. "I thought

you should know." He hesitated. "There's something else I wanted to talk to you about."

"Shoot."

"It's got to do with your mom." And it was all he'd been able to think about.

"She's been pretty quiet since you went back to Denver." Josh studied him. "You planning to do anything about that?"

"That depends on what she decides she wants."

"Yeah? What do you want?"

Roberto met his gaze. "I want your blessing. I've loved your mom for a long time. I guess maybe you know that. I'm a pretty traditional guy. Normally, I'd talk to her parents, but she hasn't got any worth speaking of. I figure you're her people now."

"You going to ask her to marry you?"

"That depends on her. You're not the only one who's been through the mill. I figure I'll ask something and if she says no, ask something else, and just keep on asking until I find a question she says yes to. After that, I'll just work my way up the ladder over time."

Josh thought about it for a minute, pursing his lips. "That's cool."

"Yeah?" Roberto asked.

Josh grinned. "Yeah."

"Good."

Down the hall, they heard the tapping of heels and saw Frannie heading toward them. And Roberto felt something squeeze in his chest.

"Hey," Josh said, "you play basketball?"

Roberto blinked. "Yeah, a little pickup. I've got a half court in my construction yard. Sometimes on Fridays some of the guys and I have a few beers and shoot some hoops. Why?"

"Stop by the house next time you're in the neighborhood. We can play a little one-on-one."

"Yeah?"

"Yeah."

Frannie came to a stop in front of them. "What are you two grinning about?"

"Basketball," Roberto said. "We're talking about basketball."

"How did your conversation with your mother go?" Roberto asked as they drove down the highway.

He'd suggested coffee, Frannie thought, but they'd breezed through Main Street and out into the open land beyond Red Rock.

She clasped her hands together. "It was good, I guess."

"You don't sound convinced."

"It was just different. Life with Cindy usually is. I said some things that were a long time coming. Nothing's fixed, but who knows, maybe things will be better. In a way, I just feel better for having said it." She looked at him. "Does that make any kind of sense at all?"

"Sometimes just saying the words makes all the difference."

How could he understand her so well and yet be so far from her? "You and Josh seemed to be getting along all right."

"I think so. We'll see. He's a grown guy. He doesn't need someone coming in and suddenly trying to be his dad. I'd like to just be his friend."

"Did you tell him that?"

"In between talking about basketball."

Silence fell. Once, they'd been able to talk effortlessly. Now, despite everything that lay between them, she couldn't come up with anything to say.

Because the only things on her mind mattered too much.

Instead, she looked at the surrounding landscape. The afternoon was clear and warm, the way it had been weeks before when they'd lain beneath the oaks.

"I've always loved the hills this time of day," Roberto said, watching the highway carefully. He slowed and pulled off on a side road.

Frannie started. "Where on earth are you going? You said coffee."

"I know." He drummed his fingers on the steering wheel. "I just felt like being outdoors for a little bit after being stuck in that courtroom."

All around them were grassy slopes and trees. They bumped down through the ford of a stream bed and back out to the open field on the other side. Just beyond that, the road rose and rose farther until they came out on the crown of a hill. Roberto pulled the truck to a stop and turned off the engine.

"You're going to feel funny if whoever owns this place comes along and boots you out for trespassing," Frannie said as they got out.

"Relax, I know the guy who owns it."

She could hear the rustle of some burrowing creature in the grass. In the distance sounded the shrill piping calls of a killdeer. On the horizon, the sun blazed out, turning everything to copper. Roberto walked around to the back and lowered the tailgate so that they could sit.

Get things settled, he'd said. But he wasn't saying anything. Frannie tried to ignore the roiling in her stomach. "What a beautiful view. I don't think you could ever get tired of this," she said. And saw him tense.

Something sank in her stomach. "I mean, just the hill country. I've always loved it out here."

She shifted to move away, but he caught her hand. "Yeah? You could maybe get used to this?"

Frannie moistened her lips. "What are you asking?"

"See that stake over there?" He pointed. "This property is mine. I closed on it yesterday morning. Six hundred some-odd acres, a couple of creeks and a natural aquifer that'll supply good, sweet well water. We can run some cattle, grow alfalfa, maybe raise horses."

"We?"

He took her hands in his. "We, Frannie. So what if we lost eighteen years? I don't give a damn. I spent every second of them missing you."

Her heart hammered. "But what about Colorado? You have a life there, a business. A home."

"My home is where you are," he said simply. "I was gone for so long because I was closing up my business. And because I wanted to give you space. The night all hell broke loose, you told me I wasn't listening, that I was pushing too hard. I thought about that in the hospital. I thought about that a lot. And I realized you were right. And I figured the best thing I could do was just walk away, leave you alone so you could work things out."

Her throat tightened. "You just disappeared."

"If I'd come to you again, I never would have left. I couldn't have. And I needed to, for you and for me, both. I needed to make myself give you the space. You need to get comfortable with your life. And I realize you may not be there yet, but I've got enough work to do here to keep me busy for a good long time. Not too busy to miss you, but love also means patience, and I do love you, Frannie, I do. I always have."

He put a hand to her cheek. "I'm sorry that somehow got mixed up so you didn't feel like I was giving you what you needed. Just take your time, build your empires, do what you need to do, but I'll be here. And if you could see your way clear to letting me be at your side while you're doing your empire building, you'd make me a really happy man."

She threw her arms around him and pressed her face to his neck. "Oh, Roberto, I love you so much. I've always known it, but the second Lyndsey pointed that gun at you, all I could think was that I'd been a fool to ever push you away. And then you disappeared and I thought you were gone forever."

"I'm never going to be gone again. I'll always be at your side. I want to marry you and make you happy. I want to get back everything we missed out on, and if we can have more kids, what the hell, let's do it."

The light turned to gold as the sun hit the horizon—the magic hour.

Frannie cradled his face in her hands. "Roberto, I love you. There's nothing I want more in the world than to spend the rest of my life with you."

"Then what are we waiting for?" He kissed her.

And in that magic hour, they sank to the grass as one.

Epilogue

Torches flickered above the masses of blackfoot daisies and purple sage in the gardens of the Double Crown. Fairy lights twinkled in the cedar elms. Music drifted through the air. It was a night for magic, for promises. Silk and white roses, the time-honored words: to have, to hold, to love, to cherish, forsaking all others, from this day forward.

It was magic and moonlight and Roberto drew Frannie away to a small path that wound among the honey mesquite.

"Our guests," Frannie protested.

"They'll have you for the rest of the night." He leaned in to press his lips to the shadowed hollow above her collar bone. "I only want five minutes alone with my wife."

Frannie shivered. "Tell me it's real," she murmured.

"It's real." He wrapped an arm around her waist and

swept her close to him for a lingering kiss. "But I'll be happy to prove it to you every day for the rest of my life."

"Mmm. Every day?" she murmured against his lips.

"Maybe every other day. I am pushing forty, you know."

She laughed. "You're so decrepit."

"Remember, you said in sickness and in health. I have witnesses." He pointed across the gardens to where the reception was being held.

Old friends and new, the two families together again, this time tied by an even stronger bond. Frannie felt a bubble of joy swell in her chest. "Come on, let's go walk around and talk with those witnesses."

"As long as you promise I get you to myself tonight."

She gave him a smacking kiss. "I promise you get me to yourself for life."

"Hey, no hiding out there alone all night, you two," scolded Maria Mendoza as they walked back to the reception area. She and José were at the edge of the dance floor, swaying to the sounds of Ol' Blue Eyes singing "All of Me." Beyond, Lily and William Sr. danced together as he held her hand his against his chest.

Roberto bowed to Frannie. "Would you like to dance, Mrs. Mendoza?"

"I'd be delighted, Mr. Mendoza."

She'd never been happier, Frannie thought as she stepped into his arms. Across the floor her brother Ross danced with his girlfriend Julie Osterman, and nearer, Isabella and J.R. laughed as they tried to practice the foxtrot with Jane and Jorge. Dress rehearsal for their own wedding in just a few weeks, no doubt.

And at a table nearby, Frannie saw her firefighter cousin, Darr, making faces at a tiny girl in a frilly white dress, his dark blond hair mixing with her golden curls. His beautiful wife, Bethany, sat beside them, smiling.

"Oh, let's go say hello," Frannie begged, tugging Roberto over to their table. "Hey, Darr, got a hot date?"

"Bethany was playing hard to get," he said, bouncing his four-month-old daughter on his knee.

"Bethany's strictly B-list these days," his wife corrected, but the expression in her eyes was fond.

"Miranda, meet Auntie Frannie and Uncle Roberto. Can you say auntie, smart girl?" Darr asked.

Miranda burbled obligingly and stared raptly up at them with her cornflower-blue eyes.

"She's beautiful, Bethany."

"Did you hear that, Randi? She called you beautiful," Darr cooed.

Frannie laughed. "I think someone might have Daddy wrapped around her little finger."

Bethany's lips twitched. "I shudder to think how it's going to be once she starts dating."

"It'll be fine, Randi, won't it?" Darr said. "Because it won't happen until you're thirty, will it?" He tickled her chin until she giggled delightedly.

"They look happy," Roberto commented as they wandered away, drifting back toward the gardens.

"If you like babies, just wait a couple of months, we'll have them coming out of our ears," Frannie said. "Darr and Bethany's, Josh's, Nick and Charlene's—" she nodded to her cousin's now very pregnant wife "—and ours."

"Good babysitting practice for when—" He stopped and stared at her. "Did you just say what I thought you said?"

Frannie nodded, watching his expression morph from surprise to joy.

He picked her up and whirled her around. "Tell me it's real," he demanded.

"It's real," she laughed.

"We're going to have a baby? When?"

"About six and a half months. I think it happened that night you took me out to show me your ranch. I guess that property's good luck."

"You're good luck," he murmured, pressing a kiss on her. "After all, you're my fortune."

* * * * *

We hope you enjoyed reading this
special collection from Harlequin®.

If you liked reading these stories,
then you will love
Harlequin® Special Edition books!

You know that romance is for life.
Harlequin Special Edition stories show
that every chapter in a relationship has its
challenges and delights and that love can be
renewed with each turn of the page.

Enjoy six new stories from
Harlequin Special Edition every month!

Available wherever books and
ebooks are sold.

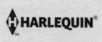

SPECIAL EDITION

Life, Love and Family.

THE WORLD IS BETTER WITH

Romance

Harlequin has everything from contemporary, passionate and heartwarming to suspenseful and inspirational stories.

Whatever your mood, we have a romance just for you!

Connect with us to find your next great read, special offers and more.

f /HarlequinBooks

𝕏 @HarlequinBooks

www.HarlequinBlog.com

www.Harlequin.com/Newsletters

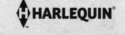

H HARLEQUIN®

A *Romance* FOR EVERY MOOD™

www.Harlequin.com

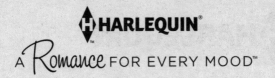

HARLEQUIN®

A *Romance* FOR EVERY MOOD™

JUST CAN'T GET ENOUGH?

Join our social communities
and talk to us online.

You will have access to the latest
news on upcoming titles and special
promotions, but most importantly,
you can talk to other fans about your
favorite Harlequin reads.

Harlequin.com/Community

Facebook.com/HarlequinBooks

Twitter.com/HarlequinBooks

Pinterest.com/HarlequinBooks

Love the Harlequin book you just read?

Your opinion matters.

Review this book on your favorite book site, review site, blog or your own social media properties and share your opinion with other readers!

HARLEQUIN®

A Romance FOR EVERY MOOD™

**Stay up-to-date on all your
romance-reading news with the
Harlequin Shopping Guide,
featuring bestselling authors, exciting new
miniseries, books to watch and more!**

The newest issue will be delivered right to you
with our compliments! There are 4 each year.

Signing up is easy.

EMAIL

ShoppingGuide@Harlequin.ca

WRITE TO US

HARLEQUIN BOOKS
Attention: Customer Service Department
P.O. Box 9057, Buffalo, NY 14269-9057

OR PHONE

1-800-873-8635 in the United States
1-888-343-9777 in Canada

Please allow 4-6 weeks for delivery of the first issue by mail.